WOKEN KINGDOM

Poppy Rose Solomon

First published by Poppy's Pages in 2023

www.poppyspagesediting.com

Written by Poppy Rose Solomon

Edited by Pauline Menchavez, Lizzie Augustine, and Ellyssa Paik

Cover art by Robert Ixer

Cover design by Haylee Buswell (HB Pencil Designs)

Paperback ISBN: 978-0-6456986-0-2

eBook ISBN: 978-0-6456986-1-9

A catalogue record of this book is available from the National Library of Australia

The author acknowledges the Gubbi Gubbi people, the traditional owners of the land this book was written and published on. Respect and gratitude are extended to elders past and present.

For all the magical, wonderful women who have come before me, but especially Mum and Nanny. You make my dreams come true <3

MAP

The World of Woken Kingdom

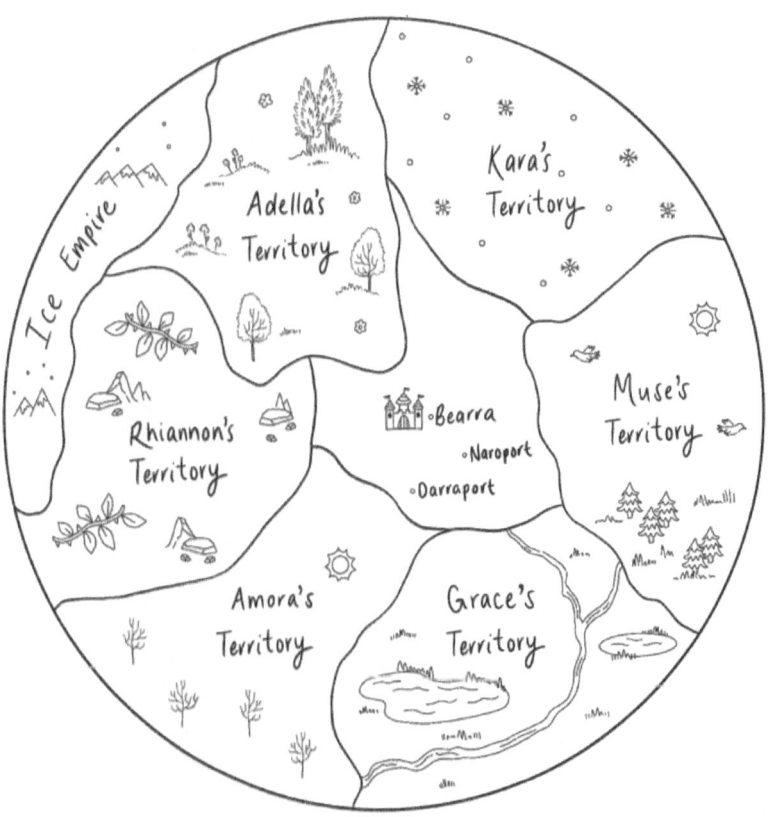

PROLOGUE

THE PRINCESS WOKE WITH a stranger's lips on hers, his hot breath like silk on her skin. His hands travelled over her shoulders, brushing away dust. His fingernails whispered down her arms. She could feel his heartbeat against her chest.

She might have screamed if she hadn't spent her entire life preparing for this moment. The fate she had never wanted. The curse she had tried to escape. The loss of the one thing she truly longed for: her true love. Because, in the end, she would always be waiting for a prince.

Only a kiss of love from *him* would break her curse. *He* was the only way she would ever be freed from the nightmare the dark fairy had bestowed upon her. The curse a fairy of wisdom had promised could be broken, even if it took centuries.

The princess wondered how long she had been asleep. How much had she missed? What had become of her kingdom, and of the world? What had become of *her*?

As she rose, pressing her strange prince gently away, aches spread through her body. Pain. Years of pain. With a shiver, she realised how cold she was, how thirsty, how hungry. Her skin was tight and dry, and she curled over as her stomach clenched.

She opened her mouth to ask the stranger for help, noting the crown atop his head of white-blond hair. Before she could utter a word, her chin was lifted, and a ring was held in front of her.

The prince stared at her hungrily, the way so many did as they observed her beauty. She could have sworn she saw a flash of lilac in that gaze, as if his blue eyes had gone glassy with devotion. 'I have freed you, my love,' he drawled, bringing her attention to his red lips. 'Now, our future together begins.'

CHAPTER ONE

I'm TYING MY SHOELACES, packing my bag, checking my map one more time. The world may have changed over the last hundred years, but I'm not planning on getting lost. Just to the grave and back again. I can make it.

The sun is barely over the horizon, and my house is still almost black. Fortunately, I'm used to getting up this early, to seeing in the dark – the last hundred years have made relentless workers of us all. Survivors. I could paint the finest detail with my eyes closed, if only that would feed my family.

I head to the kitchen and pull some bread from the pantry. Throw some cheese in my bag. There isn't a lot of space. I'm only taking the old – but precious – leather satchel my father once made for me from leftover bookmaking supplies. I have no idea how long the trip will take; I'm packing for a delicate balance between starving and being weighed down.

The grave is in a town called Glassine, if it's still called that. Apparently the world is separated into unfamiliar territories now, and it could take days or weeks to reach the grave. I know nothing of the land I'm stepping into, one hundred years ahead of what I remember.

This is all I'm able to fit in my satchel: four slices of bread and cheese, a flask of water, a change of clothes, my map, and a book. And my sketchbook, with a couple of pencils . . . just in case.

I try to be quiet, hoping that if anyone does hear me, they won't realise I'm running away. My parents are already awake, but they won't be up for a while. They're in their room, too invested in their whispered arguments to worry about me sneaking around the house. The same talk, over and over, for the past year:

'I'll find a new job,' Dad will say. 'I'll talk to the old builders. They might have something I can do, something that isn't too—'

'You won't,' Mum will reply. 'I'm not letting you hurt yourself even more. We'll get the business running again. Make new connections and find new ways to make money. Someone must want our books.'

'We can't compete with the new presses outside Bearra, if the kingdom ever opens at all. No one *here* can afford our work anymore. Our girls are suffering.'

'The girls will marry. They can take care of themselves.'

'Maya would rather starve than marry. It was my accident that bankrupted us. I won't be a burden to my daughters any longer.'

'Shh. It isn't your fault.' I imagine her placing a gentle hand on his arm.

It was, in fact, no one's fault but the royals'. *They* decided their palace needed a new wing, and *they* rushed the builders. There was no safety in place, and my father fell and broke his leg. He'll never do physical labour again.

For a while after his injury, we made enough money running Mum's bookmaking business. Collectors around the small kingdom of Bearra loved the way we bound the soft pages, the way we covered each tome in fine leather. Children coveted the picture books we made with our own drawings, and we distributed our tales past the kingdom's borders and out into the surrounding villages. Travellers bought the books to sell as they visited faraway kingdoms. Despite our business's popularity, we never made a lot of money from it, since each book took so long to craft – but it was enough to live.

Now, thanks to Bearra's precious, perfect princess, that world and that life are gone. We still aren't allowed past the vines to trade outside, and most Bearrans are too poor to buy from us anymore. Who would waste money on books when they're starving?

If my sisters and I don't find husbands, my family is going to be bankrupted, and we'll be separated and miserable forever. I'm not going to let that happen. I'll do *anything* not to let that happen.

I take a final look around my home, unable to make myself step any faster towards the door. Dark wood and unlit candles. Books, everywhere. It's a small house for Bearra, but it's cosy, and it keeps out the heat well enough. Upstairs is my parents' room, my eldest sister Prima's, and mine and Briar's. My side of our room is decorated with paintings I've created over my seventeen years of life. Briar's only has one – a sketch I drew of a boy she briefly met and fell in love with three years ago. Well, a hundred and three years ago.

Leave, Maya. My hand curls around the doorknob. If I don't go now, I never will.

But I want to crawl into my parents' bed and hide under their blankets. I want to hug my sisters goodbye. I at least want to wait, have breakfast together, anything. I'm trying so hard to be brave, to remember I'm doing this *for* them.

I left a note. That's the best I could do. I told them I love them and I'll be back as soon as I can be. It's not the right thing to do, I know that, but if they knew I was leaving they'd try to stop me. It'd be even worse.

I take a deep breath and try to suppress the aching in my chest. Twist the doorknob, turn myself around, crack the door open to the first rays of morning light. I look out at my kingdom and step into the cold.

I can do this.

I have to do this. I have to.

Take another step.

A hand clasps my forearm and spins me around. 'Maya.'

I wince. *Prima.* 'I was – I was just going to . . .' I swallow, my mind blank.

'Don't try to lie to me,' my sister says, her grey eyes narrowed and her lips pursed with disapproval. Her light-brown hair is swept into a loose braid, and she's still in her nightdress. 'You've been talking about this for weeks. And you're not very discreet.'

Though Prima is the tallest, and Briar has a rounder face, my sisters and I are mirrors. We get our hair and eyes from our father, and our sharp features from our mother. We are stamped with the Nova family name as much as our books are.

'You can't stop me. You know what this—' I lower my voice. 'You know what this crown is worth. Who knows how our grandmother ended up with it, but that thing is hidden within our family, and I'm getting it. It's going to save us.'

She sighs. She does that a lot, like our parents. Sometimes I wonder if she thinks she *is* one of the parents, just because she's the oldest. And only by four years. 'We don't need saving. I'm going to marry Matthew, and Briar will find someone too. It'll give us the time we need to figure something out.'

I stare at her.

'I know you don't want our family to be separated.'

My legs shift. I have to leave *now*. 'It isn't just about that. You won't have enough money, and Mum and Dad will be left behind. We could lose the house. Our family can't rely on your marriage alone.'

'This famine won't last forever,' she says gently, moving closer. 'Things will improve.'

'They won't.' I stare out across the kingdom, at the looming, boxy castle that sits at the top of the hill in the kingdom's centre – the *world's* centre. It can be seen from every part of Bearra, which means I get to be reminded of the people who ruined my life every day. 'Not with these royals. Things will continue to get worse until there's nothing left for any of us.'

Prima shakes her head. 'When the new prince comes into power, with Princess Dawn as his queen . . .'

'Prince Jacob? He'll probably be even worse. We know nothing about this man, yet everyone acts like he's a saint just because he kissed an innocent sleeping girl and she woke up. That doesn't mean a thing to me, except that he's good at cutting through vines. And we both know Dawn's useless. Blessed by six fairies and still can't see past her own graceful little feet.'

Prima rests a hand against the doorframe, beckoning me back inside. 'You can't hate the royal family forever.'

I raise my eyebrows and cross my arms. 'I can.'

'But you'll go and collect their crown for the reward.'

'Just because you hate a game,' I whisper, leaning my face closer to hers, 'doesn't mean you can't play it to win.'

Her eyes bulge, as if she's trying not to roll them. 'Come inside and have breakfast. We'll talk about this as a family.'

'Absolutely not.' I grip my satchel and stand tall.

'If we're that desperate, we'll ask Aunt Olivia for help. Or I'll have Matthew set you up with a job, if that's what you want. He knows a lot of the farmers, you could work the fields, and—'

'That would pay next to nothing. And why should I have to settle for a life I don't want?'

'Maya, your head is in the clouds. The world has changed, and we must make the most of what we have. Evolve, like everyone else. Can't you accept it? Find a way to be happy? Life doesn't have to be only your way or eternal misery. You need to stop wallowing and blaming others. You need to accept responsibility instead of running away.' She sighs. 'You need to *grow up.*'

I clench my jaw. I'm ready to turn and go, but I can't resist arguing back. 'First of all,' I say. 'Why must I be expected to suffer because of Princess Dawn's curse? Who thought it was a good idea to put an entire kingdom to sleep for a hundred years so one stupid princess wouldn't have to wake up alone?' My fists shake. 'We didn't even have it the worst! At least we were all in the kingdom. You know one of the school teachers had a husband and newborn before we slept? They were supposed to visit family in another kingdom, but she was sick so she stayed home while her husband and child left. It was only two days, but because they weren't in the kingdom when it closed, she'll never see them again. Her baby is over a hundred years old now, so it's probably *dead*. She isn't even allowed to leave Bearra to look for them.'

'Maya—'

'We're living in a nightmare! I have every right to blame others, I have every right to wallow, and I have every right to do the one thing I know will save us.'

'Maya,' Prima almost growls. 'You are going to throw your life away out of *spite*. You used to have friends!' She raises her voice, probably to rouse our parents. She knows I can't look into our father's eyes and turn away from him. 'You used to love people, and people loved you. You had a future – you would've been an incredible artist. You still could be! But since we woke, you've been consumed by anger. You would rather run away than face the future. Fight for the past instead of embrace the present. *Why?*'

My body fills with heat. I tuck my hair behind my ears; since I cut it to above my shoulders, it's always falling in my eyes. Right now the irritation is taking me from angry to furious. 'I'm doing what's brave. I'm doing what you're afraid to do. *You're* the one who's running away. You'll get married, and you'll abandon us, and everything will be gone. I'm not just going to save our family. I'm going to make us happy forever. We can do all the evolving we want then.'

'Girls?' My mother's voice calls from the kitchen. 'What are you doing out here?'

'*Fairies*,' I curse under my breath. If I'd only been able to walk a little faster, I'd be on my way already. This time it's me who sighs. I turn to see Mum, with Dad by her side. I look into my father's eyes, and I'm ready to cry. 'Nothing,' I say. 'Go back inside.'

'She's trying to run away,' says Prima.

Mum blinks slowly. 'Maya, we told you this crown idea wasn't . . . wasn't . . .'

'It's a bad idea,' Dad finishes. 'We know you only want to help, but this isn't the way to do it.'

I throw my head back. This has turned into a disaster. I shift my satchel further up my shoulder. It's already making my back ache. My voice nearly cracks when I say, 'Why can't you just have faith in me?'

Dad limps to the door and reaches out a hand. 'We do. But we're trying to keep you alive.'

'I'm trying to keep all of us alive!' I shout, but it only takes a disapproving look from my mother to get me to take Dad's hand and step into the house.

Briar is on the staircase, rubbing sleep from her eyes. She seems to realise immediately what's happened, and pushes out her lips in a disappointed pout. With her big, babyish eyes, despite being a year older than me, she looks younger. 'Maya . . . really?'

Dad serves us pancakes as we sit tensely around our crooked dining table. It took our local farmers a while to bounce back after their crops had spent a hundred years dying. But, a year after waking, we finally have just enough eggs and flour to bake. At least until we lose the last of our money. The royals wouldn't know this, but rotten food loses its charm after the first bite.

'Maya, remember that story you love?' says my father, scooping a chunk of pancake and honey from his chipped dinner plate.

Briar laughs. 'Heroic girl breaks the curse on her family and saves her little brother from a goblin? Or was it heroic girl slays a dragon? Or heroic girl goes on a quest to—'

'Let's not joke about those brilliant stories,' my father says.

'Which you wrote.'

I clear my throat. 'What's your point?'

Dad meets my eyes, grey on grey, though his are lined with many more years of hardship. 'You've always wanted to be like the heroes you read about, Maya. You've always had this idea that you . . . that you want to be a saviour. But those are stories. In real life, we make wise choices, not brave ones. In real life, we don't go on quests to find buried treasure. We find other ways to survive. We stick together. And things have a way of balancing again.'

'No.' I scratch my knife against my plate. 'Dad, I don't want to be a saviour. Why would I *want* to do this? I'm doing it because I have to.'

'Honestly, Maya.' Prima shakes her hands as if she might be able to shoo me away. 'I want to marry Matthew, and I'm going to whether or not you like it. Our family won't stay under this roof together forever. I don't know about you, but I'd rather we be separated than you be dead.'

I really do try not to be angry at her. She's only being protective. In her eyes, she's doing what's best. But why can't she see things from my perspective? 'If you want to marry, do it. I'm still going.'

Mum slams her hands on the table, making porcelain and metal clatter. 'I have had *enough*!' Her face is red, her lips pursed. 'We aren't allowed out of the kingdom for a reason. We are not ready for the new world yet. The queen and king know that. If you're caught trying to sneak out of the borders—' She shudders.

I take a deep breath. I can't take much more of this. 'Mum, I know you're worried, but how different can it be to a hundred years ago? I have a map. I'll find my way to Glassine. The world isn't that big.'

'You're going to walk. Across the world . . .'

'Maybe someone will be kind enough to give me a lift in their carriage.'

'And kidnap you,' Briar says. 'Never to be seen again.'

I groan and wipe honey from the side of my mouth. Our house is dark and imposing today, rather than warm and cosy. The wood is pressing in against me, and my family are holding knives to my throat. I need to be free. Now.

'You can't lock me up and stop me from going,' I say. 'We'll end up hating each other and it'll be for nothing. I'm going to get this stupid crown for this stupid prince, and you are only making it more difficult. *Help* me.'

The enchanted crown, my buried treasure, is our only hope. It is immensely magical and mysterious, probably forged by the fairy Lire a long time ago. It might even be *older* than the fairies. The royals need its power to coronate a new queen or king. And since Prince Jacob arrived and woke Princess Dawn, the royals have been desperate to get it back.

It went missing decades ago because . . . well, my grandmother stole it. No one but my family knows it's buried with her. We alone can get it back and reap the rewards of returning it. Except we're not allowed out of Bearra. They say it still isn't safe to open our borders. The world has changed too much; we aren't ready. Even though it's been a year.

Other people must have found ways to sneak in and out. I'll find a way, too.

Dad sighs. He seems to realise – I can see it in the creases of his forehead – that he can't win. 'Fine.' His voice is tired now, and I feel guilty, but I'm no less determined. 'You're nearly an adult. I won't stop you doing what you think is right. I would never try to control you. Even if I very much disagree with you. If you're going to go, however, I have some non-negotiable compromises.'

'You're letting me go?' I blurt, then I collect myself and narrow my eyes. 'Dad, what compromises?'

Mum is shaking her head. 'We are not encouraging this!'

'You'll go to your aunt's,' Dad says. 'She knew your grandmother best. If anyone has information that can help you find the crown, it's her. You'll also get yourself some new shoes. I don't care about the cost, just get some you can walk – and run – in. You'll go to the butcher's for a knife, because I'm not letting you go without a weapon, and you'll drop off some books on your way.'

A smile tugs at the corners of my lips. 'Really?'

'I have faith in you,' he says. 'And I would prefer that you go with my support, not without it, as you said.'

I nearly jump over the table to hug him. But I don't. While my sisters and mother start arguing louder and louder, I make my way slowly around the table to hug my father around his shoulders. He kisses my hands.

'You *are* a hero, Maya,' he whispers. 'I lied. You'll always be the girl in the stories to me.'

CHAPTER TWO

SOMEWHERE, SOMETIME...

ONE YEAR AGO, ALONG with all of Bearra, Maya woke.

No one remembered falling asleep. Most of the small kingdom's people found themselves on the floor, where they had been standing only moments ago, now shaking cobwebs and dust from their skin. It was as if the world had ended – the sky had gone dark, vines covered every surface, all the food had decayed. They were starving as they scoured for something to eat. They ached, they were desperate for clean water, they—

They had only blinked, and a hundred years had gone by.

Maya's first memory was clambering down the stairs in search of her family, pain searing through every part of her body, her face soaked with fresh tears despite her dehydration. She found her parents and clung to them, wiped grime from their cheeks. For a long time, they couldn't talk. It was an hour before they were ready to go in search of food. More hours before they found any.

The people tried to escape the kingdom, but they were met with a wall of impossibly thick thorns. They drank the dirty river water and speared fish, because there was nothing else. They tried to rebuild. They were so, so very weak. So very tired.

The royal family didn't show their faces.

The day they woke, most of Bearra thought they were going to die.

All of this suffering was for one girl. One princess. And the Bearrans were *pleased*. Was this not a small price to pay so their beloved Dawn would not have to wake from her curse alone? Everyone loved their princess.

Well, every Bearran except one. Maya Nova hated the royals. They had already hurt her family once, and she would never, ever forgive them for this.

CHAPTER THREE

ON MY WAY TO visit my aunt, as my father requested, I drop off some books.

The school takes three; they always pay, because they're funded by the queen. That'll be enough for a new pair of shoes. The orphanage can only afford one, though all I accept in return is a small cake from their cook. A few families buy them for their youngest children, who grin brightly when they see me coming. The children are one of the few things that make me smile. Eating my cake, I pocket my coins and hope there's some left over after today's errands.

Crafting cheap children's books has been the only way for me to make any money since Bearra woke. It's nothing more than a small way to feel useful, but a few coins are better than none. And I am *never* ungrateful for cake.

With my bag unloaded, I pace faster to my aunt's house. It's been years since I visited her – she and my mother stopped talking entirely after my grandmother passed – but the kingdom isn't large, and I remember how to find her home. Despite her relative closeness, she lives in the *expensive* part of Bearra. The streets are cleaner, the water is fresher, and though the houses are in the typical Bearran style of white walls and flat roofs, they're far bigger. Their large windows overlook the rivers and canals, and servants can often be seen behind the glass, scrubbing away to keep it pristine. To the north-east, the castle rises on its hill, and though it can be seen from all of Bearra, the view is most impressive here. It's as if they keep the grass on this side of the castle greener.

The gravel road becomes paved with orange tiles that contrast the azure sky above. My feet enjoy the feeling of hard, even ground that doesn't pinch me through my thin shoes. There are people out enjoying the sun; we're early in the warm season, before it gets too hot to want to be outside anymore. Some locals smile at me as I pass. Others sneer. Being a small, friendly kingdom, most Bearrans are polite – except the ones who really, really aren't.

I find my aunt's house: an enormous ivory building hidden behind a sprawling cacti garden with spikes that keep catching my shirt as I navigate through. I hop along the stone steps to an ornately carved wooden door and lift the golden knocker. Not for the first time, I resent my mother for estranging herself from this side of her family. This house could've been ours. This life. Instead, it belongs to my horrible aunt, while I am always hungry.

The door falls open with an echoing creak. The servant behind it nearly waves me off, and I have to explain I'm Olivia's niece so he doesn't slam the door. Reluctantly he leads me up a set of stairs to a pink sitting room with floor-to-ceiling windows. From here I can see the vines that wrap around the edges of the kingdom, thick and every shade of green, with nightmarish spikes. The fairy of strength, Rhiannon, grew them around Bearra a hundred years ago to protect us while we slept. Now they don't just keep others out – they keep us in.

A woman in a strawberry-coloured dress is seated in front of an unlit fireplace. She doesn't stand, she doesn't say hello. When the servant announces my arrival, she simply looks me up and down. Grey hair is curled back from her pinched face, which looks like my mother's if she had spent the last few decades scowling instead of laughing.

'Prima,' she says. 'I hadn't expected to see you.'

I force my lips into a smile, resisting the urge to scream. 'Maya, actually.'

Aunt Olivia raises an eyebrow. 'Classically. Well, take a seat, darling. Can I offer you some tea?'

'Yes, thank you,' I say, though I have no idea where she's getting tea from. Bearra's farmers have been struggling to grow it since we woke, but I don't question her. It's unnaturally cold in here, and if a nice beverage is all I can get from this visit, I'll take it. I sit on a large red sofa with carved wooden legs, as far from her as I can perch myself without leaving the next room.

'I suppose you aren't here to socialise,' she says as her servant pours the tea. She has my mother's sharp features – *my* sharp features – but on her, they look accusatory. Like she thinks, or knows, she's better than everyone else. 'Should I bother asking how my sister is doing?'

'No,' I say, not caring to be polite to this woman who didn't even know my name. 'I'm here because I want to know more about my grandmother. Apparently you knew her better than anyone. I hope to visit her grave. Once we're allowed to leave Bearra, of course. There's a kind of treasure in reconnecting with your family, don't you think?'

Olivia's face turns sour. *Sourer.* 'Go.' She waves a hand. I nearly argue in defence, but it's her servant who hurries out and shuts the door. 'So, you're going after the crown.'

I lift my tea and cradle it to warm my hands. 'We need the money. I intend to get the crown and bring it back for the reward.'

'You'll be caught sneaking out,' she says nonchalantly, watching the window. 'You'll die on your way, or you'll die at the grave, and even if you do make it home, they'll know our family stole it and kill us all anyway. Believe me, I've been over it a thousand times myself. It isn't worth it.'

'I'll lie. I'll tell them I found it somewhere else. No one has to find out I left.'

'You'll die,' she repeats. 'Even your mother isn't stupid enough to encourage something like this. Tell me she isn't involved.'

'She isn't happy about it.'

Aunt Olivia sips her tea. 'Then for once she's thinking wisely.'

I lift my cup to my lips as well, hoping it looks as intimidating as when she does it. The liquid sinks into my chest, the flavour strong and spiced, magical as a fairy. 'I may not be wise,' I tell her, 'but I know that I have to do something to save my family. I'm going with or without your help, so help me and I'll give you a cut of the reward.'

'I don't need money.'

'But you surely wouldn't say no to it,' I say as confidently as I can. 'Unless there's something else you want?'

She pauses. 'Something else . . . No, Maya. It isn't worth the risk.'

I press on. 'Something you can only get outside, that I could bring you. Jewellery, fabric, a new sofa – more tea.'

'I don't need *your* help to get me something from the outside,' she says, her fingers running along the edge of her teacup.

'So you know a way out?'

'I have connections. That's all. And I won't be discussing this with you any further.'

I stare at her plainly. 'Tell me how to get to the grave.'

'No.' She puts her cup down. 'I will not be part of this.'

My heart goes cold with disappointment, and I nearly consider storming out before I notice the portrait above the fireplace. In the painting, three women are portrayed with such detail that for a second I think they're real. One is middle-aged, with grey hair like Olivia's and eyes exactly like my mother's. Two young girls stand either side of her, unmistakably my mother and aunt as children. The strange thing is, they're smiling. Even in heavy-looking dresses and piles of jewellery, their hair in tight interwoven braids, they seem happy.

I didn't know my mother had ever been happy with her family.

'What happened?' I ask, gesturing to it. 'How did you—'

'Go from a happy family to one lonely woman, one dead woman, and one poor woman?' Olivia keeps her face hard, but her eyes gleam. 'People change. Priorities change.'

'I know that well enough,' I say. 'That's why I have to get the crown. My sisters and I will have to marry if we can't get money elsewhere. We'll be separated, and our family will be gone forever.' I inhale sharply. 'Just like yours.'

She stares at the painting. 'I understand your intention. I'm sure anyone with a heart would. But you need to consider the risk.'

'Family is worth risking everything for.' I lean forward in my seat. 'Maybe not to you, but it is to me.' It might be the only thing I know for certain. No matter how much we argue, no matter how hungry we are, how poor and desperate, my family is always together. We fight for each other, support each other. They are all I have, and I would die for them. They know that – it's why they're so worried about me.

Aunt Olivia's fingers clench, and her red dress matches the anger boiling beneath her hard face. 'I learned the hard way that family isn't everything. Your mother fell in love and was happy to renounce her old family to create a new one, even knowing she'd be shunned for marrying your father. Your grandmother became so entrenched in political scandals and secrets that she became one. She stole the crown and it led to her death. Neither your mother nor mine thought once about me when they left. They only thought of what they wanted.'

'My family is different.'

'They're the same. The only person you can put your faith in is yourself. You know that, deep down. It's why you want to go on this quest so desperately.'

I scoff. Maybe it's true that I have very little faith in others, but what does that matter? Prima and Briar think they'll save us by marrying and leaving – they're wrong. Mum thinks the business will pick up and we'll make money again – she's wrong. Dad thinks he'll go back to work – he's *wrong*. I am the only person able to save them, but it doesn't mean I love or trust them any less.

'Aunt Olivia,' I say, ready to end this conversation. 'Why did my grandmother steal the crown?'

She flinches, gives in, just a little. 'She knew it had power, and she wanted that power. The crown inducts the next king and queen, and if she could stop that . . . I don't know what her goal was, frankly. Maybe she only wanted to cause trouble. But if anyone ever found out, even now, everyone who ever knew her would be seen as a criminal. As her family, we would be imprisoned at best.'

I lean forward in my seat. 'Why have herself buried with it, then? What if someone found it?'

'She believed that even in death, it was safest only with her. And don't think that her grave can be easily robbed. She used the crown's magic to create wards all around it. You couldn't get to it if you tried. If you did, you'd need magical help from all seven fairies.' Her eyes narrow, as if she didn't mean to say that. 'It's impossible.'

Of course. The crown doesn't just create royals. It gives whoever holds it access to magic, so naturally my grandmother buried herself in a bubble of impenetrable power.

I tap the arm of my chair. 'So only magic can break through my grandmother's wards.'

'And why would any of the fairies help you?'

'I know where the grave is,' I say, ignoring her bitter words, 'and now I know how to get the crown. I'll find a way.'

She slams down her teacup. It clangs against the plate underneath. 'Maya, I will not allow this! You are endangering us all.'

'I can make all of this right.' My chest swells with excitement. My mind is clear. 'And when I return, I'm talking to my mother. You're going to make things right with each other. We will *all* be family again. Everything is going to be better soon. I promise I'll prove you wrong, Aunt Olivia.'

She scowls, but I can see something in her change when I mention my mother. She wants to reconnect with her. I know it. She wants me – and my family – to win. After a long pause, she says, 'I'll expect my cut of the reward, as promised.'

'Of course.'

She sighs and crosses the room to a desk covered in papers. She rifles through the drawers, creasing her dress as she crouches. As I wait, not stupid enough to question her, I watch the view outside – the vines I'll soon have to find my way through to escape Bearra.

'Here,' she says finally, handing me a compass without meeting my eyes. 'This was your grandmother's. It always points to the castle. From anywhere in the world, you can find your way home to Bearra.'

My face softens. I don't know Aunt Olivia, but suddenly I regret never visiting her. This entire side of my family, abandoned, like she said. And now she's helping me find the one thing that could help us. Reluctantly, maybe, but there must be some kind of familial love beneath her icy mask.

Olivia presses my fingers around the compass. 'She would want you to have this. She had an adventurous spirit like you. Let's hope, however, that your spirit doesn't kill you – like hers did.'

· ·*◊ 🤍 ◊*· ·

I hold the compass tight as I walk home, letting the sun glint off its surface. It's silver, round, with tiny, polished pieces of triarue around the edges. The smooth, blue gemstone is the reason Bearra is – was – so rich, despite how small and defenceless we are. It amplifies magic, so it gives fairies more power. I flip open the cap to reveal the needle inside, also made of the bright-blue crystal, which points directly to the castle above me. The compass must be worth a lot, so when I reach the busier part of town, I place it deep in my pocket to be safe.

The crowds are thick, covered in sweat from the near-summer heat. I'm detouring past the castle to get to the butcher's and the shoe shop. It's ridiculous my father is making me buy a knife, but I won't refuse. I don't know what's out there in the new world. Monsters? Demons? Doubtful, but I really might need it.

I try to stick by the sparkling canal and stay on the grass to avoid people, but it's just as busy on the shore. There are families out in the sun, children splashing in the water, and people buying cheap food from vendors. The markets are overflowing and it's hard to see anything from the streets. Then I realise why the crowds have magnetised here: the *princess*.

I sneak up the side of a market stall and sit on top to watch – not that I care, but because it's always good to know what's happening.

Dawn and her saviour prince, Jacob, shine and sparkle amongst the dull civilians around them. Bearra's fairy, Lire, is right behind them, her every step an elegant, ethereal work of art. She keeps watch as the prince and princess saunter down the street holding hands. Guards surround the trio, so people stay a good distance away, but everyone is skirmishing to get a look.

Princess Dawn giggles lightly as the prince presses a kiss to her cheek. As always, she's glowing. Because anyone blessed with beauty and every other good thing would be, wouldn't they? Her skin is a unique bronze, thanks to her father – our umber-toned king, who married into Bearra from a faraway kingdom. Dawn's golden curls fall softly over her pretty round face, and her sky-blue dress only emphasises her sunny appearance.

Prince Jacob is just as pretty, as if he's been blessed with beauty too. Maybe he has. Tall and athletic, with pale skin and hair. He's clearly a few years older than Dawn – in his early twenties. She's only seventeen, like me, and I can't imagine being engaged already. He certainly seems infatuated with her, though; he won't stop kissing her.

Still, it's the fairy who really catches my eye. Lire is always wearing shades of purple, all her pretty little dresses covered in tulle. Today it's lavender that drapes from her shoulders to her knees. Her lilac wings extend high from her back, almost translucent and stunningly magical, towering above even Jacob. She's tall, graceful, her hair falling in soft, blonde waves, and her skin pearly white.

Lire is Dawn's godmother. It was her who put us to sleep for a hundred years, to *save* the princess. Leaders of Bearra have gone to the fairy for advice for as long as the kingdom has existed – she is the fairy of wisdom, after all.

I think she's the fairy of ruining lives and kissing up to the royal family, but I can't say that out loud. No one is more beloved in this kingdom than these three people.

There's a rustling in the crowd as a young woman rushes into the street. Guards try to push her back when they realise she's running towards the fairy, but Lire smiles gently and lets her come close. The woman is holding a baby, begging for a blessing. The crowd cheers for Lire to accept.

Lire places her hands on the mother's shoulders and peers down at the baby. I can't see it clearly from here, but it can't be more than a few months old based on its size. The mother cries with joy as Lire plants a kiss on the baby's forehead, and for a moment it glows with a lilac aura, coating the market in the enchantment.

Everyone's clapping now, like the clouds have parted for a sun shower. Even Dawn and Jacob, with their annoyingly perfect hands. More people try to push their children forward for a blessing, but Lire shakes her head politely and continues her stroll with the princess and prince. They're untouchable, unflinching, as if the rest of us aren't crushed together just for a look at them, screaming their names.

Jacob goes to kiss Dawn on the lips, and she obliges. No one is watching them now – they're too focused on the baby. But I keep my eye on them, thinking as always about how much I wish I could throw shoes and tomatoes at their flawless faces. I want them to be miserable. I wish those stupid giddy smiles would be wiped from their undeserving mouths. I wish they'd go back to sleep forever. They ruined my life. Why are they the ones who get to be happy?

Then I notice it: when everyone else is looking away, Dawn wipes her mouth, a disdainful look on her otherwise perfect glowing-brown face. She takes a step back from the prince and when he steps towards her, she sighs. Unfazed, he begins kissing her again, holding her in his arms. She looks like she'd rather be anywhere else.

Then, as if it never happened, she smiles again, that sunrise beam of white teeth and dimples, and gives the crowd a wave that causes an eruption of applause.

CHAPTER FOUR

PRINCESS DAWN HAD NEVER expected the curse to truly take effect. It felt unreal – it did to everyone. How could someone as blessed, as bright, as Dawn be truly cursed by a fairy so dark? Unfortunately, it was no trick. Despite the princess having the other six fairies on her side, Kara's curse was unable to be stopped.

To most people's knowledge, curses could not be undone except by the person who cast them, with the kiss of a royal soulmate, or with immense power. However, with enough magic, curses could be *changed*. Bearra's patron fairy, Lire, protector of the kingdom and advisor to the queen and king, saved Dawn. Rather than die at age sixteen, she would merely fall asleep, frozen in time until a prince could wake her with a kiss.

Lire never told Dawn that she would also send the rest of the kingdom to sleep. And Dawn felt such guilt – her entire kingdom was held back a hundred years. Although the people seemed pleased about it, their love for their princess eclipsing any resentment at the state the kingdom was left in, Dawn lived under the weight of knowing they were all suffering because of her.

One year ago, she woke to find a man on top of her. Her body hurt, though she'd been asleep on her lovely bed in her lovely room. Thorns had smashed in the glass and vines had grown through the windows and around her door, cocooning her. Some vines were slashed, oozing sap onto the dusty floor; the prince's sword was balanced against the end of the bed.

At first, the princess couldn't seem to breathe. Her heart pounded. She wanted the strange man to leave her alone, but she also didn't want to be left by herself. Luckily, Lire found her, and soon after, her parents.

They explained everything. They met Jacob, told her he was her soulmate, her saviour, that they were all free thanks to him. The prince and princess were engaged immediately.

Ever since, she'd been making excuses to push back the wedding. She didn't love this man, no matter how certain everyone around her *knew* she would. There was something wrong with him, a side no one else saw. Jacob wanted something. The throne? The triarue mines? Maybe he just wanted *her*. Maybe she was little more than a future king's conquest.

But with Jacob came his younger brother, a sweet prince, seventeen like her, who became her closest friend. They had spent the last year hiding around the castle, sitting in silence or talking or playing – anything to get away from everyone else. To get away from Jacob. Although she wasn't *interested* in either of them, she at least wished she could have married the one she'd come to love as a friend.

Something was wrong, there must have been some mistake. She wouldn't ever love Jacob. Couldn't. Her true soulmate was long dead. If Dawn couldn't force herself to love Jacob, what would her fate be? She alone saw the darker side of the prince. If she couldn't change, would she end up as dead as her lost love?

CHAPTER FIVE

I REACH HOME AND step inside quietly, my new shoes already tied tightly around my feet and my knife tucked into my belt. The rest of my errands went smoothly; half the kingdom was so enthralled watching the royals that the shops were empty. So, I am back for my final goodbye.

My entire family is in the kitchen, and at first they don't notice me. I'm almost offended. Shouldn't they have been worried about me returning, waiting by the door? But they're surrounding Prima, staring at her hands.

'Did you hurt yourself?' I ask, rushing in, and they all turn to look at me. But it isn't fear on their faces. It's . . . joy.

Prima's brows turn up with a mix of relief and guilt. 'Maya, thank goodness you're home. You don't have to leave anymore.' She cradles her hands together, like she's hiding something within them. My stomach twists with nausea. 'Matthew finally proposed,' she says, unable to hide her smile. 'I said yes, of course.'

No.

'You're not married yet,' I whisper, more to myself than to her. 'There's still time.' I try to turn away, but Briar takes my arm.

'This is a happy moment,' she says. '*We're* happy.'

'But we – but she'll move in with him, be *his* – we won't all be together anymore.'

Briar rubs my arm gently. 'You can't keep us all to yourself forever. Please try to be happy for our sister.'

'No, I . . . It isn't just about . . .' I fight the tears stinging the back of my nose. I can't meet anyone's eyes. 'What I'm doing is going to save us, so we *can* stay together. If Prima marries, maybe Matthew earns enough to send some money our way, but how much? Not enough to feed us, house us, do anything.' I turn to Prima, who is watching me with a heartbroken gaze. 'Marry one day if you have to, but don't do it like this, when you can't be certain it's what you want. Prima, don't – don't abandon us.'

My sister clenches her fists. Her expression has transformed to rage. 'Why do you have to ruin *everything*? Why can't I have one nice day, one nice thing, without you bringing everyone down into your misery!'

'Girls!' Mum shouts. Our mouths snap shut. She turns to Dad. 'You, start making us a celebratory dinner. Briar, help your father. Prima, go to your room and cool off. Maya, outside. We are having a talk.'

I let my satchel thump on the floor and follow Mum into our mostly dried-up garden. She has her hair scooped high in a bun and an apron on for painting. She steps past some small rows of struggling vegetables and sits at the half-rotted wooden bench. She pats the spot next to her. Her face is no longer stern or upset. She just seems sad, all her features downturned. She usually doesn't let me see her like this.

My fear dissipates into guilt. 'I'm so sorry, Mum,' I say, sitting beside her.

She picks at a lettuce leaf already half-eaten by insects. 'You are already aware of how I feel about all of this,' she says, 'so I'm not going to argue with you. If you still decide to go, I don't want one of our last conversations to be negative. But you cannot speak to your sister like that. I'm sure it's hard for you, being the youngest, not wanting your big sisters to go away, but that went too far.'

My home, in its crumbling windowpanes and fading paint, will so soon be missing three of its inhabitants. How . . . How are we all supposed to leave our life behind? 'Isn't it hard for you?' I ask. 'Don't you care about them leaving?'

With a harshness that reminds me of Olivia, she says, 'Even the closest families grow up and make their own way eventually. Children leave. It's what they're meant to do.'

I stare at my new shoes, leather boots with thick soles that give me an extra inch in height. 'But that's what you did to your family, and you never spoke to them again.'

'What did my sister tell you?' she says softly.

'Not much,' I admit. 'That your mother was distracted by the crown, by her place in society. That you wanted other things, so you left. That Aunt Olivia was abandoned, all alone.'

Mum lifts my chin gently so our eyes meet. 'And you think Prima will do the same to you.'

'Olivia confirmed it.'

'Even if you get the crown, my love, your sister is going to get married.'

'But she won't have to.'

'She does have to,' Mum says. 'She's in love. You can't save someone from love. But when you get the crown, we'll be as rich as Olivia. We'll be fine.'

Something warms in my heart as she says 'when'. I take the compass from my pocket and hand it to Mum. 'This was your mother's. Aunt Olivia gave it to me so I can find my way home.'

She runs her fingers over the silver and inspects the blue triarue. 'I remember it,' she says with a smile. 'You know, it's worth—'

'Enough to feed us for a while. Yes. But nothing compared to the reward for the crown.'

'I understand,' she says. 'When you're gone, just look where that arrow points whenever you feel alone, and know I'm right at the end of it thinking about you. I'll take care of everyone while you're gone. I'm trusting you, Maya, and you can trust me.'

My eyes are burning again, so I swallow and quickly change the subject. I didn't realise how badly I needed to hear that. 'Just because things didn't work out with your family, doesn't mean it won't with ours.' I nod to myself, my confidence returning. 'We can have everyone together again, Aunt Olivia included. I can get home before Prima's wedding. It isn't over until they're married.'

Mum sighs. Of course she does. 'Why do you refuse to accept that this is what she wants?'

'I'll believe it's what she wants when we're rich. If she still wants to go through with it, I'll support her. Matthew can come live in our mansion. But if she's going to marry, it's going to be because she really wants to. Not because she has no choice.' I take back the compass. 'I wish everyone would stop acting as if I'm being childish – this isn't just about me not wanting to grow up. It's about protecting us.'

Mum squeezes my hands and presses her forehead to mine. 'You're a good girl, Maya.'

* ◦ * ❀ 🤍 ❀ * ◦ *

We have dinner, and I keep my mouth shut about the engagement. It doesn't matter anyway. If I argue with Prima now, we'll only both be more upset. In the end, she'll realise I'm right.

Dad's excited to see my new shoes and my knife, and he shows me how to hold it properly in my hands, where to shift my weight against an attacker. I slice through Briar's skirt and she screams so loud the neighbours check in on us.

Too soon, I have to say goodbye.

It's late evening, the second-best time to go, after dawn. The darkness will cover me, and the streets should be mostly empty. I have only one option for an exit – Bearra's main gates, which connect to the old road, which leads to the outlying villages – and it won't be easy to sneak through. Aunt Olivia hinted that her *outside connections* only make it in and out by bribing soldiers. There are no secret tunnels, no ways to cheat.

Mum hugs me like before, without a word. We've already said everything we need to say. I look into her eyes one last time and try to memorise their shape, their colour.

Prima and Briar hold me in their arms for a while. Briar doesn't try to hold back her tears. Prima still heaves with fury, but I pretend she's also repressing sobs. They straighten my jacket, tuck my hair behind my ears, smile at me like when I was a child. Like when I was their baby sister, not this mad young woman running away on a futile quest.

Dad steps out the door with me and we leave the others behind.

'I won't be long,' I say. 'No more than a few weeks, I'm sure.'

'I know,' he says. His grey eyes look cold in the moonlight. 'You get this crown for us, okay, love? Don't let anything stop you from getting back. If anyone gets in the way, you have your knife. Don't be afraid to use it. Keep your head down, and never close your eyes. We don't know what the world is like anymore. You have to be ready to fight for your life.'

'I am,' I say. 'If I have to, I will. Dad, I won't fail you.'

He tries and fails to smile, so he pulls me into a hug instead. 'I miss you already. I miss your complaining, and your drawings, and the strange way you butter your bread. I miss when you were happy and all you needed was stories. But I love you, so much, and I need you to know I'm so proud to be your father.'

My breath keeps catching. There's this feeling in my gut, a void inside me so deep I'm going to crumble. 'Dad,' I say. 'I love you. I'll be back soon, I promise.' I pull away from him, hike my satchel onto my shoulder, and begin to walk away. 'In a few weeks you're going to be rich. You'll be swimming in so much gold you'll forget I even exist.'

His eyes don't leave me. 'None of that matters to me. You're the only thing your mother and I care about. And your sisters, of course. We don't care about money. Never have.'

'Then we'll swim in the gold together.' I turn and refuse to look back. Step, and step, and step. I can't wait a second longer. It's impossible to hide my tears now. I knew this would have been easier this morning. That's why I *tried* to go without goodbyes.

I'm not sure I'm as strong as I hoped.

CHAPTER SIX

THE KINGDOM COULD BE another world at night. Rather than blaring sun reflecting off white walls and terracotta, the dim streets are lit only with candle and moonlight, everything a warm silver-grey. Open curtains reveal families sitting for supper. Cats and dogs sleep in alleys. The only businesses open are ones that serve alcohol and other *adult* services. The few people walking the streets are the soldiers, the homeless, and the drunks.

I'm careful to keep my head lowered, my jacket hiding my shape. While I'm gone, my family will lie that I'm ill, stuck in my room. If someone discovers I've left and they knew, they'll all be in trouble. Worse, if I get caught sneaking out tonight, my quest will be over before that's even a problem.

The castle looms above me, an ugly grey box glowing and flickering in orange and red candlelight. The princess and prince are within its stone walls, warm and well-fed, dressed in expensive fabric and jewellery. Maybe they're sleeping soundly.

They would never have to steal or beg.

My foot catches on a broken paving stone, and with a stumble I remember to focus on *myself*.

I'll visit the grave first. It's the only place I know how to reach, and it's going to be my destination regardless of the journey. Hopefully all I have to do is get in, get the crown, and follow my compass back to Bearra. Aunt Olivia might have been exaggerating about the amount of magic I'll need to break through the grave's wards. But if she's right, and I do need help from all seven fairies to get in, I don't know where I'll begin. At least once I find out what I'm dealing with, I'll know what the next step is.

I push my doubts from my mind and steady my breathing as I make my way closer to the gates. I think over my plan again and again. All I have to do is escape, then I'll be past the soldiers, and the only danger will be the *entire world*.

The main gates are the only place in the kingdom where they've cleared the vines. Like Olivia said, there's no other way in or out, and only soldiers are allowed near them. Because beyond those gates, there could be anything.

Finally I reach my wide and grand escape route. The gates are made entirely of carved triarue, blue and glimmering. The street they frame leads all the way up the hill to the castle in the kingdom's centre. And around the gates, thick vines are cut off haphazardly, threatening to creep back in and cover our only exit again.

I squat behind a carriage on the side of the road, careful to stay out of the patrolling soldiers' view. Pulling my small set of matches from my satchel, I stare at my hands, unable to fathom what I'm about to do. My idea couldn't be worse, but how else can I create a compelling enough distraction to slip through the gates unseen?

If I can simply get past the vines, I'll be okay. Even the soldiers rarely leave the border; they only will if they see me and try to catch me.

The carriage I've decided to target has the royal crest on it, so by burning it I'll at least be indirectly hurting Dawn. I squint and run my hands along the ground to find some small, dried pieces of dead vines. I pull them into a bundle, and for extra impact, I toss some leaves through the carriage window.

I light my match and set fire to my tinder. They blaze so quickly I have to throw them right into the carriage before I'm burned and—

Flames explode across my vision. I stumble backwards. *Fairies!* I only wanted a small fire. What was so flammable in that carriage? It was like magic.

Before my eyes can cloud with tears, I sprint closer to the gates, staying near the vines in any shadow I can find. Soldiers yell, abandoning their posts to race towards the fire.

'Someone get water!'

'Who did this?'

'Water – now!'

I crawl along the wall as I ensure all their eyes are far from the gates, and when I have a chance, I race out of the shadows and slip through the exit.

Into the world.

A thorn tugs at my sleeve, but I pull myself free and don't wait another moment to look back – I *run*. Sprint along the street until I'm out of the furthest reaches of candlelight and only have the moon to light my way.

Only when I'm absolutely certain I can't keep going do I stop, my chest heaving as I catch my breath. I drop onto the gravel, suppressing a disbelieving laugh but allowing myself a shaky sigh of relief. I'm *free*. I can't believe it was so easy, but I should've known. People are stupid. Stupider than even me, apparently. Most Bearrans are tired and hungry – that includes the soldiers. They aren't as strong and attentive as they once were.

Still, I shiver with a renewed sense of fear.

The darkness, despite being a blanket of protection, feels menacing. What is hiding in the murky gloom? What will I discover in daylight? Despite this area seeming entirely deserted, I can't help but feel like I'm being shadowed.

I take a steadying breath. The air seems so much fresher out here, though I'm not far enough for that to be possible. I'm still in Bearra; farmland once stretched quite far outside the kingdom's borders. But while we slept, all the outlying areas must have disappeared. They couldn't have survived without the rest of us.

I'm not sure what I expected, but *nothing* wasn't it. I've been here a million times, back when we sold our books to other villages and kingdoms. Once, travellers camped out in the fields and set up markets. They were some of my family's best customers. But of course, with Bearra closed, why would anyone be here now?

It feels apocalyptic, and a shuddering thought enters my mind that the outside world *might no longer exist.*

Is this place full of monsters? Monsters, which could be anything, anywhere. I picture dragons, wolves, ghosts, all hiding in the shadows, waiting for me. My pulse beats from my feet to my ears, thumping louder than the breeze, which sends shivers up my spine every time I dare turn my head.

That's enough – I jump to my feet. I *have* to be ready for this. Even if the rest of Bearra isn't. I need to navigate this world. Alone.

The grave is south, so I decide to follow the stars in that direction. The roads occasionally diverge, and where they aren't overgrown, I step carefully and travel at a painfully slow pace.

A noise behind me makes me spin back around. *Some- one's here.* My heart pounds. Should I try to run? Hide? *Don't freeze.* I shake my head, try to calm down. It could be nothing. An animal.

I continue pacing for a while, but my legs have turned weak with terror. I don't feel like I can run anymore; I want to curl into a ball and cover myself with my jacket. I want to hide. I want to be home.

Another rustle. Monster. *Monster.*

The soldier who steps out of the shadows looks completely out of place in the night.

'I—' I falter, tearing my knife from my belt. How did I get caught this far from the border?

Arms crossed, he says, 'Isn't it a little late for a stroll?' The young man is all sunshine, enough it shocks me into freezing as I watch him. Red hair frames his round face and the freckles across his nose. He must be my age, but he has smile lines around his eyes and mouth. I can see all of this even in the dark. The moon bathes him in blue, giving him an almost purple hue against all his warmth.

Why am I studying his *colours*? He's a soldier, not an oil painting. I hold up my knife. '*Don't* try anything.'

'I hope I don't have to,' he says. 'Where do you think you're going?' Something about him changes as he talks. He isn't like the soldiers I've seen, hard and stoic. He's animated and oddly polite. His soldier's uniform doesn't quite fit.

'I'm going to, to—'

'To run away from Bearra? You know you're not allowed to do that.'

'It's a stupid law. You can't keep us all trapped in the kingdom forever. You can't stop me leaving.' I hope the fact that he's young and alone helps me seem more daunting; maybe then he won't simply drag me back to the gates and throw me in prison.

He paces, eyeing my knife with little concern. 'The law is only to keep you safe within the vines until we can find a way to integrate your people back into the world.'

That makes me pause. '"Your people?" You aren't from Bearra?'

'Ah.' He smiles, and the sight pulls at something deep inside me. It's so warm, and out here, I am so cold, so afraid. As much as I fear him, Bearran soldiers have always been a source of comfort and protection. His uniform means safety to me.

'I'm new to the kingdom,' he says. I can hear his accent now. Unfamiliar. It hits me that I'm at least a hundred years older than this boy. 'I wanted to get into Bearra, so I posed as a soldier. When I spotted you running, I came after you. Took a while, though. You're a lot faster than I am.'

I reply with a frown. A fake soldier?

'So,' he says, 'you're trying to escape. Why?'

'I'm not trying to escape.'

'Go on, tell me.'

'No.'

'Why might a young woman like you be disobeying the law?'

I scoff. 'Are you suggesting something?'

He smirks. 'No.'

'Then let me go.'

'I can't do that.'

I roll my eyes. 'Why are you so interested in me? Send me home or arrest me. All these questions are wasting my time and yours.'

He raises his eyebrows, opening up the deep brown of his eyes. They glance at me playfully. 'Because I might be interested in running away myself.'

'I thought you just got here.'

'It's complicated.'

I turn to leave. 'Get to the point, soldier, or I'm leaving. And we both know I can outrun you.'

'Wait! Listen.' He takes a tentative step toward me. 'I'm running from Bearra as well, and we'll be safer together. I'm not here to turn you in. I'm asking you to let me travel with you.'

I laugh. My father warned me about strangers out here – especially strange men. Still, something about this boy makes me linger, curious. I don't feel threatened by him. Should I? I keep my expression cold.

'You're leaving Bearra for a good reason,' he says. 'Otherwise you wouldn't have taken the risk. You're doing something important. Something you can't fail.'

Narrowing my eyes, I silently dare him to continue. To my surprise, he does.

'You *will* fail. You don't know the world you're going into.' He smiles again. 'But if you let me come with you, I'll show you around. I'm from this world. I can keep you safe.'

The last thing I want is a boy slowing down my mission. But he *is* right. I could use some guidance.

No. I shouldn't be considering this. Why am I considering this?

But if it gets me closer to the crown, and he doesn't seem threatening, don't I have to think about it?

'Why?' I ask, standing tall. 'What's the benefit to you?'

'I'll have someone to watch my back until I figure out what I'm going to do. That's all I want. An ally.'

'Of course. *That* makes sense.' I continue along the road, and he follows me like a puppy.

'So, why are you leaving?'

The night chill is giving me goosebumps, and it's dark, and I may as well already be lost. I doubt I'll be able to shake him unless I run, and I don't want to run. So, as long as he seems harmless . . . I suppose I'll keep him for now.

'I'm looking for buried treasure,' I admit, because I can humour him just to get me through the night. I'll ditch him tomorrow, when I feel safer. It's the smart thing to do.

His eyes brighten. 'Perfect. We'll go after the treasure together, split it, and we'll both be set.'

I almost howl with laughter. 'Split it? You aren't even invited along. In fact, it's time for you to leave me alone.' Yes, I've already decided to let him stay – for tonight – but I don't want him knowing that. Especially not if he's confident enough to ask for part of my treasure.

'No! Fine.' He raises his hands innocently. 'I will only ask for a very small amount. It's the least you can offer, since I'm going to tour you around free of charge.'

I exhale. This boy is so naïve. 'Fine. But I decide the amount.'

'Fine.'

'*Fine*,' I say. 'The treasure is south. That's all you get to know for now.' I tuck my hands into my pockets, putting away my knife. 'Any suggestions on what we do first, guide?'

He laughs. 'Isn't it obvious? We need new clothes before anything else. I'm still in a soldier's uniform, and you're dressed like a great-grandmother.'

CHAPTER SEVEN

I'M STILL NOT SURE how I've found myself partnered with this strange boy, but here we are. He walks alongside me with a clumsy gait, asking me questions about myself and the treasure, which I refuse to answer. Before we can get clothes – which I think is a waste of time, but who am I to argue – we have to find somewhere to spend the night. So we're rushing to the nearest village, the cool night air sticking to our skin as we march along the desolate old road.

'What's your name?' the young man asks.

His eyes are wide and inviting, but I won't be fooled. Still, I'm not sure why I feel so hesitant to give something as small as my name. I'll be leaving him tomorrow anyway. But it's as if telling him my identity, although he wouldn't know who I am, would be giving away a life-threatening secret.

Through gritted teeth, I say, 'Maya.'

'Not very Bearran.'

'What is that supposed to mean?'

He laughs. 'You're going to love the real world.'

Glaring at him, I stammer, 'The name came from a story my father read. Maya was a word for hope, new life. More literally, spring.'

'Is that so? With your iciness, you strike me more as a winter.'

I sneer at the summer boy, secretly wondering what he looks like in the sunshine. How might his colours mix with the light?

Fairies.

'I'm Teddy,' he offers, holding out his hand – which I wave away.

There are secrets behind his smiles. That's obvious. But I'm hiding things too. Whatever his hidden motive is, he can have it. All I care about is getting my crown, and if he's going to help me get it, I'll deal with his mysteries later.

+ ⋄ ✦ ◊ ♡ ◊ ✦ ⋄ +

By the time we finally stop and sleep, my legs ache badly and my feet are raw and bloody in my new boots. We won't reach the next village tonight, and certainly not the city – that's what Teddy called it, not a kingdom, not a village or town, but a *city*, whatever that means – but we need rest. When an abandoned stone building appears on the side of the road, we reluctantly settle for using it as shelter for the rest of the night.

The idea is frightening; it doesn't feel safe or right to sleep somewhere like this. But Teddy goes in first and gives the building a thorough examination before settling on the hard floor. He insists it's safe – safer than sleeping outside, anyway – and I suppose he would know. Still, it takes me a while to get through the door. I tread carefully inside and sit both as close and as far from Teddy as I can tolerate. Not wanting to be alone, yet not wanting to be vulnerable.

We sit in silence for a long time, too wired to sleep. He keeps fidgeting, like he wants to talk, but I don't care. I always prefer quiet.

After a while, I begin to shiver. My jacket is thick, but it isn't enough. It doesn't often get cold in Bearra, and when it does, we sit around the oven while we bake bread. Right now, there's nothing but freezing stone around me.

I don't say anything – I've barely even noticed how cold I am before Teddy shrugs out of his soldier's jacket and tosses it to me. 'We'll get you some proper clothes tomorrow. Put that on for the night.'

My mouth falls open. 'W-What about you?'

'I like the cold.'

'You still don't have to—'

'Put it on.'

I sigh, tugging the huge jacket over my much narrower shoulders. His body heat lingers inside, and I resist the urge to bury my face in the soft inner material. I would've expected a soldier's uniform to smell disgusting, but it doesn't. Teddy smells like warmth and delicate, citrusy cologne.

'Try to rest,' he says gently, yawning. 'Tomorrow is going to be a shock for you. You'll want to be ready.'

I watch him as he folds his big arms and settles against the wall, closing his eyes. I curl into a ball, tucking my arm under my head as a cushion. It's uncomfortable, but his jacket gives me at least some small sense of safety.

Suddenly not ready for the loneliness of being the only one awake, I whisper, 'Teddy?'

'Maya?' He says my name slowly, as if it's a word that is now his to enjoy, as if he's teasing me, knowing how difficult it was for me to tell it to him.

'You're from really far away, aren't you?'

He doesn't open his eyes. 'It's complicated.'

'Of course. So, where?'

He bites his lip for a moment, and I'm not sure he's going to respond. My shoulders tense as he whispers, 'I don't know for certain. I never met my parents. I grew up all over.'

'Oh.'

'Goodnight, Maya.'

I close my eyes. 'Goodnight, Teddy.'

Right when I'm about to fall asleep, something in his jacket pocket pokes my stomach. A small coin pouch? I wrap my fingers around it carefully, not wanting him to realise I've noticed it. But it isn't money inside. As I reach a finger in, the contents become clear. I'd recognise this roundish but ridged shape, this heaviness, this polished smoothness, anywhere. *Triarue.* Bearra's magic-enhancing gemstone. Enough of it to feed someone for months.

Which means either Teddy is rich, or he's a thief.

I don't know which is worse – or better.

I wake to the sun in my eyes; the same sun, the same earth, but a hundred years older. I'm seeing the *real world* for the first time during the day. Last night, it was all darkness and gravel. Now, peering out the window of the abandoned stone building, past Teddy's head, I see the future. A sprawling, desolate, and dry landscape of tall grass and dead trees – is it so different? I'm struggling to remember how things were before. It feels the same, but I know, I *know* I'm very far from home.

Bearra is right in the centre of the world, the hottest location. Legend says it's because of the triarue – its magic makes it perfect for sustaining life, and it brings warmth to the whole world. The further one travels in any direction out of Bearra, the colder it becomes, until the ice is so thick the world simply stops.

We're still close to Bearra, which means the landscape is hot and dry. The stone room we're in is covered in moss and overgrown plants. Probably one of the few places around here plants can grow wild, with the shade and coolness of the building. But already the sun's heat is setting in, and I shrug off Teddy's jacket, struggling to believe I ever accepted it.

I drop it next to Teddy and examine him for a while as he sleeps, his chest rising and falling in a gentle calm that doesn't match the energetic personality I saw last night. His freckles are more pronounced in the light, his hair redder. He must've rolled up his sleeves in his sleep, because I can see his forearms, pale, freckled, and at least three times the size of mine. Unlike most Bearrans, he looks well-fed. Stocky and strong. Because, of course, he *isn't* Bearran.

He begins to shift awake, so I position myself in a way that isn't so obvious I was staring at him.

'Morning,' he says, his voice gravelly. He notices his jacket beside him and pulls it on.

I cross my arms and lean against the wall.

'Have any food?' He's smiling. As if that would be enough for me to hand over all my supplies.

'I ate plenty before I left last night,' I tell him. 'I'm saving my resources.'

He glances at the door. His brown eyes are bright and golden in the morning light. The glow changes his face a little. Opens him up. Before, in the dark, we were hiding. We're both exposed now. And either he's a very good actor, or I'm very gullible, because I'm convinced he really does just want an ally, a friend. This boy doesn't strike me as someone who can handle being alone for more than five minutes. He doesn't strike me as someone who is capable of hurting anyone.

I keep chiding myself for trusting someone I just met, because it seems ridiculous, and so unlike me, to want anyone around, especially a stranger. But in this unfamiliar world, he is making me feel safe. And if I don't feel scared, that means I'll be stronger.

Shouldering my bag, I gesture for him to follow. I don't want to stay in this mouldy old building any longer than I have to.

He stands slowly, rubbing his eyes. 'You know, we'll reach the next city by midday. We can get you more supplies there.'

I recall the bag of triarue I found in his jacket. Obviously conserving resources isn't a priority to him. 'Why waste what we have?'

'Come on. It won't last anyway. I'll get you more food. I promise.'

I fight the urge to sneer at him. 'Fine.' I open my satchel and hand him some of my bread. Although I want to prove to him that I don't need any myself, that I'm stronger than him, I'm starving. So I bite into a piece as well.

He beams, and the sun reflects off his perfect teeth. 'Thank you.' He dives into the bread, but there's something delicate about the way he eats. Like how Aunt Olivia or the royals would. Fancy, proper. Is that what all people are like now, or just him?

'Bearrans can *bake*,' he says before taking another bite.

'My sister's recipe,' I reply without thinking. I wipe the amused smile from my face. What happened to staying anonymous? What happened to keeping my guard up?

Fairies.

He takes the opportunity I've so stupidly given. 'You have a sister?'

I busy myself rewrapping the rest of the bread, then I scan the floor one last time to make sure I haven't left anything. Without looking at Teddy, I step through the overgrown grass in the doorway and back onto the road. It takes him a moment to catch up to my steady pace.

'That's okay, you don't have to tell me,' he says, but he's tapping at his leg impatiently as he walks. 'I hate talking about my family, too.'

⋆ ❊ ✦ ◍ ♡ ◍ ✦ ❊ ⋆

After a few hours, we start to pass through small villages. Nothing shocking. Some of the houses are built differently, painted in colours I'm not used to and styled with strange, slanting roofs, but it isn't the nightmarish future world I was fearing.

I spot a young girl reading a poorly-made book with thin, over-white paper, the pages already threatening to tear from the binding. Likely made by one of the new printing presses that I've heard operate outside Bearra. The cover has a tacky painting on it, clearly not done by hand.

Teddy notices me cringing at it. 'You read?'

'No.'

'Strange for a girl named after a story.'

I open my bag and split the last of the bread, handing him half to shut him up. I'm finally coming to my senses again, regaining my nerve enough to keep a safe distance from him. When am I going to get rid of him?

We keep walking, and eventually he starts pestering me with questions again. Trivial things. I know what he's doing. Tricking me into telling him more about me by starting with small, inconsequential information. Trying to get me to open up so I let something bigger slip.

I won't. I can't let him know about the crown before I'm certain he can be trusted – otherwise, what's stopping him from stealing it for himself? I'll see about starting to *consider* telling him something *if* I decide to let him stay.

'What's your favourite season?' he asks with a smile. 'Spring?'

'Autumn.'

'Mine's spring.'

'Okay.'

'Colour?'

'Blue.'

'Are you just saying that because you saw the sky and it was the first colour you could think of?'

'Yes.' My favourite colour is the dark green of a pine tree. We don't have them in Bearra; they mostly grow at the world's wintery edges, so I've only ever seen them once. I've used a lot of paint trying to replicate the colour that lives in my memory, but I've never seemed to get it quite right.

'Mine's yellow,' he continues cheerily. 'It reminds me of Muse, the songbird fairy, and her singing forest. Music has a way of reminding me of the good in the world.' He takes a moment to look at the sun. 'It's like a gift just for me, you know? Yellow makes me picture violins and baby birds and springtime.'

It takes real effort not to roll my eyes. 'Poetic, Teddy. I didn't realise you were a fan of the fairies.'

A strange look passes over his face. 'I'm indifferent about the fairies,' he says quickly. 'Wouldn't know enough about them to judge.'

I let the conversation end there, almost wishing I could let him in, answer his questions, finally have a friend. But if I want to save my family, I can't. No matter how far we travel together, I have to remember that everyone outside my family is an enemy.

Chapter Eight

When we reach the edge of the city, my head spins so fast Teddy has to wrap his arms around my waist and hold me up to stop me stumbling. It takes me too long to push him away; the city is so . . .

I can't believe my eyes, and Teddy's touch, his big arms and his steadiness, have only made me fainter.

'Sorry,' he says as I step back from him. 'I shouldn't have— I just didn't want you to hurt yourself.'

I shake my head. 'It's fine,' I mumble, not thinking about him, because what's in front of me is so much more overwhelming.

Everything about Darraport is alien to me. The unimaginably tall brick buildings, each one as big as Bearra's castle. The smoke that fills the air, choking my breath. The smells, like every scent in the world rolled into one. The utter lack of clean water, greenery, anything natural.

The city stretches further than I thought possible, and there are people *everywhere*. Crowds in every corner. People shouting, sprinting, and others sauntering as they peer in shop windows. Some of their carriages run without horses, and there are large ones, big enough to fit at least a few dozen people, rolling down the streets.

And the clothes the people wear are . . . I don't know what they are. In the warm weather, sleeves are uncommon and skirts float riskily in the breeze. Aren't they worried about sunburn? More surprisingly, many people are covered in what must be fine fabrics, in all shades. Clothes I would expect to see on princesses, not dirty street girls. Almost all of the bustling people wear pearls wrapped around their wrists in gleaming bracelets.

My hand clasps my mouth. We aren't even *in* the city yet. All we've done is make it to the outskirts. No wonder they gave it a new name – *city* – no village or town or kingdom is like this. There is nothing for me to compare it to, and I want to drop to my knees and cover my eyes and ears, but I have to be stronger than that, I have to face this.

'I knew you'd be stunned,' says Teddy, gesturing to the height of the buildings, 'and I wish you could've been exposed to something more tame before this, but . . .'

This is what the world has been doing while I was unconscious for a hundred years? It's terrifying. It's spectacular. And . . . there's grief. Because I missed so much time. I missed seeing this city be built. I missed being the version of myself that might have been part of this.

I've made the right choice by keeping Teddy around. Whether or not he can be trusted, I can't face this alone, just like he said. His hand twitches at his side like he wants to reach out to me again, to comfort me, so I shove my hands in my jacket's pockets – despite the city's heat – and straighten my back. I have to force myself to be ready for this.

'Let's go.' I step towards the busy streets ahead. Slow my breaths, try to clear my mind. I've faced worse things.

'We can wait, if you need a minute,' Teddy says, brown eyes wide with concern. His soldier's jacket is hung over his arm, and his skin is already more freckled from being in the sun all morning.

'No. I want to do this now.'

'*Maya.*'

'I'm not a child.'

'No, you're a Bearran.'

'Then you know we Bearrans don't like to be patronised.'

'No one does.'

'Then let's go.' I follow him towards the crowds wordlessly. All I can do is keep my own emotions in check. The excitement and fear, my racing heart. I try to keep myself focused, but everything catches my eyes.

He nearly loses me, and this time he does grab my hand. I let him. It's too easy for us to be separated here. He leans close to my ear as we press through a group of tightly-packed people waiting outside a restaurant. 'I told you we need new clothes,' he says over the noise of their chatter. 'We stick out here, and not in a good way.'

He's right; even hidden amongst the crowds, Teddy and I seem to be drawing attention.

I ask, 'They don't just think we're from another city?'

'I'm wearing a Bearran soldier's uniform.'

'No one's seen a Bearran soldier in a hundred years. They don't know what one's supposed to look like.'

'They've seen paintings, Maya. We don't want people asking questions.'

He pulls me through the streets, confidently leading the way. I bump shoulders with everyone I pass, and I have to cling to my satchel with the hand that isn't holding Teddy's. I'm already overheating in my jacket and boots. My palms sweat and it's difficult to catch my breath.

The buildings, made mostly of red brick and grey stone, grow even taller as we head deeper into the city. The smog is thicker. Unlike Bearra, with architecture made for the heat, Darraport is made only to create as much upward space as possible by cramming the streets with thick, tall buildings. Everything is stifling. We pass a marina full of impossibly huge boats, and the water is brown and putrid, nothing like the clear canals at home.

'Trade city,' Teddy says over the sound of a massive horseless carriage rolling down the street, transporting dozens of barrels of something that smells alcoholic. His hair is matted and sweaty from speeding and forcing our way through crowds. 'Most cities are part of the fairies' territories. They serve as capitals, places for politics and business. But there are some outlying cities, like Darraport, that don't belong to any territory – they exist on their own because they make enough money to support themselves. They prefer not to be ruled by fairies or queens and kings. Darraport is filled with businesses that provide all sorts of goods, and the marina makes it a perfect place for trading and sending products away for profit.'

'They don't have fairies or royals?' My mouth hangs open, but I close it when I get a whiff of fresh smog. Maybe I judged this place too quickly. It may be smelly and cramped, but a world without the kinds of people I hate most sounds nice.

Teddy pulls me down another street and I barely jump out of the way of a transport carriage. People keep staring at us, and it makes my cheeks flush, which makes me even more nervous. My hand keeps threatening to slip out of Teddy's, and he grips me harder, sending more warmth up my arm.

'You'd be surprised how many people don't like fairies,' he says. 'Or royals.'

So I'm not out of my mind, then. Just ahead of my time. 'But there's magic here.'

'Of course. There's magic everywhere.'

He stops and abruptly rounds us into a shop with dummies in the window dressed in ridiculous fabrics and styles. I'm relieved to find it cooler inside, the air clearer. The door is made of glass, and I close it carefully behind me, scared it'll smash if it bangs closed. Teddy smirks as he watches me. I sneer in return. I may be old, but I know what a *shop* is.

We head to the back, where a young man arrives behind the dark-blue counter. He looks bored until he notices us.

'Teddy!' He starts clapping, and smiles widely. 'It's been so long! I hope you're in town a while. Mum'll be so pleased to see you.'

Teddy beams at him. His eyes look so kind, relaxed, now we're out of the streets. 'Gus. We're just visiting. I'm heading south with my friend here – Maya – and we need new clothes for our journey.'

Of course he'd give my name out like that. Of course he wouldn't think to protect my identity from his friend.

Gus is dressed top to bottom in royal blue, the fabric draped around his body in an intricate way that makes no sense to me. It brushes the floor, so I have no idea if he's even wearing shoes. His pearl bracelet is bright and polished.

His eyes narrow as he examines our outfits. 'You certainly do need new clothes, though I'm offended you're only here on business. You've lost weight, Ted. And that soldier's uniform really doesn't suit your complexion.' He talks fast, and sometimes it takes me a moment to understand him. He glances at me. 'As for you, Maya, you're a lovely-looking young woman, but you're dressed like something I might've seen a hundred years ago . . .' He gives me an odd look, but he bites his lip and carries on. 'And I'm sure that's just your personal style, though it could use some improvement.' He holds his draped arm up to my chin. 'I'd love to see you in blue.'

Teddy quietly pulls Gus's arm away from me. 'Maya has an old soul. We aren't looking for anything showy. Just practical clothing that blends in, particularly for Amora's Territory.'

That's the region Glassine is now part of – according to Teddy. Back home, I'd heard only vague information about the new 'territories'. As Teddy explained it to me, the world is now split quite evenly amongst the seven fairies, each with a slice-like territory around the circumference of the world, with Bearra as Lire's region in the centre. Any old kingdoms or towns that fell under the new territories are ruled by fairies now. The world's south-west mostly belongs to the fairy Amora, so that's where the crown is.

Gus stares at the window, his eyes the same bright hue as his outfit. 'I've always wanted to go to Amora's Territory.'

'One day I'll take you,' says Teddy. He likes it there, and he seemed excited it's where the *buried treasure* would be. Knowing that, I've decided to keep him around longer. 'But today, Gus – clothes.'

The tailor nods dejectedly. 'Okay, let's get started.' He takes us to the back and tells us to take everything off except our underwear. I give him an expression that says *absolutely no way*, so with a condescending huff, Gus puts up a partition for privacy.

It takes some convincing for Gus to let me try on pants, since I'd 'look *so* gorgeous in a flowing red gown' but Teddy and I are quickly fitted. The charcoal-coloured pants I choose hug me around the waist but allow plenty of movement around the knees. The material is sturdy but airy.

I'm thrown a top made of flowing light-pink silk. It sits a little lower on my chest than I'd normally wear, and the sleeves don't quite reach my wrists. When I look in the mirror, though, I don't mind it. I feel new and modern, like the women of this city.

I would never have been able to wear something like this a hundred years ago – it's a colour I could never afford, a silk that must be rare. The pink makes my sharp features appear softer, and highlights my light-brown hair. It brings out the colours in my cheeks. When I tuck the shirt into my pants, my figure looks better than I've ever seen it. For the first time, I see myself as an adult. I'm not just Prima and Briar's younger sister – I'm a woman of my own merit.

Gus hands me a black coat and gently presses a pearly clip into my hair, parting and pushing back the strands on the left. My heart thaws as he fusses over me, his eyes wide as if he's in love, though I know it's about the look, not me. Suddenly I wish my sisters were here, and it was them doing my hair and dressing me up, like when we were children.

I step out from the partition to see Teddy in a pale-green button-down shirt that Gus can't get enough of. It contrasts Teddy's red hair in a brilliant way, and makes his eyes somehow warmer. Apparently, this shade of green is his second-favourite colour, right after bright yellow. Gus knew that already.

Teddy smiles at me through the mirror, looking confident in these new clothes that actually fit him. We both look so rich, and I have to remind myself this is normal now.

'Alright, bags.' Gus heads out the back and returns with new white-suede satchels. 'These will hold far more and be sturdier for your journey. Not to mention they'll be better for your shoulders.'

'Thank the fairies,' Teddy says, which gets him a funny look from Gus. Teddy ignores it to smirk at me. 'Maya, you can empty out your satchel behind the partition if you like. I'm sure you don't want me knowing what secrets you've got hidden in there.'

I groan. 'Shut up. And I'm not changing my bag.'

'But we need new—'

'I'm keeping my bag. It's from my father. It goes where I go.'

Gus tries to hide his disdain. 'It's something my great-grandmother might have passed down, and not in a cute antique way. But if it's what you *want*.'

'It's non-negotiable, and if I am compared to a grandmother one more time, someone is going to be very sorry.'

He swallows. 'Well, Teddy can take a new bag, anyway. I'm sure you'll want to carry a few days' worth of food.'

Teddy rubs his stomach. 'Oh, yes. Except, do you have one in grey? White clashes with my eyes.'

Gus laughs and collects Teddy a different bag. I watch Teddy carefully as he moves a few things out of his jacket pockets. He thinks he's being smart when he slips his pouch of triarue in his sleeve before letting it drop into the bag, but I still see. *That's* why he suggested we repack separately.

If he is a thief, at least he still hasn't seen my compass. I've kept it hidden, not dared to look yet, because it's the most valuable item on me. I also don't want to think about something that points towards Bearra, because the last thing I want to spiral about is my home, and my family, so far away.

'I hope we're getting a discount,' Teddy says to Gus. 'You know I'm a loyal customer. And a great friend.'

'Of course,' Gus says, leading us to the counter. 'Anyway, Mum would kill me if she knew I charged *her Teddy* full price.'

Teddy grins. 'Mother always provides. You better tell her I say hello, and sorry I missed her.'

Gus shakes his head. 'Absolutely not. You'll be staying the night with us. It's nearly evening, and I'm not letting a young woman sleep in the streets with only you for protection.'

'Only me!'

I clear my throat. 'We'd really appreciate it.'

Gus winks, relaxing. 'Smart girl.' He takes a moment to add up the cost of our clothes, then barters with Teddy for a price. They're more expensive than I could've afforded with the meagre money I brought along. If my money would even be worth anything.

Teddy fishes a bracelet like Gus's out of his pocket. Pink and grey pearls. What is it with this city and pearls?

Gus pulls a large one out from under the counter, its curves gleaming, and when the large pearl touches the bracelet, both glow pink. With a flash of white, two of the pearls on Teddy's bracelet turn grey.

I don't want to show my confusion, so I make a mental note to ask Teddy about it later. Currency, clearly. *Magical* currency? But if that's how money works now, why does

Teddy have that bag of triarue? And why did he keep the bracelet hidden in his pocket instead of on his wrist?

· ◦ ˙ ❁ 🩶 ❁ ˙ ◦ ·

Teddy takes me out for dinner, rather than have us eat at Gus's apartment, which I'm excited to visit later. *Apartment*. In the city, people don't have houses. Most of them live in small, separate dwellings within the huge buildings. There are several of them on every floor. It seems suffocating – and exciting.

We visit a restaurant in a nicer part of Darraport. Here, the streets are cleaner and less crowded, and with the sun down for the evening, the temperature is much cooler. Teddy opens the glass door for me, and we enter a bar with small, crowded tables. The tall ceiling boasts five chandeliers, glowing red and accentuating the rich aromas of the food and drinks. All the diners have pearl bracelets, though theirs are fully pink. On the other side of the city, most of the people's bracelets were saturated with grey. To eat here, we're certainly going to need Teddy's money.

I've never liked restaurants. Why would I settle for eating food cooked by strangers, surrounded by strangers, when I could be with my family at home, my meal made just how I like it? Yet the food here has an intoxicating scent; after the scarce food in Bearra, I'm ravenous for this.

A young woman, the hostess, leads us upstairs and seats us by a window with views of the marina. I can't see any stars here, but the moon shines bright over the water. Even at dusk, there is so much light and so much noise, inside and outside.

The hostess bats her eyelashes at Teddy when he smiles at her. 'I haven't seen you here before. Shall I go over our menu?'

'No need,' Teddy replies, before I'm able to have any say. 'We'll take the tasting board. We don't come to the city often, so we'd like to try as many of its delicacies as we can.'

'*Very* clever,' she says, her voice drawling. 'Wine?'

'Two glasses of red, please.'

I suck in a breath, sick at the thought of being intoxicated when there's already enough to worry me. 'I only want water.'

Teddy offers a light laugh. 'She'll try the wine. But you can *also* bring us some water.'

I want to yell at him, but I also don't want to make a scene, so I sit still and settle for a scowl.

She smiles. 'Wonderful. Won't be long.'

A server delivers us a bowl of bread, which we both quickly dive into. It's different to how my family makes it. So much softer and sweeter. At first I hate the taste, but as I get used to it, I find myself unable to stop eating.

'I know,' Teddy says, watching me devour it. 'It's certainly different to Bearran food. So unhealthy. So addictive.'

I speak over my mouthful. 'It's unbelievable. It must be magic.' Everything is magic these days, apparently. Somehow. I know I should ask him about it, but I'm so distracted with the food right now that I don't care.

His eyes turn to the window. 'It's the real world.'

The hostess delivers us our wine, and the scent is abhorrent. Teddy takes his with a 'thank you' and sips immediately, sighing with satisfaction. I push my glass away and pick at the remaining bread.

'You don't drink?' Teddy leans across the table, eyes sparkling.

'No.'

'Why?'

'It tastes disgusting, and it makes me dizzy and confused.'

'Oh, come on.' He seems to find this very amusing. 'Maybe the drinks of the future are better. Try it.'

'No.'

'I only want you to taste it. I'm not trying to get you drunk. It's just for *fun*. Stop being so Maya about it.'

I exhale a hot, irritated breath. Spite makes me want to tip the entire drink on the floor, but if I just take a sip, Teddy might shut up. I pull the glass to my lips, copying the way Teddy held the stem. I hold my breath and drink.

'Ergh!' It burns so badly I spit it back into the glass, but in my overreaction, I manage to spill the entire drink on the table. The white tablecloth is drenched in red.

'Maya!' Teddy hisses in mock anger, waving his hands around.

I groan, jumping up and wiping my mouth. The taste still stings the back of my tongue. 'I told you I didn't want to try it!'

The corner of his lip twitches. 'You could have refused.'

'I—' I start to laugh along with him, trying to save the bread from the spilled wine. 'I'm still blaming you.'

'Is that right?' He doesn't move to clean the dripping liquid.

'You're so annoying.'

'No, you're just unsociable.'

I try to shoot him an enraged look, but it's too difficult through my giggles. The water outside sparkles, ships drifting slowly across it. This place makes my head spin pleasantly with its luxurious marina views and rich scents. And it has been so long since I've had a friend to laugh with.

'Can I tell you a secret?' he asks.

'No,' I tell him, but I'm grinning.

'I didn't like the wine either. I just pretended to so I could convince you to try it and see your reaction.'

I'm thinking of hitting him when the server comes over with a cloth and wipes away the mess, getting between us. 'I'll get you a new drink, miss.'

'No, no more for her,' Teddy says, barely holding in a snort. 'Please.'

CHAPTER NINE

I WAKE ON THE floor of the apartment Gus and his mother share, smothered by blankets and pillows. I'm wearing a nightdress that's far too nice for me, which Gus insisted I sleep in so I don't crumple my new silk shirt, and in it I slept almost too comfortably and deeply.

I don't expect my new clothes to last long on our journey, but the care Gus shows is heart-warming. It reminds me that this new world isn't full of monsters after all.

Gus's mother was ecstatic to see Teddy, sweeping him into a hug and covering him with kisses. As a child, in that mysterious past of his, Teddy once found himself in their clothes shop, drenched from a rainstorm and half-starved. He's stayed with them every time he's visited Darraport since. At least, that's the story I've been told.

It shouldn't shock me that people love Teddy so much. He layers on the charm to everyone he meets. But he won't fool me. I'm stronger than that. Wiser. Pretty brown eyes and a sunshine smile aren't enough to make me give him everything, which he's clearly used to everyone else doing.

I rub my eyes. The sun blasts through the windows, which means I've overslept. We should be on our way. *Fairies*. I throw the blankets off me to find Teddy sound asleep with his face pressed into a cushion. He's snoring lightly, and his large back rises and falls lazily with calm breaths.

I'll let him have a minute. I could use some time to wake up, to enjoy this place before a long day on foot. Considering the grimy city outside, I hadn't expected the apartment to be so cosy and clean. Dark-red curtains and glass tabletops. Chairs upholstered in satin, and a sparkling blue bathroom.

For someone accustomed to wooden walls with chipped paint, moth-eaten curtains, and tiny windows, this is a dream.

From where we are – many, many floors above the ground – the view of the city is incredible. It's like looking out at Bearra from its hilltop castle, the land stretching as far as the eye can see. Though here the view is all buildings, they don't look grimy and stinky like below; they make the city's skyline sparkle.

It's still noisy in the apartment, with all the other people crammed into this towering building bustling around, but hearing the life around me is comforting. The city isn't just a nightmare of chaos; it can be a home, too. I feel so safe here that I could curl up on the floor again and sleep for days.

When Teddy finally rises, he meets Gus and I at the dining table, his red hair spiking all over. Heart and flower-shaped marks run along his face and arms from sleeping on the patterned cushions. His eyes are still half-closed when he mumbles, 'Morning.'

'Morning,' I say, holding in a laugh. I feel fresh and energetic, eating toast layered with thick, melted butter and rich cheese. Another Darraport delicacy.

Teddy goes directly to the kitchen to make his breakfast. Of course, nothing in this place confuses him. And because Teddy is Teddy, he has absolutely no doubt that everything is his for the taking. Why not help himself to Gus's food?

I feel as if I can't touch a thing. The apartment is a museum of the future – a reminder of all I've missed. The curves of the chairs seem uncomfortable, and must be made for style. The paintings on the walls are blocky and colourful; not made for detail and beauty, but for . . . I'm not sure what for.

Even in the clouds, all this way up, they have a functional bathroom and kitchen – water runs through the *walls*. In the kitchen, they have a cooling box to keep their food fresh, built with enchanted ice that doesn't melt.

There's magic everywhere, like the pearls they use for currency, woven into their lives like it's completely natural. I don't understand it, and every time I try to ask Teddy how they have magic when there are no fairies, we're distracted or he changes the subject. How can an entire city run on enchantments?

'Are you sure you won't stay another few days?' Gus asks Teddy. 'You know we love having you here.'

'Unfortunately,' Teddy says, combing his hair with his fingers once he's set down his breakfast, 'we're on a tight schedule.'

I nod as I swallow my last bite, my mouth feeling almost burnt from the intense taste of the cheese. How is the food here so full of flavour? 'Those magic carriages.' I swallow again. 'Can we get one to take us south?'

Gus nearly chokes, which has become his routine every time I misunderstand something. He must be sure I'm Bearran by now, but he kindly hasn't asked. 'The coaches? Most don't leave the city, and to find one that does, you'd need a lot of money and magic. Even more magic to recharge it as you go. Better to get horses, as long as you can feed them.'

'*Horses.*' I swipe a crumb of cheese from my plate and stick it on my tongue.

'Can you ride?' Teddy asks me.

'A little.' My gaze drops to my plate. 'I'm sure I can manage.' My family was always too poor for our own horse, and Bearra is small enough they aren't a necessity.

'Then we'll get two on our way out of the city.'

I blink. 'You can afford two horses?'

'Whether or not I can, we need them. So, we'll get them.'

I nearly laugh at the absurd idea of stealing horses, then I catch his earnest expression. 'Oh. Sure.'

I'm not sure why the thought of stealing horses seems so immoral to me. We're on our way to rob a grave. But Teddy, with his sweet demeanour, didn't truly seem capable of such a thing until now. Though I'd guessed as much, it pulls at my gut to know he isn't the perfect boy he pretends to be.

I *have* to remember that this person I'm relying on might only be with me so he can take my treasure when he gets the chance.

· ◦ ' ◌ 🤍 ◌ ' ◦ ·

Gus sends us on our way with our new clothes, some fresh food, and a big, teary hug. It takes us an hour just to walk to the outskirts of the city, and although I'm more confident here now, I still hesitate crossing the roads and pushing through the crowds. At least we aren't turning so many heads now we're dressed less . . . antique.

Well, that isn't the *reason* we're turning heads anymore.

No longer worried about us being exposed as Bearran runaways, Teddy smiles at everyone we pass. It seems impossible considering how many people there are, but he manages it, and does it genuinely. He waves at young children, even when their parents give him nasty looks, and eventually even turns their stranger-fearing scowls into grins.

It is infuriating.

We find a spot by the river to rest for a while before we go to find horses. Small boats and large ships continue sailing past, but here the water is clearer. It flows and laps at the shore in gently whooshing waves. I can even see fish. It's almost idyllic, if I don't think of the far superior canals at home.

Home.

I pull myself up so I'm laying on the grass with my elbows beneath me. I take a deep breath, inhaling the fresh scent of the outer city – grass and freshwater and something sweet drifting from a nearby café – and watch the sun catching the water. I think about bread and cheese. Prima's freshly baked bread topped with sharp Darraport cheese . . .

'So, are you going to tell me more about this buried treasure we're going after?' Teddy says, picking at the grass with one hand and arrhythmically tapping his thigh with the other. He's sitting too close to me.

'No,' I tell him.

'But I'll have to know eventually. So I can help.'

'I still don't really want your help, though, Teddy.'

'Oh, you're still pretending you don't want me around.' He turns to look at me, but I keep my eyes fixed on the water. 'If you don't tell me where we're really going, I can't really get you there.'

'I have a map.'

'A hundred-year-old map that barely reflects what the world looks like now.'

'Are you saying I'm incapable of reaching Glassine alone?'

'Yes!' he exclaims. 'I-I mean, no. Of course not. But you're . . .'

I exhale sharply. 'My grandmother is buried there. Okay? She was rich. I'm robbing her grave.'

'*What*?'

Oh *fairies*. He did it. He annoyed me into telling him the truth. Why did I say that?

'I—'

We're distracted by a black swan flying into view, its dark wings outstretched and its red beak pointed out like an arrow. It lands and sits at the water's edge. I gape at the creature, mesmerised. I've never seen a swan except in paintings. They usually live in the lakes and waterways in the south, which would be Grace's Territory now. As the most brilliant, clear waters of the world, they of course now belong to the fairy of justice and honesty.

The black swan stretches its wings.

'Don't be fooled by its beauty,' Teddy says, just as enraptured. 'They bite.'

I mumble under my breath, 'It's always the most beautiful things that are hiding a dark side, isn't it?'

He watches me closely. 'You *really* hate the rich, don't you? And the fairies. Is it just something about people in power? That sour look you get on your face – what goes on in your head, Maya?'

Why does everyone always assume I'm bitter or selfish before allowing me to explain myself?

I wave a hand dismissively. 'People should not be adored when they've done nothing to earn it. Bearrans would sacrifice anything for the royals – that's exactly why we're suffering now – but what did Dawn do to deserve our sacrifice, other than be born into the right family? Why did she receive six blessings? Simply because she's a princess? What makes some people more deserving of love and riches than others? It's a con.'

'Oh, I agree.'

'Well I don't—' I clench the grass between my fingers. 'You do?'

'I don't know why you believe you're the only person who sees things for what they are. Many people know how corrupt power can be. You aren't alone, and you never were.' He pauses as the black swan dives under the water and re-emerges victoriously with a bright-orange crab in its beak. 'Lineage isn't as important as it was before Bearra slept, and soon they'll catch up too. The fairies may have risen to higher power and made their territories, but there are no kings and queens and princesses. Humans get power when they earn it. Generational wealth helps, as does magic, but especially in a city like Darraport, anything is possible.' His eyes turn uncharacteristically serious. 'You could thrive out here, Maya. You're smart and determined. You could be rich without ever needing to steal treasure.'

That takes me aback. Me, live *here*? I'd never thought of creating a life in a world outside Bearra. My plan has always been to stay with my family, stay where things are familiar. But could Teddy be right? A place like this might be perfect for me. Away from royals and fairies, out of the confines of the thorns forever. Still, how could I leave my home, my family? Could I convince them all to come with me?

'It isn't your fault,' Teddy says. 'You don't know what you don't know. Maybe that's why they've kept you locked up for so long – so you don't all get a taste of what's out here and leave.'

'It doesn't matter,' I say, shaking that idea before it can consume me. 'Bearra is where my life is. My family. They're all I have.'

'But you could have so much more,' he says quietly.

'I will.' I lean in, feeling a strange excitement. More than hope. An electric *wanting*. Knowing. 'When I get this treasure, I'll be so rich that power and cities and kingdoms won't even matter. There won't be any limit to what I can have.'

He shakes his head. 'Money will only get you so far.' Our eyes meet. 'Tell me what the treasure is. Tell me what all of this is for.'

The black swan is making its way up the shore with a lazy waddle, its wings outstretched to their full span. I can see every feather, outlined by the golden sun. Its long neck seems craned towards us, as if it's listening, too. As if it can sense the thrill in our discussion.

I lower my voice, too excited to keep it from him any longer. 'It's the crown, Teddy.'

'A crown?'

'*The* crown. I'm sure you've heard of it. Were you ever a real soldier in Bearra? If you were . . .'

His face pales, if that's even possible. Apparently there is a white beyond white. His eyes dart around. 'The *crown*?'

'The one that allows the next queen and king to come into power. Yes, that one. The reward it'll fetch when I bring it home will be unimaginable.'

His breathing is erratic when he says, 'Your *grandmother* has the *crown.*'

'She didn't want the royals having it, so she stole it. I don't know why or how, but to make sure they never found it, she had it buried with her.'

'Th-The crown protects its owner. It has such an immense amount of magic that it may as well be a fairy itself. We can't just *steal* it.'

'My aunt said there might be magic protecting the grave, that I might need help from the fairies to get in. I was hoping she was exaggerating.'

'It's enough magic to do anything. If the royal family had had it when Dawn was cursed by Kara, your long sleep would never have happened. It's powerful enough to break even the strongest curse.'

The black swan, now right up the shore near us to peck open its crab, tilts its head to one side. It takes a few steps towards us, suddenly ignoring its dinner, so I push my satchel behind me in case it wants our food.

'All I care about,' I say, 'is that it's going to make me rich.'

'There's more to life than money and power,' he says with a furrowed brow, worriedly tapping at the ground.

'I'll worry about that, Teddy, when I *have* money and power. If you don't want to help anymore, you're free to leave me alone. Actually, if you could go now, that would be fantastic.'

'No.' He breathes. 'I mean, yes. I'll help. I already told you I would, didn't I?' His shoulders untense and he sits still. 'Returning a stolen item to its home is an honourable quest.'

And, he's ruined it. Didn't I tell myself I wouldn't fall for his charm and give him my secrets? I have to stop allowing him to sweep me up in the excitement of this adventure, of his friendship. What's stopping him now from going to Glassine and getting the crown for himself?

'Yes, Teddy,' I say. '*So* honourab—'

A thunderous noise makes me jump to my feet, ready to run, heart racing. People are shouting, screaming. The water collides against the shore with heavy waves. What's happening?

I hold out a hand for Teddy and help him up as we scan the area for the source of the crash. I see it before him: down the river, people are jumping off a ship and sprinting through the mud. Six teenagers, with an array of weapons amongst them.

The citizens of Darraport who were lazing by the water moments ago scramble away, leaving their things behind as they run for the streets.

'P-Pirates,' Teddy heaves as they begin pointing their weapons at those who weren't quick enough to run – knives to throats, arrows aimed at hearts. Teddy takes my hand. 'We need to run.'

I'm out of breath. My mind races. The pirates are getting closer, edges of sharp metal gleaming. I nearly trip over my own feet when they grab a little girl by her hair, keeping her hostage as her parents try to scrounge everything they have to offer the pirates.

My compass. Teddy's triarue. We have too much to lose if they target us.

I'm frozen watching them, even as Teddy tries to drag me away. But I stand my ground; he isn't strong. Shaking, I pull myself from my daze and clench my fists. I can't run away when these people need help. 'Teddy,' I plead. 'They're going to take everything these people have.'

I expect him to tell me it doesn't matter, that if we try to help we'll only get hurt, that we have to save ourselves. He would be right. But he nods, drops his bag, and runs towards the danger, pulling me with him. I let go of his hand and sprint on my own, faster. No plan.

The only thing clear to me is that I can't abandon these people.

In all the chaos, the pirates don't see me coming until it's too late. I tackle the big one holding the girl, and the three of us hit the ground with a thud. I have to ignore the pain spreading through my shoulder; the enormous boy is already taking a knife from his pocket. Luckily I'm fast – and I have years of pent up anger ready to let loose. I grab his arm and bite as hard as I can, making him drop the weapon. He leans over me in an attempt to get it back. I couldn't be in a more vulnerable position, but I manage to reach it first and I slash with it blindly.

A cut opens in his thigh and he drops to the ground.

I crawl away and remember I need to get back to my satchel before the pirates get into it and take my compass.

The little girl races to her parents, who are hiding behind Teddy. He . . . saved them? How did *he* beat two pirates?

Heaving and sore, I pull myself to my feet. Satisfied the family is saved, I turn to run for my bag – but I fall to my knees as if I'm ripped back by wind.

I can't breathe. There are hands around my throat and I'm choking, but there aren't any hands. I'm alone in the grass. *How?* I claw at my throat. I'm being suffocated, crushed, by nothing? 'H-H-Help!' I croak.

Teddy is at my side in moments, eyes wide with panic. He tries to peel my fingers back from my skin, not understanding. 'Maya?' he screams. Then he spots a pirate – a dark-haired young man with a sword – pointing his arm towards us.

His arm, which is covered in blue magic flowing out of him and right at *me*.

How does the pirate have magic?

I try to think, to plan, but I'm choking and choking and I can only claw and tear and try to scream. I can't beg for help. I can barely move. I crash back into the ground, my head smacking the grass. My vision starts blacking out and blurring. Hot tears soak my face and neck.

Dying.

Memories flash as I try to remember – remember the people I love. My mother's face. My father's. Prima. Briar.

These people, people I have failed. *Let them be the last thing I see.*

My head rings with pain, as if I'm going to explode, or implode, maybe both.

Teddy isn't with me anymore. He's taken the knife from beside me and he's running. He's still slow, but his feet don't hesitate, and he's nearly at the enchanted boy. I try to scream at Teddy, to tell him to stop, and it sets my throat on fire. He narrowly misses a slash from a young girl with twin knives and an arrow from another. But he keeps going.

The magical pirate doesn't seem to notice Teddy until he realises he isn't stopping. When it's too late, he yelps and stumbles back.

Teddy has never seemed like a fighter to me, but he must gain the willpower from *somewhere* when he uses the knife to slice open the skin on the pirate's forearm. They both scream as scarlet explodes from his veins.

The magic is cut off.

And I can *breathe.*

With a new wave of azure power, Teddy goes flying back. He lands on the grass with a loud thump. His eyes close and his head lulls, but it doesn't look like he's broken anything.

The pirates retreat, racing back to their ship with the few items they've managed to steal. They're scrambling, just like the people on the shore did when they first attacked. Are the pirates scared? Of *me and Teddy*? Did they not expect a fight from *anyone*?

Fairies. We fought them. We fought pirates. We saved all these people from harm.

And we're alive?

I crawl to Teddy, my throat still raw, my body weak, the world around me blurred. But I have to get to him. Teddy, the summer boy, lying unconscious on the grass. The black swan watches us, perched on the mast of another ship.

We're alive. He saved me? He had the information to go for the crown alone, he could have just . . . just left. But he put himself in danger to help me?

I rest my head on his chest and match my inhales and exhales with his.

CHAPTER TEN

TEDDY IS A GOOD rider. I am not. He can barely walk without tripping over his own feet, yet he looks like royalty as he leads his horse around with pure composure. It infuriates me that once again he's better than me, more experienced than me at something. Is there anything about this new world I'm good at?

We didn't have to steal the horses in the end. Teddy's seemingly endless money paid for them, though I have no doubt he would have found a way to get the horses without paying if the pirates had taken his pearl bracelet and bag of triarue.

I'm not worried any longer that Teddy might be a thief. I don't care what he is. Though, after he saved my life, I might be biased.

'Could you check your map again?' he asks, talking loudly as we ride along a narrow, deserted road. He squints through the blinding midday sun, his face pink. He'll have to buy a hat. Gus should've at least known to give him a shawl or umbrella with that pale skin.

'I just checked it!' It's hard to get words out over the rocking of the horse. It's harder still to open my satchel, and near impossible to read the map. How do people do this? 'Don't you trust me?'

'I don't like these roads. My horse is going to get sore toes.'

I groan. It burns my throat, because just hours ago I was *magically strangled*. 'Horses definitely do not have toes.'

'But I do. And they're sore.'

'The map isn't going to magically change and give us a new road.'

'Your map is a hundred years old, though.'

'So why do you want me to check it?'

We go on like that for about an hour before we find a little village and ask someone. We're fine. On our way, on schedule, alive and well. So we decide to continue on for the rest of the day. The next town is right in Amora's Territory, not far from Glassine, which means our timing will be perfect. I don't want to spend a night in Glassine if I can help it. It seems too dangerous to hang around the grave for long – I don't want anyone to see me there and get even a hint of what I'm doing.

Teddy pats his horse's neck fondly. He doesn't have a care in the world, travelling with his usual smile. Since our pirate-fight, he's picked up as if nothing happened at all. Is he used to such things? Attacks? He woke quickly after being knocked unconscious. Not even a bruise.

I'm the one who's bruised. Both physically and mentally. My arms hurt as I lead the horse, and every time my mind takes me back to the feeling of being choked, I feel the need to put my head between my legs and remind myself I can breathe. But everything is intact. I am alive. My satchel was right where I left it, compass included. Knowing I saved my belongings helps to calm me – this trip would be a thousand times worse without the objects that remind me of home.

Teddy lets his horse fall back so we're riding side-by-side. He plays with the reins. 'You need to be more careful about keeping who you are a secret. If someone like those pirates found out, imagine the price they'd fetch selling a pretty Bearran.'

I want to tease him for calling me pretty, but my gut twists with fear. Would someone really try to kidnap me? I've already changed my clothes, tried to act like nothing in this world surprises me, and told no one my identity. There isn't much more I can do to hide.

He rambles on. 'Anything could happen. People could take advantage of you because they'll know you don't know how the world works. Maybe you should've stayed safe in Bearra. I shouldn't have encouraged you to leave, made it some entertaining thing that I . . . I'm sorry.'

I shake my head. 'You're ridiculous. I can take care of myself, and I would've left even if you didn't join me.'

'You would've left alone, and you probably wouldn't be alive.'

'My choice.'

He swallows. 'I hated watching you get hurt.'

I cannot deal with him if he's going to say things like *that*. 'Teddy, I don't know why you want to keep the truth about magic from me. But if you want me safe, I need to know everything. If I'd known how that pirate had power, maybe I wouldn't have gotten hurt. So tell me, now. How are people in Darraport using magic, with their coaches and their bracelets and . . . everything?'

His face scrunches. 'Maya, I've been trying to ease you into this world, that's all. I didn't want to overwhelm you, so I thought I'd save the explanation for a better time.' He sighs. 'The pirate probably stole his magic.'

'Stole?' I'm sure there's more to Teddy's secrecy – something to do with his past. Whenever magic is brought up, or fairies, he gets a faraway look and dances around real answers. Has he been hurt by magic before?

'Magic isn't only for fairies anymore,' he admits. 'It comes from fairies, of course. They're the source. In your time, they lived separately from society and kept magic to themselves. But they evolved. They started taking leadership positions, forming their territories, and sharing their magic with humans. It helped us progress. But it also became a danger. Now, magic can be bought, borrowed, bartered, stolen. Some people use it for good, and others . . .'

Oh. *Oh.* I have no idea how to feel about that. That's hopeful, though, isn't it? That everyone has access to magic? But if anyone can have it, anyone can use it to hurt people.

'So truly *anyone* can have power?' I ask quietly.

He nods. 'Magic is like a lake. People can take water, drain it, dam it, or open up new rivers. For fairies, it always fills back up. But for humans, it always dries out. Humans are not their own source. They can only do so much, so it would be unfeasable for anyone to ever match a fairy in power. Pure fairy magic can go on forever. Still, some are more powerful than others.'

'You mean Lire? Because she lives in Bearra with our source of triarue?'

Teddy's eyes focus on the horizon. *There it is again.* His horse trots faster so he's slightly ahead. 'Triarue amplifies magic, yes. But Lire and Kara have always been seen as the most powerful fairies. The fairy of wisdom and the fairy of darkness have always been at odds, with the other fairies scattered between. When it comes to a fairy giving someone magic, if it is given directly, it will be powerful and potent. You can't steal magic from a fairy, but you can from a human. It's become something of a trading system. Magic is worth a lot. Especially if it's from Lire or Kara, because they very rarely share their power.'

How can a price be put on magic? 'That's . . . That is just . . . Magic shouldn't be used like that. That is unnatural, and warped, and *wrong*.'

'I thought you didn't care about magic.'

I wrap my hands tighter around my horse's reins. 'I have nothing against magic. Just fairies, who have never used it to help anyone – in my time, at least. And people shouldn't have it either.' I shudder as I remember the feeling of being strangled. 'No one can be trusted with that kind of power.'

'Not everyone is bad. Some people use their magic for good.'

'So you say.' I pick up a nice sugary scent from a nearby village, which distracts me for a few moments. My stomach rumbles. If I had magic, I would use it for good, wouldn't I? 'Teddy, could I steal magic from someone? How?'

'It isn't easy, and I don't recommend trying it.'

'But from what you're saying, we don't even need to find the fairies to get into the grave, because we can get magic from someone who already *has* their magic.'

Something dark catches my eye and I tilt my head up to watch a black swan soaring through the air, stark against the white clouds. Another one? Here? Maybe it's the same one, following us, hoping we have food.

Teddy smiles at it. 'Stolen magic won't be strong enough for what we need. Even if we could find enough, it could take years to track down the right people with the right magic. And then we'd have to take it. It's better to go directly to the fairies and ask for blessings.'

'Blessings? Like the princess has? But that isn't magic.'

'A blessing from every fairy will be more than enough to get us into the grave. They may not give you *magic*, but they're powerful. And people won't come after us trying to steal them.'

I rub my forehead. 'So I have to get blessed by Amora? What's she going to do, give me a makeover to help me attract a husband?'

'Amora's power is about love and passion – not just dresses and romance. Though there's nothing wrong with that, if it's what you want. I'm sure Amora couldn't do much for you, regardless.'

I chuckle. 'Oh, because I'm such a lost cause.'

He stiffens, not meeting my eyes. 'No – No, Maya. Because you don't need a makeover to attract anyone. And you already have plenty of love. Doing this for your family . . . I can't understand being able to love anyone that much. Amora would probably admire you.'

'I—' I nearly pull my horse to a stop. 'You wouldn't do something like this for your family?'

With a shrug, he says, 'I wouldn't know. I don't have one.'

It takes me a moment to respond. 'But you would. You saved me. You helped those people at the river. Even though you didn't know them, you saved them.'

He watches the swan circle above us. 'We both did.'

+ ⋄ ⚬ ◊ ♡ ◊ ⚬ ⋄ +

We spend a night in an abandoned building again, this time on the outskirts of an old town in the north of Amora's Territory. Despite Teddy saying he wouldn't mind paying for accommodation, I refused to accept the help. We also need to stay inconspicuous, which means avoiding people where possible.

Now, we're back on our horses, and my body is even achier than yesterday. I have very much bonded with my horse already, which is wonderful, because I needed something else to worry about. All it took was giving her some scratches behind her ears and feeding her some pieces of cheese, and 'Pansy' became my new best friend. I see her hazel mane and sweet face and suddenly I forget I'm on a life-or-death quest.

Teddy's horse, Sunny, isn't so nice – a huge brown thing that doesn't like scratches. But Teddy loves it anyway. He could come face-to-face with a monster and find a way to love it – and have it love him back.

I'm more confident with my riding today, and we're making faster progress than we would on foot or in a carriage. But the horses are a hassle to feed, and once again I wish we could've used one of those magical coaches.

I stuff my map into my satchel, patting Pansy's neck. 'Only a few more hours to Glassine,' I tell Teddy. 'If it's the same as when my grandmother was buried there, it won't be a big place. She chose an unremarkable town on purpose. We should aim to be in and out. We're studying the grave, seeing what we have to do to rob it, then leaving. No getting overexcited and trying to break in today.'

Teddy squints through the sunlight as we get deeper into the landscape of Amora's Territory – the south-west. As we travel further from the world's centre, the trees get thicker and bushier, the air cools, and the people's skin and hair turn darker. Out here, ethnicities aren't as mixed as in Dar-raport. It isn't rare to see people from all territories, though, so luckily our paler complexions don't stand out.

'So, if we don't need the fairies' help,' Teddy says, 'we find a place to camp and plan our grave heist. If we do need blessings, we start by heading to Amora's Capital.'

'Have you been there?'

His face is shaded by the cover of trees as he says, 'I've spent a lot of time there. I'm acquainted with Amora.'

'*Teddy.*'

He keeps his expression and tone infuriatingly casual. 'She's a social fairy, and she took a liking to me. I've stayed at her palace a handful of times. It isn't as shocking as it may seem.'

I stay quiet and try to remain collected, but I'm hit with a fresh wave of questions about Teddy. They send shivers along my spine. Who is this boy, why is he so friendly, so loved by all? And what is his real motive?

⋅ ⊹ ◦ ⋆ ◊ ♡ ◊ ◦ ⋆ ⊹ ⋅

We reach Glassine and hop off the horses to wander the town. It isn't easy to avoid attention here; everyone smiles and waves. Closely-pressed houses sit right on the street, with big porches the locals lounge on, chatting with each other. Some even come right up to us, pressing glasses of wine into our hands that we discretely pour on the ground when they can't see. It's friendly. *Scarily* friendly.

The fashion is different to Darraport. Despite the weather being cooler, the clothes are looser. More skin is revealed, and the colours lean towards rich and warm hues. Everyone is trying to get as much sun as they possibly can.

I turn to Teddy, who's watching a couple of kids drink wine from their parents' glasses.

'Are they celebrating?' I ask him. 'Is this a . . . a party, or something?'

He walks close to me, our shoulders brushing. He keeps eyeing me with a deep concern, like he's worried someone's going to jump out of the shadows and attack us.

'Amora's Territory is known for its parties,' he says. 'Fun, love, beauty, everything passion – that's what Amora represents. The people in this territory don't tend to do things they aren't enamoured by. If they want to spend all day drinking, they do.'

An intoxicated man ahead of us sloshes wine down his sunset-orange shirt, then laughs and continues on his way. I sidestep the red liquid as it creeps down my path, cringing as I remember wine's foul taste.

'But what about work? Money? Food?' I ask. 'How do they get all this wine?'

'Amora's magic keeps the territory afloat. If that's how she wants to run things, and her people are happy—'

'*Too* happy.'

'Who are we to judge?'

'She actually rules the territory? I thought the fairies' territories were more . . . symbolic? Patrons of the region, but not rulers. Like Lire with Bearra.'

He pretends to scan the wooden houses, avoiding my stare. 'Lire has always had more power in Bearra than the royal family. Haven't you noticed they've always acted more as figureheads than actual rulers? That's why monarchies were phased out everywhere else. It was found to be far more efficient to have each territory ruled by a fairy, with its cities and towns managed by elected leaders. The fairies provide what magic they choose to and exercise their control as much as they want. Cities like Darraport exist on stolen magic and trade alone.'

I tap my fingers against my thighs, frowning. Could this be why the queen and king have chosen to keep Bearra closed for so long? They could be scared to lose their power. The people love them, but if they got a glimpse of the real world, they might not for much longer.

In a bushy green park full of both children and adults playing and picnicking wildly, we stop for a moment to rest and ask for directions to the cemetery. It's at the furthest reaches of the town, past fields and fields of flowering vine-yards. Other cultures would bury their dead closer to home out of respect, but here they're only concerned with life, with fun. Why have a cemetery in the centre of it?

We head west and I expect something life-changing when we reach it. For something within me to shift forever as I sense the crown's power. But instead, the cemetery is standard, dull, with overgrown grey grass and a sprawl of headstones in various sizes and shapes over rolling hills. In this expanse of grey, on grey, on grey, finding where my grandmother is buried might be the most difficult part of this heist.

'What did you say her name was?' asks Teddy, cringing as his eyes travel across the graves. 'I don't even know where to *begin*.'

I rub my eyes and look across the cemetery again, as if her grave will magically appear. 'Olivia Shy the First. My aunt is the second. She named her daughter after herself.'

'Your grandmother sounds anything but shy.' He grins at me. 'So that's who you are? Maya *Shy* of Bearra?'

I suck in a breath, my stomach squeezing. He already knows too much, and to know my full name, to know who my family is, to know me as Maya Nova . . . It's too much of a risk.

'That's me,' I lie.

'It isn't that bad,' he says, mistaking my hesitation for embarrassment. 'And you're shy, aren't you? So, it's accurate.'

'I'm not shy.' My cheeks heat. 'I just don't like people.'

'I love when you talk about hating everyone,' he says, nudging my arm. 'It makes me feel so special to be your one friend.'

'We aren't friends.'

'I did save your life.'

'Enough.'

He kicks the dirt. 'I don't even have a surname. You're lucky.' He stretches his arms, smiles again, and says, 'So, any idea where the grave might be? What it might look like?'

I glance at the nearest headstone and can barely make out the cracked, lichen-covered name: *Sugarson*. I doubt I'll be lucky enough for the dead to be buried in alphabetical order. But what about order in terms of time? 'These are really old,' I say. 'My grandmother only died a decade ago – sorry, a hundred and ten years ago. We need to look for a less ancient section.'

Teddy's eyes brighten. 'Maya, you genius. I thought we'd have to check every last one.'

His encouraging words are nice to hear, but I'm still bothered by our surname conversation, so I don't reply. I scratch Pansy's muzzle, feed her a slice of sweet Darraport cheese, and tie her to a tree.

Teddy does the same with Sunny. 'I don't know how such a small town can have so many bodies,' he says as we walk, the fields continuing to stretch on.

I run my fingers over the top of a low headstone, and the old granite crumbles. 'Doesn't have to be many people. Just a lot of time.'

We continue scanning the names of the dead as we dawdle, slowly reaching newer sections. We're careful not to let ourselves overshoot, because a century is still many, many bodies ago. We eventually find a patch at the far side of the cemetery that's unkempt and brown, though the headstones are certainly less black and crumbled. Of course, this area would get no visitors. Who visits the graves of people who died long, long ago? It's almost as if my grandmother knew Bearra would sleep for a hundred years not long after her death, meaning no one would ever come looking for her grave.

But we come to a halt; I couldn't have been more wrong.

'Olivia Shy the First,' whispers Teddy, 'you outrageous old ghost.'

It isn't a grave. It's a *mausoleum*. The marble structure is the size of a small house, covered in the same type of thick vines that guard Bearra. Intricate details are carved into the walls and roof – depictions of flowers, of jewels, of mythical animals like dragons and unicorns.

The magic surrounding the grave has a physical force, even from where I stand at least fifty metres away. A pushing but a reeling, an attraction that simultaneously forces me away. My eyes can't focus on the mausoleum for more than a few seconds at a time. A section above the door is lined with glowing blue triarue, as if the grave is asking to be robbed, and within a circle of rubies, the name *Olivia Shy* is engraved in the stone.

My knees wobble. The crown is in *there*? And why would my grandmother bury herself surrounded by magic if she didn't want to be found out? How did she even have herself buried with it? Who created all these wards? Is the crown in there creating all this power itself?

Teddy's jaw is slack. 'There is no chance we're getting in there without help. Without *all* the help. Your aunt was right

– we'll need blessings from every fairy to fight through magic that strong.'

This is so, so, so much worse than I expected. My shoulders tense and my chest heats with frustration. 'This is why I hate magic, and hate royals, and hate—' I slump onto the grass. 'I truly thought, hoped, expected that it was an exaggeration. That this would all work out fine. That I'd be home soon. But we'll have to travel the *world*.'

Teddy steps closer to the building and inspects it. 'Even if we could hack down these vines, the magic is so strong it would probably kill us as soon as we walked through the door. And even if it didn't, there'd still be more power within. We don't know what to expect.'

'So we have no choice.' I bury my face in my hands, and my voice comes out muffled. 'We have to go to all the fairies for help. And why would they help us? We can't tell them what we're doing. Especially Lire. If she found out, she'd come get the crown herself, and my entire family would be imprisoned or killed, and we'd lose our reward money!'

He rakes a hand through his hair, shimmering copper in the sun. He looks up to the sky. Another black swan soars above. It's starting to feel like a bad omen.

He murmurs, 'It's going to be very difficult.'

'Difficult? How about *impossible*?'

'That doesn't sound like you,' he says gently, bringing his focus back. He walks all the way around the mausoleum before sitting beside me, tapping the grass with his fingers. His pale-green shirt complements the vines wrapping around the grave. 'But, you know, we could forget about the crown. Find another way to get your family money. You don't need to be rich, do you? You only need enough to not fall into poverty. We can steal something else. Get you a job. Sell something.'

'No! *No*. I can't go home with anything less than the crown.'

'Why? Maya—'

I stand, shaking the doubt from my mind, my body, until I'm rock-solid again, determined. Unstoppable. 'Because that's who I am, alright? That's what I'm *going* to do.'

'Has anyone ever told you you're stubborn? Not just a little bit, but life-threateningly so.'

'We all have our flaws.' I give him a dismissive wave of my hand. I am going to do this. How difficult can travelling the entire world be? 'I'm going to find these fairies, and get this magic, even if it's impossible. Are you coming with me or not?'

He reluctantly gets up from the ground, nearly tripping over as he does. 'Come on, then,' he says tiredly. 'Who am I to say no to an adventure?'

I take a final look at the grave as we return to the horses. We lead them to a stream for some water, then begin our next journey – to Amora's palace, for our first blessing.

To my crown.

CHAPTER ELEVEN

THE JOURNEY TO AMORA'S Palace isn't long. According to Teddy, most of the fairies have situated their capital cities towards the centre of the world, since it becomes so cold at the furthest reaches. Of course, in a place like Amora's Territory – where everything is about having fun, showing skin, and drinking – a cold capital wouldn't make sense.

Teddy uses his pearl bracelet to overpay a stable to ensure they take good care of Pansy and Sunny. Then we delve into the inner-city on foot towards the palace, avoiding the crowds as best we can. Although we don't look local, our new clothes at least make us look like tourists rather than Bearrans. And there are plenty of tourists here, looking to party their days away.

I try not to appear breathless at the sights, but in this overwhelming city, it's difficult. Amora's Capital is unimaginable. Though it's laid out similarly to Bearra – the palace in the centre and the city surrounding – nothing else is the same. The air is warm, slick, and sweet, like it's mixed with melted honey. The crowds are thick, going nowhere but nonetheless moving with rhythm. Like Glassine, the houses and other buildings are small, with larger outdoor areas; everything is meant for congregation, partying, sunshine. The roads are crimson, and the whole place is covered with a haze, like it's always sunset. Pink, red, white, and every shade between.

The palace rises above me as we weave our way further into the capital: baby-pink stone, ornate carvings covering the spires and towers and turrets, a large entryway, and sprawling gardens. Every kind of flower blooms around the palace – trees of blush-coloured cherry blossoms and jasmine, beds of poppies and lavender, and endless daisies in the grass – creating a blanket of even more pink and adding a pleasantly dizzying perfume to the air.

Teddy's cheeks are flushed and his eyes are bright as he gazes at the palace. At least *he's* excited.

I'm wondering if I've made a huge mistake. Being here, in an alien place, in front of a palace I have no business being near, hoping to ask one of the seven fairies for a blessing . . .

I'm about to shove my trembling hands in my pockets when Teddy intertwines his fingers with mine and leads me through the crowds. He takes me up a pathway of white tile and up to the tall, curved palace entrance. He presses himself close to me. In my mind, I know I should shake him off, to stop him belittling me like I'm helpless, but my body rebels and I squeeze his hand tighter.

When we reach the palace's entrance, I expect to be stopped by guards, but people wander in and out as they please. The guards I spot are too busy chatting and drinking from flasks to notice me. The palace doesn't even have any doors. The base of the structure is an open-air tunnel with various staircases along the side walls that lead to unknown places. Although everyone seems to be welcome, I quickly notice that the people in the palace are dressed more finely; they wear heavier, shinier jewels and strut about like they own the place.

Teddy leans down and whispers in my ear, 'Try to relax. Or at least act less frosty.'

I scowl at him, but attempt to release the tension from my shoulders. There isn't much I can do with my face, though I try to form an easy smile.

Teddy knows where he's going, and his confidence is enough to make us look like we belong here.

Lilting string melodies drift from the ballroom and carry through the halls of the palace. We follow the music and step into an enormous space with a marble floor, rose-coloured walls, and a range of mismatched chandeliers that drip from the ceiling. At least a hundred people dance to the romantic waltz, ballgowns swaying and shifting through the evening light.

And the *fairy*. Amora is impossible to miss, right in the centre of the dance floor. She has golden skin and a long, bumpy nose. Her hair is curled into chestnut braids that fall over the front of her flowing dress, and everything she wears is in shades of pink, from the jewels she wears to her shoes. But her wings extend from her shoulder blades in every colour of the rainbow, like a butterfly dipped in dye over and over, the colours melting together in perfect synchronisation. The fairy dances with a wine glass in her hand, and everyone's eyes magnetise to her.

Teddy watches her with a wide grin, and he squeezes my hand. 'Don't stress. I can do the talking.'

I drop his hand; I'd forgotten we were still touching.

Amora spots Teddy as she spins, wings fluttering. Her bright eyes gleam and she wiggles her arms excitedly. 'Teddy, my darling!' she calls, loud enough the entire palace must hear. As she flies over to us, the people around her disperse like steam. The music stops for a moment, but she waves a hand and the ballroom bursts back into dance. 'It's been so long!' She kisses Teddy on his cheeks, over and over.

He hugs her, chuckling. 'Amora. I love your new hair.'

She winks. 'I'm the fairy of beauty, aren't I? The most gorgeous being in the world. Who would dare *not* love my hair?'

'Well, as the second most gorgeous being, I—'

She cuts him off with a laugh and ruffles his hair with her delicate hand. A trickle of pink magic flows over Teddy's head, and suddenly his hair is shiny and sleek, as if he hasn't been journeying for days without bathing.

'My love,' Amora says, hands on her hips. 'You don't seem to be here for the ball, so what is it you need? You want to stay a while again? You know you're always safe with me.'

I nearly recoil. She's a fairy, *for fairy's sake*. Teddy said he knew her, but they don't just seem like acquaintances from parties – they seem close. Why is Teddy close with a fairy, and why didn't he tell me?

I ball my hands into fists, thinking about punching him, but he nudges my arm as if to say, *I'll explain later*.

Amora sizes me up, her gaze travelling from my dirty shoes to my matted hair. She gives Teddy a quick glance. Does she know about his past? Is she deciding what I can hear?

'I'm Maya,' I tell her, trying to cut the tension. 'A colleague of Teddy's.'

'Ah, I see.' She picks a piece of fluff from Teddy's shirt without taking her eyes off me, though I note that it's protectiveness in her gaze, not hostility. 'It is always good to have *colleagues*.'

Teddy clears his throat, giving Amora a serious look. 'Might we talk somewhere private? I do have a favour to ask. And not a small one.'

'Anything for you, sweet boy.' Amora pouts. 'I hate it when you aren't smiling.'

The fairy leads us up several flights of stairs, flying with ease while we take step after step, feet aching. We end up in a small library. Amora shuts the door and the sounds of the palace cut off immediately. Taking in the book-lined walls, I wonder if I've entered paradise. Some books are new, some ancient, and I wish I could get my hands on them all. Of course a fairy would have an impressive collection. This might only be a taste of all she has.

But that isn't what I'm here for. I blink, refocus, and join Teddy at a low table while Amora gets us tea. When she returns with steaming cups, I wait for Teddy to drink first. When he doesn't choke or die, I take a sip of my own and nearly moan at the sweet taste. Everything – *everything* – in this territory is made for the utmost pleasure. How much magic does Amora have to pour into her society to keep it running? Where does the tea even come from, if no one works?

Amora sits with us, and I try to remain calm. She's one of the less-frightening fairies, along with Muse, the fairy of music, and Adella, the fairy of generosity. Lire has always been the most powerful, along with Rhiannon, the fairy of strength, and Grace, the fairy of truth. And it was Kara, the fairy of darkness, who cursed Princess Dawn. She's the one I've had the most nightmares about – but she does hate the royals as much as me, so maybe we're on the same side.

'What do you need, darlings?' Amora says, her demeanour more serious now we're away from the crowds. The magic radiating from her turns darker and stronger, and she stretches out her multicoloured wings rather than flutter them lightly. Suddenly she *seems* immortal; not just an ethereal beauty like in the ballroom, but an intimidating force. Only a few days ago, a pirate nearly choked me to death with stolen magic. What could a fairy of infinite power do?

Teddy gives her a guilty look. 'We're on a very important quest. I can't tell you much, because it could compromise what we're trying to do, but . . . we need magic. A lot of it. Blessings from each of the seven fairies.'

She narrows her eyes. 'Six, you mean?'

'*No.*' His voice turns uncharacteristically hard. 'All seven.'

'Yes, of course.' Amora swallows, her wings sinking for a moment. 'I only meant, with Kara, well, the tension with—'

'Can you help us?' Teddy interjects. 'Please, Amora.' He looks at her with such intense, pleading eyes, it's almost as if it's *his* family at risk of starving.

'I don't like that you won't tell me what it's for.' She runs her palms along the silky fabric of her dress. 'I trust you with my whole heart, Teddy. I've known you for most of your life. I want what's best for you. I *don't* want to help you with something that could put you in danger.'

He reaches out his hands, and she takes them. 'It'll be so much more dangerous if we don't have your help. If the other fairies see you've already agreed, they'll be more likely to give their blessings, too. Then we can finish the quest and return as soon as we can.'

Her rainbow wings shift as she gives him a knowing look. 'Darling, don't try to manipulate me. You know it will work.'

I suck in a breath and say, my voice croaky, 'This quest, if we succeed, will save my family. It'll help Teddy too. And we'll owe you.'

She gives me a warm look. 'You don't want to owe a fairy anything. You're lucky I already love Teddy and can't refuse him.'

'So you'll give us the blessing?' I feel my face lighting up, so I push back and try to stay serious.

'I will.' She stares at her hands, and the jewels on them, then removes seven rings of plain silver. 'These are enchanted. Like triarue, they can hold magic.' She hands three to me and three to Teddy. She cups the remaining one in her hands, and a pink aura surrounds it for a few moments. Her wings and eyes glow.

I've seen Lire use magic, seen her bestow blessings, but I still have to stifle a gasp. I never imagined I would be able to see such a thing up close.

The colour fades, and all that's left is the ring, with a new, faint-pink colour. 'There, darling,' she says, handing it to me. 'The rings will hold your blessings – it's better that way. You'll be able to use them, and you'll feel the blessings within you, but their magic won't be part of you. If you call on the ring you want to use, it'll bring what you need. The other fairies will understand.'

Teddy puts his rings on, so I do the same, leaving the magical one for last. I'm hesitant to wear it, and I wonder why Amora gave it to me instead of Teddy.

'Go on, Maya,' she says, her features softening. 'It's yours. Passion. I hope you'll use it, and I hope it will teach you new ways to love.'

I place the ring on my finger, and like the others, it fits perfectly. The pinkish silver shines on my left hand's index finger. Immediately I feel its power – a buzzing in my heart – but like Amora said, I can't actually access any magic. I don't know how Passion will help me when I return to the grave. Maybe it'll only remind me why I'm doing all of this.

I'm so mesmerised that my cold mask slips. 'Thank you, Amora,' I whisper. 'Really.'

'You deserve it more than most,' she says, patting my hand.

I swallow the lump in my throat at the genuineness of her comment and nod.

Teddy twists his rings, all placed on his left hand. 'Amora, you're my favourite fairy for a reason. One day I'm going to repay you for all the good you've done me.'

'You'll repay me by staying alive,' she tells him.

He stands and hugs her, careful around her wings, like he's an expert at hugging fairies. 'I'll visit as soon as I can. Properly next time, I swear.'

Amora is so enamoured by Teddy, it's as if she's already forgotten I'm here. She breaks into tears and cries into his shoulder. 'Oh, Teddy, I wish you were *my* son. I always have. I wouldn't let you get into these situations. I'd keep you happy here. Without having to worry about . . .' Her eyes widen for a moment, as if realising she's said something she shouldn't. Teddy's jaw hardens and she laughs, pulling away from the hug. 'I'm sure anyone would wish to have you all to herself,' she says. 'I only wish you would visit more often.'

I realise I'm giving them a very strange look, so I cover my apprehension with a short, awkward laugh. Teddy has more of a past with her than they want me to know. He must have gotten into some trouble when he last stayed here, and she's covering it up.

Or am I being ridiculous? This is Teddy. He's saved my life several times. Sure, I've only known him a few days, but . . . it's *Teddy*. He got me this magic, the first real step to getting the crown. Who cares if he's hiding something?

Except I have a lot more to lose than him. There's an anxiety in the back of my mind that he'll take the crown for himself as soon as we get it. Does Amora know he'd do something like that to me? Is that what she's trying not to give away?

When the fairy is done crying, we move to the door. As it opens, the sounds of the palace and the ball fill the air again. Amora's voice lilts over the noise. 'You're seeking Rhiannon's blessing next, I suppose, if you're taking the clockwise route?' Teddy nods. 'Good luck to you. My sister is not as sociable as I am, but tell her I sent you, and she might just soften.'

Teddy laughs, because of course he isn't worried about anyone disliking him. 'Goodbye, Amora,' he says, pulling her into a final embrace.

She surprises me by wrapping her arms around me as well, squishing me in her dainty but strong fairy grip. Her wings brush my skin and they feel like nothing and everything at once – not quite solid, but undoubtedly real. I shiver as she says, 'Take care of my darling Teddy, Maya. He could use someone like you to keep him out of trouble.' She turns to a guard who has appeared in the hallway. 'Prepare them rooms for the night. Make sure they're well-fed and rested before their journey tomorrow. Any supplies they need, organise it.'

Teddy shakes his head. 'You don't have to.'

'As if I wouldn't.' She smiles sadly. 'If keeping you safe for one night is all I manage to do, that's still one more night, isn't it?'

He hugs her *again* before we're led away.

Step after step again. Following the guard through the palace, the monotony nearly puts me to sleep. I've now seen enough of this city to no longer be excited by every shiny pink thing.

Then I spot a girl watching us from a dark corner. My stomach drops as if I've seen a ghost, and a tingle runs up my spine. Her eyes are narrowed and challenging, dark and sleek as her long, black hair. Her outfit doesn't blend in here: fitted travelling clothes, dark and gothic; a jacket and pants made for outdoor activity, not dancing. Her eyebrows raise as if she's daring me to say something.

Why does she seem familiar? She looks my age, but I can't know her.

Teddy doesn't notice, and deciding that I'm being delusional – she must be a guard, or someone waiting to talk to Amora – I follow him silently through the palace halls.

Chapter Twelve

'Rhiannon's Jungle is as terrifying as the legends suggest,' Teddy says, and I can tell from his furrowed brow that he isn't only taunting me. 'And as deadly.'

Beneath him, Sunny trots along happily. Amora moved our horses to the palace stables for the night, which meant giant cushions and sparkly pedicures. With them so spritely, we'll reach Rhiannon's Territory in no time.

Teddy and I experienced similarly luxurious treatment in the palace. We each had an enormous bedroom with the softest of beds. I wondered if I would ever stop sinking into the cushioning, running my hands over the silk sheets. A relaxing, magical lavender scent filled the air, and I drifted into a deep sleep that left me fresh and optimistic in the morning.

The Passion-blessed ring on my finger might have helped, too. Amora did say I needed it, and I may have been sub-consciously drawing on its power. It turns out a night of indulgence and rest was exactly what I needed to gain the energy to start this next journey; to ask the fairy of strength for a blessing, and to hike through her notoriously dangerous jungle.

'Terrifying?' I tease Teddy. 'Do you have a phobia of vines?'

'Since my time in Bearra, yes. In Rhiannon's Territory they're natural, they make sense. In Bearra they're a warning – wrong and intimidating. I don't care for them anymore.'

Hm. *Try being trapped within them for a century.*

There's a distinct shift in the air as we leave Amora's Territory and cross into Rhiannon's. As the haze of fun and relaxation disappears, my senses sharpen and fear sets in again. I notice the black swan above me once more, and I shudder.

'Teddy,' I say, my voice slightly weak. 'I know I missed the last hundred years, but there's no chance animals are, well, *intelligent* now, is there?'

'They always have been.' He pats Sunny's neck proudly.

I try to keep scanning the sky, but the road is becoming so rough and uneven that I have to keep an eye on Pansy's steps. Soon there won't be any road at all – there'll only be jungle floor. If only we could fly like the swan.

'You're really worried about this bird,' says Teddy, watching me.

I point up. 'Don't tell me you haven't noticed it's been following us since Darraport. That's several days, Teddy, and that's *worrying*.'

He navigates his horse through a shallow creek, and as I follow, water hits my ankles. Teddy glances back to make sure I'm okay. I wish I had something to throw at him.

'It's just a swan,' he says. 'Maybe it wants to befriend us. Or it's tracking us, thinking we're headed to food.'

'That might comfort me if you didn't think *every living being* wants to be your friend. And out of everyone in the world to follow, why us?'

'Well, you think *every living being* wants to be your enemy. And why not us?' He gestures towards a puddle in our path. 'Careful.'

I pull Pansy around it, and I'm not sure I could be scowling more if I tried. 'Are you going to tell me, for certain, that this swan doesn't seem suspicious?'

'Fine.' His eyes, golden in the sun, bore into mine, and my breath hitches. 'It is mildly suspicious. But I'm going to focus on getting to Rhiannon rather than waste my time worrying about birds.'

The sun is beginning to set, and despite my energy from last night's rest, I'm losing patience. I want to be alone, I want to feel safe. I want to be *home*. I want my parents, my sisters. I want to be hiding under my blankets with a book in my hands, with thick pages between my fingers.

Yet I also don't want to be home, trapped again. I love it out here, I love the danger, I love travelling with Teddy, I love the . . . Passion. *You could thrive out here, Maya.* He knew it before I did.

The swan travels closer to us as the sun continues its journey to the horizon. Its huge, black wingspan is stunning against the pastel hues of the sky. Its long neck and red beak move like a snake. There is no denying that it's making a descent, as if getting ready to land right in front of us.

Why do I feel like we're its prey? My voice is frantic as I ask Teddy, 'What if someone disguised themselves as an animal, using magic? Is that possible? If it were an enemy, someone who wants the crown for—'

Teddy snorts. 'If anyone has tried turning themselves into an animal, they wouldn't be able to turn back. Animals can't use magic the way we can. They'd be stuck until someone fixed them.'

'If you say so,' I mutter. He would know better than me, but I still don't quite believe it.

The swan dives closer and closer. The trees are still far apart enough that it would have no trouble swooping, using its beak, its claws, its wings to tear open our skin. It must know it'll be harder to reach us once we've entered the jungle. It must know now is the time to attack.

'*Teddy*,' I say, gripping Pansy's reins so tight they might snap.

The swan spins around in front of us, eclipsing the setting sun, the orange light flashing in rays as its black wings beat up and down. Finally it lands on the ground and our horses stop at once, hesitant and jumpy. The swan extends its neck, stretching, staring at us as the sun makes its final drop beneath the horizon.

'Oh.' Teddy winces. 'Oh no.'

Then, a shift. A blue haze circles the bird, matching the blue of the dusk. The smoky cloud sparkles, glows, shifts and breathes. Magic. *Magic.*

'Teddy!'

The magic swirls around the swan, a whirlwind blurring the changing of the creature as it becomes—

Fairies, no.

'That's the fastest I've ever been proven wrong,' Teddy says, his face a frozen mask of shock.

The blue magic fades and leaves behind the dark-haired girl who was watching me in Amora's Palace. She steps toward us menacingly, her long legs steady even as she crosses the uneven road. She cocks her head and sneers.

Pansy whinnies. I want to scream.

'Good evening,' the swan girl says, her voice thick and sweet like a song. She's beautiful, almost regal. Her long, black hair reaches her hips, her deep brown eyes are sharp, and her pink lips are turned down.

'H-Hello,' utters Teddy.

'I know about the crown.' She doesn't bother with any small talk – something I can respect. Her arms are crossed and her fingers tap her skin boredly. The shape of her body, lithe and solid beneath her tightly fitted black outfit, tells me she's strong, a fighter. An enemy. 'And you'll find that it is now *mine* to steal.'

I try to look calm – to not seem weak – but I'm not sure what to do, and I barely manage to sit upright. 'What crown?'

She rolls her eyes. 'Stop, before you embarrass yourself. You've noticed me following you since Darraport.'

Well, *I* did. I bet Teddy wished he took me seriously now. 'And?'

'And that treasure is mine.'

Teddy throws his arms up innocently. 'What are you, a pirate? If money's what you want, you can have it. We'll pay you. Or you can join us and take a cut of the reward.'

'*Teddy.*' I look around for something to throw at him. 'Absolutely not!'

She rolls her eyes. 'Don't you dare assume I am as uncivilised as a pirate. Money is not my objective. I want power.'

'Then go and get some,' says Teddy, his face paling. 'We have none.'

'Unfortunately—' she picks a charcoal feather from the ground '—stolen magic won't be enough to break my curse.'

Teddy whips his head towards me. 'A curse! That's how she transforms, Maya, it's a *curse*. I wasn't proven wrong, because—'

'*Teddy*,' I groan.

She exhales impatiently. As if checking her story off a list, she says, 'It's simple. Every day at dawn, I become a swan. Through the night, I'm myself again. The pirates you fought in Darraport are the ones who cursed me. I've been stalking them for a long time, waiting for the best chance to kill their captain. But right when I was ready to strike, you showed up, speaking of an object so powerful it could break my curse. Of course, I decided to turn my attention to you.'

'But why?' I say, forcing myself to meet her poisonous gaze. 'Why would anyone curse you?'

'Because I am Sierra Reed,' she says, as if that answers all of my questions.

'Good . . . for you,' I say at the same time Teddy mumbles, '*Fairies.*'

She begins pacing back and forth. 'Hm. I thought even a Bearran would have heard of my family. We've been around long enough.'

My shoulders tense. 'I really don't care who your family is, Sierra Reed,' I say, but I'm thinking about Teddy's warning not to let people know I'm Bearran, and how someone else has now found out. Someone *dangerous*.

Sierra nearly laughs. 'Soon you will. We are like royalty in Grace's Territory. We are the protectors of the waters. My sisters and I were trained to fight, to defeat even the strongest, most lethal enemies to our fairy and territory. That is why pirates loathe us. Why they hatched a plan to steal magic to fight us. Not to simply kill us, but humiliate us – curse us to become *animals*.'

'Your entire family can turn into animals?' I shrug and glance at Teddy. 'I'd love to be able to turn into a cat and sleep all day in the sun. It really doesn't sound terrible.'

'No, they don't *turn* into animals.' Her jaw hardens and her eyes meet the floor. 'They've been stuck as swans since the night of the curse. My curse was only weakened because I hid. Because while my sisters were on our ship, I dove beneath the water and it diluted the magic. Now, in my shame, I am the only person who can save my family.'

'But the pirates,' Teddy says, 'can't they undo the curse?'

'You believe someone cruel enough to curse another person would ever reverse it? Besides, I'd kill him before I begged him for anything.'

'Then Grace – if it's her magic that was used—'

'You may have gotten lucky with Amora,' the girl says, 'but most fairies have no love for us. Even with my family's status, Grace doesn't spend her days fixing people's problems. She's the fairy of truth. Of justice and balance. She will always sooner let stories play out than intervene.'

'Even if it means her territory will be overrun with pirates?' I ask.

Sierra Reed shakes her head. 'Enough. I don't owe you any explanations. You're wasting my time. Hand over the rings. Now.'

I fold my fingers into fists. 'I'm trying to save my family too,' I say quietly. 'I can't let you have my treasure.'

She gives me a blank stare.

'We don't need to be enemies,' Teddy says, hands outstretched. 'You can join us. Help us, and we'll use the crown to break your curse before we take it to Bearra.'

Her laugh is husky and mean. 'I'm not looking for allies. I'm here to tell you to give up before I *make* you give up. I know exactly what you're doing. I know where the grave is and how to open it. All I need is those rings, and I can do it myself.'

'But if there's a compromise—'

'There won't be a compromise,' Sierra spits. 'That crown is mine. I'm not failing my family again. This time when I try to break the curse, it's going to work.'

I take a few deep breaths, trying to balance the anger and fear in my chest, a war of fire and frost. 'Why are you introducing yourself now?' I ask her, trying to stall her with more questions while I think of *anything* to escape. 'Why not wait for us to get all the blessings, then swoop in and steal the prize?'

She laughs again. 'Because there's no way the two of you will ever make it. You're weak. Powerless. If I wasn't following you, I'd be halfway through this quest by now. All I need is the rings. Amora wouldn't have given them to me herself, but now that you have them, I can take them. There's no more need for you.'

'So you're going to, what, attack us?' I say. 'Rip the rings off our cold, dead fingers? Because you might be able to kill me, but I swear I'll be right back to haunt you.'

Sierra steps forward on her long legs. Her eyes narrow and her voice drops to a whisper. 'I don't doubt I could kill you, day or night. I simply don't want to. Which is why it's better for everyone if you hand over the rings now, before I maim you beyond recognition.'

'If you've been following us,' I say, hands trembling, 'you know there's no way I'm giving up the crown. You'll *have* to kill me.'

She smiles. 'If you insist.'

I don't allow myself to break eye contact. I push my shoulders back, staring her down. Pansy whinnies again, but I urge her to stay.

'No,' Teddy says. 'We'll think of something, okay?'

We both ignore him. I push myself out of my saddle, remaining atop Pansy, and place my hand on the satchel so I can grab my knife. Sierra takes another step forward, her eyes bright. She is, in every way, an animal, a predator. My heart races.

She screams, jumping over Pansy's head and onto her back so fast I nearly fall. Pansy rears and nearly kicks us both off, but Sierra pushes me down and straddles me. I yelp as she tries to yank the rings from my hand, my fingers searing with pain. I use my free hand to get my knife, and try to slash Sierra with it, but she pins my arm under her foot.

I screech, my eyes filling with tears. 'Get off!' I thrash around, anything to get her away, but she's so strong – I don't have a chance. Pansy is throwing her head around, trying to tear us off her, but Sierra's grip is unyielding.

I try to look for Teddy, but his horse is ahead on the road. *He's leaving me behind?* I scream for help, but he keeps going.

Sierra has nearly pried the first ring from my finger, despite how hard I try to clench my fist. If I don't give in soon, she'll break each of my fingers until she gets what she wants. I cry out in pain, unable to do anything. The skin breaks on my finger, a wound opening where she tries to get the ring off my flesh any way she can. I kick at her as a searing sensation travels up my arm and acid fills my mouth.

She's going to kill me. She'll kill me. My family will be doomed. My *family*.

Sierra changes tactic and wraps her hands around my neck. My breath cuts off immediately, expertly. I choke on a scream. I'm not here anymore, I'm in Darraport, being strangled by magic, by a pirate. The same pirate who cursed her.

I'm dying.

I'm dying.

I've *failed*.

Then I see Teddy. How? My head is spinning. Is he only a mirage? But he's there, running towards me on foot, with a large branch in his hands. *Weapon.* He's waving. He isn't running away. He wants me to . . . to . . .

I become a dead weight and let myself fall over Pansy's side. Sierra doesn't expect it – she comes tumbling down with me. We land with a jarring thud that sends sparks through my vision, but it's enough for me to get out of her grip. Pansy nearly stomps on us both as she bolts away.

Whatever Amora's ring might have to give me, I beg for it. I give into the blessing.

Passion, I plead. *Please – any magic that might be available to me, I need it.*

Sierra pushes herself up, growling with fury. But when she touches me, the ring's power pours towards her and a wave of pink washes over her skin. She falters, her eyes drooping and rolling into the back of her head like she's drunk. She drops to her knees, black hair fanning as she falls.

Teddy raises the branch over her head and smashes it against her skull.

With a jerk, she's knocked out cold.

I sprint back, catching my breath. *I'm alive.*

And there's Sierra Reed. Sprawled on the road like this, she's just a girl my age, struggling to save her family like me. My instincts tell me not to leave her. I want to help her. But I look back to Teddy, who's staring at me with his jaw slack, vulnerable and afraid.

We have to go. Sierra will wake, and it won't be long before she finds us again. Then we'll need a real plan to get rid of her.

'You used magic,' Teddy says.

I nod, unsure what to say. It didn't feel like using magic, or at least how I'd imagine it. It was all the ring. I just asked the blessing for a favour.

Teddy nods in return, wilting with exhaustion. He doesn't look like himself. 'We'll need to ride through the night. We better start.'

Not just ride, but race.

Because now? Now, we have an *enemy*.

CHAPTER
THIRTEEN

ANY ENERGY OR SENSE of calm we had earlier today is gone. Hours after leaving Sierra Reed behind, Teddy, me, and the horses are ready to drop. But we can't let her catch up. For days she flew circles above us, almost teasingly, showing us how slow we are. As soon as she becomes the swan again, we're doomed.

After a while, we hop off the horses and walk beside them. Neither of us thinks it's fair to make them keep carrying us, and the jungle terrain is so difficult to traverse, I'm worried that at any moment Pansy could fall with me attached. It's difficult to see, and every time a cloud passes over the moon, we almost have to stop. Otherwise it's only a matter of time before we're prey to some kind of jungle hazard – a hole, or a river, or some animal lurking in the shadows.

I shudder.

The jungle thickens and thickens the further we travel, a humid tangle of green and brown and sharply-coloured blossoms. There are small villages here and there, but the territory mostly consists of people living on their own in huge structures built high in the trees and vines. Teddy says there are cities closer to the heart of the territory, including the capital, but out here people prefer to be alone.

The weather, even into the night, is warm and sticky. A layer of dampness, sweat, and grime coats my skin, and insects bite at any flesh I have exposed. For it to be this warm, we can't be far from Bearra – unless it's only the heavy canopy of trees trapping the heat, or Rhiannon's magic. I'm just thankful for my new shoes and their ability to grip the wet rocks, fallen trees, and squishy ground.

I wipe sweat from my brow and hold back an enormous leaf. 'When Sierra said Grace refused to help her . . .' I say, panting to keep my breath. 'Do you think she was right? Even Lire only makes rare public appearances. We were lucky with Amora. How are we going to get a fairy like Rhiannon to help us?'

Teddy slicks his auburn hair back. He's struggling to walk, clumsy and fumbling; he has no spatial awareness even at the best of times. It would be funny or endearing if I wasn't so frightened. We need to be stronger. We need Rhiannon's Strength blessing.

'We have the rings,' he says. 'The other fairies will know Amora helped us, so that'll bring us at least some level of trust with them.'

'If they'll even talk to us. And won't they ask for something in return?'

'We'll be fine,' he says as I let go of a palm frond and it smacks him in the head. He clears his throat. 'Anyway, we'll lie. Tell Rhiannon we're going on a brave quest and need Strength. Tell Adella we're using the blessings to help people. Et cetera. It's only blessings; we aren't asking for real magic.'

'You think we can lie to Grace, the fairy of truth? And what about Lire? She doesn't care about anyone, and she's the fairy of wisdom – she'll see right through us.'

He looks ahead. 'I'll think of something.'

'If you say so.'

'I won't let us fail, Maya,' he says, which takes me aback.

This far into our quest, knowing all that's still to come, I once again wonder why he's really here. He could have turned back at any time. This is dangerous, ridiculous. Especially now Sierra is in our way. Yet he's treating getting the crown as if it's life-or-death for him as well. He has money. He knows a *fairy*. What is it he's hanging around me for? Can it really be that he only wants something to do?

We walk for a while longer, and my legs feel as if they're going numb. The few stars I can see through the canopy of trees move slowly across the sky, and all I can think about is Sierra right behind us, ready to kill. The sky is a ticking clock, and I'm not sure if I want it to go faster or slower. Before long, it's completely dark, but we still don't pause.

Teddy stumbles again, falling onto his hands and knees. He yelps, and Sunny startles as her reins are yanked down. 'Ah!'

'Shh, Sunny!' I calm down the horse before she tramples him, then help pull Teddy up, our warm hands connecting.

'I'm fine,' he says, brushing at the rips in the knees of his pants. His skin is scratched beneath. 'Let's keep going.'

'You're not fine,' I tell him. 'You're exhausted, and we're going to kill ourselves trying to get away from Sierra.' I glance around, looking for answers, for a saviour, but we have only one option. 'We need to rest. If we can find a way to hide in the trees for a few hours—'

'No, not until we get to the capital, or at least somewhere safe.' His expression is difficult to read in the darkness, but I'm certain he's pretending to be braver than he is. 'It can't be much further.'

'And then what?' I sigh. 'By the time dawn breaks, we'll both be so shattered we won't be able to travel, and we'll be completely exposed to Sierra. It's better that we're rested. Then we can figure out what to do next. We can't fight her if we're both half asleep. We barely got away last time.'

He shivers. 'But the jungle isn't safe.'

'The only real danger we've had in this jungle so far has been a swan. Unless you're afraid of trees and shadows?'

'A little. And where will we hide? We could attempt to make a shelter for ourselves, but what about Sunny and Pansy?'

I spot a flat piece of ground and sit on it, pulling Pansy down with me. Her body heat is stifling, but I let her press her large back against me anyway. I open my satchel and give her some food. 'I'm not going any further, Teddy. We can take turns sleeping so someone's always keeping watch.'

His shoulders fall. 'Maya, I'm not okay with this.'

It's even darker here, the canopy of trees obscuring us nicely, and a nearby waterfall provides a steady hum to hide any noise we make from passing swans and monsters.

'Too bad,' I tell him. 'You'll have to drag me if you want to keep going.' I do want to keep going. Desperately. But I'm braver than I'm desperate, and I know what the smart thing to do is.

Teddy reluctantly falls beside me, sitting on his jacket as a cushion. His horse drops next to him and places its head in his lap. He strokes Sunny's neck. 'Then you sleep first,' he says. 'I'm too anxious to shut my eyes.'

I stiffen. Despite the nights we've already spent together, agreeing to have him watch me sleep makes my skin crawl. I don't want him to view me as weak. And even if he doesn't use this as an opportunity to betray me, I can't trust his ability to stay alert and keep us safe. He doesn't have my attention to detail or stamina.

'Go on, Maya.' He pats the leaf-strewn ground. 'You were the one who demanded we stop. Otherwise we're sitting here for nothing.'

I exhale. 'Two hours, then wake me. *Promise* you'll wake me.'

'What if I still don't want to sleep?'

'I don't care. I need you rested for my safety as well as yours, so promise.'

With a shake of his head, he whispers, 'I promise.'

✦◦✦❀♡❀✦◦✦

I jolt awake to something tugging on my hair. Teddy nearly gets headbutted when I sit up – he was combing through my knots.

My head. Was in. His *lap*.

'Teddy! Creepy!'

He gives me a fake pout. 'Your hair was all matted from the day's journey. And from sleeping on the ground. A little different from Amora's silk sheets, isn't it? Thought this would be a nice, gentle way to wake you.'

My voice is hoarse and groggy. It's still dark; I'm not sure how long I was asleep. 'Gentle? You nearly pulled half my hair *out*. And I'm serious. Don't touch me.'

He sinks into an uncomfortable-looking position, propping his jacket under his head. 'Okay, grumpy. I'm *sorry*.' He rolls over. 'My turn to sleep.'

He's out within minutes – I can tell by the way his breathing slows – and I'm not sure what to do with this rare peace. It's a different kind of solitude, when you're with someone who isn't conscious. Even the horses are sleeping soundly, though Sunny's snores could wake the entire jungle. Wherever their dreams have taken them, it's far from me.

I dig through my satchel and pull out my compass. When I open it, the blue triarue arrow points to my right, to Bearra. To home. Mum, Dad, Prima, Briar. To my bedroom, to my art supplies and our bookmaking workshop. I can almost smell the freshly cooked bread, and my chest aches with longing. My real life seems like another world, and my childhood a lifetime ago. A hundred years – it *was* a lifetime ago.

At first I try to hold my tears back, but I remember Teddy is asleep and he won't see me cry, so I let them fall. I rest my head in my hands and sob silently, letting out all the emotions of the last few days. All the pain floods out. All the fear. All the swirling thoughts and feelings.

My fingers wrap around the compass tightly. I wish I could ask my mother what she thinks of Teddy, and if I can trust him. I wish I could ask my father to tell me a story about a brave girl on a daring quest, a girl who doesn't feel the way I feel right now. I would even take Prima pulling at my hair as she tries to braid it, or Briar rambling about the latest handsome boy she's spotted in town.

I glance at the compass one last time and wish for my family's safety. Then I try to send them a mental message: *I'm okay, I'm not going to fail, I'll be home soon.*

Wiping my eyes, I pull out my sketchbook. It's too dark to draw anything well, but I still touch my pencil to the page and begin to sketch some of the things I've seen. Amora's wings. Teddy's profile. Gus's silk clothes and Darraport's skyline. I even draw a black swan, her wings extended as she flies amongst the clouds.

As I draw, I munch on some Amoran crackers dipped in chocolate. They're Teddy's, but he's eaten enough of my food that I decide it's fine. And with each bite, my worries lift.

By the time the sun rises, I feel so much better – cleansed, despite being covered in dirt – that I could almost cry again. I feel like myself for the first time in days.

⋅ ❖ ⁺ ۞ ♡ ۞ ⁺ ❖ ⋅

Teddy wakes naturally, the sun's rays hitting his eyes. Sierra will now be taking to the skies again, flying far faster than we can walk, with an aerial view of the jungle. At least the canopy is dense. If we stick to shaded areas, we might be able to hide.

But already, as we eat our breakfast and start hiking for the day, it's clear we'll have no such luck. We make so much noise moving through the jungle that there's no chance Sierra's bird-ears won't sense us.

'We'll get new clothes when we reach Rhiannon's Capital,' says Teddy, straightening his shirt. Only a few days ago, our clothes were perfectly tailored and high-quality. Now they're in tatters. *Sorry, Gus.* 'It'll help disguise us while we're here and as we make our way north-west to Adella's Territory.'

Teddy believes we aren't far from the capital now. And as the villages become less sparse, more crowded, and larger,

I know he must be right. They're built around lakes and rivers, stone buildings on the ground and huts built into the treetops. There's no farmland here; they must get all they need from the thriving jungle. With the midday sun, everything is highlighted gold and emerald.

Someone tosses strange fruits from the top of a tree, and one narrowly misses my head. 'Out of the way!' he yells, and I scramble to the side. The people in Rhiannon's Territory tend to have even darker complexions than in Amora's; they're highly-contrasted, with prominent features and wavy hair. There's less diversity, and it's clear why: anyone from outside this eerie jungle would be afraid of this place, and struggle with the intensity of its people. They seem perfectly comfortable climbing high into the canopies and diving into the rapid rivers. I watch one man sharpening a wide, arced knife with another smaller knife, and a group of children tossing a hammer between them for fun. No one walks hunched over or talks quietly – there is a universal confidence here.

What more could I expect from the territory of the fairy of bravery? It looks like a wonderful way to exist – free, and uninhibited – for those who are fearless enough for it.

At least now we're closer to a city there are proper roads again. We ride much faster towards the capital; the horses trot along gratefully. Time begins to speed up and I feel less afraid of Sierra catching us. Before I know it, we've made it to the capital and once again dropped off the horses so we don't have to drag them through busy city streets.

The *city*. The capital and fortress of the fairy of strength and bravery are exactly as I imagined. Sharp and solid, the colour red woven into every surface. It starkly opposes the green of the jungle growing above us. The city is cut into a stone floor, like a ravine, and half built into the trees as if overrun by them. It reminds me of some of the buildings we found, destroyed by vines and claimed by nature, when we first woke in Bearra.

The palace consists of several large, rectangular buildings made of a moss-covered dark stone. People jump off its rooftops into the lake below. Above the palace, within the trees, is a statue of giant red wings cut from vines and flowers, wrapped in a magical ruby glow. With the canopy growing over and around the city, caving us in the dark, the wing statue paints the city crimson.

Everywhere I look, magic is rampant. Like in Darraport, enchanted appliances are part of their culture: coaches, glowing shop windows, food stalls serving cold food despite the heat. Our first stop is a clothes shop, where we pick up items without the type of fussing I feared after last time. We're in and out, changed into fresh cotton clothes. I've chosen a dress this time, which is unusual for me, but with its short length and airiness, it's perfect for Rhiannon's Capital.

People rush around even more violently and packed together than in Darraport and Amora's Capital, knocking into me unapologetically. I hold my satchel tight to my side and Teddy grips my other hand. I'm so used to him holding my hand now that I barely notice – until I do notice, and my palm becomes sweaty and I can't help but observe every layer and curve of his skin on mine.

He spots a food stall and gasps so loud I almost jump out of my skin. 'Ice cream!'

I glare at him, but he's already dragging me towards the stall. '*Teddy*!'

He stops us in front of the assortment, staring at the carts of frozen, coloured cream. It smells sickeningly sweet, and the desserts are artificial mixes: bright-red dotted with glazed cherries, lime green run-through with chocolate chips, saturated yellow covered in rainbow sprinkles, and so many more. I can feel the cold coming off the tubs and see the heat bouncing from the glass divider.

Magic.

'One chocolate, one raspberry,' Teddy says to the owner, almost breathless in his excitement. 'Please.' They nod and hand Teddy two crispy waffle cones topped with the dessert. Teddy pays with his pearl bracelet.

'Teddy,' I hiss as we leave, 'We don't have time for this – we're running, remember? From the girl trying to murder us?'

'But it's *ice cream*,' he whines, leading me to a less-crowded park to sit and eat at a lone wooden bench. Giant, jungle-green palms sway on either side of us, and a multicoloured bird squawks above.

'I don't want your cold cream,' I say, pulling my dress under me as I sit beside him. 'I want to go and see the fairy.'

His face falls. 'Oh, Maya. Have you never had ice cream? Of course you haven't. You're an old lady. You don't understand.' He hands the chocolate one to me. 'Go on. You've at least had chocolate before, right?'

I huff. 'Of course I've had chocolate.' I'm hesitant to try it, aware that Teddy's recommendations have so far proved to not be reliable.

'Try not spitting it out like the wine. And don't bite it – you'll freeze your teeth. Just lick.' His skin is bright and hot, his eyes creased with joy.

I don't trust him. 'But you've already licked it.'

'And?'

'That's disgusting.'

'No it isn't.'

I groan. 'Fine!' I press my tongue to the untouched side and the cold instantly makes me gasp. But as the flavour hits, and the coolness seeps into my too-warm body, I sigh with delight. '*Not* disgusting.'

'I know.' There are already pink stains on his lips from eating the second cone. He switches them. This time I bite in, despite Teddy's warning, and the raspberry explodes in my mouth with a sweet, strong flavour – it's like eating cold fire.

We keep switching until we're done. The mix of sugar and ice makes me tap my feet with extra energy. 'Let's go,' I say, hopping up excitedly. 'Let's get our next blessing.'

Teddy grins, also bouncy, tousling my hair. 'Looking like that?'

'What?' I pull my dress down, suddenly self-conscious.

'You have chocolate on your cheek.' He reaches his thumb to my face and wipes it away, all the while gazing into my eyes, his fingers brushing my neck, and I . . .

'Let's *go*.'

He quickly stands, his eyes downcast. 'Yes – of course.'

I stare at the pink ring on my hand. *Passion.* A dangerous thing.

CHAPTER
FOURTEEN

THERE ARE NO GUARDS or soldiers at Rhiannon's Fortress. The stone looming above and the vines wrapping the building are intimidating enough on their own. The fairy of strength and bravery has no fear, after all. Who would dare to attack her, or even bother her for a favour?

Well, despite the dread this place gives me, I would.

We step into the fortress's entrance, unnoticed in our new clothes. The inside of the palace looks like the outside: plants everywhere, climbing the walls and covering the floors, growing across the hallways and rooms. With the windows blacked-out by vines, the only light comes from faintly-glowing red spheres floating on the ceiling.

Teddy leads me through the puzzling halls and passageways. I shouldn't be surprised he knows his way around here. Still, it fills my stomach with anxiety. His past – whatever reason he has for knowing Amora so well, for having travelled so much of the world, for having so many friends – is the reason he's my perfect guide. But I also know it could be the death of me.

We step down to the throne room, where red-uniformed guards lean against the doors with bored expressions; they pay us no mind.

I have to stifle a gasp as we enter the cavern-like space. There isn't a single window, but fire burns across the skirting of each wall. Murals on every surface – the walls, the ceiling, the floor – depict bloody battles from both history and legend. People mill about with serious expressions, deep in conversation. And at the end of the cavern, with all the fire, murals, and people pointed towards it, sits a throne of elaborately carved silver. Its tall back is encrusted with rubies, and the silver of the arms drapes and climbs like vines.

Atop the throne is the fairy of strength, Rhiannon. She's as stunning as the other fairies I've seen: tall, elegant, lethal. Her red lips are downturned, and her brown skin glows in the red lighting. She wears a thin burgundy dress, unrestrictive and war-ready but strikingly feminine, and her feet are bare. Her black hair is braided back, and her eyebrows are thick and angry.

It's her wings, though, that stun me. They aren't floaty and translucent like Amora's or Lire's. Hers are bloodred and scaled like a dragon's. I can even recall one I painted in a storybook as a child that reminds me of Rhiannon; it frightened me so much I hid it under my bed.

I want to run away screaming, and Teddy must sense my fear, because he gives my hand a squeeze. I remind myself that if I can't handle Rhiannon, I'll have no chance with Kara – the fairy of darkness. I can't have fear. Strength is what we're here for, so it's strength we have to show.

She notices us and slightly raises her brows. Teddy takes this as an invitation and makes his way towards her. I reluctantly follow him as he weaves through all the people. I put my hands at my sides, trying to look brave. The fairy's throne places her above us, and I stand only as close to her as I can bear.

Rhiannon waves a hand, and the crowd gives us some space. Her dragon wings beat as she peers down at us, waiting for us to speak.

Teddy stands tall, his usual charisma masked with stoicism, which I attempt to copy even though my legs are shaking. 'We've come to ask you for a blessing,' he says, putting an uncharacteristically powerful volume behind his voice. 'We're on a quest, and we need your Strength to complete it. Amora has already blessed us. Rhiannon, will you help?'

There are a few snickers in the crowd, but I force myself to disregard them. *Show no weakness.*

The fairy's eyes move to my hand, like a hungry bird watching a worm. 'I see. I can sense it.' She offers an amused smirk. 'Amora may have freely given you her Passion, but I am not so generous. Not everyone deserves my blessing. What gives you the audacity to enter my fortress and ask for a favour when you are not even of my territory?' She looks

Teddy up and down. 'You look familiar, boy. Have you visited my capital before?'

He lifts his chin. 'I have not. We've come from Muse's Territory.'

I *try* to ignore how easily he lies.

'Children of the singing forest,' she says apathetically. 'I have no reason to bless you, and no desire to.'

'Please,' I say, sounding more confident than I expect to. Heads turn in our direction. 'It's for my family. We're looking for a treasure that could save us from certain death, but it's guarded by such strong magic I need blessings from every fairy to reach it.' I swallow, remembering that I can't say too much in front of this crowd, but I don't dare ask Rhiannon to speak privately – I'm too scared of her. 'Amora chose to help us because she believed in our quest. What can we offer you to deserve your blessing?'

Her wings stretch as she watches me. 'I don't ask humans for favours. When I share my Strength, it is because I have chosen someone worthy. Someone I believe will make good use of it, and someone I trust not to lose it.'

I cross my arms. 'We've made it this far with Amora's blessing. We even escaped an attack from someone who wanted it for herself so she could steal our treasure.'

Rhiannon's eyes light up. 'You're in competition for a treasure that will save you?'

'She wasn't just any rival, Rhiannon,' I say quickly, dramatising my tone as I realise I can tell her exactly what she wants to hear. 'We fought and escaped Sierra *Reed*.'

Now everyone is watching us closely, dozens of stares trained on me, but I force myself to maintain eye contact with the fairy.

'Oh?' she says, her expression turning wicked with intrigue. 'Well, why didn't you say so? That certainly makes things more interesting. The Reed sisters have been missing for months. And they're known for their ruthlessness.'

Missing? Rhiannon mustn't know about the curse. Maybe Sierra's family kept that part quiet.

'Sierra wants the treasure to save her family,' says Teddy. 'We tried to convince her to make an alliance with us, but she attempted to take our lives instead. Maya—' he nods to me '—was smart enough to use Amora's blessing to stop Sierra. We raced to reach your capital first, to get the Strength we know will help us defeat her if – *when* – she attacks again.'

Rhiannon mulls it over, tapping her silver throne. 'I find myself almost convinced to give the Reed girl my blessing instead. She's more worthy.'

'No!' I shout, then I feel all the blood rush to my cheeks. 'She's a murderer. Sierra only wants to hurt people. I'm trying to save people! Isn't that more worthy?'

'It makes no difference to me.'

'Then consider this,' says Teddy. 'Sierra Reed is a trained fighter with power of her own. We were able to escape her once, but she will not be fooled again. Without your Strength, Rhiannon, there will be no competition between us. There will be no fight, because she'll kill us easily.'

My chest lifts with thrill as Teddy and I spin our argument. Is this how he feels all the time, charming and lying his way through life?

'But with your blessing, Rhiannon,' I say, 'there's a story. Unlikely heroes defeat a villain, saving their family with the aid of the fairy of strength and bravery.'

Rhiannon grins as if she were on our side all along. 'You two certainly come from Muse's Territory, with tongues like that. And since Amora did already bless you . . .' The people in the throne room hush entirely to hear her verdict. 'I do hope you survive,' the fairy says, 'so you can return to tell me about your adventure.'

'We'll survive,' I say at the same time Teddy says, 'We'll come back.'

She steps down from her throne, her dragon wings fanning, and the crowd moves backwards. Teddy and I stand in place, staring at this being who has lived longer than we can ever hope to, and who will be here long after we're gone. Of course this is all about stories to her. Everyone needs entertainment, and in her immortality, she must deal with infinite boredom.

Teddy holds out his left hand, with his three rings, but Rhiannon shakes her head. 'You don't need more strength,' she says to him. 'And you won't get any from me. What *you* need is to find and use the power within you, boy.' She turns to me. 'This, however, is a woman who has no lack of inner strength. Who wants what she wants, and knows that she will get it. My blessing goes to her.'

I swallow. I would rather have this blessing – I would rather have all the blessings – but there's a reason Amora split the rings between us. It feels wrong to take two blessings before Teddy has one. Still, I need the Strength blessing. Rhiannon is right. Teddy doesn't know how to use it like I do.

She takes my hand, and her magic becomes thicker than the air around us. 'I am also the fairy of temperance,' she says. 'While you wear Amora's ring of Passion, my blessing will allow you to retain balance. Passion and Strength may be similar, but the self-discipline to pull back from passion is vital. You lack patience, and this blessing will help you.'

Her magic flickers around our hands like fire as it enters the ring. It buzzes through my fingers and throughout my body, and for a moment I really do feel strong. Rhiannon's power pours into me, and I feel sure, steady, invincible. Then it eases back into the ring and the scarlet glow subsides until it's only faint, matching the pink-tinted ring to its left.

The fairy spreads her scaled wings as she returns to her throne. Her movements are so unlike the gracefulness of the other fairies; she isn't afraid to seem harsh and imposing. I still fear her, but I respect her. Authenticity is a trait most fairies and leaders seem to lack.

'Thank you,' I say, shivering as the lingering effects of her magic ebb out of my skin.

Teddy touches my shoulder supportively. 'We really do appreciate it, Rhiannon. And we will be back.'

The fairy nods. 'If I see your opponent, I'll be sure to send her your way. I assume you're seeing Adella next? Or will you attempt to break into Bearra to talk to Lire?' She smiles excitedly. 'Never mind. I'll find out soon.' She waves us off. 'On your way. Be strong.'

Teddy is about to say something, but she clears her throat and we take that as our cue to leave. The crowd parts for us as we exit the dim throne room. I allow myself one last look at Rhiannon and take in her startling beauty, her unwavering confidence. Everything about her is intense. Everything about her is what I wish I was – unstoppably powerful and terrifying.

She gives me a final smirk before I turn and walk to the fortress's exit with Teddy, trying to look like I'm as strong as I should be.

But a voice rings in my ear, a sound I'm certain no one else can hear, and I nearly trip. 'We will see who wins the crown . . .' whispers Rhiannon, with an eager and malicious laugh, 'when he betrays you.'

CHAPTER FIFTEEN

RHIANNON'S BLESSING RENEWS THE stamina in all of us. We travel faster and reach the edge of Adella's Territory within two days, running on ice cream, bananas, and cooked beans from Rhiannon's Capital. Still, it's forty-eight hours of barely being able to look Teddy in the eye. I keep hearing the fairy's words over and over, wondering why she told me Teddy would betray me. Was she warning me? Was there something she could sense about him? Or did she only whisper those words to me as part of her game, to instil doubt in me?

I shouldn't trust Teddy. I've known that from the second I met him. But it isn't only that I need him anymore. I want him here with me. I can't let him go, and the thought of forcing him away, of fighting him, is unfathomable. Just like everyone else in the world, I've fallen prey to his charm. And I've been so easy to manipulate, haven't I? I'm the ideal target, perfectly vulnerable. Of course I would grow to rely on him, to care for him.

Is that all part of his plan? To steal the crown from me? Or worse?

No. No, it can't be. He's my friend. My only friend. He wouldn't hurt me now.

But gaining Rhiannon's blessing was too easy. How could it take only a short conversation? She knows there will be a battle between Teddy, Sierra, and me – and to her, that's exciting enough to give us her blessing.

At this point, only two fairies in and five to go, I wonder if it would have been easier to simply kidnap Princess Dawn and use *her* blessings. Then we would only need Kara.

The horses canter through the outskirts of Adella's Territory, north-west of Bearra, thrilled to be out of Rhiannon's difficult terrain. There's a lightness in the air here, and whenever we need food, we seem to happen upon an apple tree or friendly village. The sun shines warm, cut through with a mild breeze, and rivers snake along the hilly landscape.

Teddy keeps tilting his head up to soak in the daylight. Whenever we pass anything that isn't a sheep-clouded grass field, he feels the need to point it out and give me an excited lecture. I don't know why I need to know about every type of tree in the world, or how different types of roofs are made, but I find myself *mildly* enjoying it.

We come across a waterfall and his mood dips. 'Every time I see water,' he says, tensing, 'I start thinking about swans again.'

'Me too.' I groan. 'This open landscape is beautiful, but it is not good for hiding from birds.'

As if to laugh at our bad luck, birds sing above us, and we share a disbelieving glance. In these moments, it's so easy with Teddy that I can't believe I have doubts about him, and I chide myself for taking Rhiannon's words so seriously.

Teddy winces. 'At least Sierra is the only enemy I can imagine we'll have to worry about here.'

He's right. This place is safe and lovely and seemingly utopian. The territory of kindness. I take a breath and try to allow myself to just enjoy the peace. 'Rhiannon must love the thought of that,' I say. 'Our murderous rival lurking above when we're in such a kind land. It keeps things interesting.'

'You know,' he says, 'I have no intention of returning to tell her our story.'

'Oh? I was going to make a special trip for it.' I grin teasingly. 'Maybe move into the capital for a few years, have a home there – with all the money I'll have when I get my crown, I'll have houses everywhere. I'll be best friends with Rhiannon, and all the fairies, and all the richest people, and I'll buy all the most expensive enchanted items and live like a queen. People will gather around to hear how I defeated Sierra and saved the crown. I'll even have my own pair of wings someday.'

'I know an easy way to get a pair of wings,' he says, shielding his eyes from the sun as he watches me.

'Yes?'

He points to the sky. 'Yes. Just ask our friend Sierra.'

I force back laughter.

'I wouldn't mind being a bird,' he says. He lets go of Sunny's reins and raises his hands to his sides, stretching them out like wings. He sways left and right, letting the breeze catch his light shirt and red hair. 'It would be easier than this.'

I tear my eyes away from him before I begin to melt at how adorable he is. Rhiannon's words linger in my mind. *When he betrays you.* 'I'd miss my hands too much, I think,' I tell him.

'I'd only miss the ability to talk.'

'I wouldn't miss your ability to talk.' I offer him a sweetly-sarcastic grin. 'Don't they say the animals speak in Muse's Territory? You can go there.'

He laughs lightly. 'Only if you come with me.'

'What's our story going to be?' I ask Teddy. 'We'll have to tell her we're using the Kindness blessing to help people in some way, won't we?'

'She's the fairy of generosity,' says Teddy. 'I'm sure all we'll have to do is ask. I don't think the people here have heard of the word *no*.'

We've stopped inside Adella's Great Library, a sprawling structure that serves as a museum and gallery as well as an infinite hoard of books. I insisted we visit as soon as we walked past the grand castle-like building. There was nothing I could do to pull myself away from the endless towers of light brick and gold trimmings – and the promise of infinite stories within. To my absolute devastation, we won't have time to explore the entire place, but each room we wander is different: some are small spaces full of dusty old books; some are large, open galleries with stunningly colourful paintings; others hold artefacts in large glass cases. People sit at desks, studying tomes and artefacts or copying sculptures into sketchbooks.

It's like a maze. Apparently, there's a field in the centre, with trees from all over the world and exotic animals roaming free. Can this place be *real*?

Still, it's the books that interest me most. The old ones, from my time, which bring such beautiful nostalgia, and the new ones, a lower quality than any I ever made, but fantastic in their own way. And so, *so* colourful. There are books made of animal skin and papyrus, books that still look like the bark they came from. Books with illustrations and books filled with countless words.

The most wonderful part, however, is that in Adella's Great Library, people may take or leave anything they like.

Clearly this doesn't cause issues with the collection, since there is so much still here. But the idea that I could take something so special and leave behind a special item of my own . . .

What books might I read from here? And what treasures could I leave for someone else to find?

I was only joking with Teddy about having homes all over the world when I'm rich, but I really could spend years in this place. It's almost as if I *must*. And it feels so good to long for something real in the future after so long of only wanting to preserve my past.

Adella's Capital is somewhere I could really see myself living. It isn't a city like the other capitals. It's more like home, with older, shorter buildings, and villages surrounding an ancient castle. But where Bearra is decorated with triarue, Adella's Capital is lined with gold. Everywhere, it glimmers in the bright sun. Truly, everything that can be gold, is gold: window frames, bricks, statues, coaches, even hats.

The city is close to the inner edge of the territory to make use of the temperate weather, which means we aren't far from Bearra. I've been away for just over a week now, and the temptation to revisit before we head far north-east to Kara's Territory is strong – but now, I'm stronger. And in a place as lovely as this, it's easy to tear myself away from my sadness and throw myself into curiosity.

Here, there is no clear disparity between the rich and the poor; everyone plays and eats and smiles together. I should expect this in a territory of generosity, but it's still jarring to see. It isn't like Amora's Territory, either, where everyone is in a drunken, reckless haze. There's real, genuine joy. It's so infectious I can't stop grinning.

The people wear bright colours and outlandish patterns, expressive and cheery; the material bounces off their midnight-black skin. As we entered the city, laughs echoed all around us, and Teddy kept staring at the blissful people, his gaze enchanted, longing. They returned his smiles with enthusiasm. This is the sort of community he belongs with. Sweet, caring people who love humanity, just like he does.

I glance back at him. I was so entranced with blowing the dust off the leather cover of a novel and watching the particles drift in the light that I forgot he was there. I say to him, 'Just asking Adella seems too easy, doesn't it? When we began this journey, it all felt impossible. Now we've gotten two blessings already, and nearly a third, with almost no difficulty. Sierra I didn't expect, but otherwise . . .' I run my fingers across an illustration of a soldier charging into battle, thinking of the stories I read and wrote in my childhood. I always wanted to be part of them, part of an adventure, and now I am. But I'm not saving a kingdom or slaying a dragon – I'm robbing a grave. 'We've travelled a quarter of the world. Shouldn't this be harder? Shouldn't we prepare for the worst?'

Teddy watches my fingers as I turn the page. 'The world isn't such a terrible place,' he says. 'It only feels like it to you because you don't know it. Maybe we should give my abilities as a guide some credit for our good luck.'

'And your ability to know everyone, and to have been everywhere, and always know what to say.' I'm trying to joke, but I can't keep the cynicism from my voice.

He nearly laughs, then he crosses his arms. 'Are you trying to say something, Maya?'

'No.' I exhale. 'I just didn't think we'd have two blessings already, and all we'd have to do is ask.'

He sits at an old library desk and furrows his brow. 'Rhiannon was ready to throw us out before she found out about Sierra. Amora only helped us because she's a friend. We can assume Adella will be easy, but we still can't be certain. And the others – I don't expect Kara, the fairy of darkness and death, to be friendly. Sierra said Grace doesn't help people. You can never know what to expect with Muse, and as you said, Lire barely makes public appearances.'

Is Teddy trying to be pessimistic? That's not something I thought I'd see in my lifetime.

'I still think we need a story,' I say, 'like with Rhiannon. Are we saving little animals and need blessings to help? Do orphans need toys? Has the swan's lake dried up?'

His expression softens. 'Adella loves the idea of family and friendship. We should stick to the truth as much as we can. We're looking for treasure to save your family, because you're all so close and love each other so much, but you desperately need money. Since you don't want to take money from anyone else, you're looking for a treasure that already belongs to you. You just need magic to get it.'

'What if she asks what the treasure is?'

'We'll tell her that letting anyone else know about it risks them taking it from us.'

'I thought she was all about sharing.'

'Then we tell her you'll only use the money for good.'

'She has no reason to trust us,' I say.

He shakes his head. 'How many times do I have to tell you that most people don't expect the worst from everyone, like you do?'

I shut my book with a *thud*. 'They should. Where I'm from, people are selfish. They don't care about others, and they don't do you any favours unless there's something in it for them. Especially not fairies. I'm certain the world hasn't changed so drastically in the last century that that's no longer true.'

He gets up and walks along a wall of books, gazing at the titles while tapping at the spines. 'Maya, I know you've been hurt, but that doesn't make everyone evil.'

Not this again. 'I don't believe *everyone* is evil. I believe that everyone has the potential to hurt others, and it isn't worth taking your chances.'

'How about we agree to disagree?'

'No. I disagree.'

He picks a book off the shelf and places it in front of me. 'You are so stubborn.'

The leather cover is soft in my hands, and only a little worn from time. I absently open the book and touch its thick pages. 'I'm not stubborn. I'm right. And—'

I look down to find a manuscript filled with hand-drawn illustrations of a girl with light-brown hair and grey eyes, and a red dragon with eyes of gold. The story is about a young girl who travels deep into a dragon's cave to search for its treasure, but the dragon saves her from the other monsters lurking in the dark, and she returns home not with gold, but with a new ally. I know the tale, because—

'It's one of yours,' says Teddy, as mesmerised by his find as I am. 'I heard of your family's books when I was in Bearra. Although you told me your surname was Shy, like your grandmother, I eventually realised you must be one of the celebrated Nova bookmakers. When I spotted this, I just knew it was by you.'

On the cover is printed 'By Maya T Nova, of Nova Books', and on the inside is a dedication to Prima. But other people have written on the first pages, with notes of gifting as the book has been passed on. To a friend ninety years ago, to a lover fifty years ago, to a newborn baby twenty years ago, and finally to here, the library. Since then, many readers have written their names within to mark that they've borrowed and returned it.

How many people have read and loved my work?

Fairies, I am choking back tears. 'I made this when I was ten,' I tell Teddy, my fingers trembling as I turn the pages. 'It was my first book. My mother and father wanted me to keep it, but I was so excited to have created a book like my parents did – I wanted to sell it, too. I regretted it as soon as it left my hands, even though the money bought us a few days' worth of food.'

Teddy sits beside me, inching close but not too close, as if he's afraid to break the old book. 'It found its way back to you. You have to take it.'

I could swap it for the book in my bag – one of my mother's. I would hate to lose something of hers, but it isn't nearly as precious to me as my first story, and it wouldn't feel right taking something without leaving something behind.

This old book shows that, maybe, I didn't miss the last hundred years at all. Part of me was out in the world, going from home to home, watching time tick by.

'If you don't take it,' Teddy says, 'I will. It's amazing. Maya, if this was what you could do at ten, how good are you now?'

'It doesn't matter.' My shoulders fall with the weight of my grief returned. 'We're obsolete. No one wants my books anymore.'

'But look how many people loved this one.'

I shut it, and dust blows everywhere. I take my mother's book from my satchel and lift it to my book's place on the shelf. With one final glance and a kiss on the top of the cover, I give my mother's book to the library.

We don't have to enter Adella's Castle to find the fairy. She's out in the streets, surrounded by people, walking amongst them like a friend. As we ride down the street, following the faint glow of her wings, people turn in our direction.

They clearly all know each other. Even if we wore the best disguise for a place like this, we'd stand out amongst their tight community. But they aren't unfriendly. In fact, Adella opens her arms and waves us in when she sees us. We hop off our horses and walk with them towards the fairy.

Her brushed-out curls sit like a huge black cloud above her head, and her skin is pitch-dark. Like the other fairies, she strictly sticks to her colour – orange. Her dress, falling around her ankles, is the shade of Teddy's hair: a deep, shining ginger. Her wings are simple and small compared to the other fairies I've seen, spread thin like a dragonfly's, with golden veins.

She gazes at Teddy as if hypnotised. Her eyes are honey brown and wide, and I'm overcome with an urge to fall into her arms and let her hold me, as if that would make everything within me heal. 'You need my help,' she says, her voice high-pitched and floaty. 'For something of great importance, of life and death. I sense your desperation.'

'*We* need your help,' I say, shifting awkwardly as I avert my eyes from the dozens of smiles being beamed at me. 'Could we speak to you? Privately?'

Adella peers at my rings. 'Young one, you do not need my help,' she says. 'You can take care of yourself. You have everything you need. It is your friend who needs what I can offer. Both of you understand generosity. You know sacrifice.

But sometimes—' she reaches out a hand to softly touch Teddy's cheek '—we give too much, and it hurts us.'

Of course. Because everyone loves Teddy. Everyone thinks he's perfect. And *yet*.

'You can see we already have blessings from Rhiannon and Amora,' he says to the fairy. 'But we need all seven. It's to save my friend's family. We need magic to find a treasure that can—'

Adella raises a hand to stop him. 'You need not explain yourself to me. I see your soul. And if three of my sisters have already decided to help you, there's no reason I shouldn't trust their judgement.'

'Two,' I say, brushing my hair out of my face, feeling more than a little uncomfortable – and ignored. 'Only two fairies have chosen to help us so far.'

The orange fairy looks Teddy up and down. 'Of course. That is what I meant.' She takes his hand, and a gold circle of magic encompasses it. His shoulders shake as Adella's magic pours into the ring.

It can't be this simple. It just can't be. But a few moments later, she lets go of him with a smile, and the blessing is right there, sitting on his finger. I can feel the magic from here.

Three fairies done. Four to go. Half the world still to travel.

I look at Teddy's orange ring with a jealous heat in my stomach. He shouldn't have one of my blessings. Why have I given this boy more power to betray me?

This boy, who is favoured even by the fairy of love and the fairy of kindness. But just because he's a 'good' person, doesn't mean we're on the same side.

⋅ ⊙ ⚬ ◊ ♡ ◊ ⚬ ⊙ ⋅

Adella offers to have us stay the night – in fact, half the population of her capital does – but she isn't offended when we choose to move on. Kara's blessing is next, and I'm sure it's going to be the most difficult to get. The fairy of darkness and death is well known for being, well, evil. She and Lire have been against each other since time began, and while Lire sits happily in the centre of the world with her stashes of triarue, Kara lives at the north-edge, deep in the snow and ice.

To get a Darkness blessing, we have two problems: a land that's known for being difficult to survive in, and a fairy who hates humans. Having Amora's blessing helped us get Rhiannon's and Adella's, but Kara doesn't trust the other fairies. If anything, having blessings from them will only make it more difficult to ask Kara for a favour.

It's going to be our longest journey yet, a week at least in deep snow. Not something a Bearran is made for. But at least it's something swans aren't made for, either.

We spend the rest of the day riding until the sun sets, and we stop at an inn towards the inner-edge of Adella's Territory. We're closer to some outlying non-territorial cities now, but we won't be going into them – which suits me fine. These smaller towns are nice. Quiet, friendly, and free of swans. They also have less magic, so I feel a sense of peace, like home.

My body is heavy as we lazily ascend the stairs of the inn, and I pull off my jacket before we get to our rooms. *Rooms*. Because after days and days of sleeping on the ground, we're in a town where we can spend a night somewhere civilised.

'You didn't need to get two rooms,' I say to Teddy. 'You should save your money in case we need it.'

He gives me a strange look, unlocking his door with a rusty bronze key. 'I thought you would be more comfortable,' he says, his cheeks flushing. 'With your own space.'

He's overreacting to my recent distance from him. We've slept in far worse places, far closer quarters, than a bedroom. I don't know why it makes my heart fall that he's accepting the way I push back. I don't know why I say, 'Actually, I hate sleeping alone. I'm used to sharing a room with my sister, so I don't like the feeling of being, I don't know . . .'

'Vulnerable?'

I nod. My eyes meet the wooden floorboards, which I kick at absently.

'I'm used to sleeping alone,' he says, tapping his leg with his fingers. Then he adds quickly, 'But I don't like it, either.'

I look up. 'You don't?'

'Sometimes I get scared by myself. I'm *slightly* afraid of the dark.' He cringes. 'I should keep that secret. But it's true.'

I suppress a laugh. 'It's okay. We all have our fears.'

'What's yours?'

The laugh disappears on my lips.

'What if I—' He falters. 'What if I brought in some blankets from my room, and I slept on your floor? Would that be . . . Would that be okay? Then neither of us has to be alone.'

I meet his eyes. Sincere. *Always* so sincere. Suddenly I feel awful asking him to sleep on the floor when he has a bed. 'Teddy, no, don't worry about it. You don't want to sleep on the floor, and there's no room in the bed for both of us. Not comfortably, anyway. You already paid for the extra room.'

He shrugs. 'As long as I'm not alone in the dark, I'm happy.'

'*Okay.*' I try to sound nonchalant, but my heart is fluttering. Why is it doing that? Why am I encouraging this? I'm supposed to be pushing him away. I'm supposed to *not* be vulnerable with him. 'I'd like that,' I add, and it mustn't even be me talking anymore. I must be possessed.

'You're sure?'

'I'm sure.' I smile. *What?*

We enter a cosy room with an unlit fireplace and black curtains. It feels private, secure – exactly what I've been craving since I left home. By the time we're clean and nestled in our sheets, we're both struggling to keep our eyes open. We try to talk about our trek to Kara's Capital, but it's impossible to concentrate. My head hangs over the bed, neck sore as I try to talk to him on the floor.

He's wrapped in blankets and pillows, and my chest wrenches with guilt. I want him with me, next to me, his warmth right here. How could I let him sleep on the ground like that? I seem to forget all the distrust, all our arguments, and all I want is his presence. I've come to rely on it so much that maybe I can't live without it anymore.

'Teddy,' I whisper. 'You don't have to sleep on the floor. Get in bed.'

'Maya, no,' he mumbles through his pillows. 'There's no room. I made my decision.'

I pull back the covers. 'In. Now. Before I change my mind.'

He pushes the mountain of pillows and blankets off his face and stares at me for a few moments, mouth open, before blinking and pulling himself up into the bed. With a stumble, he brings his blankets with him, wrapping them over us.

I shuffle over, but it's impossible not to be touching him. Our legs are tangled in an uncomfortable knot, heating quickly, and my arm gets stuck for a moment under his back. I pull away, but it's too late. My skin already prickles where we touched.

He breathes slowly, settling into the sheets. He glances at me for a moment, and I hope he can't see the blush on my cheeks.

'Good night, Teddy,' I whisper, turning my back to him.

He exhales and turns onto his side so our spines are pressed together. 'Good night, Maya.'

How can someone's presence make me feel so calm, so strong, so sure, and yet so, so desperately fiery and afraid?

Don't get distracted. Don't let yourself trust him.

Amora's ring burns on my finger.

It's too late.

CHAPTER SIXTEEN

THE NEXT DAY, AFTER savouring our first warm breakfast in many days – and our last for even longer – Teddy and I collect our horses from the inn's stables and pack our bags with enough supplies to last a week. Teddy managed to get us some warmer clothes for the journey to the world's edge, and I begrudgingly shrug on my new coat. I whine, '*Must* we go to Kara's Territory first?'

I struggle to look at him. The feeling of our bodies warm and pressed close together last night has left an impression on me that I can't shake. Every time I shut my eyes or we brush hands, I'm reminded of us together. In bed. Doing nothing but falling asleep.

'I've thought about it,' I add, shaking my head as if it'll clear all of these confusing feelings, 'and Bearra is closer. We could go home and get Lire's blessing, then head north again.'

Teddy pales. 'No— No. We're going clockwise. Around the world. Then we'll cut through Bearra before Glassine.'

I shiver in anticipation of all the snow we'll be facing. 'I understand that's the plan, but—'

'If you go back and see your family, you'll only be distracted. We need to get the crown before Sierra does. We don't have time to waste. And Bearra isn't easy to get into.'

'*You* got in.'

He won't look me in the eye. 'I was being reckless and cocky, wanting to explore a place that was hidden for a hundred years. As soon as I got in, I wanted to leave.'

I grit my teeth and wave a hand dismissively. I'm almost certain he's lying, or at least not telling the entire truth. But unless I want an argument, pressing him won't help. 'Fine. If we make it that far, the other blessings will help us get in anyway.'

Two long days and nights pass without any sign of Sierra, and we're suddenly halfway through Kara's Territory, getting closer and closer to her palace at the edge of the world.

This far from Bearra, we have no reprieve from the icy cold. My fingers are stiff to the bone, and my eyelashes are coated with frost. Every time we stop, Teddy and I huddle with the horses for warmth. There aren't any inns or villages. This territory is a white wasteland of rolling hills and snowstorms.

If we didn't have the blessings we had already, I'm not sure we'd have survived the first day. The biting chill was eating into my heart and soul when I called on the Strength ring to help, and since then I've found it easier, but still unbearable.

Teddy's ring has made sure we've always had food and shelter when our supplies have proved useless. It's as if it attracts luck; travellers we pass give us their extra drinking water, and on the second night, when we were both desperate for a hot meal, we came across campers baking bread atop a huge fire, which we slept by.

More than ever, I long for the warmth of Bearra, even its hottest days. I long for my bed, my stifling room in the middle of summer, the oven after it's been lit. I wish to hold each member of my family and absorb their warmth. Even Aunt Olivia, though I'm sure she'd hate it. *Fairies*, I'm tempted to hug *Teddy*. His stifling warmth that night in the inn seems like heaven now.

His teeth chatter as he tries to make conversation, our arguments from a few days ago long forgotten in this un-forgivable cold. His nose, cheeks and ears are as red as his hair, and his lips are cracked and dry. 'They must have some sort of m-magic out here,' he says. 'The people who live here, I mean, to f-fight the cold. I've seen magical heating systems in some of the colder cities – pipes that run through the buildings, filled with magic that w-warms every room. Surely, surely, it isn't all like this.'

I shake my head. Pansy's feet sink into the snow with every step, and she trembles as much as I do. Several times we've gone over ice so slippery I had to hop off and lead her so she didn't slip. I give her a grateful stroke of the neck.

'Are there other places like this?' I ask Teddy. I don't shiver and stammer as much as him – the Strength blessing is helping me, but mostly I'm just trying to act tougher than I feel. 'Other . . . inhabited areas, this far out into the cold? Or is it only the fairy of darkness who lives in such a nightmare?'

'I don't know why anyone w-would choose to live so far from the warmth, but in the world's west, past Rhiannon's Territory, there's a mountain range inhabited by a p-people who call themselves the Ice Empire. They're basically their own world. But they think themselves conquerors. They're trying to expand, training more soldiers to take more land to the east. No one is t-too concerned about them, though. They don't have a fairy.'

We pull our horses along the winding road, which can barely be seen beneath the snow and ice. The only way we've been able to tell where we're going is the position of the sun when it peeks through the clouds, and the occasional vague road markers. Very rarely do other travellers pass, and if they do, they have warm carriages.

Ice Empire. I think I've heard the name before, but it's difficult to place, and I certainly know nothing about it. 'So the fairies could stop this Ice Empire if they had to? Why haven't they, then?'

'The fairies interfere when and how they choose to, and it isn't s-something I understand.' Teddy flicks Sunny's reins to have her sidestep a slippery-looking patch of ice. 'I've heard stories of a magical person there – a rich, p-powerful woman who's amassed so much magic she claims to be a true fairy. She has many followers, and she's g-greatly helped the Ice Empire's army. So, they're similar to Bearra, in that they still have a r-royal family guided by a fairy. But their prince has been missing for over a year, and their fairy isn't real. The Ice Empire isn't as powerful as they t-try to convince the world they are.'

'Their prince? I thought Bearra's royal family was the only one left.'

'No one sees the Ice Empire as legitimate. And like I said, he's m-missing anyway.'

I hug my coat around my body as a chilling wind picks up. I have to raise my voice so it doesn't get lost. 'What about Prince Jacob, the prince who woke Princess Dawn? Is he from the Ice Empire? How can he be a prince if there are no royals left?'

A look of shock flashes across Teddy's face, but he quickly recovers. 'Jacob isn't an official p-prince, but he is of a royal bloodline – from a kingdom that was phased out after Bearra went to sleep. That doesn't mean his family isn't still extremely w-wealthy and powerful.'

'But he's *claiming* to be a prince. I wonder if the princess knows.'

'That's the least of her concerns,' he says darkly.

'What do you mean?'

He turns away. 'N-Nothing. I just mean Lire would've advised them otherwise if it was an issue, don't you think?

The kingdom is just grateful Prince Jacob s-saved them. It wouldn't matter if he was a king or a servant.'

'I think it *would* matter,' I say. 'Lire has never shown interest in anyone other than the royal family. If anything, she would've made sure Princess Dawn's true love would be someone of the right standing.'

'She's protective of Dawn – *Princess* Dawn – that's for c-certain.'

I'm already sick of talking about her, so I change the subject. 'So, this false fairy in the Ice Empire. Is it possible for someone to gain so much magic they're seen as equal to a fairy?'

'No.' He laughs, then breaks into a cough from the icy air. 'People will believe in anything if they want it badly enough,' he says, sputtering to recover. 'The Ice Empire wants a saviour, that's all.'

I guide Pansy past a mound of soft snow that wants to swallow us whole. 'Why do people insist on believing in things that bring them no benefit? I don't even like *Lire*, and she's a real fairy who hasn't done anything explicitly wrong. Everyone else in Bearra loves her, and I'm the only person who seems to see she doesn't do anything to actually help us. Sure, wanting to have faith in something powerful must ease your mind, but I would prefer to not live in a mindless fantasy.'

He's quiet for a while before saying, quietly, 'I wouldn't mind something to believe in.'

'Oh?' I'm about to tease him, but my arms cover in goose-bumps as darkness washes over us, turning the snow grey.

'*Maya*,' he whispers, going white.

With the cloud cover so thick, I hadn't noticed the sun setting. The white world around us has turned a deep grey, and somehow the freezing temperatures become even colder. We should've realised sooner – we haven't found any shelter.

But I sense something worse, something magical, and when I look over my shoulder, sure enough, there she is.

A freshly-human Sierra stands with tendrils of blue magic still wrapped around her as her transformation ends. She crosses her arms and gives us a wicked smile.

Fairies, fairies, fairies!

My shivering worsens, my arms and legs stiffening as the instinct to freeze overtakes me. My heart is too cold to race, and the air is too icy to hyperventilate, so instead of feeling truly afraid, I only feel an eerie numbness.

Her black hair is in two braids that whip around her in the wind, and she's wearing a thick white coat that looks incredibly expensive. Paying no mind to the snow, she paces towards us gracefully. 'Maya, Teddy.' Her voice is icier than a glacier. 'I missed you.'

'Well, you don't have to despair a moment longer,' I say, cowering behind Pansy. My Strength blessing barely disguises the quivering in my voice.

There's a sword in her hand, with a red gem encrusted in its hilt. It must be from Rhiannon. Because *of course*

Rhiannon would help Sierra too. Of course she'd want this to be harder for me. Does Sierra also have a Strength blessing?

'You like this?' She swings the weapon in an arc. 'Yes, it's from Rhiannon. She was *so* welcoming when we met and I explained my situation. She told me exactly where to find you, and so much about you. I thought at first that she regretted giving you her blessing and wanted me to end you before you used it, but it turns out she just loves fights. She wanted me to hurt you, just because she was curious if you would survive it. A strange fairy, but who am I to complain? I'm even stronger now, *blessed*, and there's no way I won't get those rings this time. All four of them.'

'Three,' I grumble. Is everyone bad at counting in the future? 'And we're not giving them to you.'

'Oh, right, you don't have Lire's yet, not *really*.'

'Of course we don't have it. We haven't been to Bearra.'

She winks at Teddy. 'Rhiannon and I had a funny conversation about *you*. Maya still doesn't know, does she?'

'Know what?' I say, a new fear setting in. Whatever Teddy is keeping secret, whatever Rhiannon warned me about, Sierra knows. *Why*?

'Keep talking, Sierra,' says Teddy; they both ignore my question, and I want to scream in frustration. 'We'll wait until the sun rises.'

'No need,' she says. 'I'll kill you long before then.' A blizzard is building around us, and her eyes glint menacingly in the oncoming storm.

Teddy's ring begins to glow. What he thinks he'll do with Kindness, I'm not sure, but any advantage right now is good.

I have no plan. That's been the problem all along – Teddy and I aren't fighters. We can walk for days, we can talk for days, we can survive. But we can't win a fight against an enemy far more powerful than us. We have no idea how to stop her, so our only tactic has been to run and hide.

I call on the blessings I have – Passion and Strength – and beg for help. Immediately I feel a little more sure, a little more confident. My tensed muscles become relaxed and ready, and my senses sharpen. Deep in my heart is a storm ready to be unleashed. My family's faces appear in my mind's eye. Sierra won't stop me. I won't wait to die. This time, she's going to lose.

I yank my knife out of my bag, jump from Pansy, and run at Sierra. My feet sink into the snow with every step, but I don't slow. The cold slips away as my body and mind focus on one thing only – winning.

Teddy is yelling, but I can't understand him.

Sierra's already fighting back. She tries to swing her sword at me, but I take a gamble and tackle her waist. We thud to the ground. Snow sprays around us, blinding me. A slash of metal just misses my left arm, and suddenly she's thrown the sword to the side and is trying to take my knife instead. I blink the snow from my eyes and press the weapon towards her face, but she's too strong – she manoeuvres it away, spinning it so it's suddenly in *her* hand instead. She flips us over and she's straddling me; I gasp as she places one hand around my throat and the other just below it, sharp metal threatening my skin.

If I scream or try to talk – even move – the knife will slash my neck open. I settle for my one option: I give her the nastiest expression I can.

She sneers at me triumphantly, chest heaving. 'You should have given me the rings,' she says.

I'm not cold anymore. I don't have the capacity to be. *Fight her.* My hands are stuck uselessly at my sides, and I'm desperately trying to think of any way out of this. If I had magic – real magic – I could do anything. Anything to get her away. I could throw her off me, dull the blade, make her mind go so numb she'd fall apart.

Her *mind.* Of course – that's how I survived her last time.

My eyes dart to my hand, to my ring blessed by Amora. I remember how it sent Sierra to sleep and ask it to do the same thing.

But Sierra realises too quickly what I'm trying to do. 'Not this time.' She removes her hand from my throat so she can grab my fingers. She squeezes them so hard I cry out involuntarily, and my knife, still pressed to my throat, nicks my skin. Hot blood trickles down my neck.

What do I do? I can't beg Teddy to help. *Teddy.* Where is Teddy? Why isn't he helping?

'Stop moving!' Sierra yells, her voice hoarse. She peers around for her sword, still not removing the knife. I struggle despite the threat – there's nothing else to do – but it's no use. Sierra finds her sword where she abandoned it on the ground.

Why hasn't she killed me yet? Does she need the rings first?

She raises the sword above her head with both hands, and I gasp and pant, trying to get up as soon as the knife is gone from my throat. I look around for Teddy and spot him standing nearby, still as a statue, watching me. *Why?* Before I can scream for him to help, Sierra arcs the sword directly down at me. I expect a slash or stab, for my skin to break open, for blood to pour all over the white snow, but she uses the hilt of the sword to bash my skull, and with a flash of blinding pain I crash back to the ground, unable to move.

For a moment I can't feel anything at all. My vision is blurred and filled with stars, and I can just see the two figures of Teddy and Sierra, so colourful against the grey, moving around each other. I can't hear anything but a gushing noise in the back of my ears.

My mind swims incoherently. If I didn't have the Strength ring, I would be dead right now. Unconscious, at least. *It's keeping me alive.*

Why didn't Sierra take the rings?

Oh. She's too busy fighting Teddy. She has to knock him out before she can risk stopping to pry them off our fingers. They scream at each other, loud enough for me to hear. He could never beat her. He tries to punch her, putting all his weight behind it, but she merely takes his arm and uses his own force to push him into the snow. She kneels beside him and stretches one foot out to press her thick boot against his throat while she studies the rings on his hands.

Tears sting my eyes and cheeks, freezing in the blizzard. I can't watch Teddy be hurt like this. I try to crawl towards him, but my head spins with blinding pain and I fall back into the snow.

He coughs and screams. He's saying something. It takes a while for my hearing to come back enough to catch parts of it, and longer for my mind to start comprehending anything.

Sierra is laughing. Wind pushes falling snow all around her, turning her black hair white. Her coat billows with the intense gusts. 'You really won't use your magic to beat me?' she says to Teddy. 'You would rather die?'

He chokes beneath her, and she wraps her fingers around his, thumbing his rings.

'Or is it *her*?' she says. 'You don't want her to know who you really are.'

My head swims. *Who you are.*

Who *is* he?

'N-No,' he says, his breaths laboured.

Sierra pushes his hands down onto his chest, holding them easily despite them being so much larger than hers. 'Rhiannon could sense it. It's easy to tell what you are when no one else in the world, except one fairy, has that kind of magic. She whispered it to me, right before I left her palace. Oh, how that fairy loves her drama.'

I want to push myself to my feet, run at her, just get closer, but I can't. I can't move at all. I can barely breathe. My vision is still covered with sparks, and I can barely process what Sierra is saying. The numbness is subsiding, and the ache in my head is becoming unbearable. My body begs me to fall unconscious, but I can't, I *can't*.

If I can't fight, I have to at least listen. Even if it's with my last bit of strength, I might find out who Teddy really is. If I survive this, I need to know what I'm dealing with.

'Come on,' Sierra says. 'Use your magic. Give me a real fight.'

'I won't,' he says. 'Even if I had magic, which I don't, I-I would never use it to hurt someone.'

'Really?' A sinister grin spreads across her face. Her foot is still against his throat while she holds his hands and she presses her heavy boot against his windpipe. 'I would.'

He starts blacking out, his eyes rolling back and forward, white and brown, white and brown.

'I'd use magic to hurt you, torture you, kill you,' she says. 'I'd use it to make Maya wish for death as you watched. But I suppose I don't need magic for that, do I?'

If he just used his ring, called on its power of Kindness, couldn't he get her to ease back? Has he even considered it? Why won't he use any magic? Unless he's already using the extent of the ring's capabilities, and that's why Sierra hasn't killed us yet. Why she's only hurting us, why she's taking her time. But it doesn't feel generous.

'If you let Maya go,' Teddy says through ragged breaths, 'I'll come w-with you. I'll help you get the remaining blessings, the three we need, and you can have the crown. You can even kill me when we're done. But spare h-her life.'

Three. I should care about his bargaining, feel grateful, feel something, but I don't. I can only focus on that number. I thought everyone else kept slipping up. But I can see, finally, that I was the one miscounting. We're a fairy ahead of what I thought.

Because . . . Because Teddy . . . He already *has* magic. And according to Sierra, it's no small amount. Magic no one else has, from a fairy we've yet to meet. But no one can steal magic from a fairy unwilling to give it. Who gave him this power? Why?

Who is he? And why, why in the world has he chosen to go on this quest with me? A quest for money? Magic? He already has both. What more could he want?

I'm still too weak to make sense of any of it. To even feel the betrayal Rhiannon promised me. Pansy nudges my shoulder, trying to rouse me, and I don't have the energy to push her back. She slumps beside me.

Sierra laughs. 'It's a tempting offer,' she says, 'having you to myself, dragging you unwillingly along on my mission. But I could never trust you, could I? You would betray me as soon as you got a chance, as soon as you knew Maya was safe. You would probably try to take the crown for yourself. And even I know that if you actually used your magic, I'd be no match for you.'

'If you already know you'll lose, don't make me hurt you,' he says, his expression full of pain. 'Please.'

'I won't make you hurt me,' she says sweetly. 'I'll be kind enough to kill you before that's possible. But I'm going to slash Maya to pieces first. It's so much more exciting that way.'

His jaw tenses, and his hands begin to glow. *Lilac.* A light, warm purple that shines with rhythm against the grey snow, bouncing off falling snowflakes and radiating through the wind.

I suck in a breath.

Sierra grins. 'There he is.' She turns to me. 'See who your sweet boyfriend is now, little Bearran? You could never trust him. I don't even need to beat you anymore. Together the two of you might be a threat. But apart? Useless. And you'll never stay with him now you know the truth.'

The magic courses through the air until it's all around us. Sierra jumps back from Teddy and races to grab her sword from the ground. He stands, glaring at her, a hard look on his face as swirls of purple circulate around and through him. His eyes glitter with the magic as he examines Sierra, and the light shines off her gleaming sword as she swings it down over him.

I expect a loud noise from him, a scream at least, but there's nothing.

The sword hits a wall of magic and bounces. Sierra cries, and I hear her shoulder cracking. She throws her sword away, realising she's miscalculated Teddy's plan of attack, and sprints lightly over the snow until she's next to me. Her face is illuminated in a faint blue light – the moon peeking through the clouds – and for the first time, I see true fear in her eyes.

She hauls me up with her good arm and hides behind me, using me as a shield. I'm still too weak to shove her away. Pansy and Sunny gallop off, frantically abandoning me to our enemy. Sierra is usually predictable in her ruthlessness, but Sierra *scared*? I shake with terror.

'What are you going to do?' she shouts at Teddy. 'Use your power to kill us all? If you want to kill me, you'll have to go through *her* first!'

He shakes his head. 'I told you I didn't want to hurt you.' He doesn't look at my face, but I'm still staring at him, unable to move, my mouth gaping open. *Who . . . How?*

Sierra's hands shake as she tries to grip me. 'You won't hurt me in front of her! Not if you don't want her to see you for the monster you are.'

Teddy steps toward us. The wind picks up again, but it doesn't seem to disturb him. Teddy, the boy who stumbles over his own feet. 'You had so many chances to stop, Sierra. I was willing to give up everything to help you.'

She hides her head behind my back. Defeated? No, that can't be it. I wish I could laugh at her for hiding, for relying on me for protection, but I'm so confused, so afraid. I am entirely numb.

Teddy kneels in front of us, and his magic snakes across the snow, coming towards me. His. Magic. But it goes around my body, crawling past to reach Sierra. I'm no use as a shield.

'I shouldn't exist,' Teddy says solemnly. 'But I'm here, and I have chosen my side. I won't let anything happen to Maya.'

Sierra lets go of me, and before I fall face-first into the snow, Teddy gently takes me into his arms. He drags me back as his magic surrounds the girl now on the ground.

Her black hair is stark against the white blizzard, spread around her as she shivers. The lilac mist clouds her body, and she screams, but I can't hear it. She thrashes, trying to shuffle back through the snow, but the magic presses in, in, around her until she's surrounded by a thick, purple haze. Her hands reach up as if she's swimming, and she tries to push herself to her feet. But she keeps falling, floating, her eyes rolling to the back of her head.

Then the magic crystalises, turning into amethyst-like ice, run through with cracks and splinters. Sierra is frozen within, her eyes and mouth open in terror.

'She . . .' I whisper, but I can still barely move, barely think.

'She's alive,' Teddy says. 'But it'll take her a while to recover.'

I begin to whimper as the pain becomes too much. I want to run, get away from him, but I can't even scream. I can't beg him to explain, I can't hit and punch him until all my anger is released. So instead, I fall unconscious in his arms.

CHAPTER
SEVENTEEN

I FEEL HIS HANDS on my head before anything else, pressing something ice-cold to the spot where Sierra bashed me. I'm tempted to jump awake and try to run away, but I know I'm too weak. I open my eyes slowly, remembering it all in such vivid detail, even though I was too hurt to fully comprehend it as it happened.

What do I feel now? Fear. In every inch of my body. Pure. Fear.

We're sitting on the ground in a circle of dirt surrounded by thick snow. It's warm; a bubble of lilac magic. The sun shines high above us, which means I've been unconscious for at least a full night and half day. I can't tell any areas of Kara's Territory apart, so I have no idea if we've moved.

Sierra isn't in sight, at least. The thought of her frozen, terrified body sends a fresh wave of nausea through my core. What's going to happen to her?

Teddy takes his hand away and instantly a deep pain runs through my skull. As I groan, he helps me sit up, lifting my head from his lap. 'Maya, I . . .'

'Don't talk,' I say. I don't even want to look at him, but I force myself to.

His face falls. His hair is matted, and his eyes are red and glassy. 'You don't know how sorry I am.'

I inhale sharply. I expected more lies. More charm. I thought he might no longer be Teddy. My Teddy. I didn't think he'd be sorry, that he'd let his guilt show like this – at least not yet.

'I'll tell you everything,' he says. 'I promise. I won't lie to you again.'

I mumble, 'After everything you said about me not trusting people . . . *this*,' and another wave of agony hits me. I let out a sob before I can stop myself, and then Teddy's hand is on my head again, pressing ice to the wound. The pain eases, but I don't want him touching me, so I grab a handful of snow and brush his hand away so I can cool the wound myself. 'How long was I unconscious?'

His mouth turns down at the corners, his lips puffy. I think he's been crying. His eyes are half-lidded and his brows pull up at the middle. The sadness doesn't make sense on his face. Teddy is supposed to be happy. His smile lines don't make these shapes. 'Only since last night,' he says.

'Last night, when Sierra attacked, and you . . . you . . .'

'I—'

'Didn't I tell you not to talk?'

'Sorry.'

I weigh my options. I could leave him, try to get him to give me his rings and make him go away. But I can't complete this quest alone, and I'm so injured I don't think I can even stand. How can I go on without him? At this point, if I tried to go on by myself, I really would die.

So my only option is to continue travelling with this liar?

I exhale. He could've hurt me, stolen my rings, done anything he wanted, but he's here keeping me alive. Which means whatever his motive is, if he is going to hurt me, he won't yet. That gives me time to recover, then lose him as soon as I possibly can.

'Okay, fine,' I say. 'Tell me the truth. How did you get Lire's magic? Are you a thief? Or something worse? A pirate? A spy? Is that why you were in Bearra? And don't even think about lying to me again, Teddy, if that's even your name, because if you do . . .'

He nods dejectedly, wrapping his arms around his knees. Sunny's head rests on his shoulder, and I realise Pansy is pressed against my back, keeping me warm. 'It's so difficult to explain,' he says. 'I don't tell anyone the truth, because I wish it *wasn't* true, Maya. I wanted to escape the life laid out for me, and you were it. You were my hope, my perfect plan, and more. I didn't want you to know about my past. And this quest for the crown, there's more to it than you think, okay? So much more. There's so much to tell you.'

I glare at him, grabbing a new heap of ice and switching the hand on my head. 'Then get on with the story before you have time to make up more lies.'

He looks at me like he wants to help, to lower me down into his lap again, to take care of me and brush my hair like he did that night in Rhiannon's Jungle. I wish I didn't want that, too. He stays back. 'I didn't steal my magic,' he says. 'It wasn't given to me, either. I was born with it.'

'Do you really think I'm that stupid?'

'Of course not. And I'm not lying.' He taps at his knee arrhythmically, wincing. 'I have Lire's magic because . . . because . . .' He covers his mouth and finishes with a whisper, 'Lire is my mother.'

'*Teddy.*' My stomach flips, because he knows not to lie, and why would he say something so insane unless it really was true? 'No – I – don't be ridiculous, Teddy. No. Teddy—No.'

'I—'

'*Teddy.*'

'It's bad, I know. That's why I don't tell anyone.'

'Oh, Teddy. *Fairies*, Teddy! So what are you . . . one of them? Where are your wings?'

Oh no. Oh *no*. There's no . . . No. No, I can't deal with this. I won't deal with this. I have a simple life and a simple quest. I need to get a crown and get back to my family. I need to stop being distracted by a boy, and I need to be as far from his fairy drama as possible. I cannot involve myself with a conspiracy like this. I can't be anywhere near him.

A son of Lire? One of the people I hate most?

Not Teddy. Not my Teddy.

No.

He pats Sunny's head, blushing. 'I'm only half fairy. My father is human, whoever he is. I'm not immortal and I don't have wings. I don't dress monochromatically. I'm nothing like Lire at all, except that I have her magic. A lot of it.'

'It's impossible,' I say, cradling my head in my hands. 'The fairies don't have children. They're *fairies*. Can they even get pregnant? And with a human? They would never. Would they? That's disgusting. Half-fairies don't exist. They can't. If they do, they would be like . . . like . . . I don't know. Wrong. Not right.'

'I'm aware of how bad the situation is. And Lire didn't do it for fun. She's had this all planned for a long time, this is her way of gaining power.'

My head droops with realisation. 'A long time? Should I take a guess and say a hundred years?'

'You would be right,' he says.

I blink. So Lire put Bearra to sleep on purpose? I shouldn't believe him, about any of this, but what other explanation is there? Why shouldn't this be real? 'I . . .' I start, then take a breath. '*Fairies*, what did I expect from an immortal being who's basically called *liar*? But why? Why did she do . . . any of this?'

'She's always been the most powerful fairy, but as the world has changed, she's felt threatened.' He gazes out at the snowy landscape, absently brushing out the knots in Sunny's mane. 'Politics have always been tense between her and Kara, and if the other fairies turned against her, she could have everything taken from her. I don't know if fairies can die, but it wouldn't be good.'

'So she hides Bearra away for a hundred years to keep her stash of triarue to herself?'

'That's part of the reason,' he says. 'Bearra is the heart of the world, and the heart of magic, which is why it's Lire's domain. She knew she needed to keep it for herself, but her influence was weakening. Over time, each fairy became patron of a section of the world, and even as they integrated more into society, they kept their immense power. This was happening long before the territories were official places. But Lire never carved out a territory for herself, so her political power started falling. She only has one small kingdom, and she isn't even the ruler of it. Lire was merely an advisor to Bearra's royals. She needed a way to regain her authority without starting a war.'

'But what does an immortal being have to gain from having a baby?'

He glances at his hands. 'I'm not her only child.'

It takes me a moment to understand, but when it clicks, my hands cover my mouth. 'Prince Jacob.'

'My older brother, and the world's only other half-fairy.' Teddy rubs his temples and exhales slowly. 'It was always about him. Lire had a son and created a perfect plan for him to marry Princess Dawn. When he became king, she would really be the one in charge. No one would ever know she intervened. She'd keep her place as the beloved, powerful fairy of Bearra, while becoming its true ruler.'

I want to bury myself in the snow and give in to the cold. No. No. No. I hate Lire, so I'm not surprised to hear she's behind terrible things. But for Teddy to be involved, and for me to be involved by extension, and, and— What about my family? What's Lire going to do to Bearra once she has all this power she's striving for?

I wrap my arms around my body, forgetting my sore head, and watch snowflakes drift across the endless white landscape. My mind feels the same as this place – a colourless nightmare where nothing makes sense, with a blizzard eating at my very soul. 'So you're saying that just to gain more power, Lire put Bearra to sleep for a hundred years, had a child of her own to marry Dawn, sent him to save Bearra, and made it look as if he was Dawn's soulmate?'

He looks so ashamed, so embarrassed, I'm really starting to feel sorry for him. 'She organised the entire thing from the moment Dawn was born,' he says. 'She saw an opportunity in the princess and manipulated Kara into cursing her to die. It was all to make Lire look like the hero when she changed the curse, and solidify the world's distrust of Kara. It worked.'

'Why a hundred years?'

'It's poetic. A century makes a much better story than fifty-three years, or a hundred and twenty-four. It also gave her time to have a child and form her plan. And Bearra would be so weakened after a hundred years that it would *have* to rely on Lire more than ever.'

I feel beyond sick. I'm in an entirely new space, where dizziness and nausea are all I know. My life was ruined so a fairy could gain political influence? I was right about her. She's never cared about people. And if she ever cared about the royals, it was only because she had something to gain from them.

If Teddy isn't just making up more lies.

'It all worked perfectly,' he continues. 'Jacob was the first person to be able to break into Bearra, because he had the right magic. He was able to break the curse because my mother made sure he could. He isn't Dawn's soulmate. He's a fraud.'

'And you?' I ask, trying to keep my face flat, to not show him how confused, how upset, how afraid I'm feeling. Trying *not* to show that I understand and want to forgive him for all his lies, because why do I have to feel like that? 'If Lire already had Jacob, why have you, too?'

'For backup. Luckily she never really needed me. I managed to be mostly invisible for much of my childhood, which is how I travelled so much. Amora took me in for a few years, knowing who my mother was. She was more of a parent to me than Lire ever tried to be. She taught me to be a better person than my brother and mother. But mostly . . . I was forgotten.'

'Until it was time to return to Bearra.'

He nods, tearing at the frays in Sunny's reins. Even his horse looks dejected, as if it can feel his pain. 'Lire staged us as princes from a distant kingdom,' Teddy says. 'She kept a close eye on me, for the first time in my life, to make sure I didn't ruin her big plan. I *hated* her, Maya. I still hate her so much. I didn't want to go, but I had no choice. She knew I didn't like what she was doing, and that I hated my brother, so it was time to keep me under supervision. It was terrible. I had to lie constantly and, worst of all, watch Dawn try to be around a man she loathes, knowing she had no choice but to marry him. Dawn was the only good thing about living in that castle. She was my only friend for a year.'

Yuck, Dawn?

He smiles faintly. 'She kept saying that if she had to marry a man, she wished it could at least be me. She's spent the last year doing her best to put off the wedding, but it'll have to happen eventually. She'll be stuck with him forever. But the girl she really loved died a hundred years ago. Maya, I almost wished I *could* save Dawn by marrying her, but we knew it had to be Jacob, her "soulmate", or there would be scandal.

'After a while in Bearra, watching her suffer, I couldn't take it anymore. My brother and I had a fight and . . . and although it meant abandoning Dawn, I had to escape. My plan was to run to Amora and seek refuge with her, to find a way to hide from my mother. I wanted to distance myself from it all, never use magic again – even change my face if I had to – and disappear forever.'

I breathe, take it all in. Teddy and the princess . . . *friends*. This is worse than I thought. 'But then you met me?' I say. 'How did I not recognise you as Prince Jacob's brother?'

'Did you even know he had one?' His posture goes limp and his chin touches his chest. 'I kept myself inconspicuous, stayed in the castle or only left in disguise. On the rare occasion people saw me as a prince, I was overshadowed by Jacob. I'm an afterthought, Maya. Why would anyone notice me if I didn't want them to?'

I take a new handful of snow and place it on my throbbing head. '*Teddy*. And— And Princess Dawn? She was never . . . I always blamed her. For all of it. The curse, the sleep. I thought she ruined my life. But it was Lire? All of it was her? She's the only reason my life was ruined?'

'Dawn is innocent,' he says. 'She would have been a great queen, but now Jacob and Lire will make sure she's powerless. I didn't want to leave her behind, but she refused to abandon her kingdom.'

A gust of wind tugs at my hair and my jacket, and I pretend to be shielding my eyes from the white glare of the snow while I wipe away welling tears. Everything feels so blurry, and I want to sink into the ground and sob. But I can't show him how weak I am; I don't know who he is anymore.

I try to meet his eyes, but I'm caught with a shudder as the ice on my head drips onto my neck. 'So y-you found me running away and decided to f-follow me around instead.'

He takes off his coat and wraps it around my shoulders. I don't have the heart to shove it back to him, though my mind says I should. He attempts a small smile. 'You seemed to need my help. And I suppose I threw myself into helping you because, well, I needed a distraction. Then I found out about the crown.'

Fairies. 'The final piece of Lire's puzzle.'

'If she gets it, and Jacob is crowned, he'll be unstoppable. It isn't just that he'll officially be king. The crown's magic will amplify *his* magic. He'll become not just powerful on his own, or as a king, but also as the bearer of all of Bearra's triarue.'

'You're saying you only came with me to *stop* me giving the crown to the royal family?' My shoulders fall.

He never wanted to help me. He only used me to help get him closer to the crown. A lump forms in my throat, but I swallow it back.

He turns away, raking his fingers through the snow. 'I'm sorry, Maya. I wanted to convince you to destroy it, but the longer I've known you, the more I realised that would never happen. Then Sierra turned up, and it was one more person who I couldn't risk getting its power. I couldn't say anything. I had to hope I could get to it first and break it. And that one day you might be able to forgive me.'

'I need that crown, Teddy.' I shuffle backward. 'Your mother's politics mean nothing to me. I *have* to save my family.'

'I know that's how you feel.'

I clench my fists, hardening my expression. 'So you understand I won't let you destroy it.'

'I understand I still have time to change your mind,' he says. 'But it's yours, and your decision. I have magic and money. There's a lot I can give your family. We could find a way to get them out of Bearra, set them up in Amora's Capital, give them everything they could ever want. You don't need the crown.'

I shake my head. Who does he think he is? 'I don't want any favours from you. I want what's mine.'

'If that's your decision.' We finally meet eyes, and I see a genuineness in his face that only confuses me more. Would he really help me, even if it meant giving in to his mother's plan?

'I need to rest,' I say, lying back on the ground. My head is still pounding. 'Then we can continue to Kara's Palace. I don't trust you. But we need each other to get what we want, so for now we'll keep working together. *That's* my decision.'

'You're still my friend,' he says softly. 'Maya, I'm still the same person. I won't stop trying to convince you to destroy the crown, but I'll never lie to you again. I'm on your side. Please know I'm sorry. Please know how much I care about you.'

I close my eyes.

My summer boy's mask is slipping away, revealing the autumn decay beneath. Maybe he's more like me than I thought. We're both falling in the dark, grasping desperately for some light.

But if we're reaching for each other, we're both headed for oblivion.

Chapter
Eighteen

Somewhere, sometime...

TEDDY GOT HIS MAGIC and his talent for lying from Lire. He must have gotten his red hair and his heart from his father, though Teddy didn't know who he was. Teddy's charm, however, was all his own: a mask created to hide his true self, a skill honed for survival. Of course, he was no prince. He had no last name, no identity. No one would ever know who he was, and no matter how powerful he became, he would always be trapped under his mother's thumb.

Climbing the stairs to Princess Dawn's wing of the castle, he cleared his throat to announce his arrival. It had been another long day trapped in this hot, ancient kingdom, and seeing the princess was the one thing that Teddy could enjoy – when he could find her, at least.

In one of the darkest corners of her large wardrobe, there was a shift in the ballgowns hanging along a pink wall. He brushed the curtain of material aside and found the princess nestled on the floor. She flinched, and he whispered quickly, 'It's only me.'

Her wide hazel eyes relaxed. 'Teddy, be more careful coming back here,' she breathed. 'If you were ever caught— You don't know what your brother would do. Not to mention the scandal it would cause.'

He had been living in the castle for almost a year now, since his brother – Prince Jacob – 'broke the curse' and woke the kingdom. A long, painful year for both Teddy and the princess. Their unexpected friendship had been the only hope they'd had to hold on to.

Teddy ran his hands across a silk dress. 'We can't be expected to ignore each other just because you're engaged to him. Don't let him tell you what to do.'

Dawn sighed, her golden hair falling in soft waves across the tulle she was hidden within. Her warm, brown skin was radiant even in this dim nook of the castle. The princess was beautiful, lovely in every way, and maybe in another life Teddy would have wished for more than friendship with her. Anyone in the world could love Dawn. Everyone did. Possibly it was the woman herself, or possibly the blessings bestowed upon her, but she really was flawless in every way. From head to toe, inside and out, everything about her was the perfect picture of a princess. Except that she had no interest in princes, and Dawn and Teddy's situation was more than complicated. Their friendship was of such high importance to them both that neither knew what they would do if it were lost.

'I don't *let* him tell me what to do,' Dawn retorted with a slight wince. 'But I fear for you. Even if he were a monster – and I'm not sure he isn't – I must marry him. I would much prefer the arrangement to be on good terms.'

Teddy squeezed in beside her and pulled a bright-yellow dress across to hide them. Bearra was already warm enough without being pressed against each other under layers of fabric, their breaths hot on each other – but this was all they had, so they would take it. 'If you're planning to abandon me just to appease Jacob,' he said, 'you'll have to find me a new best friend first. Or someone in this ancient kingdom to marry.'

She laughed lightly, then covered her mouth to keep quiet. 'You know I wish it could have been you.'

Teddy and Dawn had gone over the discussion of marriage many times, hidden in their secret places, whispering about what might have been. They were the same age – both seventeen, and both very similar in mindset. Their friendship was easy, unlike Dawn's relationship with Jacob, who was several years older and more an empty shell than a real person. Where Teddy was sensitive, Jacob was blunt, soldier-like, and plain. He tended to say things as if he were a puppet, repeating what was expected of him and never offering a true opinion. If he loved Dawn – not only physically, but genuinely – she did not know it. Worst of all, she could tell there was a violence hidden in Jacob, one that might explode at any minute. But no one else seemed able to see his true nature; they were too enamoured by their fairy tale hero.

Dawn and Teddy, however, were linked by the weight of the magic bestowed upon them at birth: Teddy born into power, and Dawn showered with blessings. Though she knew nothing of his magic or his parentage, Teddy knew that in a twisted way, Lire was what drew them together. They both had her magic within them, and had experienced her whispering in their ears all their lives. Both would have been happier without the weight of the responsibility their magic gave them. Both desired to run far away and never return. And both knew the weight of selflessness – of knowing that they *couldn't* ever run away.

They did not fit into the lives laid out for them, and they were terrified.

Teddy wished he could tell her the truth – about Lire's plan, about who he really was, about Jacob. To Dawn, Teddy would always be the prince who came along with her future husband, a boy dragged into another world. If she knew he was Lire's son, that everything happening to her was part of a conspiracy that would shake the foundations of her world, would she still care for him?

'I'm sorry, Dawn,' Teddy whispered. 'I'm sorry you're so unhappy.'

She shook her head, her curls bouncing endearingly. 'Don't say sorry. You don't wish to be here either. Both of us are victims of my curse and your brother.'

In answer, he brushed her hair from her face and pressed a kiss to her forehead. He pulled her back into his arms so they were leaning against the wall and unable to see each other's faces. There was nothing to this intimacy but comfort, nothing but their desperate need to cling to each other.

After sitting and breathing gently for a while, Dawn tensed as if a painful memory had crossed her mind. 'There's something wrong, Teddy, isn't there?' she whispered with haste. 'Something you can't tell me about Jacob. I'm not supposed to marry him, am I? Something went wrong with the curse – he can't be my soulmate. He's so much older than me, nearly eight years, and he's a *man*. You're his brother. Don't you know the truth?' She was so uncharacteristically frantic that it shocked Teddy. 'You would never hurt anyone. I know that. But he's different. I fear that he'll . . . That once the marriage is done, he'll . . .'

Teddy dropped his head, leaning it against her shoulder. He wanted to warn her, to fight Lire and Jacob, but what could he do? Teddy had spent his life being a coward, avoiding his mother and trying to make his own life so he wouldn't have to face his reality. He could have tried – he still could – to stop Lire. He could even find a way for Dawn and himself to run away together. But he wouldn't. He could not run away like he did as a child – no, now he had to sit and watch as his mother's plan unfolded. Even if it hurt him. Even if it hurt his best friend.

'I know,' said Dawn, sighing. 'You would tell me if you could. I just wish I had some way to stop it, to protect myself.'

Teddy shifted, his eyes wet. 'Just say no. They can't force you to marry him.' He wasn't sure why he said this. He just needed to say *something*. Of course she couldn't refuse.

'After the worst year Bearra has ever had, this engagement has been one of my people's few sources of hope – a reason to see a bright future for the kingdom. If I refuse Jacob, I'll be letting everyone down.'

A sudden noise startled them, and as they jumped, a dress nearly slipped and fell off its hanger. Dawn covered Teddy's mouth.

A door had opened.

'Princess?' Jacob's voice called. 'I want to speak with you, and I know you're in here.' They heard him shuffling around the room, but Teddy and Dawn stayed quiet and huddled, backs against the wall and feet tucked in. 'You'll have to stop avoiding me eventually. We're going to be married soon.'

Teddy knew that a secret meeting in the princess's rooms was off-limits, and if Jacob found them, he would assume the worst. He would be furious, and Jacob's fury could burst out in terrible ways. Teddy's breaths shook even as he tried to hold them. Their small hiding place was growing hotter by the second, but he was frozen. Dawn pressed her face into his chest as if that would protect her.

Jacob's footsteps approached and the dresses were yanked back with a screech. Fresh air rushed into Teddy's lungs as he gaped at his older brother. He stood tall above them, his teeth clenched, and he growled at Teddy. Although he looked every bit a royal, the light-haired man seemed more animal than human.

Teddy sat up, almost jumping away from Dawn. 'I heard her crying,' he stammered. 'I only came in to comfort her. Nothing happened. We didn't even talk.'

Jacob snarled, looking between them with a fiery gaze. 'You're a liar, little brother. You always have been. Don't think I'm so easily fooled.'

'I'm sorry,' Dawn whimpered. 'We really weren't doing anything improper. I swear.'

He ignored her. 'Of course jealous little Teddy would try to steal *my* bride. Is that what you want? To take her? To take Bearra? To have all that's mine for yourself?'

Teddy shook his head. His brother was unpredictable, the one person other than their mother that he never knew how to react to. 'I want nothing to do with Bearra. I wouldn't be here at all if I had a choice. You know that. Dawn and I live here together, and we'll be brother and sister in law soon. Why shouldn't we be friends?'

'Because I know you,' Jacob spat, 'and I don't trust you, *Prince Teddy.*'

Teddy stood to leave. 'Fine. I'll leave you two alone. I won't talk to the princess ever again.' He said it half-heartedly, knowing his brother was right – he was lying. There was no part of him that could give up Dawn. But if it meant keeping them both safe for today, he'd go.

Dawn's face was pleading, begging Teddy to not leave her alone with Jacob, but Teddy didn't know what else to do. To stay would be to fight his brother, and that would have far worse consequences. Jacob wouldn't physically hurt Dawn, would he? He hadn't yet. But that didn't make Teddy feel any less guilty for leaving her vulnerable with a man she hated.

He tried to walk away, but Jacob caught his arm and looked him dead in the eye. 'We aren't finished.'

Dawn scrambled to her feet. 'It's okay. It's okay, Jacob, I swear. Just let your brother go.' She touched his arm gently, but her hand was trembling.

He shook her off, not looking away from Teddy. 'Not this time.'

One moment things may have been fine – the next, Jacob's fist landed with a *crack* on Teddy's jaw.

Dawn screamed as Teddy fell. A purple glow filled the room as Teddy's vision swam with stars. Dawn ran to the window, waving for help. Jacob's hands alighted with magic that spread across his body; even his eyes glowed with it. They narrowed menacingly.

Teddy tried to stand, a hand on his bleeding lip, but Jacob punched him again. This time it landed on his stomach, and Teddy retched and doubled over, thumping on the floor. His body glowed with magic where it had been hit, the force of Jacob's power hardening the blow.

'Stop, Jacob!' Dawn yelled. 'Guards will be here soon, and they—they—'

He whirled on her, magic flaring around him. 'You think guards can stop *me*?'

She hurried back, her eyes bulging with every gasp for breath. 'H-How are you doing this? How do you h-have magic?'

'I am the most powerful person in this room.' His voice was deep, with a dark laugh beneath it. 'I will not be betrayed. I will not be disobeyed. I do not wish to hurt my wife, but if you plan on spending your time with *him*, one of you must pay.'

Teddy shuddered, balled up on the floor. Jacob stepped toward him, building up his magic as if to use it for an even stronger blow. It could kill him – Teddy knew his brother had the power – but he wouldn't. He only wanted to hurt Teddy. Just like all the times before.

Magic poured from Jacob's fingers. Dawn pleaded at him to leave, but his animal eyes were latched on to Teddy. His hands pushed forward, forcing the magic at his younger brother with the strength of a hundred strikes.

Teddy was still. His face fell flat, and—

And the magic simply curved around him.

Jacob growled, angry like a child. 'Coward!'

Teddy's own magic was building like an aura over his skin, protecting him. He stood, his power so potent that it healed his wounds. He stepped in front of Dawn, who was pressed against the back wall, her cheeks covered in tears – she wouldn't look at him, though she accepted his protection.

Jacob kept sending magic Teddy's way, but it did nothing. Teddy was sending so much back that it only hurt Jacob the more he attacked. He was thrown into the wall of dresses, knocking the rack down and exposing the window. Sunlight blasted into the room. The floor cracked beneath them, and dresses began catching fire.

The amount of lilac magic filling the room became choking, blinding. When the brothers realised neither could overpower the other, they turned to using their fists once more, tackling each other to the ground – hitting, kicking, biting, clawing. Jacob was going to win, there was no doubt about it. Teddy coughed and sputtered while Jacob roared.

Teddy covered his head, expecting a final blow.

Then the room froze, and all the purple haze and fire disappeared at once. The boys were thrown apart and landed at opposite walls.

In the doorway, Lire stood like an angry storm in her violet dress, her huge, wispy wings pointed upward to extend her height. Teddy knew, then, that there was no coming back from this. There would be consequences. Terrible ones.

Lire glared at Dawn. 'Forget what you saw,' she hissed. 'If you tell *anyone* about this, you will regret it.'

Dawn looked relieved to see the fairy, but she must have known something was wrong. Lire's mask had dropped. Teddy had never seen his mother act this way in front of the princess – usually she took the role of a wise, caring aunt. A better mother to Dawn than she ever was to him. Was it obvious to the princess, yet, that Jacob and Teddy were Lire's sons?

'Tell me you'll stay quiet,' Lire pressed.

Dawn finally seemed to realise the fairy hadn't come to save her. Her face fell and she nodded, fresh tears welling in her eyes.

The fairy turned to her sons, her lips turned down in disgust. 'If the two of you ever use your magic like that again . . .' She didn't need to finish her threat.

Jacob stood sheepishly, giving Teddy a nasty sneer before storming out of the room. Lire shook her head at Teddy, then followed her eldest son.

For a long time, Dawn and Teddy sat beside each other in silence. When he tried to reach for her hand, she shrank away. 'You need to leave.' Her words were sharp, but not without grief. 'Get away from here.'

'I'm so sorry . . . I'm sorry.' His voice wobbled. He shuffled away from her slowly, examining his wounds. 'I'm sorry you had to see that. I won't visit you again.'

'No.' Dawn wiped her eyes. 'I don't mean get away from *me*. You need to get out of Bearra. I don't understand what's happening here, but I know that next time, you might not survive a fight with your brother. I can't abandon Bearra, but you still can.' She still wouldn't look at him.

Teddy sat in shock, looking at his friend with heartbreak. She was wrecked, her skin blotchy, her dress torn, her curls all out of place. He knew he had to protect her however he could. 'Do you understand now?' he said, his voice cracking. 'Do you see why I won't leave you alone with him?'

She pulled him up and pushed him towards the door. Already she was collecting herself, relying on every one of her blessings, all of her training as a princess. 'One day, if you ever can,' she said, 'return to me with a solution. I want you safe and alive, Teddy, but I have a kingdom to protect. A duty to fulfil. And now that I know *something* of the truth, I'm the only one who can protect my people. Save yourself from Jacob and Lire. Then, when you can, come back and save the rest of us.'

CHAPTER
NINETEEN

I HATE HIM. I do. I hate him.

Except I don't. I couldn't. I only *wish* I could hate him.

Maybe when I get Kara's blessing, it will be easier. The power of Death and Darkness might stop me from making the mistake of befriending another human being ever again. If Teddy even counts as a human being. Fairies certainly aren't people.

We've travelled for three more days since the *incident*, and now Kara's Capital is in sight. It's covered in a large, transparent-grey dome, which I assume is to protect the city from the harsh weather.

Since we left Sierra behind – frozen in that horrifying enchanted ice – I've not let Teddy out of my sight for a second. I ride behind him at all times, so I'm watching him and not the other way around. No more vulnerability. No more niceness. I don't care that he explained everything. That his story made sense. He lied, and he could *still* be lying.

So I barely talk to him, and he lets me sit in my silent anger. There isn't much to say out in this desolate icy world. But every time I glimpse his hands, I imagine that lilac glow of magic, and my head spins, making me want to turn and run. How can I believe a word he's said about being on my side?

My skull still aches from where Sierra hit me. Teddy asked if he could use his magic to heal it – as if I'd let him. I'm sure I'm fine now, anyway. I've seen enough of his magic. Whatever the extent of his power is, I don't want to know. I'm furious at him, and afraid of him, and I'm grieving what we had before, and now I want to be home with my family more than ever.

'Only a few more hours,' Teddy calls from ahead.

I ignore him. There's no longer any need to be friends. I'll get rid of him as soon as I have the crown. And if he tries to steal it from me, I'll die before I give it up. Or maybe Sierra will take him out for me.

✦ ❖ ✦ ◗ ♡ ◖ ✦ ❖ ✦

I expect trouble getting through the dome over Kara's Capital, but the magical wall simply curves and stretches around us, the light scattering into rainbows as it lets us pass.

As soon as we're within its circumference, the temperature heightens considerably. Still cold, but bearable.

I let the dense, sprawling city warm me, and as we continue toward Kara's Citadel – after first dropping off the horses – the feeling in my hands and feet finally returns. But as the numbness subsides, the pain it was hiding resurfaces. Days and days of travel, my fight with Sierra, *Teddy*, all of it pours into me until I want to curl into a ball and press snow against my body to numb myself again.

The houses here are robust, made of thick stone that steams as the heat within seeps through. There are fewer people in this city. They have skin paler than Teddy's, and most have light hair, too. They look like Bearrans if we didn't get so much sun, which makes me wonder if Bearrans were initially from the outer reaches of the world and wandered in over time.

There are countless questions I want to ask Teddy about this place, but I refuse to let myself open my mouth. I can't give him the upper hand so easily. He's never been here either, so it wouldn't help anyway.

Kara's Citadel is much like I would have expected from the fairy of darkness: a huge, haphazard structure of shining, sharp obsidian, with a few small windows. It isn't as large as the other fairy's castles, though. Like the rest of the capital, it's modest, despite its intimidating appearance. *Everything* is cramped together under the dome to preserve warmth, but it doesn't feel claustrophobic. It feels cosy.

Strangely, it reminds me of home.

Teddy taps his thighs nervously as we make our way closer to the entrance. He's probably afraid because Kara hates his mother so much. *His mother*. Lire. The fairy, Lire. *Stop it*, I think, shifting my gaze away from his face and focusing on following his feet.

When he stops, I almost walk into him. I look up and realise we're already at the citadel's entrance. People smile at us. This place is completely contradictory to what I thought it would be. If Amora's people are passionate, Adella's people are kind, and Rhiannon's are brave, then what are the people here? Clearly being in the territory of death and darkness doesn't mean they're all evil, so what values do Kara's people live by?

Steps of dark wood lead up to the citadel, snow pressed into the cracks. There's already a line of people at the gate, waiting to speak to the guards. Some they let in, and others they wave away. Teddy and I step into a line, following others who must be hoping to get an audience with Kara. It takes an uncomfortably long time for us to reach the front as we stand apart in total silence. I keep shifting from foot to foot, and Teddy claps rhythms onto his crossed arms.

When we make it to the gate, a guard asks, 'What do you want with the council?'

I lift my chin to see her properly – she's already tall and burly, but being a step above us makes her all the more intimidating. 'We need to see the fairy,' I tell her. 'Kara.'

She chuckles, her pale skin freckled but smooth. '*Really*? Why would that be?'

I grind my teeth, trying not to lash back at her patronising tone. 'That isn't your business. Let us in and she'll decide for herself whether to see us.'

'It's important,' Teddy says, with a bright smile that sends bile into my throat. 'And private.'

The guard looks down her nose at us. 'The fairy isn't seeing anyone at the moment. If it's an issue you can talk about with our elected council, you're welcome to tell me what it is. Then I'll decide whether to let you in.'

'No,' I say, brushing snow from my sleeves. 'It has to be Kara.'

'You aren't from here, are you?' She moves to better block the gate. 'Kara rarely leaves the citadel, and rarely speaks to anyone. She comes out every so often, takes care of a few magical problems, and sorts out anyone who needs sorting out. She isn't here to serve us. She may not be in the city again for a long while.'

'*When*?'

The guard raises her eyebrows with amusement. 'Could be hours, could be months. Years if you're very unlucky.' She pauses, clearly trying to irk me. It's working. 'Even then, she has no reason to talk to you. Why don't you go to Adella, if you need a fairy? She's only a week or two's travel south-west. And she *is* known for her sociability.'

I tap my foot. 'No. We need to see Kara. Now.'

'*No*. You don't need to see Kara. Not now, not ever.'

Teddy stands tall – *prince-like* – beside me. 'And what if we have something she might want?'

'*Do* you?'

'We . . . might.'

'Then show it to me.' She waits a moment as we stare at her dumbly, then she waves us off. 'Go. Both of you. Stop wasting my time.'

I scowl. 'I hope you freeze and all your toes fall off.'

Her shoulders shake with laughter, and snowflakes drop from her hair. The citadel looms above her head, dark and impossible. Within it is the *only* thing I need from this territory. 'Have a lovely day,' the guard says.

That night, in our chosen inn, Teddy pays for separate rooms. This time I don't complain. I lock the door behind me and sigh with relief – it's been so long since I've had my own space. After a long bath, I sit on the bed and work on sketches.

First, I draw that guard getting knocked over the head with Sierra's sword – something I've been fantasising about since earlier today. Next I draw Teddy's hands surrounded by magic. Sierra's face, frozen in fear. The back of Pansy's head, a view I'm so familiar with now. Then I draw her eyes.

If these were illustrations in a storybook, how would my story be told? I thought I was a brave hero on a daring quest, danger and adventure everywhere, with new strength and new sights to behold. But my story isn't worth telling. I'm definitely not a hero. What I'm doing is to help my family, of course, but now that I know the truth about the crown, shouldn't I let Teddy destroy it?

Lire is the reason my family is in poverty – but I don't hate her as much as I love them. Does giving her the crown to protect my family make me a villain? Will Jacob becoming the king of Bearra even be such a bad thing? The current royal family are useless. Maybe with him, things will be better. Does it really matter if Lire's methods have been deceitful?

I cross my pencil over a half-focused drawing of wings. They're how I imagine Kara's might look: sharp as blades, pitch-black.

It doesn't matter if I feel guilty. I won't change my mind. I'm getting the crown and giving it to the royal family. It doesn't matter what the stakes are; it's life or death anyway. I'm not going to back down now.

I press my face into my pillow. Blankets are heaped over me and the fireplace is roaring. It's never felt so good to be warm. As I lie here alone, I think of Teddy in the next room. I hope he's scared of the dark. I hope he feels as lonely and afraid as I do.

I fall asleep furious.

+ ⸰'ⓞ ♡ ⓞ'⸰ +

'Who knows what you are?' I ask Teddy as we have breakfast at a restaurant in the city. I don't want to speak to him, but this piece of information feels necessary for me to know.

He winces, glancing at the people near us. The tables in here are cramped together, and the doors block out the sounds of the city outside. But who would understand what we're discussing, anyway? I eye him, pushing him to speak.

'Not many people,' he says with shame in his tone. He puts down his steaming plate of waffles, overflowing with honey and butter. 'I don't tell anyone, and my mother has always preferred to keep me a secret. Her allies may know of me, but they wouldn't know my face. Amora knows, of course. And Gus and his mum. I tried to keep it secret from him, but he eventually found out by accident.'

He watches the room for eavesdroppers again, as if he isn't powerful enough to deal with them. 'Those are the only people confirmed to know. But Rhiannon certainly noticed I had Li—' He stops himself. 'She knew I had magic, whether she thought it was stolen or otherwise. I met her before, as a child. My mother was meeting with her, and I happened to be dragged along. As for Adella, I'm not sure if she could tell, but she must have. It seems to be instinctive – the fairies can sense each other's magic if it's strong enough.'

I swallow a bite of waffle; a piece cut into a perfect square with honey pooled atop it. 'Surely your *mother* knew the other fairies could sense who you were, then? Why'd she let you spend your childhood running around the world wherever you liked?'

He stares at his plate. 'She didn't see me as much of a threat, and if people did find out, she could always claim I stole her magic and have me killed.' We each take a few tense bites of our breakfast. 'Anyway, most of the time that I was running around the world, I wasn't just having fun. I was running *away*. She'd still always find me eventually. She's smart, and she has eyes everywhere. Sometimes she'd let me be gone for years. Finding me was never a priority. Until my brother got into Be—' He sighs. 'When that happened, she brought me back to stay.'

I don't care to offer him any comfort or validation, so I continue asking questions. 'Where did she live for a hundred years while Bearra was closed off? Where was your home?'

His eyes darken. 'Her home was never my home. My brother and I were raised by maids sworn to secrecy. They were replaced every few months so they never knew too much. We lived in Naroport, a smaller city near Darraport, in an apartment my mother would only visit in disguise. She had an estate closer to Bearra, but we were never allowed there. Not as ourselves, at least. She could never wait to get back into Bearra. She always talked about waiting for the right moment to finally return to her kingdom.'

'Well she certainly took her time,' I say into my waffle.

Teddy cracks a small smile, which I don't return.

Two women in thick furs wander into the restaurant and sit at a table pressed close to ours. The staff immediately bring out plates of bread for them. Heavy jewels glitter from their necks, drawing eyes from around the restaurant. One has dark hair and features similar to Sierra, so she must be from Grace's Territory. The other looks like one of Kara's through and through, with hair and skin so pale she's almost transparent.

The pale one thanks the staff for the thickly buttered bread and leans in to speak to her companion. 'They're saying Kara is desperate for it,' she says quietly. 'All the fairies would love some of their own.'

'It does put them at a disadvantage,' the dark-haired woman replies. 'Politics are only becoming more fragile as time goes on, especially with Bearra on the brink of reopening and crowning a new queen and king. All the fairies are nervous, unsure what the others are planning. Their borders are beginning to crumble. Especially with the threat of the Ice Empire. No one knows who's loyal to who, or what the world could become if a war starts.'

Teddy begins to say something, but I widen my eyes and tilt my head towards the two women. He realises I'm trying to listen and his sentence trails off. We dig back into our food, pretending to be engrossed in it. Which is almost true, since the waffles are beyond incredible.

The pale woman nods. 'Which means now is the time to get our hands on Lire's magic. Every fairy has a stash of stolen power somewhere, hidden away in unassuming people or objects. But Lire has never once shared her magic. She remains the most powerful fairy not just because of her access to Bearra, but because she's the only one whose power can't be taken and used against her. She'll have access to all seven kinds of magic, while the other fairies only have six at most.'

'That magic is more precious than a *mountain* of triarue. If we got our hands on some, and offered it to any of the other fairies . . .'

'We would be very, very rich.'

She nods excitedly. 'Wealthier than we could even imagine.'

'So that's our next mission. A hunt for Lire's magic, wherever it might be hidden, even if we have to steal it from her ourselves.'

Her friend waves a hand, blue magic crawling around it like a shadow. 'How could I say no to that?'

The two of them laugh and dive into their food without any more talk.

Are they some kind of treasure hunters? Pirates?

Teddy frowns as he listens, but I can't fight the grin crawling onto my lips.

I lean over to him so I can whisper. His eyes turn hopeful and his gaze drifts to my lips. I don't pull back; I'm too excited. 'Teddy, I have an idea.'

CHAPTER TWENTY

WE HEAD STRAIGHT FOR the citadel, leaving behind our unfinished food.

I stand tall, feeling more confident than ever. Yesterday evening we shopped for new clothes; Teddy now wears a thick knitted jumper over a white shirt, a thicker jacket atop that, and pine-green pants. I absolutely refuse to think about how much I love pine green, and how much I love to see him in it. Instead, I focus on enjoying my new outfit: a black corset over a black blouse, stockings under my grey pants, and a stunning brown coat. All things Teddy can afford, and all things I wish I had while we were travelling here in our measly coats from Adella's Territory. After being rejected by the guard yesterday, we both knew we wanted to look our best the next time we returned. And we do.

'What's the plan?' Teddy asks, hurrying beside me in his clumsy gait.

Kara's Capital extends around us in its dark iciness, the obsidian citadel towering above. People shuffle out of our way as we race past.

'We offer her your magic. If you're going to be the child of that—' I stop myself. 'At least it'll be useful.' I drag Teddy along, not giving him the opportunity to stop me.

'No – *Maya* – no! What if Kara kills me when she finds out who I am?'

'That's your problem.' I race into the line at the citadel's gates, and he steps beside me. The line is long, but the guards turn so many people away that it's moving quickly. 'You already said she'll be able to sense who you are. We'll just be confirming it and making a fair trade.'

'Some of my magic for some of hers,' he says, out of breath. 'I'm not even sure I can share my magic. I've never done it.' Despite his hesitation, I know he'll do anything to get to the crown and have a chance at destroying it. He won't refuse this idea.

'You're about to learn.'

'And if it doesn't work?'

'Then she'll kill you, and I'll go on my way to the crown by myself.' After an uneasy pause, I ask him, 'What will we do if she isn't even here? In the capital, I mean.'

He shifts from foot to foot. 'When she finds out what we're offering, she'll come. Fairies can use their magic to travel incredibly fast – Lire does it all the time. Kara could be here within a day.'

'Perfect.'

When we reach the front of the line, the guard from yesterday laughs in our faces, her large chest thundering above us. 'I told you two you're not seeing the fairy.'

I meet her eyes. 'That was before. Now we have something she wants.'

'What's that, girl?'

'Magic.'

Another laugh. The citadel looms high behind her, flecked with snow. 'Kara does not need any magic,' she says, gesturing to the already enchantment-filled city. 'And certainly not stolen magic from a pair of teenagers.'

My nostrils flare. 'My friend here has magic that is *not* stolen. And he isn't even a teenager, probably, because he isn't a real person.'

She gives Teddy a mildly disgusted look. 'Do I want to know?'

He gives in and helps my case. 'Kara would be at a great advantage if she had some of Lire's magic. I know you know that, and I know you would agree to help us if you knew we had some. No one else can offer this power – but we're presenting it to Kara in exchange for a blessing.'

'Impossible,' the guard says.

Teddy lights up his hand with that indisputable lilac magic, so only the guard can see. 'You would think so,' he says, holding it close as if it's a match he's cradling in a breeze, 'but unfortunately for me, it is not.'

She steps back, the purple reflected in her pale eyes. 'Lire would never share her magic. Everyone knows that.'

I grin. 'Yet here we are. So are you going to let us see the fairy, or are you going to cost her the greatest advantage she could gain against Lire?'

The flustered guard stammers to her colleagues, 'Someone accompany them for an audience with the fairy. Tell Kara she'll want to see this.'

They seem hesitant but don't disobey. There's some clanking and clattering as they open the heavy gate for us to slip through, and a huge male guard keeps his eyes on us as he leads us into the citadel.

The whole place is dark, lit only by dim torches along the walls. We travel far into the citadel's labyrinthine depths – so much bigger than I anticipated from seeing it on the outside – and I'm not sure if we're being intentionally misled to confuse us. As we go down, down, down, the air gets warmer and suddenly we're in a cavernous space with walls lined with gleaming obsidian. It glows with magic, rippling in shadows of light. I wish I had my paints so I could capture the colour, the texture, but I'm sure it would be impossible.

There is no one else here, but I spot a pair of blue-green eyes piercing through the darkness. As my sight adjusts, I take in the rest of the woman surrounding the vibrant gaze. Her skin is white as if painted with snow, and her shoulder-length hair is deep brown and dead straight. She wears a long black robe with thick-soled boots. Her wings are brown, black, and white – moth-like. Each wing has a white spot in the shape of an eye, staring down at us.

'What is this?' she says, inching towards us. Her voice is clear and deep, and the way she watches us is more analytical than angry.

The guard clears his throat nervously. 'We tried to turn them away, but they say they can offer you magic – Lire's magic.'

She tilts her head to one side, her eyes narrowing. 'Step forward, then,' she says, waving us towards her. I feel a kind of pull, as if she's using magic to summon us. Her features are sharp like mine, and her impatient expression reminds me of myself, too. She takes a seat on a cushioned chair in front of a desk. The room is slowly beginning to appear around me; a finely-furnished office. But there is no clear beginning or end to the room – each wall, and the ceiling, if they exist, disappear into blackness. Mist flows around the floor at Kara's feet, as if the heat of her magic is steaming off the cold tiled floor.

'Kara,' I say, stepping towards her. 'Thank you for seeing us.'

She nods at me, leaning forward with her elbows on the desk, then her gaze shifts to Teddy. 'You *do* have Lire's magic, and a blessing from Adella. And you,' she adds, coldly examining me, 'have Amora's and Rhiannon's blessings. That's very interesting. Why exactly are you collecting magic? And why offer some of it to me?'

Teddy begins, 'We—'

'We're searching for treasure,' I interject. Because she reminds me of myself, I decide to skip the manipulation and get to the point. 'It's protected by strong wards. To get through them, we need blessings from every fairy, or we won't be powerful enough. We don't need Lire's magic, since my *assistant* here already has it, but we do need a blessing from you. So that's our offer – a blessing in exchange for some rare magic.'

'A trade . . .' She nods to her guard, who leaves the room and shuts the door behind him. Without the extra light from the hallway, I have to squint to see. 'Lire gave you her magic?'

'No,' Teddy says. 'Not exactly, I'm . . .'

'Her son,' I finish.

Kara raises a dark brow. 'Sorry to hear that. There's a reason we fairies choose not to procreate, though it seems Lire has conspired to do it anyway. We never should have let magic get into the hands of humans, and certainly not through birth. I mean no offense to you, boy, but I'll be glad when you're dead.'

'That's okay.' He glances at me. 'You're not the only one.'

'So,' I say, 'will you accept our trade?' I hold out my hands, revealing my rings.

Her moth wings turn down, the eyes staring at me. If their purpose is to intimidate, they work. 'Like Lire,' Kara says, 'I am hesitant to share my power with humans, though I have been known to do it on *occasion*. I have no reason to trust the son of Lire, but I suppose, for a blessing only, and for what you can offer me . . .'

'I don't trust him either,' I say, hoping she can at least trust that I hate Lire as much as she does. 'But he has power, and that's what we all want, isn't it?'

'Go on, then,' she says to Teddy. 'Give me the magic.'

He swallows. 'Of course.' He deliberates for a moment, then takes an old bronze coin from atop her desk. He holds it in his palm, cups his hands over it, and closes his eyes. Lilac magic forms around it, curving through the room in transparent waves, ebbing around his hands. When he's done, the coin shines with a deep purple.

Kara stands and flutters her wings to float down in front of us. She's taller than me, and her wingspan must be the same as her height. I blink dizzily and take an involuntary step back. She observes the coin thoughtfully. 'That's a lot of magic,' she says.

'You're welcome,' I say as he hands it to her. I cross my arms with impatience – and discomfort. 'Now can we please have a blessing?'

She gives me a knowing smile – though I'm not sure what exactly it is that she's knowing. 'Strange girl, with strange morals. You think highly of yourself, don't you? Always believing you're doing what's right, what's best, but never hearing the concerns of others. Now you're hit with doubt and must decide which is the right path to take. Darkness and light, death and life . . . these things need to be kept at a balance. Death *is* life, girl. Do not fear it. Sometimes we must learn to let old things go if we want to let in all the good the world has in store for us. You cannot start a new chapter without turning the page.'

My eyes hit my feet, her words hitting me right in the stomach. Where did all of *that* come from? 'Maybe I like the page I'm on.'

She shrugs, though her eyes remain serious and probing. 'Either we write our own lines, or the world forces our hand and writes our story for us. You're a soul who needs to be in control of her own fate.' She takes my hand and examines the rings. Darkness seeps out of her fingers and into a ring, and it fills me with a chill deeper than any I felt travelling across her territory for a week; a coldness that comes from my heart. 'My blessing holds lessons for all humans to learn. Listen to it, and let it guide you.' She releases me, and I gasp as the magic leaves. My chest fills with warmth again, and Kara gives me a soft smile.

'Thank you,' I say. 'I-I'll listen.'

Kara flies up to her desk. 'If we do end up in a war – and I imagine we will – I could use the two of you on my side. A Bearran and a son of Lire could be just the allies I need.' She taps her long fingernails against her desk, as if she's already forming plans. 'One day I may call upon you.'

Teddy exhales with exhaustion. 'I hate my mother as much as you do,' he says. 'But I don't think a fairy war is something I want to become involved in.'

'And I don't like the cold,' I say. 'But I appreciate the offer.'

Her expression shifts to a calm acceptance. 'Very well. Don't freeze on your way to Muse's Territory. Ask the guards for two perma-heaters to use as you go. And when you reach my sister's forest, be careful. The land of the songbirds may sound sweet, but there are monsters there that can destroy you before you even notice they aren't innocent. Everything in Muse's Forest talks, and you should beware of listening.'

I nod, almost not wanting to leave. Kara is a fairy that makes sense to me, and although I didn't lie about hating the cold, I wonder if this is a place I could fit in. It isn't the terrifying city I expected, and Kara isn't the evil fairy I once had nightmares about. There's a gentleness and intelligence to her that I didn't expect. She *cares*, so genuinely, without needing falseness or charm to show it.

'What about Grace?' I ask. 'Do you have any advice for dealing with her?'

'Of course,' says Kara, flipping her new enchanted coin between her fingers. She speaks apathetically, as if she would rather not discuss her fellow fairy. 'Don't lie to her or manipulate her. Go in with a plan. She doesn't do favours. Give her a reason to help and make sure it's true.'

'And if she doesn't like the truth?'

Kara tilts her head. 'Then your journey will have been wasted.' She waves a hand. 'Go on, children. Get your treasure and leave me in peace.' Right before we reach the door, Kara finishes, 'And destroy the crown, boy. Do what you must.'

CHAPTER
TWENTY-ONE

A WEEK PASSES IN silent, miserable trekking as we head south: out of the snow, and towards Muse's Territory. Kara's hot perma-heaters – enchanted scarves made of thick, fluffy wool – help immensely. They never lose their warmth, and I wrap mine around my body like a hug. This time, the journey isn't so bad. The new ring helps, too.

Death and darkness aren't powers in the way the other fairies' magic is. But like Kara said, I'm finding that a Darkness blessing isn't a bad thing. 'Death' is not only about dying – it's moving on, cutting old ties to create new ones, closing and opening doors. It's learning who I really am.

I was always confident in myself and my decisions, but I'm beginning to wonder if I was completely wrong about everything. There's still so much of myself I'm yet to discover, so many decisions still to make. And I may be afraid, but I'm also excited to keep moving forward.

The Darkness ring also helped me reach an important conclusion: I'll forgive Teddy. I'm still unhappy about his lies, and I'm still holding him at arm's length. But retaining all this anger towards him is not helping our quest. All it's doing is draining my energy. I believe him when he says it's my decision what we do with the crown. Teddy is self-sacrificing, as Adella said, to his own detriment. If it means appeasing me, he really will let Lire have this object she'll only use as a weapon.

For now, I am safe, so I won't make this journey harder on myself.

When we reach the edge of Muse's Forest, tucked into the bright, warm mountains of her territory, it's like the oxygen comes back to the air. We shed our coats and leave them on the road, certain we won't need them again. It's surprising that Muse and Kara's Territories are next to each other instead of on opposite sides of the world; while Kara's Territory is death, Muse's is life. Everything in Muse's Forest is music. It's alive and conscious.

A towering stag wanders over to us, his antlers making him as tall as my horse. 'Good morning,' he says. When I gasp so hard I nearly fall off Pansy, he huffs and turns around, muttering, 'Foreigners.'

Teddy laughs hysterically, then stops when he sees the deadly expression I'm giving him. 'I did tell you what to expect here,' he says. 'The fairy of music, words, life – everything in the forest talks. Even the dead, they say.'

I feel the blood rushing from my face. Suddenly the beautiful springtime hills, the landscape of every shade of green, the swaying trees, and sweet-looking animals all become petrifying. 'I thought that was an exaggeration.'

'It is not.' He pulls his horse forward into the trees, the ground laid with flat leaves and grass where others have passed through. He shields his eyes from the light. The bright sun leaves a yellow mist over the landscape, as if the forest itself is glowing. 'At least it isn't cold.'

I pat Pansy's neck and get her to follow. 'The horses aren't going to start talking too, are they?'

Teddy grins. 'As much as I would love that, no. Only a living thing from the forest can talk, and only within the forest's enchantments.'

'Good,' I say. 'And it won't make you talk even more, will it?'

He glances at me, a smirk tugging at the corners of his lips. 'Who knows?'

⋆ ❦ ˚ ◍ 🩵 ◍ ˚ ❦ ⋆

Two days into the forest and I'm ready to cut my ears off.

Everything talks. Constantly. Loudly. Unashamedly. Trees sing high above us, the dissonant sound echoing across the mountains. Blades of grass screech as they're stepped on. When we pass streams, fish beckon us in for a dip, and when we pass caves, dark things call out. At the edge of the forest, this place could be considered spectacular, but in its depths is infinite chaos. Teddy, naturally, has to strike up a conversation with everything that'll listen, and our travel is slowed drastically. At night, I stuff my ears with the two ends of my perma-heater, trying to drown out the noise.

'Kara was right about the hidden danger here,' I say on the second night. 'If we don't get attacked soon, I might pick a fight with a nest of wasps. I don't care if it's painful. I do not want to be *alive*.'

'It isn't so bad,' Teddy replies, looking up at the stars. From the side, his face looks stronger – less soft, more certain. Maybe it's because I can't fully see his eyes. 'I grew up in a city, so I'm used to noise. At least here it's impossible to feel alone.'

Is it? I may be surrounded by conversation, but I feel as if I'm behind a window, observing but not participating. Lonely despite being so crowded. I hadn't known I could feel that way. I never wanted any friends. I loved my family enough, and I was content. Now I'm so far from that old life, despite my entire quest being an attempt to protect it. Prima might already be married by now. My family could suspect I'm already dead. I've been gone *weeks*.

'At least it isn't cold,' I say quietly.

When Teddy is asleep, I take out my compass and stare at it. An ache blooms in my chest as I conjure memories of home. Closing old doors to open new ones. What if everything I've been trying to do is for a version of myself who no longer exists?

· ❁ ✦ ⓪ 💛 ⓪ ✦ ❁ ·

'What the . . .' Teddy starts, his eyes wide in panic.

We've nearly reached Muse's capital when we both sense something is wrong. The hairs on my arms rise, and my chest tightens.

The horses grind to a halt, the ground shifting beneath them. Shouts turn to whispers, shuddering through the valley we're passing through. *Fairies, fairies, fairies.*

With a slithering tear in the earth, dozens of snakes crawl out of the dirt and wrap themselves around the horses' legs. Pansy squeals and drops to the forest floor, throwing me off her – I land with a searing jolt to my shoulder. I jump and shake as I land on a pile of the wormy creatures.

'*Teddy*!' I scream.

They coil around my body, locking tight. When they squeeze my head, the wound Sierra made by hitting me reopens with a trickle of blood and an earthquake of pain.

The trees above curl in, forming a canopy that blocks the sun. A flurry of animals skirts around us violently, hissing, growling, gnashing their teeth. Teddy is shouting, but I can't move to see him or even talk – the snakes wrap around my face and keep my jaw clamped shut.

What is *happening*? Why now?

As something curls around my throat, once again I'm taken back to Darraport, to a pirate's magic choking me, to dying, to terror. I sputter, tremoring, but I can't move, can't move at all. *I am not going to survive.*

'You're in *trouble*,' a bird sings shrilly, soaring over our heads as it laughs. 'Your mummy is very upset.'

Teddy makes a guttural noise that tells me he can't speak either.

Oh, fairies – Lire sent talking animals after us?

'But it's alright,' a deer says, trotting towards us. 'She asked us to stop you if you passed through our territory. And now here you are.' Is it *grinning*? 'Lire will reward us greatly for this.'

The snakes holding me hiss in delight. I spew up bile, but with my mouth forced shut, I have to swallow it back down. The acidic smell rises in my nose as tears sting my eyes and blur my vision.

Why isn't Teddy using his magic? Why isn't he saving us? These creatures already know his secret.

As if in response, a lilac glow forms in the corner of my eye. As quickly as it comes, it's smothered by the animals. They're blocking him, overwhelming him so he can't focus enough to use his power.

My limbs shake; every movement I make is met with bites. Are we going to die here? Now? After everything we've already been through? Mauled by animals?

No. Surely Lire wouldn't kill her son. She must know how precious he is – to her, I mean. His magic can't just be destroyed.

I try to call on the blessings sitting in my hand – Darkness, Strength, Passion – but nothing happens. With the snakes shifting and squeezing all over my body, I can't think. I don't know what I need or what I'm asking for. My head is pounding, and I'm unable to create any plans past the pain and panic.

Please, magic, keep me alive.

'Let's deliver them to Muse!' says a rabbit. Its mouth forms strangely human shapes as it talks. It gives me a sinister sneer, and I vomit in my mouth again. 'Then she can call on her sister!'

Teddy must get free for a second, because he shouts, 'What is it that she's giving you? We'll offer better! Anything! I have her power too!'

The snakes pull my body up, entangled around me like vines choking a tree, leaving me in a seated position. The snakes around Teddy do the same, and he's struggling, pained, but I'm just happy to be able to see him.

A bird swoops on us and says, in its whistling voice, 'We do not wish for your mother's power. Lire promised we can join her army. She promised us freedom.'

Teddy screams through his nose, his mouth shut once more.

I'm in a nightmare – that's it. This cannot be real. A nightmare. Just a nightmare.

A snake bites the flesh of my upper arm with a sting that travels through my entire body. It lets go and laughs. All the snakes laugh, writhing and wriggling over me. With a shudder, I realise I'm not lucky enough for this to be imaginary.

Fairies. I cry. I sob. Because I could be at home. I could have simply gotten married, like Prima said. Everything else I've been through so far was worth the idea of escaping a life in which I'd be trapped and hungry and alone.

But now? Being attacked by talking animals? I'll take the poverty. I'll get a job I loathe. I'll do *anything*.

I struggle again, try to scream, but I am entirely bound. I don't want to give up – I can't give up – but there is absolutely nothing I can do. There are no tricks, no moves, no way to survive unless someone saves me. And I *hate* it.

'And when we join her army,' the bird continues, 'we will no longer need to be confined to this forest to speak. Lire will let us live out in the world – the *real* world – as ourselves. As the conscious, intelligent beings we are. When she wins the war, we will be kings and queens.'

Two more deer appear in front of us and the snakes lift us onto their coarse-haired backs, still not loosening their grip on any part of my body. Where do they plan to take us? Pansy and Sunny squirm on the ground as more snakes suffocate them and bite at their ankles. I sob at the sight of their torture.

The trees laugh above, their leaves rippling with sadistic pleasure.

I scream again through my closed lips, push with all of my strength, with all of my blessings, and let out a final burst of energy—

Nothing happens.

If we don't die now, Lire will finish the job. My only hope is Teddy being able to concentrate long enough to use his magic.

The deer begin carting us away, and I cry over the horses as they're left behind, sure to die, and I'm more upset for them than for us. I silently curse the forest and I'm ready to close my eyes and give up. If I stop struggling, maybe I'll be able to breathe easier and calm myself as much as I can before death.

So, with a cry, I settle, let every muscle in my body relax, and resign myself to reaching the end.

Then something black streaks across my view, deep-dark against the bright forest. An inverse shooting star.

My eyes burst wide open as Sierra surges in swan form through the trees. I whimper as she dives, viciously swooping at the deer carrying me. She pecks it right in the eyes and it falls. I thud onto the ground still wrapped in snakes, onto my freshly-bruised shoulder. The creatures are stunned from the impact long enough that I'm able to let in a deep breath and properly call on my blessings.

My body immediately fills with heat and strength, and I fling the snakes off me. Sierra pecks at them, hurling them away and brushing them off as they try to wrap around her slender neck. Her wings are so large and strong that she could swipe away any weapon or creature with ease.

'Teddy!' I shout at her in a hoarse voice, not wasting my time worrying why she's helping us. 'Help Teddy!' I can't help her, I can't save us, but he can.

Her head dips as if nodding. The animals come for me again, snakes whipping their tails at me to grab my limbs, but I throw them off using Rhiannon's Strength. Sierra soars to Teddy and picks the snakes off his body. Animals try to attack her, but she expertly hunts them down as they come. When he's finally free, lilac bursts past the boy and the swan, magic beaming through the animals like sunrays through leaves.

As the creatures swarm back to Teddy, he builds a blast of lilac magic that sends them flying in all directions. I crawl to him and Sierra – they've thankfully ended up back with the horses. Teddy forms a protective dome around us, colouring us in purple. I'm weak, and my shoulder and head hurt so terribly they could be on fire. But with my blessings I manage to pull myself to the horses, ripping the remaining snakes off them. They dissolve as they hit Teddy's magical shield.

And we are safe. Our bubble isn't large, but he still runs to me. He's followed by the black swan, and we huddle together. We don't talk, we just wait and catch our breath. They must be as shocked as I am.

Animals try to break through Teddy's magic, but they bounce away. The dome is so thick it's hard to see anything beyond it – I only watch as the creatures' silhouettes rise and fall.

When I finally open my mouth to speak, I can't make a sound. Teddy taps my arm and I realise it's part of his magic. He's stopping the animals by blocking Muse's power. It's completely silent in here. Sierra tries to squawk but chokes instead.

My ears pop in the strange stillness, and though I've been craving peace for days, I find I don't like it as much as I might have thought. I stifle a cry behind my hand and I use my sleeve to wipe my face. I take some water from my bag, which is luckily still strapped to Pansy's saddle, and sit for a moment, wiping my other sleeve over my wounds, breathing. I stare at the floor and hold my throbbing shoulder.

Then it hits me who saved us. *Sierra.* Sierra is here.

With a burst of blessed Strength, I lunge at the swan and wrap my hands around her narrow neck.

Teddy grabs at me, but I push him away and focus all my fury on Sierra. Her beak opens in shock and pain, her animal eyes boring into me. I don't care. I feel the feathers under my palms and squeeze harder. It makes my shoulder scream, but it doesn't matter. This is my chance to get her.

I'm holding her neck high enough that she can't bite at me, so she uses her wing to hit me in my wounded head – *hard* – and I fall. A burst of pain thunders behind my eyes, and she uses my weakness against me, jumping over me and arching her neck to peck at my face. I try to use my hands to get her off, but she's too powerful. Her wings keep batting my hands away.

Just as she's about to launch her beak into my eye, Teddy tackles her.

'Stop!' he yells, the sound breaking through his magic. 'Both of you!'

Hearing his voice shocks me enough that I stay back this time. I can't kill Sierra without Teddy. But I'm so angry, and so . . . confused. I hate her so much. I want to hurt her. I've never felt so helpless, and I need to do something, anything, to remind myself I have power, control.

Sierra stays back too, likely not wanting to be turned into a glacier again, but I can see in her eyes that our loathing is mutual.

Teddy uses his magic to create a second, smaller bubble within his noise-blocking one, and the sound returns around us while retaining the shield above. We could be in another world in here. Finally, I exhale and press my sleeve against my head, pulling it back to find fresh blood. Between my shoulder and my head, I'm barely alive, but I have enough blessings and enough rage that my wounds won't stop me for long.

Teddy tries to help me, gaping at the blood on my sleeve, but I brush him off. He turns to the swan. 'She saved us,' he breathes. 'Sierra – that *is* Sierra, isn't it? We aren't mistaking her for another swan?'

'What are you doing here?' I scream at the bird, wishing it really wasn't her. 'Why did you do that?'

She only squawks. She can't reply, not even in this place.

So I whirl on Teddy. 'If you're not going to let me kill her, what are we going to do with her? Freeze her again? Clearly she can't be stopped. Not alive.'

She flaps her wings impatiently, and I imagine her rolling her eyes.

'You can't kill her when she just saved us,' Teddy says, exasperated. 'You shouldn't kill anyone at all!'

I rub my head. 'I think just this once it would be okay.'

'No!'

'Then what do we do? Waste a day sitting here until nightfall to let her talk? Then what? How do we get out of here?'

He swallows. 'I don't know any more than you do, Maya, but I'm not letting you kill someone.'

I groan. 'Well can you fix her?'

'What?'

'Use your magic to change her back. Reverse the curse for her.'

He gestures around incoherently, waving his arms like he's in a hurricane. 'I can't break curses!'

'How do you know?' I glare at him.

'Because that isn't how magic works!' His face goes cranberry-red with exasperation.

'Can't you fix her temporarily? Your magic is stronger than the pirate who cursed her. Change the curse, like Lire changed Dawn's.'

I refuse to think about how we were both hurt by the same pirate. If it wasn't for that one man, this quest would have been far easier. We might have met Sierra while crossing through Grace's Territory. Maybe she would have been normal, kind. Human. She might have been the warrior, the protector she claims to be as a Reed, instead of the violent, petty bird in front of me.

Teddy eyes Sierra closely, magic glowing dimly in his right hand. It reflects in her dark eyes. She waddles back, shaking her small head.

'It won't hurt,' he says. 'But Maya is right. I have to try. We can't waste the day.' He lays a hand on her wing and closes his eyes. Is he using Adella's Kindness blessing to help him? Does it make his power stronger?

Purple magic surrounds the black swan, engulfing her. She shudders, surely out of fear of what happened to her last time. The magic turns a hard, opaque lilac, surrounding Teddy too. For a few moments I have to look away, breathing hard. When the magic subsides, Teddy's arm isn't resting on the wing of a swan, but on the arm of a young woman.

Sierra gasps, and she looks awful. Her usually silky black hair is matted, and her clothes are torn and dirty. 'How did you do that?' she demands.

Teddy only shrugs. 'I have a lot of magic. You know that.'

She loses interest in him and glares at me. 'I can't wait to kill you.'

I stare back coldly. 'Really? After putting so much effort into saving us?'

'I didn't save you to do you a favour,' she spits. 'I saved you because the only person who gets to kill you is *me*. And you still have two blessings to get. I've decided I would rather you get them first, and I'll kill you after. It makes my job much easier.'

I throw my hands up in frustration. 'Really?'

'I didn't think I'd have to save you, after our last encounter. Turns out I'm still better than the both of you.' She gives me a cocky smile.

Teddy reaches out a hand, as if for a shake. 'Sierra, see how we helped each other today? Don't fight us. Join us.'

I slap his hand away. 'We've been through this! No!'

'Listen,' he says. 'I don't want us to keep fighting each other. We all have the same goal, so why not reach it faster by working together? Then we can have the bloodbath at the end once we've secured the crown.'

Sierra slumps down, brushing her hair over her shoulders. 'I can't say it's a *terrible* idea.'

'I can,' I say. 'You'll only stab us in the back! Or I'll stab you in the back. Either way, someone will be stabbed.'

Teddy takes a *very* long breath. 'Okay, yes, someone is going to be stabbed, but if we can put aside our differences just until we reach Glassine – with all the blessings – it'll speed up the process. Then we can fight for the crown, and whoever wins, wins.'

I'm unresponsive as I watch the purple dome of magic above us reflect off our skin, ebbing and flowing in water-like pools of light. The sun is a lavender circle above us. I don't want to think about all of this – I want to take this moment of silence and go to sleep.

'That only seems fair,' Sierra says. She shakes Teddy's hand. '*Temporary* allies.'

He grins painfully.

I cross my arms, trying not to cry as I squeeze a bruise. 'I don't agree to this. You know, Teddy, for a man whose mother is the fairy of wisdom, you can be so, *so* stupid.'

'I'm sorry,' he says, crinkling his nose with a wince, 'but you've been outvoted. The three of us need each other to finish this journey, so if an alliance is what we have to make, we're going to make it work.'

'Until someone is killed.'

'Yes.'

Sierra offers a wicked smile. 'Absolutely.'

I wonder if I was right to forgive Teddy, or if I've only opened the door for more trouble.

CHAPTER
TWENTY-TWO

SOMEWHERE, SOMETIME...

PRINCESS DAWN, QUEEN OF Bearra's hearts, was strong.

She was passionate, brave, and kind. Spirited, just, and wise. For the first time, however, she longed for the one blessing she was missing: Darkness. Over the past few weeks, she had felt entirely unblessed. She was scared, alone, and helpless. She longed to sink into the shadows, to let go of the weight she felt; maybe Kara's blessing might have helped her.

Dawn, though loved by all, had only ever had two true friends: Relia, her lost love, and Teddy, her lost prince. Now, she was trapped as the only person in Bearra who knew the truth about her kingdom's situation, and she could do nothing about it.

She had tried to warn her parents, but they had spent their entire reign relying on the fairy's counsel – they did not know how to rule without Lire, and so they trusted her entirely. Dawn understood, as she too had always been able to rely on Lire, almost as if the fairy was a second mother. Still, her parents' betrayal struck her with a terrible heartache. How could they not care how badly their daughter was hurting? How could they leave her with Jacob, even when she told them how dangerous he was?

Everyone the princess had ever relied upon had left her.

At night she cried, trying to stifle her sobs so Jacob wouldn't hear her. He had spent nearly every night in her bed since Teddy left, despite it being against etiquette. He never touched her violently, but with the way his hands would rest on her arms as she slept, she felt just as attacked. He was trapping her, making sure she would have no chance to escape him.

Did he not realise that even if she could get away, she would never leave Bearra alone to deal with his and Lire's cruelty? Dawn may have felt weak, but she would always be a princess before she was a person, and she would always sacrifice her needs for her kingdom's.

On the morning that marked three weeks since Teddy escaped, Dawn's maid – Kelina, who had brought her breakfast every morning since she was a little girl – made the mistake of entering Dawn's room without knocking.

Dawn was already awake. Nowadays, it was rare for her to get any sleep at all, but Jacob usually snuck out before anyone would notice his presence. Even he knew he could be prey to scandal.

As Dawn's eyes met Kelina's, the princess shook her head at the maid, silently begging her to leave.

But Kelina gasped at the sight of the prince, and spilled the pot of tea she was carrying, burning herself with the scalding liquid. As it shattered against the floor, Jacob jumped awake, his gaze feral.

He could kill her for this – to protect his secrets, to protect their mask of perfect happiness and purity. Dawn knew he was capable.

She jumped to action, placing a hand on his chest, trying to push him back into the bed – trying to protect Kelina, even though touching the prince sickened her. 'Jacob!' Dawn pleaded. 'Shh. Don't worry. She'll leave.'

Jacob heaved, magic already stirring around his skin. Kelina tried to back out of the room, but Jacob shouted, 'Don't you dare! Get in here and shut the door!'

Dawn flew out of bed and stood between them. 'Please, no – go, Kelina. Tell no one what you saw. I am begging you. For your own safety—'

Jacob stood beside her, his towering, muscular frame domineering over her. He was sweltering, his hair tousled and his eyes half-lidded from sleep. 'Stay, maid.' There was almost a laugh in his voice, as if he were glad to have an excuse for violence.

'You will *not* hurt my people.' Dawn raised her chin and gritted her teeth, staring him down, though inside she was filled with ice-cold terror. 'Hurt me all you like, Jacob, but stay away from Kelina.'

This time he laughed clearly, a sound that came from a dark, deep place within him. 'You are so adorable, my princess.' He brushed a curl of her golden hair behind her ear, and she flinched. 'I would never hurt you. I *love* you.'

'Then let Kelina go.' Dawn's hands trembled and her eyes teared up, but she would not give in.

Jacob's gaze darkened. 'I wouldn't hurt you. That doesn't mean I won't hurt anyone else who gets in the way of our never-ending happiness.'

Dawn remembered his fight with Teddy, which only ended because Lire stopped them. Kelina, however, would not survive Jacob's rage.

The maid choked on her tears, ready to scream, but Jacob reached past Dawn and took Kelina by her throat. He yanked her further into the room and threw her onto the floor, slamming the door. Kelina's knees were cut by the broken porcelain of the teapot, and her plain black dress tangled around her as she scrambled across the hardwood.

Dawn rushed to help her, using her nightdress to wipe at the blood on Kelina's knees. With gasping breaths, the two held each other, crawling away from Jacob. Dawn wished she could hide, cover her eyes and escape this reality, but she couldn't leave Kelina.

Jacob was covered in magic now, ready to strike, and Dawn knew it was hopeless to help her maid. But she would have to try. Even if she couldn't save Kelina, she would ensure she did not suffer.

'Jacob. Jacob. *Please*.' Dawn's voice was a weak mess. Her hands were cut by the same porcelain that wounded Kelina. Her shoulders shook, despite her effort to remain unwavering. When Jacob ignored her, staring at his own hands, watching his magic with egomaniacal awe, Dawn took Kelina's face and forced the maid to meet her eyes. 'Kelina. Kelina, look at me. Don't be scared. I'm going to help you. Don't be scared.'

The maid had no words. She was frozen, tears streaming silently down her cheeks. It was as if her mind was entirely gone.

Dawn was alone, again.

'Out of the way, my bride,' said Jacob, toying with his magic.

With a scream that came from the depths of all her pain, as loud as she could muster, she shouted, '*No!*'

She could already hear guards pounding their way to her rooms, but Jacob heard them too. He threw a wave of magic against the door, and although the guards hammered against it, it was no use.

'Bad idea,' said Jacob. His eyes were dead; he wasn't human, Dawn was certain of that. There was no soul in that man.

Dawn shut her eyes and held Kelina, ready to die with her maid, because there was no other way she would let this end.

Then the door crashed open.

Dawn's eyes flew wide and she gasped as Lire entered alone. She did not know what to do – if this would make things better or worse. *Please help me.*

The fairy of wisdom took less than a second to take in the scene. Her lilac dress was long and ruffled, her light hair tied up in an intricate bun and her arms covered in crawling silver cuffs. Her wings were lifted high, entirely still. With the surety and power she exuded, she may as well already be wearing a crown.

Dawn sucked in a breath. '*Help*,' she wept to the fairy. What else was there to do?

Lire watched apathetically. 'Such a shame.' With a lightning-fast flicker of purple magic, she—

She snapped Kelina's neck.

Dawn felt the crack through her entire body as she held the woman, her head now bent at an unnatural angle. Blood poured everywhere, and Jacob was laughing, and Lire was stepping away, and Dawn screamed.

And screamed.

And screamed.

Until she couldn't anymore.

CHAPTER
TWENTY-THREE

BETWEEN SIERRA'S FIGHTING SKILLS and Teddy's magic, reaching Muse's Capital was easy. I felt almost useless next to them. All I could do was take care of myself. I can't fight. I can't use magic. I can't do anything worthwhile, apparently. Who knew being a regular person was such an inconvenience?

How long do I have until Teddy and Sierra realise they don't need me?

Though I don't want to admit it, having Sierra on our team is an astonishing advantage. We need her strength and abilities. I'm just grateful that today, in the daylight of Muse's Capital, she's back to being a swan. Sierra is terrible at being human.

'Muse! Muse!'

The thick crowds sing loudly as we journey through the streets. Every person is dressed in some shade of yellow, their eyes almost glazed over as they dance in senseless delight, occasionally bowing towards the castle. Their boisterousness is irritating, but at least I'm out of the enchanted forest, where it felt like constant screaming in my ears.

Sierra the swan watches us from above. Falling asleep next to a young woman and waking next to a bird was bewildering. Teddy hasn't offered to transform her again, and she hasn't asked. *Good.*

She currently sits in the treetops over the town centre, black feathers deadly against all the yellow, her red beak like a bloody arrowhead. We tried to convince her to stay behind and watch the horses, since she wouldn't be much use as a bird anyway, but she refused. So, as usual, we left the horses at a stable at the edge of the city.

Although we try to stand apart, Teddy's arm keeps brushing against mine as we walk through the tight crowds. Every time I take a small step away, he's back again. I give up and decide to step closer, too, enjoying the barrier he creates between me and the revellers.

So many people have red hair in Muse's Territory – from scarlet to ginger to strawberry blonde – that I can't follow Teddy's bright head through the crowds like I usually do. I want to hold his hand. I really do. But it's too soon.

Muse's citizens parade through the streets in a whirl of dance, singing even if they absolutely cannot sing, and waving around yellow ribbons and flags.

'Is this a festival?' I ask Teddy. Shout at him, really. I'm so used to yelling after all this time in endless noise that it's a habit now – a habit I quite like, considering I'm still a little bit mad at him.

'Looks like it,' he replies. 'Though after the chaos of the forest, I wouldn't be surprised if it's just a regular day.'

We wander past an intimidatingly tall statue of a fairy – presumably Muse – her wings painted bright saffron and her skin olive green. A fountain of sparkling golden water spits from her mouth, which is open as if singing. People sit under the statue with their heads lowered and their hands pressed together, humming. Some throw coins and pieces of jewellery into the pool at the base. As others pass it, they turn to bow their heads.

Above us, Muse's Tower looms over the city. It reminds me of the bizarrely tall buildings in Darraport, except this is built like a castle. The pale-yellow stone reaches high until the tip points into a baby-blue turret, and windows wind down the wide circular structure in no discernible pattern. By comparison, the rest of the capital looks miniature, and while the buildings are colourful, many are in a state of decay. Windows are rotted, gaping from their hinges. The cobbled roads are chipped and uneven. There's a too-sweet scent to the air, like a perfume used to hide a bad smell. And once I start to think of the painted exteriors as stained white rather than yellow, I can't unsee it.

No one seems to care, about anything. People bump into us without apology, lost in song. Even the children run between our legs and sing in our faces, unafraid of being trampled. Their feet are bare, and one little girl leaves bloody footprints in her wake as she twirls down the streets.

I soon realise they aren't just singing – what they're doing is *praise*. They're worshipping the fairy. If I could press my hands over my ears without offending the entire population, I would. I wish for the cold, quiet streets of Kara's Capital.

'Muse! Muse!'

Teddy has never visited this city, and Sierra only has in passing. Our unpreparedness makes me more uneasy. After the wickedness of Muse's Forest, what dangers could be lurking in her capital?

Muse is living in a shiny tower while her people are down here in poverty, so why do they worship her? It's a stark reminder of Bearra – of the royals and Lire comfortable in their castle while the rest of us were left to starve. I've learned a lot since leaving my home, but that kind of disparity will never seem normal to me.

Sierra squawks above and flaps her wings to get our attention. She points her beak to our right. There's a banner hung between two tall buildings over a main square, painted with the words *Welcome to the Festival of the Fairy*.

'So it *is* a festival,' I say.

'It doesn't seem right,' says Teddy. 'The way they're singing for Muse, praising her as if she's . . . There are some small sects around the world of people who worship fairies, but there is no way the other fairies approve of this behaviour.'

Someone screams ecstatically from a rooftop. 'She's coming! The fairy is coming!'

Every eye in the city square travels to the tower as the fairy flutters out of the very top window. It's difficult to see her at first – she's so high above us – but her yellow wings glitter and glow, and her arms wave at her subjects generously. Her wings come to harsh points, the tips sparkling so intensely it's as if she's attached stars to them. Red hair trails down her white shoulders in waves, and her long, golden gown shimmers blindingly. She could be the sun itself, a song of light.

At once, the people fall to their knees, their singing even louder and more ravenous.

Sierra squawks again from her new rooftop perch, flapping desperately, her head bobbing. I understand her signal: *get down*. We're sticking out of the crowd like trees in a sparse field. I pull Teddy to the ground and we almost fall on top of each other as we scramble onto our knees.

Canary symbols are painted in yellow across the city; on the walls of shops and on the paved ground, on people's clothes, and carved into hedges. As Muse comes closer to us, they alight, glowing harshly and beautifully. Real birds whistle all around us and Muse sings along with them as they join her in flight above, swimming around her in dance. A mystical harmony echoes across the city, a sound that makes me want to raise my hands and worship the fairy like everyone else. She's laughing, her dark eyes creased at the edges and her nose scrunched.

The people gasp in delight. On our tiny square of pavement, Teddy presses against me, and I find myself reaching for his hand. He takes it, and I'm certain I can feel his eyes on me, but I can't stop watching the fairy.

It's easy to see how Teddy could be the child of a creature like her. She would make sense as his mother – the red hair, the way the people adore her, the magnetic, alluring presence. Muse's charm, like Teddy's, is indisputable. I could imagine him in the fairy's place, with people following and praising him.

Yet his mix of gentle humanity and Lire's wisdom shine through his charisma. While Muse is an enchanting spectacle, Teddy is a calming presence.

I turn to him and we meet eyes. His warm gaze reflects all the yellow, his mouth turned up into a smile, and I could kiss him. I could reach up, cup my hands on his cheeks, pull him close and lay my lips on his. His gaze drops to my mouth as if he's thinking the same.

Haven't I resolved to forgive him? Is it too late to feel, well, whatever I might have been beginning to feel about him before the truth was revealed?

He shifts, and my pulse quickens.

But the fairy's song changes melody, and we're brought out of our trance. His eyes lose their brightness and meet the ground. He clears his throat and his palm becomes sweaty in mine, but he doesn't let go.

Good. A terrible idea averted. He knows as well as I do that nothing can happen between us. Right?

Muse lands somewhere out of our sight, but the people remain on the floor, waiting. They move from their bowed positions and sit with their legs crossed.

'She'll come soon!' a man says to a little boy bouncing around and singing loudly. 'Muse always visits every street.' He smiles at the crowd timidly. 'It's my son's first festival.'

They burst into happy cheers for the child, and he presses his face into his father's chest bashfully.

Teddy leans towards my ear, his breath brushing my skin. 'If she's out visiting people, we have a good chance of getting her to talk to us.'

'Or we'll be crushed trying to get to her,' I reply, still *mildly* flustered. I try to will the heat from my cheeks, but then I just start to think about wanting to kiss him again, and—

Fairies.

We sit there for a long while, the ground becoming harder under us with the passing time. I keep watch of Sierra, who occasionally flies above to monitor what's happening. She doesn't give us any suggestion that we should move, so we don't.

Which I hate. Sitting here while my enemy is above, telling me what to do. I still hate Teddy for letting her live, and even more for letting her into our quest. *That* is why I am not kissing him.

Overcome with sudden irritation, I drop his hand.

I see the fairy's glow before I see the fairy. It's as if the sunlight is following her, and as she turns the corner into the square, light shines out, temporarily blinding me. The crowds scream and sing and wave their arms frantically. I cover my head with my hands.

Muse gestures for everyone to stand, so they do, dancing and bowing around her, leaving a small bubble of space for her to move.

Teddy and I stay put, too confused by everything happening around us to do anything. Muse smiles, and every person in the crowd acts as if the smile is just for them. They're *obsessed*.

Occasionally Muse stops and makes displays of her canary-coloured magic, to the people's delight. She gives blessings to a few of the children, and pours her power into the air in waves of lemony glitter. Sometimes she flies up, just above us, dancing and singing while beating her wings, and even as people scream at her, she retains her small, steady smile.

Until she notices me and Teddy.

Her eyes magnetise to us and she flutters over, not expending any strength to cut through the crowd of people trying to touch her. Some fall right to their knees as she passes by. Still, she doesn't avert her gaze. If I hadn't only seen her smiling, I might not have noticed the aggravated look on her face. But in the small inflections of her features, there's something dark. Does she know we're not from here? Are we not welcome?

I shuffle back as she stops right in front of us, and the crowd quietens, murmuring and whispering instead of singing.

'Help me to understand,' Muse says, her voice the most beautiful instrument I've ever heard. Her golden, starry wings are mesmerising. 'Do they not sing where you are from?'

Teddy places his shoulder in front of mine, a hand at his side as if to reach out and cover me if there's trouble. 'We're sorry to cause any offense,' he says. 'We only arrived here this morning, and we aren't aware of your people's customs. We didn't know about the festival, but we are honoured to attend.'

'We also don't know the lyrics to your songs,' I tell her.

The corners of her mouth turn down further. 'Would you walk through someone's home with dirty shoes? Would you throw crumbs on their floor? One should have respect for any place they find themselves in. Because of my mercy, and because it is a special day, I will let you go with only a warning. But next time you fail to sing, do not expect to be welcome here again.'

I don't tell her that I don't want to ever come here again anyway.

Teddy bows his head. 'I respect you greatly, Muse. You must understand that we were so enthralled with watching and listening to you that the festival slipped from our minds completely. All we could do was stand in awe.'

Fairies, Teddy. Does he ever not know what to say?

She lifts one of each of our hands, her touch warm and delicate, as if she's barely corporeal. Her thin eyebrows raise. 'You have blessings from nearly all of my sisters,' she says. 'And, I suppose, you have come to ask for mine.'

'We feel blessed enough just being in your presence,' I say, though as soon as the words leave my lips, I'm certain I've overdone it. 'But yes, we want to ask you for a blessing. It's for a very important—'

'I don't need to hear why,' she says, her voice rising and falling in pitch with a soft melody. 'I, the fairy of life, of music, of communication, give my magic freely when I feel it is needed. I take care of my people!' The fairy smiles, and the crowds scream in delight, falling over themselves and singing. 'I even offer my assistance to those who wrong me, because they are the people who need me most.'

'Really? You're just going to—'

Teddy nudges me. 'Thank you very much.'

Muse smiles at Teddy, then inches her face close to mine. 'Don't question me, little girl,' she mutters so quietly that no one else can hear. She turns away and starts singing a song about singing songs, the people and birds harmonising around her instantly. It makes me shiver. The sound forms an almost physical essence, pulsing in my ears the way Teddy's wall of magic did in the forest. The melody is both satisfying to the ear and damaging to the mind.

Yellow magic forms around Muse's body, concentrating in her hands, and she lifts Teddy's fingers to examine his rings. She picks an empty one, and Teddy's eyes roll up to their whites as she pours her melodic magic into him. I so badly want to block my ears, but I think Muse would kill me if I did.

So I focus on Teddy's hand. Three fairies each. Once, I thought that even if he one day betrayed me, I could fight him. Our friendship was as safe as any could be. Now, as he becomes even more powerful, I'm struck with the fact that I'm completely helpless against him.

Yes, I want to kiss him occasionally, but I can't take the risk of fully trusting him. He could decide to hurt me at any moment. Still, I can't do anything about these haunting fears, because I need him.

What happened to the sweet boy I met? Why has my Teddy been replaced with someone I don't recognise? Or is he the same, and I'm only seeing him under a different light? Charming, clumsy Teddy and lying, powerful Teddy might be one and the same. But I don't know if I can accept both sides.

I force my eyes to move to Sierra, who cranes her neck curiously – hungrily – as she watches Teddy receive the blessing.

Muse's song ends, and the music turns to cheers as she releases Teddy's hand and raises her arms victoriously. He rubs his fingers silently as the fairy shouts, 'I am the patron fairy of this city!' Her voice reverberates through the streets. 'I am the deity who watches over her people with grace and compassion – with power and strength and music! All who reside in my territory are blessed, and all who leave are lost!'

She turns without another word, and flies over our heads into the next street.

People converge on me and Teddy, their shouts nearly deafening, so we quickly follow Sierra as she leads us out of the crowds from the air.

·•'◊ ♡ ◊'•·

When we finally reach a small, empty park in a quiet area away from the city centre, we slouch on the grass under the shade of a thick weeping willow. Teddy buys food from a nearby stall. Root vegetables cooked into a sour stew – because of course the only vendor not at the festival would have to make disgusting food. Sierra flies to a nearby stream to catch fish . . . or whatever it is that swans eat.

'How does it feel?' I ask Teddy, motioning to the ring.

He frowns at it, putting down his spoon. His other hand runs absently through the grass. 'It's strange,' he says. 'Like my other blessing, it isn't anything that's really there, not accessible like my magic. When I called on the power of Kindness in the forest, it made my natural power stronger. But it also made me feel weaker, because the goodness in the ring played on my conscience. I'm not exactly sure what Muse's ring does . . . makes me a very good singer?'

'Maybe it's more about harmony? An intellectual bless-ing?' I shake my head. 'No, that can't be right – as I've already told you, you're stupid enough for a child of the wisdom fairy. Even Muse's blessing couldn't help you.'

He gives me a look of teasing curiosity. 'Or am I incredibly smart, and it's just you who's wrong about everything?'

'That's not possible. I'm always right. And I'm older. Wiser.'

'Only by a hundred years.' He laughs softly for a moment before his face turns sombre. 'But you were wrong about me.'

I inhale sharply, shocked at the turn in conversation. *Communication*, that's what Muse said she was the fairy of. Not just song, not just life, but the act of understanding, the act of honesty. Oh, no – this can't mean that Teddy will start talking even more. I can't take it.

'I never would have guessed the truth about you,' I tell him, 'but I always knew you were hiding something. I just didn't have a choice – I had to trust you for my survival. That *is* intelligent.'

'Maya . . .' He winces. 'I need you to know it wasn't easy for me. It really hurts, having to lie, to not be able to be myself, whoever that is. Especially with people like you. People I care about.'

I'm tempted to end the conversation there and start eating my food, but the pain in his voice pulls at my heart. My stupid heart. 'Teddy, you know normal people hide things too, right? Mistakes, pain, love . . .'

His eyes shift up. 'Have you ever hidden love?'

I swallow. 'Why would I?'

'If,' he said carefully, 'you fell for someone you knew you shouldn't.'

I chuckle nervously. 'Like an affair?'

'No. Like someone you couldn't trust. Someone who made no sense to you, yet they occupied every part of your mind.'

'Someone like Dawn, your princess?'

'No! I know you hate her, but there was nothing between her and me.'

My mind completely fails to think of any other avenue to change the subject. I watch for Sierra, hoping she'll be back soon – and I know if I'm wishing for *her* presence, I've completely lost all sanity. Again, my stupid heart.

'Maya,' Teddy says. He's so serious now I want to run. And I nearly do – my legs keep shifting beneath me. 'I wish I could have been myself with you from the beginning. You still might've hated me, but at least you would've been able to make that decision.' His head hangs and he stirs his bowl of vegetables absently. 'I need you to know that when I was with you – before you found out about my mother – that was the most myself I have ever felt in my life. My past and my blood are part of me, but they aren't who I am. You still know me, better than most, and I can't bear the thought of you only seeing the part of me that I wish didn't exist. I wish we could have been something else, something normal. Friends, or more. Now you just hate me.'

I run my hands through the grass, picking at it, getting dirt under my nails. 'Teddy,' I say with gentle warning, 'you don't know me well enough to say all these things. How can

you be sure we'd have been friends if things were different? You would still be too giving, too kind. I would still
prefer my own company, and be cold and stubborn. Even
if there weren't all these . . . *politics* to keep us apart, we
still would never be friends. We're allies, and that's all.
You need to let any other ideas go.'

'I don't believe that. I *do* know you – just like you know
me. The real me.' He turns his body to fully face me. 'I saw
you once, in Bearra. It was a few months before we left.
You were walking through town alone, selling your books.
You didn't smile, and it was so clear the contempt you
felt, because your eyes darkened every time you glanced
at the castle. Then a young woman walked towards you –
your sister, I presume – and the way your face lit up . .
. I was just wandering around, hoping for fresh air, but
then I saw you and I couldn't stop watching. I was drawn
to you even before we knew each other. I never forgot
about the beautiful girl with the books. And one of the
reasons I wanted to help you that night we escaped Bearra
was because I could tell how much you cared about your
family. I wanted to see your face light up that way again.'
His steady gaze locks mine in place, not letting me look
away for even a moment.

And I'm speechless. Even the singing in the air of Muse's
Territory isn't enough to inspire words in me. Not even
thoughts. I just *feel*. The pumping in my heart, the flush
in my cheeks. The same way I felt earlier when we were
crouching in the street, when I wanted nothing more than

to kiss him. When I tried to pretend I didn't, and couldn't even fool myself.

Teddy. The son of a fairy – the son of my enemy. A boy who grew up without a family, a boy who has magic, who always listens to me but never agrees. My bright, charming summer boy. That is who he is.

'Maybe I lied,' I say, the words spilling out before I can stop them. 'Maybe I do know what it's like to keep love a secret.'

No, it couldn't be love. I haven't known him long enough – haven't been able to trust him long enough. But the beginning of love, the way they talk about it in stories . . . This must be it. The *falling*.

'I wish it didn't have to be a secret,' he whispers. 'I wish we could be ourselves and nothing else. I wish we had the privilege to simply be us.'

CHAPTER
TWENTY-FOUR

SIERRA GETS US ON a ship to Grace's Territory, which Teddy pays for. For three days I'm queasy from the constant rocking on the water, but otherwise the travel to our next destination is uneventful and much faster than if we'd have gone on foot.

Our boat ride also happens to fall on the worst days of my period, so I'm more than happy to hide under my blankets and sleep away the hours. It took my body a while to return to a regular cycle after the curse, and I still find that it shocks me each time it arrives. There *must* be a magical way to deal with periods now, right? I make a mental note to ask Sierra, if I ever stop being deathly afraid of her.

When we dock in Grace's Capital, we exit into heavy rain. The horses trudge through the mud while Sierra, in swan form, flies expertly ahead despite the wind. We follow her, clumsy after days on the water; if Teddy could barely walk across flat gravel without tripping over his feet before, he's entirely useless with river legs.

It's so irritating. I have to keep holding him upright even though I'm trying to stay as far away from him as possible. I can't let the tension between us fool me into doing something I know I'll regret.

We planned to explore the city for the rest of the afternoon, while waiting for Sierra to become human again and organise our accommodation. But with the weather soaking us already, we decide to leave the horses at a stable and head into a small café – which Teddy also pays for – so we can hide away with hot tea.

The population of Grace's Territory is diverse, like most places in the world now. Still, the majority of the people in the capital look a lot like Sierra, with black hair and dark eyes, though their skin colour varies vastly. Many of them seem perfectly comfortable around the water, including the rain, so Teddy and I look ridiculous to them as we cower from the weather. They keep laughing at us. Lovely people, just like Sierra.

Still, the city isn't as alien as others have been. It looks a lot like Darraport; just another port city built around river systems. *Grace of the Crystal Fountain*. That's what the legends call the fairy. No wonder Sierra's family were granted their power protecting the waterways from pirates. All the world's major lakes are in this sprawling territory, the water always crystal clear. People travel by boat as much as they travel by carriage, and pirates are more likely to attack than talking animals.

Teddy and I are halfway through a conversation about algae when Sierra, drenched but freshly human, saunters through the café door. The owners seem to recognise her, quickly backing away to whisper. She sneers at them and waves for us to follow her out. It's so dark outside with the heavy rain that I never realised dusk already fell.

'We can keep the horses at the house,' Sierra says once we're outside. 'We'll only need one night there, but we need to plan. Then we can go to Grace, get the final blessing, and make our way to Glassine.' *Where I'm going to kill you,* she generously doesn't add.

Fairies. We are so close to the end. Being able to skip Lire's blessing has given us at least an extra week, and with Sierra's help as well as our other blessings, we've been moving fast.

No part of this quest has happened in a way I expected. Everything that I thought would be difficult hasn't been so bad, while things I never imagined now plague me. When I feared the possibility of monsters outside of Bearra, I was picturing dragons, not a girl who turns into a bird.

I shake my head and pull myself back to the moment. 'What house? Yours? I thought your family were all swans.'

She rolls her eyes. 'Where do you think we lived before that? Underwater? It was only my sisters who were caught in the curse, when we were on a patrol. My parents still live in the manor.'

'The *manor*? I knew you were powerful, but are you . . . *rich*, rich?'

'We're basically royalty,' she retorts impatiently. 'Our influence is why the pirates wanted to get rid of us. Why I got cursed. We've been over this.'

I cover my head with my jacket to protect myself from the relentless rain. 'If you're royalty, why can't you get Grace to help your family?'

She changes streets so we can travel under the cover of a building's awning. 'The fairy of justice and truth steps in when she feels like it, not when she's begged to. No matter who you are. My parents asked, and she said we had to break the curse ourselves. Which is why they banished me until I could do it.'

I nearly stop dead. 'Your parents banished you because you got cursed?'

'Of course.' She walks straight ahead and answers without looking at me. Her black hair swishes hypnotically. 'Wouldn't yours?'

'*No*,' I say. 'That's not what families do to each other.'

Her expression is blank. 'It's my responsibility to break the curse. I should have been able to stop it from happening in the first place. When I get the crown, I'll fix my family and use the magic to regain control of the waters. Then they'll accept me.'

Teddy clears his throat. 'I suppose we aren't spending the night with your parents, then.'

'No,' she says. 'Would you want to spend a night with *Lire*? One of my sisters has a house near the river. It should be unoccupied. We're breaking in.'

Teddy and I share a doubtful glance.

· ⚬ ' ◍ ♡ ◍ ' ⚬ ·

She breaks us in quite easily, which unsettles me more than it comforts me. The house is far bigger than mine, but according to Sierra, it has 'nothing on the manor'. Her sister lived here alone to be closer to the river and patrol when needed. Of course, no one lives here now. Unless a swan tries to fly through the window, we should be fine. The horses are making a big mess, though.

The house is dark – Sierra refuses to bring in any light in case people realise someone's inside – but I can still tell how nice it is. Like my Aunt Olivia's house, everything has a place, and everything is well-made and fitted. There's something about the organisation of it that's so luxurious. I envy the ability to live in a house that's made to look beautiful and isn't just for surviving in. Large windows, high ceilings, oversized furniture, chandeliers; all things my parents would never be able to afford.

'There should be enough rooms for us all,' she says, leading us through to the kitchen, where she scours the cabinets. 'Just shake out the sheets. They'll be dusty. I don't think anyone's even been here in months. Maybe a year.'

I nearly laugh. 'A year ago, I woke up covered in a *century's* worth of dust. Believe me, I've seen worse.'

Sierra rolls her eyes. '*Bearrans.*'

'Thank you, Sierra,' Teddy says. 'It's a beautiful home.' His brown eyes look black in the dim light, and I wish we could light a candle. I want to look at him clearly – which is why it's probably best that it's so dark. He beams at me with that charming smile. *Fairies.*

'Sierra,' I say, forcing my attention away from him. 'Please don't tell anyone I'm Bearran. I'm not supposed to be out of the kingdom, obviously, and if I'm caught by Bearran soldiers, or worse, someone who wants to kidnap me, or something . . .'

'Whatever,' she says, rummaging through another cupboard. She throws a rotten *something* on the floor and it lands with a squish. 'I have nothing to gain from turning you in. Well . . .' she contemplates, 'maybe I would, but that would mean we can't get the crown. I suppose I'll consider turning you in next time I try to kill you. Get the reward, instead of getting blood in my hair.'

'So what's our plan?' Teddy interjects before I can yell at her. 'For getting the last blessing. Not for turning Maya in.'

'Kara said not to lie to Grace,' I offer.

Sierra sits at the long dining table, opening a jar of almonds she found at the back of a cupboard. We join her and she passes them out. 'Kara was right,' she says. 'And Grace doesn't simply see people like other fairies do. We won't be able to walk in and talk to her. If we want a chance at asking her for a favour, we'll have to break into her fortress, get her alone, then ask for what we want – without pretence or manipulation. She should see it only fair that she gives us the blessing after we've bested her security.'

'We're . . . breaking . . . in?' I say. 'To the fairy of justice's fortress?'

Teddy winces but doesn't argue. 'What else can we do? The three of us together are powerful and skilled enough. All we need is a foolproof plan.'

The three of us. So he hasn't yet noticed they don't need me? I sigh. 'A foolproof plan? I should hope so, because this is so, very, incredibly, *undoubtedly* foolish.'

'Hush, Bearran,' says Sierra, with the slightest hint of humour in her tone. 'It's possible, even if it won't be easy. That's the point. Then we can return here for another night, rest, and be on our way to Glassine by dawn.'

'You told us we'd only be here one night,' I whine.

'Then I remembered I can only *break into a fortress* after dusk, and I can't see us doing it right this second.'

My mind is spinning so much I feel dizzy. I am overflowing with apprehension. And . . . why am I suddenly *happy* Sierra is here? I can't begin to think how we'd reach Grace without her. Maybe – and I'd never, ever say this aloud – Teddy was right to bring her in. Without either of them, I'd never have had a chance at getting the crown and saving my family.

Maybe we're all working against each other, but does it really matter? I'm starting to wonder if enemies and allies are so different.

· ◦ ◦ ꙮ 🖤 ꙮ ◦ ◦ ·

Sierra goes upstairs to be alone once we've finished planning. She must relish her few hours of humanity; she almost always spends them awake. I don't know how each of her forms affects the other. Does she need to eat as both swan and human? Drink, sleep, bathe? Actually, I don't want to know.

Teddy and I stay up for a while, pressed together, lying in the cool night air on one of the house's many luxurious sofas. We're covered in blankets, sideways so we can both lay down. My head rests against his arm, and his warmth is an endless supply of comfort. I'm not sure how we even ended up here. A slow, magnetic migration of two people who want to be touching, eventually colliding. Again, my stupid heart.

But if we're this close to the end, and this is one of our last nights together, I'm not going to hold back anymore. 'I don't want to sleep in an old, dusty bed,' I tell him. 'I might just stay here.'

I don't look at his face, but I feel his body tense. He says, 'Mind if I join you?'

'You're already here.'

'But you don't mind if I don't get my own room?'

I swallow. 'Teddy, I would rather have you next to me.'

'Me too,' he whispers. 'I'd rather be next to you.'

I nuzzle his arm, and he puts it around my back so I can rest my head on his chest. I fall asleep instantly.

CHAPTER
TWENTY-FIVE

SOMEWHERE, SOMETIME...

SIERRA HAD NEVER, IN her life, felt cold like that.

She'd known frost before. She had patrolled the waters of Grace's Territory on the most intense winter nights, with wind and snow stinging her face. She had been to the southern border of the territory, where if travellers weren't careful, the ice would bite at them until they were a distant memory.

She had spent her entire life being frozen out of her family, her world, everything she longed for. She had known the pain of failure, of cowardice. The pain when she first realised she would never be loved as her sisters were, or even loved by her sisters.

Often, youngest children were doted over, but Sierra had spent her life invisible, overshadowed by her six sisters. They were all at least a decade older than her, while she was a mistake, a shock, and ultimately unwanted. Her sisters had long been a team of brutal warriors – a perfectly trained unit that had protected Grace's Waters for years before Sierra was even born.

Sierra, though skilled, did not belong. She was hated by her family for being a blemish on the perfection they had already created. Despite doing all she could to prove herself, she could not find her place. When her parents and sisters weren't pretending Sierra didn't exist, they were screaming at her or hitting her. And when she and her sisters were cursed, the blame was set on her alone. She was banished.

Yes, Sierra had power, but she didn't always feel powerful.

Still, even with all the endless cold she felt, the worst pain she ever experienced was being trapped by Teddy's magic. Stuck in place, with the cold pressing in from all sides, ice lodged in her open mouth and down her throat, in her veins, prickling into her heart and lungs. Her eyes, forced to stay open, watched as the sun rose and fell for days, until she was nearly blinded by the way it bounced off the white snow. She hadn't seen the sun through her human eyes for so long, but trapped this way, under such strong magic, even her curse lost effect. Each dusk and dawn, her body would tremor, begging to transform. Magic warred within her, searing her from the inside out, until she wished she would never see the sun again. She was still unable to die or so much as sleep. Whether this was part of Teddy's enchantment, or the blessing she had received from Rhiannon, or even her curse, she

did not know. Her mind swam at random, piecing frag-
ments of information together, but it was as if her
thoughts were as frozen as her body. She was not human
or swan – she was a being of perpetual pain.

It took three days for anyone to find her. The passing
travellers used magical axes with heated blades to cut
through the ice.

When she was free, she did not stop to thank them.
Her body was too busy convulsing, shifting and flashing
between swan and human as the curse tried to catch up
with its missed transformations. By the time this was
done, she was fully healed, new. Not even thirsty. One
of the few advantages to her curse was that each time
she transformed, her body was renewed. She could reach
near-death and be fine by the time the sun rose or fell.

As the swan, she could not speak to the stunned travellers, so with new strength she flew south-east towards
Muse's Territory. She knew Teddy and Maya must have
reached it by then.

She had a new plan. She knew now that she could not
best them. But she could convince them to join her. She
would tell them they needed her to get Grace's blessing,
which was true. She would also tell them she'd kill them
as soon as they got to the grave. Also true. There was no
point in lying. They were as desperate for the crown as
she was – they would not be able to refuse her.

As her mind so often did over her long hours in the sky, with her strong, black wings outstretched and gliding, she let her imagination wander to the past.

· ◦ ✦ ◍ ♡ ◍ ✦ ◦ ·

Sierra sat by the river, her arms and legs outstretched and bare as she took in the sun. She let one hand drift in the water, swirling in refreshing, magical blue, while her other held up a book. She was eleven, and this was how she spent many of her days. She had tried to break into her family's enterprise – tried to join her sisters on their ships and her parents in their offices – but since realising they did not care to waste any of their time on her, she had resolved to step back and enjoy her privilege instead. She may not have been a warrior or a leader, but she was still the daughter of a rich family, able to lay in the sand while others worked until their eyes burned and their hands bled. She could spend every day tanning by the river and picking up new hobbies – so why wouldn't she?

The waters near her parent's manor were always clear blue. Grace's magic flowed from her crystal fountain throughout the rivers and lakes, giving the water a diamond effect. Sierra's family controlled the waterways, and therefore the supply and demand of goods, as well as who got to come in and out of the city. Pirates would occasionally get in and attempt their pillaging and swindling, but thanks to Sierra's sisters, few were successful.

All Sierra wanted was to join her sisters in battle, protecting the waters and the people of her city. But her family would probably prefer if she was dead. Why carry around the dead weight of a young, unwanted girl? The Reeds were merciless warriors – they would not take the time to train Sierra when they had already reached perfection. Sierra only served as an embarrassment to her entire family.

She watched the swans and ducks playing in the water, followed by their grey babies. Fish swam beneath them, occasionally caught, and crabs crawled along the shoreline. Sierra threw some breadcrumbs into the gentle waves, creating a flurry of wings and splashes. She laughed, then sat back once again, nothing at all to do.

After several hours, she was stirred from the pages of her book by the hum of a ship passing, its inhabitants giggling venomously. The vessel shook waves through the water that rocked up the shore and lapped at Sierra's legs. Sitting up and rubbing her eyes, she saw her sisters on their patrol. She brushed the sand off her body and stood straight.

The women were so adult compared to Sierra, their bodies strong and lithe from the years of training and fighting. They looked just like Sierra, and Sierra would have fit in with them perfectly if they didn't loathe her so much. Why couldn't they see that if they just let her in, she could help them?

'If it isn't our little black swan,' her oldest sister jeered, jumping off the boat and splashing into the water before wading into the shore. Her other sisters anchored the boat and followed.

'You're back from patrol early?' Sierra asked as they reached her, wishing she could make herself invisible. Her sisters were bored, she could see that, and when they had no criminals to chase, they had to torment *someone*. Sierra was such easy prey to them.

One of the girls shook her head, running her hands through the water. 'We wanted to check in on you, Cygnet,' she teased without a trace of true concern. 'We heard you've been spending your days lazing by the river. Mother and father may be alright with you doing whatever you like, but we won't allow such a taint on our family's image.'

Sierra stepped back, nearly losing her footing in the soft sand. Her sisters were circling around her like a family of sharks. She tried to keep an impassive expression. 'I'll go home,' Sierra said. She picked up her bag, but a girl ripped it from her hand and threw it on the ground, its contents spilling in the shallow water.

'I'm *sorry*,' Sierra pleaded. 'I didn't know. No one told me I shouldn't . . .'

'This is why we don't want you around, Cygnet.' The oldest sister – the princess of the waters – stood in front of her, staring down her nose with disdain. 'We have to watch over you, coddle you, tell you the obvious, and take care of you so you don't bring shame on our family – on our territory, our patron fairy.' Her voice stayed low and striking. She did not shout, but her fury could be felt in the air. 'You have always made us look weak. You do not deserve to be part of our bloodline.'

Tears burned at the back of Sierra's nose, and she tried to hold them back; she knew crying would only make things worse. 'I said I'm sorry. I swear I'll go home.'

Her sisters kept circling with a dance they all knew, a balance they existed in without her.

'I'm so—'

Sand flew as her sister slashed her hand across Sierra's face. She crashed to the ground and cried out. Her hands burned from landing on the abrasive shore, her face scorching from the slap. She spat sand from her mouth and stood quickly – if she didn't, if she stayed down, her sisters would only take the advantage.

Don't be a coward.

She held her sister's gaze, refusing to touch her cheek or brush the sand from her skin. Tears welled in her eyes, but she did not wipe them – she let them silently fall, straightened her spine, and took a few deep breaths. 'It won't h-happen again.'

'No, it won't,' another sister hissed, stepping in from behind. She shoved Sierra forward and she fell face-first, sand cutting her gums.

This time she couldn't hold back her sobs. Her nose and chin were bleeding, fiery with pain. Her shoulders shook. 'Stop,' she moaned. 'Please stop.'

A hand on the nape of her neck yanked her up. She screamed, but the women were all around her now, grabbing her limbs and dragging her through the shallows. Sierra struggled to break free, but they were so strong.

'You need to learn your lesson, Cygnet,' one of them spat, but Sierra barely heard it.

Her head was shoved underwater. She shook, trying to cough out the water she inhaled. She flailed her limbs helplessly. There were too many of them pinning her down. Even if there were only one, she'd be overwhelmed. How could Sierra compete now? Below the surface she screamed, but no sound came out, only her last breaths.

Every effort to escape was met with another hand shoving her down. She was so weak. She couldn't breathe. Black spots filled her vision – the thrashing and fighting were only making her lose more oxygen. Her lungs and muscles ached so terribly she wondered if she would fall apart, disintegrate.

She heard the torturous sound of her sisters' muffled laughter as water rushed across her ears. As she balanced on the edge of unconsciousness, the pain began to subside. Was she to die this way? By the hands of the family she had only ever wanted to be loved by?

She had an idea. A cowardly idea, but the only one that would save her: Sierra played dead.

She stopped moving, went limp, and when the hands around her loosened, she took the moment of distraction and pulled herself down as hard as she could through the water. She spun – liquid flooding through her nose – and flipped over to escape their grip and put distance between her and her sisters.

Sierra did not hesitate. She ran, water splashing as her feet sank in the soft sand of the shallows. She reached the shore, the wet sand firmer and easier to sprint across. New breaths heaved into her lungs, and she felt stronger again. If she could just outrun them, get home, beg her parents for mercy—

The women caught up. Black hair fanned everywhere, and suddenly Sierra was on the floor again. This time her ankle twisted and she shrieked. 'I didn't ask to be born!' she wailed, hot tears streaming out of her eyes as her sisters pressed her body into the ground, punching, kicking, tearing at her hair. 'I'll go away!'

The oldest girl yanked her by the hair to force her eyes up. 'You'll stay,' she snarled. 'And next time you make us angry, we'll get to hurt you again. Maybe we'll even get to end you one day. But you had better get yourself home now. You've learned your lesson, Cygnet.'

Sierra tried to speak, but she found she couldn't. Not through the pain.

Her sister shoved her face back into the sand, and her head rang in pain at the impact. Sand scraped her eye and stuck itself in her throat. Something hit her head – she did not know what – and she heard her sisters distantly laughing and jeering as they left her to fall unconscious. No one came to her rescue.

When Sierra woke, she crawled to the river and pressed the salt water into her scraped and open skin. It stung, but she was used to it. This was not the first time Sierra had gotten herself into trouble. It would not be the last.

She flushed out her mouth and eyes. She detangled her hair with her fingers.

Her sisters' ship was long gone. Now, the still waters mocked her as she stood broken on the shore. Except for the blood in the sand, it was as if the women had never been there at all. But with the memories of the fight forever imprinted in her mind, Sierra knew she could not let herself be overpowered like that again.

She was used to being beaten, but this time was different. This time, they had nearly killed her.

She could not be weak, be a victim, any longer. Humiliated and crushed, she vowed in that moment to never be a coward again. She would no longer laze all day by the water – she would be like her sisters, just as she wished, and—

No. She would not be like them. She would be greater than them all. Sierra would find her place, even if she had to kill, torture, and cheat to do it. She would not be kicked down by her own family again. Sierra was a princess of the waters – a woman born of Grace's chosen bloodline. She was a Reed whether her family wanted her or not.

It was time for her to take her rightful place.

CHAPTER
TWENTY-SIX

'IF YOU CAN GET a favour from Grace by breaking into her fortress,' I say to Sierra as we amble through the light-stone streets, past the canals and towards the fairy's blocky, intimidating structure, 'why not do it before?'

'Because I didn't have the two of you. I couldn't be certain it would work. It was too risky. If I failed – not that I *would* – I'd have been imprisoned, and how could I break the curse then?'

'But it's fine to take that risk with us.'

'Exactly, Bearran.' She brushes her dark hair behind her back, and it blends into her black outfit – we're all in clothes we stole from her sister's house to camouflage in the dark. Though if I ever see Sierra wearing anything outside the range of black and white, even stolen, I'll be astounded.

When I woke this morning, I was still in Teddy's arms. I quickly removed myself and tiptoed across the room to make tea. It was strange watching him then, still fast asleep. It reminded me of the last time I saw him like this: our first night together, in that abandoned building just outside Bearra. I had watched as the rising sun lit him up for the first time, making his auburn hair almost yellow. When he woke, his brown eyes shone so brightly. The version of him I saw that day was something entirely different to the boy I see now.

My feelings keep changing. Once, they were all apprehension towards him, maybe excitement. Then, all warmth – as much as I tried to ignore it. Now I don't know anymore. The warmth is still there, but there is so much dishonesty between us, so much ice to splinter each good moment we have.

Today, while waiting for Sierra to turn human again, Teddy and I spent our free time wandering the glittering canals of the city. Sierra would occasionally soar into view above, most likely searching for the flock that's really her sisters. Grace's Capital is a lot like Darraport, if only Darraport were mixed with a paradise. This is a clean city, a place that feels fresh, clear, and safe. It's the perfect blend of commotion and serenity. Yesterday, in the unrelenting rainstorm, it was difficult to see past my own feet, but today I could appreciate Sierra's drive to protect Grace's Territory.

Teddy nearly trips over a loose stone in the brick pathway, and I realise I've been absently staring at him. I have to remember where we are, what we're doing. I move my gaze to Sierra's long, dark hair instead, watching it sway. She has a hard, determined look on her face as she stares at the fortress. It must be painful for her to be back here, but she doesn't show it. She doesn't seem to show any emotions at all, ever. She's exactly who I wish I could be: invulnerable, independent.

At midnight we reach the back edge of the massive fortress; the moon is hidden by clouds, darkening the already foreboding structure. The fortress is made of a light stone, extending out in a square that's flat against the ground. Except for the pearls and opals lining the base of each storey and every window, it doesn't rely on the splendour or height of the other fairy's homes. Instead, Grace's Fortress has the size and brutality to instil fear in anyone who sees it. There's a moat all the way around, and the famed crystal fountain is at the front, beyond our sight. The magical water floats past us, shining clear blue even in the dark.

And we have one bizarre plan to get us in. *Fairies.*

Teddy links his arms through ours, and lilac magic forms around him in the navy night. The three of us simultaneously take a deep breath, and my body tingles as the magic takes hold.

'Try to stay still,' Teddy says with a tremor in his voice.

'Scared of heights?' Sierra shifts so her arm is over his.

'No,' he replies in a tone that makes me think he's hiding a 'yes'.

I grip Teddy's arm hard, then chide myself for clinging to him out of fear. Hopefully he thinks it's for his sake. 'This will work, won't it?' I ask. 'If this is how we die—'

'Of course it'll work,' Sierra says flatly. 'If it doesn't, we'll only fall into the moat. It isn't high enough for us to get hurt.' She clears her throat. '*That* hurt.'

I swallow.

'Ready?' Teddy rolls onto the balls of his feet.

'Ready,' we reply.

There's no one around, no guards watching from here. Very few people would have the magic to do this. Fewer would be stupid enough to try.

My feet begin lifting as Teddy pulls us up with a cloud of lilac – first my heels, then my toes, until I'm no longer touching the ground – and suddenly my heart is racing. I glance at the others, who also look doubtful as we rise inch by inch until we're hovering over the moat. The water glitters below with a welcoming shimmer, but we keep flying further from it.

I let out a deep breath, doing my best to stay still. I want to struggle, or scream, or both. My body fights the feeling of being in the air, but if I let my instincts win and drop, I'll really be in trouble. How do fairies do this so gracefully?

We hover and hover until our feet land softly on the flat stone rooftop. I take just a second too long to let go of Teddy.

Sierra is already ahead of us, waving us along. 'No time to stop and look at the view. The guards will be making their rounds. We need to be r—' She grinds to a halt. 'Oh, wonderful.'

Two women in navy-blue uniforms round a corner with heavy footsteps. I'm about to run in retreat, but Sierra is already sprinting right up to the guards. She uses her long legs to trip them, then punches them each in the back of the head – simultaneously knocking them down. She has them motionless on the floor before they can react, before I can even gasp in shock. Even as a human, Sierra fights with the swift, dance-like movements of a bird.

'S-Sierra,' I breathe. 'Are they dead?'

She gives me an indifferent look. 'Probably not. It doesn't matter. The real threats will be inside. These are only Grace's expendable guards.'

I shiver and follow Sierra through the now unguarded rooftop entrance. We step down a dark wooden staircase, spiralling until we reach a heavy door and enter the top floor of the fortress. Teddy places a reassuring hand on my back and walks beside me, pushing me forward, making my heart rush. My cheeks heat despite the coldness of the fortress. As Sierra wordlessly leads us through the labyrinth of hallways, I call on my blessing of Strength to keep me unafraid.

Teddy takes my hand and my mind tells me to push him off, to not encourage him, not now we're so close to the end, but I can't make myself do it. Amora's ring – that must be it. Maybe *all* the feelings I've had towards Teddy are because of it. Wouldn't that be a relief.

Teddy knocks out the next lot of guards with a wave of magic, and it really is that simple. Sierra was right. Between the three of us, the impossible is possible. Between the two of them, at least. But they still need me.

As long as I have these blessings in my hands, I think, pushing back my shoulders, *they need me.*

Without any light reaching us from outside, the fortress darkens with every step we take. Teddy uses magic to give us enough glow to see ahead. He and Sierra take turns taking out guards, dropping them silently as we go. It shouldn't be so easy. If it were, couldn't anyone with magic get—

An alarm blasts through the walls and the corridor lights up midday-blue. I shield my eyes as Teddy and Sierra stiffen, going back-to-back and gasping through confused expressions as they ready themselves for danger. The echoes of footsteps thunder through my body. There must be dozens of guards on their way.

It's fine. I know we can handle them. What we *can't* handle is Grace, if she comes to face us herself. We have to find her first if this is going to work.

Teddy and Sierra are shifting, ready to fight – they may be strong, but they aren't very strategic. They rely on their power. Everything is easy for them. But Grace isn't Rhiannon. We can't win her favour on strength alone. I'm reminded of my escape from Bearra, distracting the soldiers with fire so I could slip past them and through the gates.

Distraction.

That's it – we can make this work for us.

'Teddy,' I hiss, trying to call to him through the blaring alarm without bringing attention to us. He looks up and hurries over to me, his lilac magic circling my feet as he comes close – too close. I stare at him, heaving with the wild idea. 'We need to fly again.'

Sierra raises her brows, her eyes darting between me and the corridor as she awaits our next attack. 'Maya, I can handle some guards.'

'No – we need to get to Grace before she gets to us. If we take out all her guards, she'll come and fight us herself. We're supposed to impress her, remember?'

She exhales, nods, though I can tell she's a little offended.

'So you want to fly?' Teddy asks me. 'That wasn't a trick I wanted to make a regular habit of.'

I rub my temples. Why can't they just agree with me? Why is everything an argument? 'If we're going to reach Grace's rooms,' I say, 'we'll have to sneak past all the guards coming our way. The alarm is a great distraction, because they'll be looking for us in the wrong place. They won't expect us to be in the air. If we can crawl along the roof—'

'That's *insane*.'

'Is it?' I shoot back, daring him to challenge me as our time keeps ticking.

'It's perfect,' says Sierra, winking at me, and I nearly trip over my own feet although I'm standing dead still.

Without wasting another second, Teddy pours his magic out of his hands and around our bodies, and we float up into the air as if rising through water. With confidence from our last flight, and a healthy dose of adrenaline, it's much easier this time. Not a moment too soon, we're pressed to the ceiling and the guards are marching below us.

The rough stone scratches my hands as I pull myself along it, putting all my faith in Teddy to not let me fall. How much of his power is he using to do this? Will it weaken him, or will his magic fill right back up again like his mother's?

Sierra leads us through the hallways, and every time a group of guards passes below us, we hold our breath. The ceiling is high and dark enough to hide us well. Teddy's magic surrounds me like a warm blanket, hugging my waist, and before I know it we're outside Grace's wing of the castle. I try to hide my disappointment as Teddy releases me, even if it was his magic holding me, not him.

The guards nearer Grace's rooms are armed with magic. Crystal-blue light laces their hands as they approach us, and the magical glow slashes through the darkness as they move. They have bigger muscles and sharper eyes.

I stay back as Sierra runs at them and Teddy sends his own magic their way. Sierra almost fails against them as their numbers grow, more magical guards pouring from the corridors – how many guards does Grace *have*? – but Teddy's magic easily overpowers theirs.

Without their power to rely on, the guards are no match for Sierra as she takes them down one-by-one. A punch to the gut here, and a kick to the face there, the crack of wrists and ankles as Sierra topples them onto the hard floor. She turns to me and smirks through her cuts and scrapes, as if proud to have beaten more challenging opponents.

We're absurdly close to Grace already, and I stand shivering as I gawk at the pile of unconscious guards. Why did I ever think to be afraid when I knew I'd be with Teddy and Sierra?

I realise with sudden clarity that although I fear them, I don't have to envy or feel lesser than them. Why shouldn't I enjoy their protection? If it weren't for my idea to fly above the guards, we wouldn't have made it this far. I'm so afraid they see me as weak and useless, but maybe I'm the only person who believes that.

I walk with my back straighter and my chin lifted as we reach a set of flashy, triarue-lined double-doors which must be the entrance to Grace's wing. Sierra turns a diamond handle, and as she pulls, a bright-blue light washes over us, as shocking as the sky itself.

'*Sierra Reed*,' a clear, strong voice calls. 'I wouldn't have believed you would ever return, if I weren't seeing it with my own eyes.'

The fairy who steps toward us is taller than the others I've seen. Her black, shoulder-length hair brushes the sleeves of an azure dress that waterfalls in delicate drapes down to her feet. Her brows are raised at us, and as my eyes adjust to the magical brightness of the room, I realise her skin has a slightly blue tinge to it, as if the fairy is under water. She's perfectly symmetrical, from her analysing black eyes to her smooth cheeks, short nose, and round lips. Grace's wings spread out clear as diamond and thin as sheets of ice, with swirls of sapphire bending through them.

'I've already told you I won't break your curse,' Grace says to Sierra with an irritated tone, completely ignoring Teddy and me. 'And now you dare to enter my fortress unannounced and uninvited, to do what, exactly? Do you believe that just because you have brought a son of Lire and blessings from my sisters that I'll be inclined to treat you any differently?'

We've entered what must be her private library: a few leather armchairs, books around the walls and on shelves throughout the room, and a large oak desk. Not a throne room, and nothing as spectacular as Adella's Great Library, but it does match Grace. Simple, clean lines and bright, blinding blues. A set of crystal scales sits atop her desk, each side filled with glistening water. The several doors off the library's back wall must lead to the rest of her rooms.

Sierra gives the fairy a flat expression. 'We're here for a blessing, Grace. I would hope that since we bested your defences and made our way in here, you would in return give us what we want. Does that not sound like fairness to you?'

The fairy's eyes narrow. 'Your strength is a merit of your own, Reed, but bringing the boy does seem like cheating.'

'I hope your waters are safe without my sisters and I,' Sierra responds. 'How are you dealing with the pirates on your own?'

I'm speechless as I watch them, absolutely certain I'm out of my depth. I fight the urge to hide behind Teddy and his faintly glowing fingertips. These are women who exist in an entirely different world to me – a world of power and riches and politics.

Grace grins viciously, showing straight, white teeth. 'Tell me what the blessing is for.'

'We know where Bearra's crown is,' Teddy says. I can tell he's trying to stay still and copy Sierra's indifference, so I do the same. 'It's buried under layers of magic, and without blessings from all seven fairies, we won't be able to break through. We knew getting enough magic to do it would be difficult – if not impossible – so we've travelled the world petitioning the fairies to help us by providing blessings.'

Grace hums. 'Even you, a child of Lire, cannot break through these wards? I knew the crown was powerful, but *this* is intriguing.' She pauses to give Teddy an examination, her calculating eyes travelling over him. 'I remember you. It may have been years since you visited with Lire, but you have a distinct aura. Since you were a child, you have been more concerned with the greater good than anything else. Though your values have to compete with *her* now.' She gestures to me. 'Interesting, interesting.'

'Don't worry about all of that,' I say. 'We know what we're doing, and what we need. If you could just give us the blessing we broke in here for, we can leave.'

'Please,' Teddy adds.

Sierra rolls her eyes at him. 'What they mean is, you can trust that we have a plan – all we need is this one thing from you, Grace.'

'So you can reach the crown,' says the fairy, 'and fight to the death over it.'

'Great, you understand,' Sierra says. She's glowing in Grace's blue light, and I can see why she's meant for this territory. She could be a creature living in the shallows of a river, a siren. It isn't right that she was banished from her home.

Grace's tone shifts. 'Okay,' she says lightly. She turns, her icy wings extending from the centre of her spine where her dress dips to fit them. She glances back. 'You can have the blessing on one condition: you must come to an agreement on what to do with the crown.'

'But we've already—'

Grace shushes Sierra. 'This may come as a surprise, but I do not want any of you to die. I am harsh on you, Reed, but only because I must be. Although I cannot break your curse, I would like to nudge you along on your journey to breaking it on your own. You were correct – by coming here, you have shown your worthiness of this favour.' Her eyes travel to Teddy. She steps up to him and gently lifts his chin with her fingers. He shudders. 'And the fairy boy. I certainly cannot let *him* be murdered, especially by one of my own warriors. That could start a war with Lire.'

Teddy winces.

'As for the Bearran,' she says, watching me through the side of her eye but moving no closer, 'she's a piece of history. So different from the others in her kingdom, so wise beyond her years, inquisitive and cold. She could do incredible things. Already has.' She reaches a doorway on the other side of the room and runs a watery hand down its frame. 'Formulate a plan for how to each gain what you need from the crown without killing each other, and I'll give you a blessing.'

All the blood rushes from my face and pools at my feet, making me sway. 'But we can't do that! We can't compromise. We already agreed to fight.'

Grace raises a brow. 'Said like a girl blessed by Rhiannon, Kara, and Amora. I'll leave you alone to come to a conclusion. Justice, Bearran – that is what I create, what I support, and what this final blessing will provide. If you cannot show me that you can create fairness, you cannot have any from me. Whoever possesses the crown will need this wisdom. It is not enough to be willing to die or kill for what you want. You must be prepared for more difficult things than that.'

I am, I want to say. *Just not this.*

Sierra's eyes are dark and daggering. She presses her lips into a tight line and nods. The fairy exits the room with a short wave, shutting the door behind her. At the click of the lock, the three of us stare at each other.

I wrap my hands around my head. 'At least one of us was going to get the crown. Now none of us will.'

'As if we could share,' Sierra grumbles.

Teddy taps his nails against his rings. 'We've managed to work together to get this far. We can find a way to all get what we want. I want us all to win.' He may as well be saying,

'*Look how kind and wonderful I am, while you're both selfish monsters.*'

'We all want the crown,' I say, pacing the room. 'Except you, Teddy. You want it destroyed. So how can two people have something that doesn't exist?'

'Grace has set us an impossible task.' Sierra sits at the desk, putting her feet atop it – her legs are impossibly long. 'She doesn't want any of us to have the crown. She's already thinking about how she can get it for herself.'

'No.' Teddy shakes his head. 'Grace is the fairy of justice and truth. She wouldn't play games. If she's asking this of us, she knows there's a way. She wants to see if we're able to find this compromise, because she wants to help us. Because that's what we've earned.'

'It doesn't matter,' I say. 'I can't give up the crown. For anything. You know that.'

'But it isn't the crown you want,' Sierra says. 'What you want is money. Security. You don't need the crown for that. I *do* need it.'

'That isn't fair,' I say. 'The crown is mine. Neither of you would even know where it is if not for me. You don't get to claim it just because you believe your need is greater than mine.'

'Sierra,' Teddy says, 'you don't need it either. What you need is magic. Not necessarily the crown.'

She narrows her eyes. 'What, like yours?'

'That isn't enough. But you can get the person who cast the curse to reverse it.'

She fumes. 'I've told you – he would never do that. The crown is my only option. Unless you can beg your mummy to fix me, the crown is the magic I need.'

I start to zone out of their bickering. My eyes have adjusted enough to the light now that I can see the intricate details in every book on every shelf. There are carvings in the wood of the desk, like water spilled through in veins, and the floor is inlaid with diamonds and triarue. I long to search through Grace's books, to study the artwork that is the library itself, but we're on limited time to do the impossible.

'Teddy,' I say, 'you don't need the crown at all. You just don't want your mother to get her hands on it. That doesn't count. It only makes sense that I should have it. Once I've got my reward money, I don't care what happens to it. You can steal it back and destroy it then. Use it to fix Sierra's family if you want. But that's your problem to deal with, not mine.'

'Considering I could snap your neck without losing a breath,' Sierra says, 'I'm not so concerned with *your* problems either.'

I cross my arms, barely containing my frustration. 'And yet, if you don't come to an agreement with me, none of us get anything. At least if I get the crown first, you can take it back. I don't want to keep it. I only want to get what it's worth.'

She throws her hands in the air. '*Anything* else in the world can get you money! We can sort through my sisters' things and you'll find enough jewellery to feed you for a lifetime. Or simply have Teddy use his magic to make you rich!'

'I have not come all this way,' I say with as much venom in my tone as I can muster, 'to not get my crown.'

As I say it, though, my heart isn't in it. It's pride that keeps me arguing, keeps me attached to the idea of my treasure. They're right. I sound ridiculous arguing for it just because I feel like it's mine. Saying I deserve it because I want to be rich. I'm acting like a child. But I don't want them to win. I don't want to admit I'm wrong.

Teddy has the most honourable claim to the crown, because he's Teddy, so of course he does. He wants to stop Lire getting it, to stop her hurting more people like she hurt me and my family when she put us to sleep. He wants to stop magic getting even more out of control, so people like Sierra will be less likely to be hurt by those using it for their own gain. He wants to stop a war.

For Sierra, the crown really is her only hope for saving her family. Can I really take that away from her just for the sake of my pride?

Right now, far away, my sister is planning her wedding. She's readying to leave us because she can no longer afford to stay. Soon Briar will be next, then me. My parents will be left behind to rot while my sisters and I live out our lives in miserable marriages.

Once, I thought this quest was the only way to secure our futures. Now I've seen a world where anything is possible, where magic is shared, where different cultures thrive and mix and don't just survive but really *live*. Cities of passion and cities of bravery. There are so many other ways to help my family. I don't need to steal riches; I now have the ability to earn them. It's the future, and I can either stay wallowing in my old, stubborn ways, or step into this new world and thrive.

A world with a boy who has all the power he could need to do anything he likes, but only wants to help people. Help *me*. And a girl who, despite being cursed and banished, still wants to protect her beautiful territory.

I fear that if I let go of everything old, my family will slip through my fingers faster than the last hundred years. I still can't lose the crown, still can't take any chances of losing them, but like Grace said, I can compromise.

'I won't give up now,' Sierra says, standing up from the desk and joining us again. She towers over me, her black hair shining in the blue light. 'I wouldn't care if you were using the crown to save a hundred innocent orphans. I need to save my sisters.'

'Okay, fine,' I tell her. 'You get the crown first. We'll bring it back here and break the curse. Then when you're done with it, we can move on to Bearra.'

Sierra crosses her arms. 'I don't agree to that. The crown could change everything for my family. We would have the power to undo all the bad done to Grace's Waters over the last year while we've been gone.'

'We're trying to compromise,' I say, taking a seat in one of the armchairs and hoping I look aloof and not idiotic. 'You can have your curse broken, and that's the best we can offer. Then I'll take the crown to Bearra's royals so they give me the reward for it. *Then* Teddy can find a way to steal it back and destroy it before his mother uses it to destroy the world, or whatever.'

Sierra's lips purse as she mulls it over. 'Fine. I'll accept this deal, but if either of you are lying, Grace will know. Don't think you can pretend to agree just to cheat later.'

'I also accept,' says Teddy. 'And I'm not lying.'

'I wish I was,' I mutter. 'But I can't see the point in it.'

'Will you work with me to steal the crown back?' Teddy asks us. 'Since I'll have helped you both with your goals first.'

Sierra sighs. 'We'll see. I'll have plenty to deal with, with my family. But if this works, and you call for my help, I'll do what I can.'

'Me too,' I say. 'I don't know what I can do, but if there's a way . . .'

'That's all I need to hear,' he says, the tension releasing from his brown eyes as they brighten, even in this monochromatically cool-toned room. 'Thank you.'

Grace re-enters, her footsteps so soundless it's as if she's barely there. But her presence is intense. The light glimmers off her wings, making waves of brightness dance across the bookshelves as if they're under the travelling sun. 'That took you long enough,' she says. 'Sierra is right, you cannot and should not lie to me.' She eyes each of us like she can read our minds. 'Luckily, none of you are. It's very heart-warming to watch enemies become friends.'

'Allies,' Sierra and I correct.

'Very well.' Grace flutters her wings, and suddenly she's in front of us, aqua glowing all around her. She holds Sierra's hand up with one hand – not mine nor Teddy's, though we both have a ring left – and with her other, tips a finger over it. Water-like magic drips from her wrist, down her hand and along her finger, then splashes into Sierra's palm. Sierra tenses, her eyes wide and childlike.

Grace stops after a few drops, smiles contently, then pulls away. 'May this blessing show your family the worthiness *I* see in you, Sierra.' She waves her hands. 'Now, out of here. And do not break into my fortress again. This was your first and last favour.'

Sierra watches her as she goes, a distant but hopeful awe in her eyes. In this moment, I find it hard to hate Sierra. We *could* be friends, couldn't we? If we were only ourselves. If we weren't tainted by what our world has turned us into.

CHAPTER TWENTY-SEVEN

TEDDY AND I SIT on the same sofa as last night, legs and arms pressed together, knowing we only have a few hours until dawn. Until our final trek to Glassine, to the grave. Until it's over. Until we go our separate ways and never see each other again.

Although part of me wants to talk to him, to hold his hand, *anything* more than this, I savour our silence. Because in this quiet, alone together, we can be ourselves without consequence. I wonder if he feels the same way.

After a while he turns to me, and I meet his watchful eyes. I don't feel tired. Does he?

In this rare moment, I feel . . . happy. Warm. In the darkness, on this soft sofa, touching him, everything else disappears. The crown, the fairies, Sierra, even my family.

They're all gone and I just want to be with Teddy forever. I want so much more from him than I can have.

His eyes move down to my lips, and I would normally turn away, but I don't move. I no longer want to. If this is our last night together, like this . . .

'Teddy,' I whisper. 'When we talked about hiding things—'

He moves swifter than magic, and suddenly his mouth is on mine. His hands are on my jaw, and at first mine hang uselessly at my sides as I sit in shock, then I regain my wits and move to hold the outsides of his hands, not letting them shift away from my face. Heat runs from my lips to my heart to my stomach. As if enchanted, I lean forward and kiss him back.

Us, together. Just us. As ourselves.

Not the girl from Bearra with the starving family.

Not the magical boy shrouded with conspiracy.

I take in every second of the kiss, every feeling that sparks across and within my body, because I can never, ever forget this.

When we break apart, my lips still tingling, I whisper, 'I don't want to hide this – how I feel – anymore.'

He kisses my cheeks, his soft mouth warm and magical as he moves his hands up the nape of my neck, through my hair, then down to my jaw again. He stares at his hands, brushing my bottom lip with his thumb. His mouth is hanging open, and his brown eyes are the most awake I've ever seen them.

What do I look like to him? It doesn't matter. But it does. It does. I want him to see me. I want him to see what's beyond my eyes, but I also want him to think I'm beautiful.

'I want to love you,' he says quietly, and his words come out in tumbles. 'I want to fall in love like they do in stories. I want to touch you, kiss you, every moment of every day. I never want to leave your side. Maya, I want you. I want to experience what this can become. Grace was right – everything I've ever thought I wanted, you cloud it all. You're all I can think about.'

'Me too,' I say. 'You – you too.'

Then his hands drop, and tears form in his eyes. 'But we both know it isn't possible.'

'*Teddy*,' I say, but I sit back, because what else can I do? Lie and tell him that it's all going to be okay? Tell him that I'll help him destroy the crown, that I'll give him everything he wants? That I'll run away with him so we can hide from his mother and be alone and free together?

He wants us to just be ourselves because he doesn't have anything else. Unlike him, I have everything to lose. Priorities that must come before whatever I might want from him. He knows that. But we keep pushing each other away so intensely that we're only bringing ourselves closer together.

It's so easy when it's just us. When we're sitting here in the dark. But always, as soon as day comes, as soon as things become serious, the spell will be broken. The way we fight, the way we're on such different sides, even if he's supposedly willing to sacrifice what he wants for me. The versions of ourselves who argued while creating a compromise for Grace aren't the versions of ourselves we are right now. But which is real?

We lean back and spend the final hours of our last night huddled in each other's arms.

◆ ⊙ ˙ ⊘ ❤ ⊘ ˙ ⊙ ◆

The trip to Glassine will take four days, and there's no time to waste. The tension between the three of us has eased since getting Grace's blessing, but it has almost made things more unbearable, knowing we have all this weight to carry for each other.

Although it's on our way, Teddy says we shouldn't make a visit to Amora's Capital – probably because we'll waste too much time there. So we ride north-west instead, Sierra flying ahead to guide the way. Strangely, in the first couple of evenings before we sleep, our interactions are . . . pleasant.

On the third night, Sierra drops from the sky as the sun hits the horizon, and flips her hair back as she stretches out her human body. We camp by a small lake, the weather warm and sweet. Which means one thing: we have to swim.

Sierra strips off her shirt and pants and runs to the water first, black hair flying behind her as she dives in. I've never seen a genuine smile on her, and the sight of it is as shocking and beautiful as magic. Her eyes tilt up as she floats in the water, staring at the stars. She breathes slow, heavy breaths.

I leave my shoes with Pansy and follow Sierra into the shallows of the lake, soft sand between my toes. We laugh together, and out of all the things I've experienced since leaving Bearra, this is the most ridiculous. I'm not worried that she could turn around and drown me at any moment. I'm not worried about being vulnerable, letting her see me happy.

The water feels so good on my body, fresh and cold, washing away the last three days of grime. I duck my head under and let my hair fly around me. The bottom of the lake is visible even in the dim evening light, and small fish dance around my feet. Sierra catches a round jellyfish, then tosses it out towards the depths, laughing like a playful child.

I look to the shore. 'Teddy!' I shout. 'Get in!'

He raises his eyebrows. 'In *there*? No.'

Sierra's jaw drops, but her tone is teasing when she says, 'You can't swim?'

'I can! But you don't know what's in there. I'm not getting myself eaten by a fish when we're this close to getting the crown!'

I giggle. 'Come on!' I heap a lump of algae into my hand and toss it in his direction. He jumps back and cringes. '*Teddy*. Just dip your feet in.'

He kicks his shoes off, shaking his head. 'Fine.' At first he only stands in the shallows, but as the night gets darker, Teddy ventures further into the water.

When he's finally reached us, Sierra and I are floating, telling each other stories. About her sailing the rivers of

Grace's Territory, learning to swim and to fight. About my sisters and I splashing each other on hot days in Bearra's canals.

Sierra teaches us her methods of treading water and of diving. She shows us how long she can hold her breath underwater. She catches fish with her bare hands and tosses them onto the shore so we can eat them later. 'The skills you learn as a swan,' she says with a grin.

Clouds come in quickly, despairingly, covering the light of the moon, and we sigh as we realise it's time to get out of the water. We start swimming to the shore when Teddy stops us. 'Let me try something,' he says.

His hands begin to glow lilac, the light and colour spreading through the lake. The magic reflects through the water, highlighting every swish, every wave. Soon the tendrils of power are touching our feet, warming the water and gleaming off our wet skin. When Teddy is done, *everything* is dusk-purple.

Rain pours over us, glowing as it falls from lavender clouds and scattering the sparkling water in stunning ripples and splashes. The three of us laugh in awe.

Teddy's face goes soft, staring at his hands as if he's experiencing his magic for the first time.

It's the most beautiful thing I've ever seen, and I know, when I see his smiling, lilac face, that this is *my* Teddy.

Sierra points behind us, her expression relaxed in her rare joy. 'Look,' she says, her voice loud over the rain.

I turn to see three black swans floating towards us, shaking their long necks and fluttering their wide wings in the rain, their dark coats reflecting the lilac glow. Four grey cygnets follow close behind. Their heads occasionally dive under the water and come back up with fish, making Sierra laugh.

I take a few deep breaths as I tread the water, watching the moment unfold. I swim to Teddy and hold his hands under the water, letting his magic encase my arms and wrists. It tingles pleasantly. He smiles at me, his wet hair stuck in a funny way to his forehead, his eyelashes dripping over his eyes. My boy is a summer night, and I think I might love him.

He moves us so he's standing up in the water, and he wraps his big arms around me. I rest my head on his bare chest and he leans down to kiss my hair. We watch Sierra, but my mind isn't thinking about her, or the magic, or the rain. Just him.

Just us.

The feeling of being in Amora's Territory is physical, the ring on my finger pounding as it begs me to give in and give him my world.

I hope the rain covers the tears on my cheeks.

Sierra waves at me, and my chest fills with warmth. In these few days we've had, I've finally been able to really know her, and now I don't see a killer I hate – I see a woman who has fought tirelessly to protect her world while getting nothing in return. We both grew up in the water, we both have sisters, we both want our families' approval.

I think she's my ... friend? Yes, she could kill me, and she's wanted to, and she might want to again. But doesn't that make our care for each other even more special? I know what it's like to hate her and be hated by her, and this is something new.

By the time we go to sleep, I know without a doubt that I love her and Teddy with parts of my heart and soul that, a century ago, did not exist.

+ ₊ ° ꙴ 🗘 ꙴ ° ₊ +

That night, in my dreams, I'm in a forest. It's just like Muse's Territory in the night, the trees close-together and sprawling, with multicoloured blossoms that sparkle under the stars. Except, apart from the low humming of a red-haired girl I don't recognise, it's entirely silent. In this place, I feel at peace.

'You're fascinating.' The girl appears my age, but she's grey and lifeless. Her face is round, doll-like, and her eyes seem kind. She would be pretty if she wasn't so ghost-like. 'I was right to find you, to see who you really are.'

'Who are *you*?' I ask her. In the dream, my voice is lighter, and I move slowly, as if through water. When I glance at my hands, they're translucent.

She ignores my question, looking me up and down. 'The princess always dreams about the fairy's son, and he always dreams about you. *Maya, Maya, Maya*. You might just save us all, Maya.'

'What do you mean?'

'Don't trust Lire,' she whispers. 'The worst is still to come, and this war is so much bigger than you. I'll be watching over the princess, but there is only so much I can do.'

'But who are—'

I jump awake, shuddering, and I don't quite remember the dream except for a flash of red hair. Feeling violated, I curl into Teddy's arms until I'm warm again.

CHAPTER
TWENTY-EIGHT

GLASSINE IS QUIET AND covered in the soft-pink haze of Amora's Territory, but the sprawl of grey gravestones echoes with gloom. It's dusk as we reach my grandmother's marble mausoleum. Teddy and I meet eyes. In the light of golden hour, there is something final hanging in the air between us.

An, *I could have loved you, and we could have loved each other, if not for this world.*

I feel as if I'm not entirely in my body. I'm certainly not happy, like I thought I would be. My eyes are blurry and my palms are damp. The grave is right here, the small building wrapped with thick vines and gemstones.

The magic is so strong it's like wind, a physical thing surrounding me, pushing, pulling, pulsing.

The black swan, sitting in the grass with her neck craned and wings flexed, flashes blue and turns into Sierra. She winks at me as she runs her fingers through her hair and stretches her arms, yawning. 'Stop looking so scared, grandmother. All your dreams are about to come true.'

When the three of us are separated, I won't miss the jokes about how old I am, but I'll miss Teddy and Sierra. For now, we are linked. We cannot do this without each other. I have blessings from Amora, Rhiannon, and Kara. Teddy has Muse's blessing, as well as Lire's magic. Sierra has blessings from Rhiannon and Grace. We have all the power we need to do this.

I wring my hands. 'I'm ready.'

We step towards the grave, into the hurricane of magic.

'*Olivia Shy.*' Sierra squints at the faded, vine-covered engraving of my grandmother's name. 'Were you close with her?'

'No,' I say. The ebb and flow of our magic and the grave's is so strong it nearly trips me over, like I'm drifting through a river rather than walking on grass. 'And I'm glad I wasn't, or stealing from her would be incredibly upsetting.'

Teddy takes a breath. 'Family is complicated. There's give and take, and—'

'And sometimes a lot more take,' Sierra finishes.

We reach the mausoleum door and I'm suddenly sweating all over, my heart pounding. I've travelled the world and made it back here. I've *won*. I will be back with my family, successful, so impossibly soon. So why am I scared?

Teddy looks nervous, with his brows creased and his bottom lip twitching. Sierra only looks determined, maybe even hopeful.

Teddy slashes through the vines with swords of lilac magic. When they immediately try to regrow, Sierra and I hold our hands up against them, both our Strength blessings enough to cut off their magic – at least around the entrance. We grin at each other as Teddy uses more magic to push open the heavy marble door.

He goes in first; I don't need to prove myself by stepping into danger like that, even if I want to be the first to get my hands on our prize. But before I can follow, waves of magic in every colour shine out of the doorway. The rainbow is blinding and palpable, forcing the hairs on my arms to stand on end. Sierra and I race back, giving each other a worried glance. But after a moment, we put on braver faces and step into the magic anyway. Like the shield around Kara's Capital, the magic begins to bend around us, but there's far more force.

The rings on my fingers glow and I feel their power in my body and mind, working and changing, helping me get through the wards. Passion to remind me why I'm here. Strength to help me be brave. Darkness to remind me it's okay to let go. With each step I am a better version of myself, until I'm the Maya I need to be to get my treasure.

The wards falter under my blessings and I slip through the doorway. Inside, Teddy is using his own magic to shield himself. The rainbow of wards slowly fades, making the world seem unnaturally undersaturated. Still, the magic left over is enough to keep the room bright.

Sierra follows me, and her eyes widen as she takes in the room. She places a hand on my forearm, and I'm not sure whether she's trying to reassure me or herself.

I run my fingers across a shelf that's miraculously spotless; there isn't a drop of dust anywhere. The coffin rests at the back of the mausoleum, tucked into the corner like a bed in a child's bedroom. The rest of the room is full of *things*. My grandmother must have brought all the expensive material goods she collected over the years. There is so much magic in here, shimmering from enchanted objects. Stacks of jewels, plates and teacups of fine porcelain, paintings and sculptures, all of it in piles around us. No wonder she made sure the grave was protected with all this magic. Even without the crown, there would be enough riches in here for a lifetime.

Or an afterlife.

'It's . . .' I start, but I'm speechless.

The rainbow of power we came through still emanates faintly from an object on a high shelf above where my grandmother's head must lay. *The crown*. Teddy and Sierra watch it with matching awe.

It's blue – made entirely from triarue – with gold and silver lining the edges and creating swirling patterns across its scope. There are other gems inlaid into the shape; rubies, emeralds, amethysts. In fact, there are gems to match every fairy. Each one is dark, beautiful, full of magic. The crown must be the purest piece of triarue I've ever seen, and maybe the biggest piece to ever be found, carved into tiered and pointed sections. I can't help but picture it atop my head, and can't help but picture it giving me everything I've ever wanted.

Sierra laughs gleefully and reaches for it, but Teddy uses magic to pull her back. She spins in outrage. '*Don't—*'

'Just wait a moment,' he says, eyeing it warily. 'What if it's a trap? What if we grab the crown and the floor opens to a pit full of knives?'

Sierra turns to me, disbelief sharpening her features. 'Would your grandmother do that?'

'She was certainly capable.' I glance around the room with hair-raising suspicion. 'Still is.'

'Just let me try first,' Teddy says. He wraps a layer of purple magic around his hands, and the magic of his blessings glow dimly within it, like tea seeping into water. With a nervous look, he reaches to the blue crown and places a hand on either side of it. He picks it up slowly, as if it's heavy, and—

'Ah!' He drops it onto the stone floor with a clang. Sparks fly as the crown screeches across the ground and halts at my feet.

'What happened?' I jump backwards, then forget my fear and step back towards it when I realise the crown is almost in *my* hands.

'Not knives,' Sierra says. She crosses her arms and peers down at the crown. 'But another layer of protection?'

Teddy nods, nursing his hands. 'It got heavy, then it burned me. Like it'd been dipped in boiling water. Even with my magic I couldn't hold on. It's protecting itself.'

'From what?' I ask.

He shrugs. 'From being stolen again? This thing is old magic, older than even the fairies, according to some legends. If it doesn't want to be taken . . .'

Sierra stares at it. 'Maya's grandmother managed to take it and bury it in here. If someone on their deathbed can steal it, I'm sure we can.'

'We need to take it together,' I say, before my idea has even fully formed. 'That's what all the blessings are for. It won't work if it's only one of us. The wards my grandmother made must be powerful enough to stop *anyone* else taking it. She was smart; she would have used the power any way she could. But between the three of us, we can get it out of the grave and break the wards. Then it'll be ours.'

'Are you sure?' Teddy asks, his face alight in the multi-coloured aura of magic swirling around us. 'Because I don't want to get burned again.'

'Of course I'm not sure. My grandmother can't have had blessings or magic when she took it. They're our advantage. The more magic we use against all the wards my grandmother made, the better.'

'Thank the fairies you two have me,' Sierra says, hands on her hips. 'You're far too weak to do this alone.'

'*Sierra*,' I warn. 'Let's all take a side, both hands, and lift together.'

Teddy wraps his hands with magic again, and spreads the lilac shield to Sierra and me. It fits over my hands like a protective glove, though I can feel the cold crystal of the crown as I edge my fingers under it.

When we all seem to have a firm grip, I say, 'Now,' and it lifts so lightly that for a moment I think we'll lose our grip and it'll fly away.

'Gentle!' Sierra screeches. 'Now, outside. *Slowly.*'

We shuffle out of the mausoleum, into the blueish dusk and away from the aurora of power. As soon as the crown is out, all the magic seems to dissipate at once. The weight is suddenly lifted, and it's like I can breathe again. The light, the rainbows, everything in the mausoleum goes dark. Finally the dead can rest.

I begin to laugh, and within seconds Sierra is joining in, both our hands still on the crown as if frozen.

'Wait a second,' Teddy says, his expression serious. 'Can you let go for a moment? I want to see something. Before we take it away. Just to make sure it's safe.'

I nod and let go without thinking.

Sierra narrows her eyes, her hands still on it. 'What are you going to do?'

'You still don't trust me?' he says, pulling it towards himself. 'Do you think we're both going to hold it all the way back to Grace's Territory?'

'Maybe,' she says, but then she seems to think better of the idea and lets go. Still, she keeps a suspicious eye on him.

It's ridiculous to not trust him now, but I don't like seeing the crown only in his hands. Why did I give it to him so easily?

My heart grows cold. That's my crown. *My* crown in *his* hands.

'*Teddy*,' I say. 'What are you doing?'

Something is wrong. Am I only being selfish, distrustful, paranoid? Why does my heart suddenly feel so cold?

He inhales sharply as he stares at each jewel, every turret of blue, every line of gold and silver. When he looks up, his eyes are glassy with tears. With *devastation*. His cheeks are red and he looks at me with guilt, with heartbreak as he starts backing away from me. 'Maya.'

I shake my head, and I don't know why I argue, because I already know what's going to happen; maybe I always did. 'Teddy. Don't. Don't even start with this. Y-You promised.' I step forward and place a hand back on the crown, a shiver crawling along my spine.

Magic sends me flying and I hit the ground with a painful thud. I scream as my shoulder scrapes the side of a gravestone. 'Teddy!'

His breaths come fast and his foot taps the grass. 'I'm so sorry,' he says, unable to meet my eyes. 'Maya, I didn't mean to do that!'

Sierra steps in front of me. 'You can't betray us,' she warns. 'You can't. Grace said—'

'Sierra,' he says, his expression haunted, 'I have spent my entire life lying to fairies. I was never going to let the crown fall into the wrong hands.' He cradles it, holding it back from her.

'*Teddy*!' I shout again. I'm dizzy from the shock, unable to get up, and my vision is swimming. 'We have a-a plan! A *deal*! What are you— What are you doing?' I want to tell him that he can't do this – he can't do this to me because – because – because, *fairies,* I love him. But the words get stuck in my throat.

Tears fall down his cheeks. 'You are everything to me, Maya, but I have to destroy it. If my mother gets hold of this, you don't know what she'll do.' He trembles over his breaths, his head shaking quickly. 'I'm so sorry. I thought you would have changed your mind by now. I didn't think I'd have to do this.'

Sierra tries to jump at him, but he uses magic to hold her back. She shrieks as lilac wraps around her forearms, lifting her hands above her head. Her eyes are wide with fear, tears pricking at the corners. 'I'll go!' she shouts. 'Don't hurt me again! *Please.*'

He looks almost confused. 'I'm not going to hurt you.'

She silently gestures to the magic surrounding her.

'No. You know that I didn't mean— You know I wouldn't do that again. I only want to help you.' His fingers grip the crown until they're red, and its magic begins radiating out of it, mixing with his own. He's using it, *calling* on it.

'Stop it!' I try to shout, but my voice is so fragile. I feel like I've been kicked in the stomach, the pain of what he's doing boring into my core. My throat is raw from sobs. 'Don't touch her!'

Sierra tries to struggle, but the magic is too strong. She's barely able to move. Rainbows flow from the crown in Teddy's hands and out towards her. While she thrashes uselessly, Teddy closes his eyes to concentrate.

The colours of all the fairies' magic wrap around Sierra completely, encasing her with magic. I can't see her, but a blue light shines through.

Her curse. Grace's magic. He's breaking the curse?

I try to stand again, to go to her, but I slump back to my knees, my hands smacking the grass. Did I hit my head?

When the magic subsides, Sierra's face is broken with tears, all her usual nonchalance eradicated.

'What did you do . . .' Her voice is raspy, and her eyes blink slowly. I crawl to her. She takes my hand and the magic is still pulsing around her. It hurts my fingers where it meets my rings.

'I *helped* you,' Teddy says. His eyes are wide, pleading. 'I used the crown's magic to help you. I only ever wanted to help you both.'

My body heaves. 'Don't you dare act like you're helping anyone but yourself! You do *not* get to do that!'

'Don't I?' His jaw hardens with frustration. 'You two want this magic for yourselves. I'm taking it to save *everyone*. To stop people like you getting hurt. Magic is a danger, and this crown provides enough of it that whoever has it could destroy the world. Do you still not understand that?'

I don't get to answer, because suddenly Sierra's hand falls out of my grip and her body tremors. With a flash, she's the black swan. The bird's wings flap in fright for a few seconds, her beak opening in piercing squawks before she turns human again just as fast.

I jump back, afraid she's going to transform again and hit me with a wing.

Sierra sits with her long legs sprawled on the ground, panting. She sneers at Teddy. 'You changed the curse!'

He holds the crown to his stomach the way a child might hold a doll. 'Now you can transform at will. Never be the swan again if you don't want to. Without your sisters here, I can't *break* the curse, but I can give you this much.'

'Why would you do anything for me?' She hits the ground with a fist.

'Because I want you to get what you want,' he says. 'You can find your pirate, make him fix the curse himself.'

'Are you insane?' Sierra says. 'We could be at Grace's Territory within days. You can destroy the crown after the curse is broken, like we *agreed*.'

'I can't take that risk.' He takes a few more steps back from us.

I want to step forward and grab him, kiss him, get him to change his mind, pretend this never happened. Equally, I want to strangle him.

'I can't wait for you,' he says. 'Now that the crown is back in the open, it has to be destroyed. My mother is already looking for me. She'll know by now I've been collecting blessings.

She'll guess I'm up to something, and when she finds me, I won't be able to prevent her taking the crown. I have to stop her and my brother – I have to help Princess Dawn, and all of Bearra. All of the *world*. Including the both of you.'

The sky darkens with each passing moment, and Amora's pink haze eats at the ground, circling our feet. The grave-stones sparkle between the magic and the moonlight. I want to hide away in the shadows, break down into sobs.

'You used us,' I say breathlessly, still trying to catch my mind and heart up to this unfolding nightmare. 'You used our desperation to get the crown. This is all for you. It isn't to help people. It's just *you*. You, and your resentment of your mother.'

He steps toward me, and when I try to scramble away, a wall of magic gets in my way. My hands are held in front of me and I can't move. I scream and struggle to break free, and his face falls, but he doesn't stop.

'I know how much I've hurt you,' he whispers, his voice cracking and his long eyelashes wet with tears. 'But I have to do the right thing. I'm sorry.' He kneels in front of me, even as I screech at him, and takes each of my three rings from my fingers. 'I'm *sorry*.'

The blessings being ripped away feels like my hair being ripped from my skull or my nails being pulled from my fingers. My skin burns in the spaces left behind.

He puts them on his own hands. 'I can't leave them with you,' he says. 'I need all the power I can get to destroy the crown.'

I push myself to my knees and stare daggers at him. 'Why did you kiss me,' I whisper, tears dripping into my mouth. Because *that* is all I can think about. 'Why did you kiss me if you knew you would do this? If not to be cruel?'

His eyes meet the grass. 'Because . . .' He hesitates. 'Because my feelings for you are so strong that I nearly *didn't* do this,' he says. 'I stopped it. Don't you remember? I tried to not let anything more happen.'

It's all I can do not to throw my hands around his throat. 'I should have left you the moment I found out what you are,' I hiss, and from there it all tumbles out in a flash of venomous insults, as if I have no control over my speech. 'I should have run. I should have done this myself. I don't know why I would *ever* choose to trust you. You're not human. You act like it, but you aren't. You're *exactly* like your mother. All charm and nothing more.'

'*Maya*,' Teddy says, his chin trembling. He reaches for me, then drops his hands. 'If you return to Bearra, I'll meet you there as soon as the crown is destroyed. I swear I'll give you anything – everything – you want. I'll give your family all the money you can imagine. I'll be my mother's son. I'll be the prince. I'll go back to Bearra and face Lire just to be near you. I will give you the world, Maya. There is nothing more that I want. But please forgive me and let me do what I have to.'

I spit at his feet. 'If you do this, don't *ever* return to Bearra. You go away and get what you always wanted – to be as far from Lire as possible. *Coward*.'

'Enough,' Sierra says. 'I'm not sitting here listening to your divorce.' She slowly stands, body still shaking, and she puts herself between us. I try to reach for her, but she shrugs me off. 'You're right, Teddy, you've helped me. I have two blessings. I'm no longer bound by my curse. You have given me the ability to find my own way to save my family, and I thank you for it.'

My hands hit the floor as I fall. *She can't leave me too.* 'Sierra!' I sob. 'He b-betrayed us!'

'Shut *up*,' she says. 'Do you think we care about your stupid, petty struggles? You act like a child, Maya. You know nothing of the world, of the battles that Teddy and I face. You need to run back home to your parents and learn to grow up.'

My heart caves in as cries retch through my body. It's hardly the worst thing she's ever said to me, but it hurts the most.

'Don't talk to her like that,' Teddy says darkly. 'Just leave.'

She nods, fury all over her features. 'Again,' she says, 'thank you.' She reaches out to shake his hand, and an understanding look passes between them.

Teddy smiles hopefully. 'I owe you a favour,' he says. 'You helped me get the crown, and I know changing your curse isn't enough, and I know how badly I've hurt you. Sierra, one day, I'll make all of this up to you.' He shuffles the crown into one hand and reaches to her, wrapping his hand over hers.

She pulls him down so hard he falls over his own feet. She's on top of him before he can react with magic, and she kicks him hard in the head. Then she's beside me again, this time holding the crown.

'Move, Maya!' she shouts. Sierra helps me to my feet, and I feel the magic of the crown pulsing through me as she drags me along.

It strengthens me, and suddenly I feel awake again, my mind clear, which brings on fresh panic. *Fairies, fairies, fairies* – oh *no*.

Teddy struggles to get up, his eyes rolling around dazedly. His magic seeps out of his fingers towards us, but a blue force from the crown stops it in its path. A huge wall of rainbow manifests behind us, separating us from Teddy.

'Keep running!' Sierra shouts. I try to keep up with her, but I must be too slow, because she grabs me around the waist and pulls me into the air.

We're flying. She isn't a swan – she's using magic. *All* the crown's magic.

'What are you doing!' I shout over the harsh wind. My hair is blown back and my face burns. She doesn't reply. We don't slow until we're by the big tree we left the horses tied to. I pant as we land, tumbling across the grass as sobs push my chest up and down. '*Sierra*! What just happened?'

She uses her hand that isn't holding the crown to brush the tears from my cheeks. 'He lied to us,' she says harshly, but for once I appreciate her callousness. 'He used us. But it's okay. He should have known not to cross me.' She looks to the distance and lets out a villainous laugh. 'Fool.'

I inhale a shaky breath. 'But—'

'Stop,' Sierra says. 'Don't waste your time on him. I've been there. Men aren't worth it. Never believe *anyone* is worth more than your victory.' She gives me a firm expression, but I can still see the panic in her eyes. 'Tell me no one is worth it.'

'They . . . They . . .'

'They aren't worth it,' she presses. 'Promise me you won't ever trust him again.'

I nod, eyes wide, and my voice comes out as barely a whisper. 'He isn't worth it.'

'You'll be okay.' She pulls me over to the horses and unties Pansy, then helps me into the saddle. 'Maya. Ride home as fast as you can, okay? The crown will support you.'

I stare down at her. 'Wh-What about you?'

'Teddy did help me,' she says. 'I know what I have to do. But *you* need this.' She presses the crown into my arms. It's freezing. Pansy shivers as the magic brushes against her mane.

'You're just giving it to me?' I can't hide my shock. 'I don't want it, Sierra, you need it. Just take it.'

She shakes her head and quickly stares around us as if Teddy might be lurking in any shadow. 'That's the fear talking, Maya. You take your crown and get what you deserve. We can only hope Teddy ends up rotting.'

'Come with me,' I beg, gripping the reins tighter as Pansy nervously stomps. 'I don't want to be alone. Come to Bearra. *Please*. I'll give you some of the reward money. Or we'll go to your sisters first. Something . . .' I search desperately for a reason for us to stick together. After everything, I can't just leave her.

'Shut up,' she says. Am I imagining it, or are there tears welling in her eyes, too? 'We're both going to be okay. You're going to owe me a favour, alright? When you're rich and powerful in Bearra, you might be able to help me out someday. We're going to stay friends.'

'Allies,' I whisper, and somehow we both laugh lightly. 'Sierra, I owe you so much.'

'There's no time for this,' she says, cupping my hands. 'You need to go. The crown will protect you, but Teddy knows exactly where you're headed. He'll probably get there first. You need to secure your reward before he gets in your way.'

I nod, determination washing over me. 'I will. I'll make sure I get it. To spite him if nothing else.'

She smirks. 'There's the Maya I know.' She pats my leg. 'I'll see you again, I swear it. Next time, hopefully under nicer circumstances. We'll meet for tea, okay? No murdering or betraying.'

Before I can reply, she shifts into the swan, expands her wings, dips her long neck to me in a goodbye, and soars away. Within a few moments she's just a black speck in the dark sky, the moon glinting off her wings with each heavy beat. And I am all alone.

Alone. Without Teddy. Without Sierra. But I have the one thing I wanted.

I breathe in and out, fetch my compass from my satchel.

I'm going home. I'm going to save my family. This is my quest, and I have won.

Pansy jumps into a sprint and we race through the night.

CHAPTER
TWENTY-NINE

WITH THE MAGIC OF the crown, the ride back to Bearra – which should take at least four days – is cut in half. Power like this makes everything easy. Pansy is practically flying, and for those two days, we're little more than wind.

I reach Bearra's walls late at night, and it takes me almost no effort to break through the vines and sneak in, even with Pansy. Rhiannon's red magic pours from the crown and into the wall of vines, and once I'm past, they grow back as if no one ever went through. I take the horse straight to Aunt Olivia's stable – I made sure to enter the kingdom's edge where it touches her back garden – then I pull my satchel from Pansy's back. The crown is tucked deep inside, safe, so I tiptoe up to the house while avoiding any light from the street.

And I'm here, in Bearra. *Bearra.*

Even at night, the kingdom is a wonder. I can't see any water from here, but even from Olivia's house, tucked far from the centre of the kingdom, I can hear the sounds of the canals; ducks splashing, the current flowing. The air is warm but not damp, the houses are topped with terracotta roofs, and the plants are dry and brown. And oh, it *smells* like home. Above it all, the hilltop castle is alight with torches, watching over the kingdom and piercing the darkness.

I once resented this place so much – once thought it a prison – but now, back within Bearra's walls, I have never felt safer.

I sneak through Olivia's sprawling cactus garden, towards the eastern-facing wing of the house, careful not to get poked or scratched. There's a side entrance for servants, and the crown's magic unlocks the door before I even ask it to.

Using magic is perplexing. It listens like a living thing, but sometimes it listens too much, and other times I feel like I have to shout. But it always, eventually, does what I want – as long as it's within magic's limits. Wielding it feels like energy buzzing through me, like ideas forming within my soul until they burst out with a flash of light. I can understand why some fear this kind of power, why some steal it, and why some would go to war for it.

I suspect Teddy is already here, waiting at the palace, watching my house, ready to attack and steal back what he believes is his. That's why I've come to Aunt Olivia's house instead of my own. She'll keep me safe here. For a while, at least. We'll figure out what to do.

Teddy and Sierra aren't my concern anymore. I've spent two days getting them out of my mind, preparing for what I'll do when I get home, and it's time to move on. I have officially repressed them from even the furthest reaches of my brain, and I will not let them back in. I don't have the capacity to care about them. Not until this is all over and I can be sure my family is safe.

I push open the heavy side door to Olivia's house and barely get a few steps in before I screech. A servant stands in front of me, a single flickering candle in her hand, and her eyes expand. She opens her mouth to scream.

'Shh!' I hiss, and without meaning to, I wrap a cage of magic around her head to block the scream. The sound reverberates through the magic and into my body, but it doesn't leave the room. The servant drops to the floor in fright and the candle blows out.

She's fainted. Which, actually, might be a good thing. I have to find my aunt, and I don't need her staff getting in the way.

'Sorry,' I whisper sheepishly as I skirt around her flailed limbs. I creep up the stairs with my satchel clutched to my side. It takes a few rooms – this house is *so* big, and the doors are indistinguishable with their matching gold handles – before I find Olivia's. When I do, I almost reel in shock. Asleep, even in the dark, she looks so much like my mother. The mother I haven't seen in weeks.

I could break down into tears right here, but I don't.

'Olivia,' I whisper. 'Aunt Olivia?'

She slowly wakes as I step into the room. Then her eyes snap open and she jumps up with a yelp as she realises it's me, her estranged niece, filthy and bruised in her bedroom. Aunt Olivia clamps her gaping mouth shut, shuffles into a sitting position on her four-poster bed, and motions for me to close the door.

'I didn't mean to scare you,' I stammer. I'm not sure why I expected a warm welcome or congratulations. I suddenly feel awkward standing in my aunt's room in the dark. 'I'm back. From getting the crown.'

'Yes, your mother told me you went,' she says, and as she relaxes, a small smile plays on her lips. 'She and I reconnected after you left. I'm sorry your mission didn't work out, my dear, but I'm glad to see you home safe.'

I frown. 'It did work out. I have the crown right here.'

She leans forward. '*Excuse me?*'

'I got it. Had to travel the whole world to do it, but—' I grin '—I used your compass to find my way home.'

'Maya!' She leaps out of bed, surprising me as she races over to pull me into a hug. 'Really? I am so proud of you! Most Bearrans wouldn't have survived a day out there, and you travelled the *world*? Is magic really everywhere, in the hands of regular people? And you – you – how did you survive it all?'

I lead her back to the bed and slump onto the silky sheets. 'I'll tell you everything soon,' I say. 'But first, can you bring my family here so we can all talk together?' I pull my dirty feet up onto her cushions, and she cringes, but I'm too exhausted to care about manners. 'Oh, and your servant is unconscious on the floor downstairs.'

+ ⊹ ⋆ ◍ ♡ ◍ ⋆ ⊹ +

Olivia keeps me hidden in her study in case Teddy is having my relatives watched. My entire body aches to run through the halls and to the front door, but I sit on my feet and try to be patient.

The study is a nice enough place to wait. Anything with a roof is nice after my last two days travelling without shelter. There are leather couches that sink me into their cushioned depths, a beautiful white desk covered with quills and ink, and most importantly, not a single window, which eases my nerves about Teddy jumping out of the shadows.

The moment I hear my family's footsteps shuffling down the hallway, however, all my patience disappears and my concerns are forgotten. I burst out of my chair and race to the door, flinging myself into the arms of the first person who steps through.

Briar. She's cut her hair shorter, and she seems thinner. I close my eyes and bury my head into her shoulder. After a lifetime sharing a bedroom with my older sister, it's been so difficult to be without her. Immediately I feel at ease.

Mum and Dad pull me out of her arms and into their own, and we stand there for a while just holding each other. I embrace everything about them. The shapes of their hands, the smell of their clothes, the softness of their hair, the way they breathe – Dad in slow, heavy breaths, and Mum in short, sharp ones. They hold me so tight that for a while I'm not sure I'll ever escape, ever breathe again. I'm not sure I want to.

Once they finally let go, Prima gives me a funny smile. '*Maya,*' she says, a teasing lilt in her voice. 'We were having such a quiet few weeks.' I throw myself over her, wrapping my arms around my eldest sister's shoulders even though she's taller than me. We laugh incredulously. 'I'm sorry,' she whispers, gripping me tighter. 'I'm sorry I didn't believe in you.'

I pull back and meet her eyes. 'I'm sorry I acted so childish. Even though I was right.'

She smirks and ruffles my hair. 'That's my sister.'

'Now,' my father says. He looks so tattered, his hair thinned and his eyes circled with purple; he immediately lowers himself into a seat. They all look so sickly, so tired. Is it because of me, or has their financial situation worsened in just the past few weeks? My father must see me worrying, because he reaches over and places a hand on my wrist. 'We have a lot of talking to do.'

'We do.' I sit beside him, my mother on my other side. As close to everyone as I can be. I don't let go of their hands. 'I have the crown, and we need to figure out how I'm going to give it to the royals without getting us all in trouble.'

'Yes, yes,' Mum says, leaning forward and examining my face. 'We can deal with that later. We want to know what happened to you! Where have you been this entire time? What's it like out there? Did you make any friends?'

I sigh. 'It's all so complicated.' I ready myself to launch into the story, just how I rehearsed it over my days riding home, but I don't make it that far. Dad squeezes my hands, and I break into sobs.

♦ ❀ ◊ ♡ ◊ ❀ ♦

When I've finished telling them everything and managed to stop crying, they each have a turn admiring the crown. Then we sit in stunned silence. Olivia and my mother keep meeting eyes, and I don't understand the communication passing between them. I suddenly feel like I've aged backwards ten years. Outside, on my own, I had to be self-sufficient and strong. My parents weren't there to hold my hand. Now here they are, and the feeling of always being the youngest in the room floods back.

With the shock of a punch to the face, I realise that my goal to keep my family together, to never truly grow up, is far from what I want now. Why did I so strongly resist stepping forward? Outside, everything was so different that I didn't notice how much I changed. But back in Bearra, with my family staring at me, I don't recognise myself.

As thrilled as I am to be back with them, I don't like the way I feel like such a child around them. I'm ready to live my own life – still with them close by, but as my own person.

Briar leans back in her chair. 'I'm going to kill this Teddy boy.' She strangles the air with her hands. 'Violently.'

'And what about Sierra, the swan girl?' Prima asks, leaning forward. Her sharp features soften with curiosity. 'Did she ever make it home?'

'I . . . I don't know,' I say. 'Sierra has survived a lot, so I don't doubt that she's fine.' It doesn't make sense for Teddy and Sierra to exist here, in my old life. I can't quite put it all together. I don't know how to talk about them as if they're real people. Not just as characters in the story of my adventure – which my sisters find very entertaining – but as real, flawed humans. Friends.

Olivia claps her hands together. 'Alright. Enough storytelling. We must get the crown to Lire as soon as possible – before this Teddy boy does something to sabotage you again. It's time to make a plan.'

This Teddy boy. I suppose that is all he is. All that talk about being ourselves together . . . it was nonsense. All he really is, all he ever was, when it comes down to it, is a boy. And *maybe* the son of a fairy, *maybe* the enemy. Or *maybe* he's just doing what's right, while I'm the villain.

Does it really matter?

Fairies. Of course it does.

I run my fingers through my hair, detangling the knots from my hurricane-speed travel. 'Teddy could already be here, and if he is, he might have told his mother about me. He could've said anything. The most important thing is we make it seem like I just happened upon the crown. But we need to make it believable, or they'll know I escaped Bearra. Worse, they'll know the entire family is involved and we'll all be in trouble.'

Aunt Olivia rubs her temples. Her candlelit study is dim, and with all of us here, she hardly looks at home. This is a very different woman to the cold aunt I met a few weeks ago. 'I can organise an audience with the royal family,' she says. 'I'll make sure they know it's urgent, but with our royals . . .'

'They're useless,' I finish. 'You could ask to speak to Princess Dawn. Teddy knew her. He said she's a lot smarter than her parents. She'd have to be, with all her blessings. And I'm sure she wants to know as well as anyone where her family's crown is.'

Olivia nods. 'I'll do what I can. Though I'm still not sure how we can stage this to make us look innocent.'

'Can we put the blame on someone else?' Briar says, and we all turn to her in shock. 'I don't know! You could tell them Teddy kidnapped you and made you go with him to get the crown. Hopefully he'll get in real trouble, and—'

'No one would ever believe me over Teddy.' I picture him in a crown of his own, posing as a prince. Even if I borrowed a nice dress from Olivia, I'd look like a peasant next to him.

'So you need to have found the crown hidden away in Bearra,' Dad says, 'but not so deeply hidden away that it's unrealistic for you to have found it.'

'The mines?' Prima suggests.

'I'd have no reason to be there,' I say. 'What if I stumbled upon something while out delivering books?'

'No,' Mum says. 'No one has seen you in weeks. We told anyone who asked that you were bedridden with the flu. If the royals ask around, they'll know you lied.'

'People asked about me?' My heart swells.

'Mostly the children,' Dad says, his eyes creasing as he smiles. 'They wanted more books. One concerned mother came around and dropped you off a lovely apple pie. You really enjoyed it.'

'I bet I did.' I only give myself time to enjoy a short laugh. 'So how, if I've been bedridden for weeks, did I happen to find a crown the royal family has been seeking for longer than I've been alive? And if Teddy shows up to dispute my story, or worse, make up an even more damning one, what am I going to do?'

Briar slouches, rubbing her eyes. 'Shall we decide in the morning? Otherwise none of us will be of any use tomorrow, when it really counts.'

'Yes - yes, of course.' I'm hit with the sudden feeling that I'm burdening them, having them here to help me. Why did I just assume they would drop everything and stay up all night for me? They have enough of their own problems to deal with. 'Go home and try to come back here first thing tomorrow.

It's too dangerous for me to come home yet. But make my bed for me, okay? Or don't. After tomorrow, we'll be moving into a mansion so big you can't even imagine it.' A smile tugs at the corners of my mouth. 'In fact, start packing.'

Chapter Thirty

We reach the castle with perfect timing, the sun bright and the kingdom loud; it's a perfect Bearran day. We took Olivia's carriage so we wouldn't have to walk up the hill to the castle and be completely dishevelled and sweaty by the time we arrived.

It's mid-afternoon – the earliest Aunt Olivia could get us a meeting with the royals. Now, she and my mother escort me up the stairs and into the castle's main chamber, which is bustling with guards, servants, and finely-dressed aristocrats. Some try to say hello, but we don't let ourselves get distracted for even a second. We keep our plan in mind with every step, knowing the dire consequences of any slight mistake.

I've only visited the castle a handful of times, but its grandeur never fails to put a bad taste in my mouth. I can't look at all the decorative triarue and gold, the huge paintings and harsh sculptures, without thinking about how, while the royal family were still living this way a year ago, hoarding all this wealth, the rest of us were starving in a dead kingdom. It gives me a petty kind of pleasure that this castle is hardly as spectacular as others I've now seen.

I pull at the hem of my nicest dress, which I've always hated. The loose yellow lace never suited me, and it's utterly old fashioned compared to what I wore outside Bearra. I tightened it with an old white corset of Briar's to give me some shape, but I still feel like an ancient version of myself. I don't want to look like a child – I want to look as powerful as I am.

The crown is tucked into my satchel, which is gripped in my hand. Though I'm sure the fairy will sense it immediately and take it from me, I feel the need to protect it with my life.

But I am no longer afraid. I have spent years waiting for this moment, waiting to *win*. A familiar crimson ball of fiery anger and determination roils in my core. This fury is mine, it has been for a long time, and today is the day my bitterness and misery become worth all the energy they've taken from me. I do not forgive, I do not forget, and I will not be a victim any longer.

Mum reaches out and squeezes my hand. She's wearing her hair in a tight but elegant braid, her brown dress touching her feet. A smile is pasted on her red-painted lips. This is the version of my mother I never met, the heiress who left her riches behind to marry my father.

Ahead of us, Olivia struts along the stone hallways with pure confidence, her scarlet dress scandalously colourful in the old, dim castle. People gawk as we pass them, taking the three of us in, their judgements clear on their faces. Olivia's gaze doesn't waver. She doesn't care if people stare.

Meanwhile, I'm using most of my energy trying not to scowl at each one of them.

The crown's magic grows impatient with every step through the castle, glimmering and glowing even past the leather of my satchel as it responds to the mines of triarue beneath us, the fairy we're headed towards, and the rulers who should be holding it in their possession. This crown may not be for wearing, but this kingdom needs it all the same. It represents hundreds of years of Bearra's culture and blood.

For the first time, I wonder if my grandmother took the crown for a reason – if she knew Lire's intentions were always wicked. What if she was more than just a selfish socialite? Now I'll never know.

It doesn't matter. None of it does. My reward is so close in sight. I lift my chin and grip my satchel tighter, letting the magic tingle across my fingertips.

The birch doors of the throne room extend high above us, covered in elaborate carvings of flowers and adorned with triarue handles. As we approach, a guard clears his throat. 'This way, ladies. Do not forget to bow.'

He throws open the doors and light floods my eyes, momentarily blinding me as I adjust. The windows are massive, travelling from the shiny marble floors to the high, painted ceilings. The walls are full of stunning artwork, and the floors are lined with statues, as if this is a gallery more than a throne room. The harsh sunlight that streams through the windows highlights the two triarue-embedded thrones at the end of the long room. The place is a masterpiece, and I have to force myself to look ahead to the royals instead of ogling until I'm lost forever.

The three of us are outnumbered. Guards line the walls, shields and swords at their sides. The queen and king are each seated on a throne, and Lire stands behind them, her tall lilac wings fluttering delicately. Princess Dawn and Prince Jacob are seated on smaller chairs below, to the left.

And to the right, standing with his arms clasped tightly in front of him and a pained look on his round face, is Teddy. He's wearing the tailored, expensive clothes of a royal. His hair has been cut since I last saw him, and his eyes, even from here, appear bloodshot. I hold back a gasp as I take him in, and I don't know whether I want to run at him to hold him or hit him. He stands in a shadow, and I've never seen him look more out of place.

My heart begins racing and something pulls in my gut. *Stop*, I think. *Remember who he really is.*

I follow Olivia's lead as she ambles up to the royals and offers a deep bow with perfect posture. My mother and I do our best to copy her. Bent down, I catch a glimpse of my hand, white from clutching my satchel so tightly.

When I rise, I do everything I can to avoid Teddy's eyes. Everything I do or say could be damning. Who knows what he's already told them? What he might tell them? Even if he says nothing, it wouldn't be difficult to add up that we both disappeared at the same time – especially now that the crown has mysteriously appeared. They'll know I ran away with him. They'll kill my entire family as an example, then officially crown Prince Jacob, and Lire's power will be secured.

Fairies. *Fairies.*

I can tell from looking at Prince Jacob now that he's Lire's son. He in no way resembles Teddy, and Teddy doesn't look anything like Lire. Jacob, however, has her pale colouring, and the same sinister look hidden behind his flat eyes.

The king watches us, his eyes half-lidded with exhaustion. 'We have been told you have our crown,' he says, his voice deep and accusatory. His skin is a few shades darker than his daughter, Dawn's. He must be from the north-west regions of the world, once a prince of a long-gone kingdom now absorbed into Adella's Territory. Does he mourn it, knowing he can never go back? Or is he happy to have the power of being married into Bearran royalty?

Olivia nods politely. 'Yes, my niece found the crown, and we have brought it to you so it can be placed back into the hands of its rightful owners. She has been searching for it in secret, the clever girl. Not just so she could restore the crown to our beloved royal family and help bring Bearra back from the brink, but to save her poor family with the grace of whichever reward you see fit for its return.'

This was the story we settled on. We wanted to stay close to the truth, despite fearing the trouble it may land us in.

The greater our lies are, the more easily Lire will be able to see right through them.

I catch Teddy watching me as if he's trying not to roll his eyes. *I'm* trying not to hit him in the face, so I suppose we're even.

Lire's brows crease, her lilac wings flattening against her back. Her light hair is loose and soft, and her dress is almost white, with just a touch of lavender. Purple flowers are embroidered into the sleeves and across the hem. 'May I ask how a young girl with no means and no information found a crown we have been seeking for many years?'

To avoid her question, I fish the crown out of my bag. The blue crystal is heavy, especially with the magic echoing off it and around us. Its rainbow glow seeps out, hitting the sunbeams and making the entire throne room shimmer. The queen and king rise to get a better look, their mouths hanging open.

Lire flutters over to me and snatches the crown from my hands. 'Let me see this.' She inspects it closely. 'Before you get any kind of reward, we must ensure it is real.'

'But, Lire,' the queen says, 'clearly it is. Look at the magic! Look at the depth of the triarue's blue!'

Prince Jacob stands beside his mother and runs a finger across one of the crown's jewelled peaks. His gaze is ravenous. The rainbows around it mirror in his light eyes. Sparks of lilac magic come off his fingers as they touch the triarue. 'It's real,' he says. 'It's . . . *real*.'

Cacophony erupts as everyone leaves their places to circle Lire; even the guards close in cautiously. My nerve falters as the crown nearly leaves my sight. I restlessly massage the places on my fingers where my rings were.

The queen pats my hands enthusiastically. Her eyes meet mine with a bright, genuine gratitude. 'Thank you. *Thank you.* You have brought to us a treasure we thought we might never see again. You may have saved Bearra. Anything you want, girl, tell me and it is yours.'

'Hm,' Teddy mutters from just outside the circle, Dawn standing behind his shoulder. All eyes turn to him. His silhouette is lined with lilac, as if the light slightly misses him. Is he protecting himself in some way? 'First, why don't you tell us where you found it, *girl?*'

I try to keep all recognition from my face as I meet his eyes, but surely my hatred of him is obvious. 'The crown was hidden away in a library that was abandoned after Bearra woke. Someone had buried it deep within their holdings, amongst many other enchanted artefacts that masked its powerful presence. I found it only because I was looking for a rumoured enchanted mirror. I heard the collector might have it, but suddenly the crown was in my hands, and I could not deny what it truly was.' I smile at him in mock sweetness. 'I was overjoyed to know I could return this object to the royal bloodline of Bearra. And,' I add quickly, 'be able to ask the queen and king to help my family in return.'

'Of course you will have your reward,' Dawn says. Her voice is deeper than I expected, than I've known. There are dark circles under her hazel eyes. She and Teddy are a matching set of perfect people turned hollow. 'You've brought us the power that will allow my future husband and I to truly rule our kingdom.' She glances at Jacob, and I almost catch a sense of fear in her eyes.

Guilt kicks me in the stomach – and it's more bruising than any blow of Sierra's. The tension in the room rises. Too much power, too many people who can get hurt. It's as if a hundred knives are floating above us and with one wrong move, one breath out of place, they'll fall.

Above me, a painting on the ceiling depicts Lire crawling from the earth, her wings extended as she carries the crown to Bearra's first queen and king. Centuries have led to this moment, to me with the crown, to handing Lire a weapon – yes, in her hands, a weapon – that will give her all she wants. Jacob will be king, Lire will rule Bearra, and together their power will be unmatched. Dawn will be stuck by their side, forever a helpless pawn forced to smile as they take apart her kingdom.

Oh, *fairies*. My breaths quicken. Have I made the wrong choice? Am I a terrible person for sealing the princess's miserable fate?

I turn to my mother and see the gaunt face beneath her red lipstick. She offers a small smile in return. I clench my fists and remember that even if doing this means hurting Dawn, and maybe the entire world if Lire gets her way, it's my family I'm trying to save.

I mustn't lose focus. Lire already has the crown in her hands. I couldn't get it back if I tried.

Anything you want, the queen said.

Teddy stares at me with raised eyebrows. But he doesn't understand. He doesn't have family like I do. He can't judge me when he doesn't get it.

He tilts his head in Dawn's direction. Her jaw is tight, her body tense. Jacob squeezes her hand tightly. No one seems to be paying her any attention, and who would bother to look past her perfect mask? But I notice the tears welling in her eyes.

The queen turns to the princess. 'We are saved once again,' she tells her daughter. 'Now we can give Jacob what he deserves for breaking your curse, and we will all be happy forever.'

Dawn doesn't speak, only swallows. Suddenly I feel as if I can read her mind. She can't talk because she's holding back a sob. She can't talk because no one would ever believe her if she tried to tell them Jacob isn't the saviour he claims to be. She can't talk because I am taking away her final hope.

I tear my eyes away from her. I can't— I can't think about her right now, not when everything I've ever wanted hangs in such delicate balance.

No, no, no, no.

Why did I do all of this in the first place? So I wouldn't have to enter a marriage I would hate? So my sisters wouldn't have to either? But I would sentence Dawn to the same thing?

Something in me breaks. The chatter in the room seems to fade away.

I ... *Fairies*.

I can't.

The walls of the throne room press in on me, the statues and paintings watching me with condemning eyes. Don't they know how far I've come? Don't they know all I've been through? I can't give up my family for a mere *princess*.

But Sierra saved me. She protected me even though we were enemies. She gave up the crown for me because she saw the danger in Teddy. We hated each other so much, but the second we understood each other, we were friends. How could I let Sierra do all that she did for me, then do this to Dawn?

I can't justify this anymore. It was so easy when I didn't have to look Dawn in the eyes. As badly as I want to give my family the world, I cannot sacrifice someone else's happiness for it.

'Maya?' says Olivia. She must notice me staring out the window, trying to reach for any kind of answer. I barely hear her. She places a hand on my shoulder. 'Well done, darling. It's over. It's time for us to go home.'

My heart shudders to a stop and my shoulders fall. *Oh, no. Oh no.*

I scowl at Teddy, knowing he'll understand, and he grins. Something bursts in my chest, but I ignore it. I close my eyes for a moment, take a breath, clench and unclench my fists. Lire will kill us for this. I am damning my family for a princess I have never, ever liked.

I blink, hard. How does Sierra prepare for a fight?

I summon all the rage I've ever felt, and channel it towards Lire. *Her fault.* Everything. The curse. The hundred years we lost. Dawn's engagement. My family's demise. Teddy's very existence, and why we can't be together. Why we're here like this.

Teddy clears his throat. 'Mother.'

Lire turns to him automatically before the consequences of that word crash through her ancient mind, providing an infinitesimal moment of distraction.

I step forward and grasp the crown, yanking it out of her strong grip before she can use her magic to stop me. I use my left foot to trip her over as I take the crown. I sprint to the end of the room, silently thanking Sierra for the fighting tips.

There are screams, but I don't stop until I can spin around with my back to the wall. *Fairies fairies fairies!*

Heaving and smoking with magic, Lire flies up and tries to throw arrows of lilac at me. I build up a wall of power between us – a shield – and she screeches to a halt. As she howls in outrage, the king and queen cower beneath her, running back – scared of me, not her. Because they don't know. They still think she's helping them.

'Mum!' I shout. My breaths come quickly. I can't think, can't make a plan, don't know what to do. I'm not sure I feel anything right now. I'm out of my mind. What am I doing?

Keep the crown away from Lire. Save Dawn. 'Mum, get over here!'

She snaps out of her shock, her features sharpening, and races over to me, sliding behind my expanding wall of magic. Teddy grabs Dawn's hand and together they join us.

There's so much going on I can't keep track of everyone, of everything. Scrambling and screaming. Short breaths and sparks of panic. Weakness and adrenaline. Guards trying to break through my magic. Magic that smells like smoke.

What am I missing? Who?

How can I protect everyone?

Jacob tries to break through my magic, his own turning deep purple as he presses through. I shove back with more of the rainbow power – conjuring a shield like the wards around my grandmother's grave – and momentarily he's pushed away. Then he comes roaring back at the wall in a tidal wave of mauve. Even as Lire calls him back, he rages towards us like a rabid dog.

I ready myself to stop him again, but then I realise – I can use this. I open the wall, just for a second, and he stumbles within. I use magic to freeze him in place. *Hostage.* 'Hold him!' I shout to Teddy.

Oh fairies oh fairies. I want to crash to the floor, cower, hide, but adrenaline has my eyes forced open and my mind whirring to find ways to fight.

Teddy quickly adds his own magic to hold down his brother. Dawn takes a few steps back, pressing herself against the wall. There are tears in her eyes now. Real ones. She's shaken. Isn't she supposed to be Strong?

Teddy wraps his arms around his brother, their magic fighting in a swirl of lilac, but it doesn't matter. The crown's power is strong enough for me to keep Jacob down.

I am winning.

We've done it. I have the crown again. I have everyone I need to protect. I have a hostage. I can have it all. I can save my family, save Dawn and Teddy, save myself.

Then, *oh, then* – someone shrieks. My heart shatters all at once, broken glass cutting through me from the inside out. My eyes travel up, and it's hard to see through all the magic. As if in response to my blindness, the rainbow wall turns crystal clear, and there she is, held in the fairy's arms, so high she's almost touching the ceiling, struggling uselessly.

Aunt Olivia.

Mum cries out, looks to me for help, but it's no use. I can't get her back. I can't—

How could I forget Olivia?

She's sobbing. Lire grips her with one hand around her waist and the other in her hair. She tilts Olivia's head down so I have to look at her tortured face. She looks so much like my mother; it's as if I'm watching both of them up there. There's magic all around her body, almost like it's *in* her body. When she moans in agony, lilac pours from her mouth. It ripples in sparkles down her red dress.

I fall to my knees, clutching the crown to my chest. I know what this is. I know what Lire is wordlessly telling me: Olivia for the crown. Olivia for Jacob. Olivia for Lire's future, for all her schemes to come together.

It's a sacrifice I can't dare to make now I've come this far. 'What do I do?' I ask no one in particular. I'm not sure my voice carries, I'm not sure I have any breath left in my lungs, I'm not sure I'm alive.

'We can bargain,' Dawn says, wiping her tears with a torn scrap of her tulle dress. 'We have more than she does. We can come to an agreement.'

Jacob snickers. 'My love,' he says, his voice silky and snaky, 'if you think I'm worth *anything* to my mother, you're about to be very disappointed.'

Teddy lets go of Jacob and rummages through his pockets. Jacob thrashes around uselessly in the invisible bindings Teddy and I still hold him within, but he stops when he sees what's in Teddy's hands. Our rings.

He hands me mine – glowing in their respective colours – without meeting my eyes. 'Let them help you,' he says, placing his own on his fingers. He clenches his fists around them a few times before wrapping his arms around Jacob again.

I hold my rings in one hand and the crown in the other. My mind quiets as if I'm balanced again, whole. The same way I felt stepping onto land after the days we spent on the ship to Grace's Capital. I place the rings on my fingers so I can grip the crown properly, and their power flows through me.

Kara's blessing might be the most important of all today. Death. Because I know how this is going to end, and I know

I'm going to need it. There are doors I'll need to permanently close. I can't sacrifice my aunt, of course I can't, but, *fairies*, I think I have to.

All the blood in me turns ice cold. I have no tears as I peer up at her again. A family member I was estranged from. Who helped me anyway. Who I thought I was going to spend the rest of my life getting to know, making up for all the years we missed.

I thought I could fix everything. I thought we could have it all.

But it's time to let it all go.

'The c-crown!' Olivia shouts before Lire moves her hand from her hair to her throat. Olivia's legs dangle uselessly as she struggles. She manages to squeeze out the rest of her message, her voice a small squeak, amplified by the magic of the crown as I beg it to help. 'U-Use the crown to d-destroy the—' she gasps '—the crown!' Her mouth gapes open as she tries to catch her breath. A fish out of water, gulping desperately. Nothing about my aunt's cool exterior remains – just fear.

Lire's face turns down, becoming dark and furious. Her eyes bore into mine and I know – I know this is the end. Olivia has doomed herself by telling me to make sure Lire can never get what she wants. Lire's fresh fury negates all bargaining power we may have had. Bearra's perfect fairy has snapped, once and for all, and I am the target of all her wrath.

I do the one thing I can: send as much magic to my aunt as possible, knowing I can't stop Lire, but I can at least make it less painful. I send Olivia acceptance, peace. A closed door. *Kara, help me.*

Aunt Olivia's face falls into a sad smile and she meets eyes with my mother. She nods.

Lire throws her body to the ground, and my aunt's life ends with a *snap* against the marble floor.

Mum screams. Maybe I do too, I don't know. I barely feel as if I'm in my own body anymore. There's no feeling left in my fingertips, no feeling in my heart, and it's as if I'm floating.

Dawn shouts, and I don't even see where she pulls the knife from. She pulls Jacob out of Teddy's grip, roughly spins him onto the ground, and—

And she stabs him through the heart.

I gasp in horror as blood goes *flying*. It seems to pour in all directions, like it's coming from everywhere. Red is all I can see. The princess is covered in it, and there are spots of it on the crown, on my hands too, and in Teddy's hair. It trickles across the floor and seeps through the magical wall, meeting the blood from my aunt's body. My mother is curled against the wall, sobbing, and I— I'm not even here.

Jacob takes his final breath, his magic ebbing out of him in dark purple waves as he dies. *Dies.*

Teddy's eyes widen, along with Dawn's. I can't tell if they're feeling joy or dread. They step back and he wraps his arms around her; she drops the blood-dripping knife to the floor. So the princess *is* Strong.

I . . . I don't know what to do. I am frozen, I am nothing. Grief and blood and devastation. Olivia. Olivia. And the fairy

– she's still there, waiting, grinning wickedly, because Jacob was right, she doesn't care, and she's waiting for our next move.

Olivia.

She told me what to do.

Use the crown to destroy the crown.

I breathe. Breathe again.

Of course the only way to destroy something this powerful is to use its own power against it. But if we lose the crown, we lose any chance against Lire. She'll kill us all, like she killed—

'What is happening?' the queen shouts, her small face tilted up to the fairy. She doesn't look at the body on the floor, the pool of crimson spreading out beneath it.

Lire flutters to the ground, her light hair floating around her as she descends. 'Are you *truly* that stupid?'

The king steps in front of his wife. 'You will not talk to your queen that way, fairy!'

'You think you rule this kingdom,' she snarls, and the once ethereal, lovely fairy of wisdom is acidic and venomous, 'but who has really been leading Bearra since it was first built? *Me.* And now I'm taking back what's mine. Do you think it has been easy? Tricking Kara into cursing Dawn so I could put you all to sleep for a hundred years? Making sure I would have enough time to ensure Bearra was so defenceless against the rest of the world that I would be its only hope?' Her voice turns even darker. 'Bearing two sons to become the kingdom's saviours alongside me. Creating the perfect husband for your daughter – a soulmate – who could become king, allowing me to really rule this place, without anyone the wiser. All this work. Everything I've done. Hundreds of years. The only thing I need now is the crown. I will not have it taken from me by a child, and I will *not* have the most useless monarchs in Bearra's history question me!'

With a flick of her wrist, she sends a wave of magic at us so strong it nearly bursts through my magical shield, shaking through me like an earthquake. It's just for show – she knows she's equally matched with the crown and can't break through – but she wants to scare us.

Jacob's blood is leaking everywhere, seeping into my shoes.

I still can't think. Can *any* of us think?

'You are Bearra's patron!' the queen says. 'You protect us! You guide us!'

My head spins, and their voices become muted again as I place a hand on the wall to keep myself upright.

The fairy sneers at the queen. 'Not anymore. This world will be mine.'

My mother must have risen from the floor at some point, because I notice her presence beside me. With her arm around me, she whispers, 'You must destroy it. Now.' Her face is red and blotchy, her expression frozen in something between anguish and horror, shock and determination. Does it look like mine? 'Maya, it doesn't matter what the consequences are. It doesn't matter what happens to us. We cannot risk her getting the crown's power. Do you understand? You must destroy it. Do it for my sister.'

Dawn doesn't take her eyes off Jacob's body as she says, 'Lire will kill us as soon as we lose our magic. What will we do then?'

'I can protect us,' Teddy says. 'I know I'm not nearly as strong as my mother, but I can fight her. Maybe I can create enough time for us to run.'

'And my parents?' asks Dawn, a hitch in her voice.

He holds her hands delicately. 'We can't save everyone. But we won't save *anyone* if the crown isn't destroyed.'

The princess exhales, nodding, though I see the repressed cry in the set of her shoulders.

'Okay,' I say. 'Okay, I'll do it. If this is what we have to do.' I look at my mother and try to smile, wrapping her in a tight hug. 'If we don't make it, Mum, I'm so sorry about all of this. I'm sorry I didn't listen to you. I was so stupid, trying to run away, trying to keep us all together. I was just scared. I didn't want things to change. I didn't want to be alone. I let my pride and anger cloud everything else. And now we're here. And Olivia . . .' I choke on my words. 'Mum, I'm so sorry.'

'Don't be sorry.' She speaks quickly. 'You have no idea how proud I am of you. Your father, too. I had a few weeks with my sister back, Maya, and that's because of you. I believe we'll make it through this. And if we don't, I don't blame you for any of it. If we die here, we die knowing we did the right thing.'

I nod, trying to blink the tears from my eyes and hold back my sobs so I can concentrate on the crown. I pull out of her arms and brace myself for what comes next.

Lire tries again to break past the magic wall. She must sense what I'm about to do. Her scream is muffled by the crown. She's still powerless as long as we're separated. The crown and the fairy. One cannot destroy the other. They can only destroy themselves.

Breathing, knowing I am safe in this bubble with my mother and Teddy, I sit on the floor and hold the crown in my lap. I close my eyes.

The crown usually listens to me, but this time, there's resistance. I have to use my blessings to get the message through. It tries to fight, to save itself, but eventually it caves. The tension in my muscles eases as it does. All its magic travels through me at once; the power of a fairy. My stomach flips. It feels so wonderful and so wrong.

The crown raises into the air, out of my hands. I open my eyes and breathe deeply. The triaruo is almost navy, darkening the throne room as its power spreads out in angry shadows.

Lire stares up at the crown, throwing her hands against the wall. 'Stop this! Stop this!' Waves of her magic sear through the paintings on the ceiling.

But I don't lose focus. Teddy takes my hand, and that's all I need. He lends me his magic, his will. And we command the crown to destroy itself.

The stunning jewel bursts apart like shattered glass, falling slowly as if through water. Magic of every colour pours out, falling around us in sparks as it bounces off the floor and walls. Some of the crown's escaped magic is so potent it burns right through the marble floor. Teddy protects us in a layer of his own magic as my wall disappears.

'Stop!' Lire screams again. The magic rains over her, and in her anger she doesn't think to protect herself. It burns holes through her wings and she cries out. Lilac magic coats her, but it's too late. She's injured, badly. Screaming and screaming and pulling at her own hair.

Olivia and Jacob's bodies are eaten away by the magic, while the queen and king cower behind their thrones and bewildered guards lift their metal shields above their heads.

Blue shards of triarue sit all over the floor, and the bursts of light finally begin to dissolve. Teddy wraps his arms around me, holding me close to him as I sob. I'm too weak to push him away. Too weak to make myself pretend I don't want his touch.

I hear footsteps, running, and I look up to see Dawn racing to her paralysed parents, their eyes glazed over.

'Where has she gone?' the king says.

Pain splinters through my hands, an ache resounding through my body. I turn to the side and retch, vomiting all over the floor, right in the puddle of Jacob's blood. I'm ready to faint. The power was too much. Too much. I can no longer talk, no longer move. I shut my eyes and drop to the floor. Teddy puts his hand on my head to hold it up.

'The fairy!' one of the guards says. 'Lire! She's disappeared!'

'She ran,' Dawn says. 'She *lost*.'

The voices blend together as I fall unconscious in Teddy's arms, the last beams of sunlight falling black behind my eyelids.

EPILOGUE

SOMEWHERE, SOMETIME...

IN THE WEEKS AFTER Lire disappeared, Princess Dawn organised a whimsical wedding for Prima and her fiancé, Matthew.

Maya, though she never liked extravagance, felt that this was the least the royals could do for her family. And she was enjoying it, just a little. There weren't many attendees, but Dawn let them have the entire ballroom to themselves for as long as they wanted. She saturated it in flowers, with petals scattered across the floor. A string quartet played slow music as the sun set.

After the ceremony, when the guests broke apart to dance and eat, Maya's parents stood close together, holding hands and whispering to each other. Her mother had not yet recovered from losing Olivia. Maya wondered if she would recover either. They smiled through the days, but their joy was rarely real. Maya's father, at least, seemed better than he had in years. He began storytelling again, sitting with

Maya for hours as she recounted her adventures. He turned her words into beautiful stories as she painted the blue of Grace's Waters, the yellow of Muse's Forest, the deep jungle green of Rhiannon's Territory. Maya was overflowing with inspiration, as if she had a never-ending well of ideas. This helped, she knew, with the pain.

Prima and Matthew spun around the ballroom floor in their beautiful clothes, laughing and kissing and feeling all the joy in the world. Others joined in, dancing at their own pace. It was nice to watch from her seat in the corner, but Maya couldn't force herself to join.

She was still so tired, but today was a good day. It had to be. She would feign joy for a few more hours.

Dawn and her parents – the royals Maya had spent so long hating – had kept their promise and made sure Maya's family were looked after. Even though they didn't get their crown in the end, Maya had stopped Lire and prevented Dawn from entering a terrible marriage. She had saved Bearra – for now.

Teddy, however, had an unsettled fate. No one, besides those there that day, knew who he really was. For his own protection, they kept up the pretence of him being a prince. They spread the lie that Jacob died in a tragic accident, and due to the pain of seeing Dawn's soulmate's life taken, Lire fled in grief.

But Teddy was still the fairy's son. The queen and king only let him stay because Dawn insisted upon it. Even living at the castle, he was kept at a safe distance from everyone.

Something between a prisoner and a guest, but also a source of protection for when Lire undoubtedly returned.

Maya was still not sure what to make of Teddy. She had been busying herself with preparing for the wedding and, a week beforehand, the funeral. She had not seen much of him, and that was exactly what she needed.

'Enjoy it,' Dawn said, walking up to Maya in a sweet yellow dress that made her brown skin glow and her golden hair beam. She was finally back to looking like the princess Maya once knew from a distance – perfect, beautiful, carefree, and kind. Except now, Maya saw far more of the bravery and power within her, and she was strangely happy that Dawn would be her queen one day.

Maya picked a loose thread at the hem of her dress, an uncomfortable but pretty pink slip. 'I can't seem to enjoy anything since . . . Well, you know,' she admitted to the princess. 'It's like my body and mind are always racing, even though I'm safe. I can't relax knowing that Lire is somewhere out there.'

'I know the feeling.' Dawn sat beside her. The princess's energy was calming. Maya had enjoyed spending time with her to organise the wedding. They had come to find a protectiveness of each other after that day in the throne room. 'I fear for everyone in Bearra every day, now even more so. But I have you to thank for saving us from a worse fate. You have given us the chance to regroup and regain strength before Lire returns.'

Maya frowned. 'But she'll return stronger, and next time we won't have the crown.'

'But we *will* have Teddy. And your blessings.' She smiled. 'The rest we will figure out in time. There must be a way to defeat her.'

'I hope there is,' said Maya. 'War is coming, isn't it? No one likes to say it, but—'

Teddy appeared in front of her in a cornflower-blue suit. His red hair was shaken out, wild compared to the way it was when she first saw him here weeks ago. The day neither of them were themselves.

His soft gaze travelled to her fidgeting hands, then to her eyes. He tried to smile as he reached out a hand. 'Maya, might I have this dance?'

She sighed, but her heart lit up at the thought, as if a thousand magical crowns glowed in her stomach. Could they be themselves, now, after everything? Was this her chance?

Closed doors. Open doors.

Letting go of the past didn't mean they couldn't start again.

When she took his hand, part of her awoke, and the distress of the last few weeks began to melt away. He led her to the floor and held her at a small distance as they stepped to the slow rhythm. They stayed comfortable like this for a while, but by the end of the song, they were pressed close together, her head resting on his shoulder.

'You know how sorry I am,' he said softly. 'You know how much you mean to me. I can't thank you enough for destroying the crown.'

Maya swallowed. 'I know, Teddy, but I didn't do it for you. I did it for Dawn. I did it for Bearra.'

'Good.' He held her tighter. 'It's better that way.'

'I'm sorry, too.' Her throat felt rough saying those words, but she forced them out anyway. 'Sorry for hating you. For letting my pride get in the way of . . . of everything right.'

'Shh.' He brushed her hair behind her ear and ran a thumb down her cheek. She shivered. 'Don't ever be sorry to me. Just be honest. Just be you. Maya, you are all I want. As yourself, as you are. Be prideful. Be selfish. Take everything from me. I don't care. I just want *you* by my side. Promise me you'll always be you.'

She faltered, melting inside and out. How could this be *real*? 'Only . . . Only if you promise to always be you.' She let herself smile. 'I want you, too, Teddy. I want us. If that's what you want.'

He nodded, his grin lighting up his face with the charm that could pull the sun from the sky.

'Even if the world is falling apart?' she asked, her voice suddenly small.

Teddy held her face between his hands. 'No more lies, no more hiding. We can do it all together now, really together, without everything else. War is coming. Our situation is going to get far worse. But I'm myself, for the first time. With you. Please, if you can forgive me—'

She kissed him.

He was tense at first, stunned, then he laughed and tilted her face to a better angle. As they crashed together, she fell apart. His magic wrapped around them both, holding them up. Her legs gave out beneath her, and her heart thumped madly. Everything was warm. But, conscious of where they were, she did her best to hold back the true extent of her joy. Today wasn't their day.

'I could love you,' Maya said when they broke apart. Her words slurred as if she were drunk. She certainly felt like she was. 'I think maybe I do. But I know without a doubt that I will.'

'I know without a doubt,' he said, his brown eyes gleaming, 'that I have loved you since the day we met.'

A shadow passed over them, something travelling across the setting sun, and they gazed out of the window. A black swan soared across Bearra, level with the hilltop castle. Maya thought it looked happy – for a swan.

Teddy and Maya laughed together, and she pressed her head to his chest, listening to his heart, feeling his magic.

Maybe this *was* their day. She touched the dark ring on her finger, and thought that, maybe, she could only open this door if she knew she'd be willing to close it. She could only let Teddy in if she accepted the risk. If she acknowledged that it may not work, may not last. That the world could end, and they could be gone forever.

Could she accept so much impending heartbreak?

They met eyes and he smiled, all his summer leaking into her like fire melting ice, and Maya decided that Teddy was a door she would never, ever close.

Acknowledgments

I HAVE BEEN SO lucky to have so many people on my side who are passionate and supportive of not only Woken Kingdom, but my entire author career. These people have made publishing this book possible, *and* made it such a joy. I am grateful to so many more people than I can list here, but I'll do my best.

First, my family, of course. Mum! Oh my god I love you so much. Nanny and Polly, Bob, Mary, Gypsie, Stanley, Chelsea, Ronny, and all the rest. Couldn't have done it without you all.

And the friends who have supported my writing the most: Brady, Jazmin, and Bradman. But especially Haylee Buswell, for her beautiful design skills (and friendship skills). Also, an overall shoutout to my bookstagram community, because I love y'all so very much.

My beta readers: Savannah, Angie, Emma, and everyone else who has read any part of WK and offered feedback. I owe you the world. My editing team: Pauline Menchavez, Ellyssa Paik, and Lizzie Augustine, thank you so, so much for everything you put into this book for me.

And finally my gratitude must be extended to Barbie and Tchaikovsky, the major inspirations behind Woken Kingdom. You taught me to love sparkles and magic and fairies and princesses and orchestras and romance and dance. Woken Kingdom exists because of real-life magic.

Can't wait for more Woken Kingdom? Follow Sierra's journey to break her curse in *Woken Kingdom #2: Cygnus Curse*, coming late 2023.

Follow @PoppysVintageBooks on Instagram and TikTok for Woken Kingdom content, and sign up to the Poppy's Pages newsletter for sneak peeks at upcoming stories!

poppyspagesediting.com/newsletter-sign-up

About the author

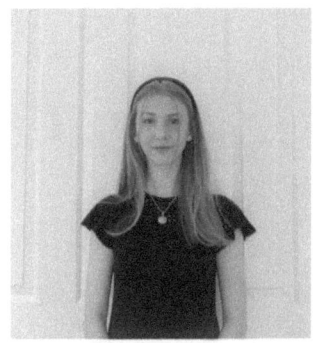

Poppy Rose Solomon's YA novels reflect the traumas and lessons she experienced as a teenager, and she loves creating 'unlikable' characters who learn to heal themselves. Evoking inspiration and escapism is the goal of her storytelling. From her home on the Sunshine Coast, she freelances as a YA editor and coach through her business Poppy's Pages, and runs the Writing YA With Poppy podcast. Woken Kingdom is her first series, with plenty more to come.